Kept

Evelyn Flood

First published by Evelyn Flood in 2023

ISBN: 9798865723684

Imprint: Independently published

Cover by JODIELOCKS Designs

Contents

Content overview

This book contains fictional references to torture, murder, abduction, physical abuse, child abuse (off page and relating to background characters), blood, rope play, drug use and prostitution.

If this is okay with you, please keep reading!

Evelyn x

In loving dedication

For every girl who secretly wishes for a psychotic, obsessive, serial killer lover.

(Hey, we didn't choose the book life. The book life chose us.)

Zella

Tick.

Tick.

Tick.

The mechanical sound burrows into me. It pulses inside my brain, drumming against the back of my skull and making my eyelids flicker.

My eyes stay closed, my forehead wrinkling with the effort of keeping them shut as I listen.

There are no footsteps. No music plays in another room. There's no cheerful whistling from a companion. No sign of life anywhere around me.

Just silence. Endless, empty, echoing silence.

Tick.

And that *stupid* clock.

Sighing, I give up on any thoughts of going back to sleep and sit up, pushing the tangled covers away from my bare legs. As I scan the room, my eyes are drawn to the dress I carelessly discarded last night, crumpled in a heap on the floor.

My feet pad across the deep cream carpet as I reach down to pick it up. The white material crumples further as my fingers burrow into it.

Turning, I place it carefully into my empty washing basket before I head to the bathroom.

My feet press into the same slight grooves in the carpet, years of following the same routine showing in the wear and tear of the room around me.

Routine is important, I remind myself. Shucking off my sleep shorts and camisole, I detangle myself, yanking at a thin silk strap irritably when it catches on my braid. Stepping into the huge shower, I gradually pull the braid in with me, tugging off the various bands at the end and running my fingers through it to loosen the intricate weaving that keeps it at least partly out of my way.

The tightness in my scalp begins to ease as I work my way through, and I send a moment of thanks as I slap my hand to start the hot water that I live in an apartment with a gigantic walk-in shower.

Ignoring the mass of hair waiting to be washed, I take a moment to enjoy the way the water pummels against my back, loosening tension in my spine I didn't even notice was there until I'm sagging against the spotless white tiles.

It's only when I'm in danger of turning into an actual prune that I begrudgingly reach out, starting to pull my hair through the water until it's soaked and heavy against my scalp.

Routine.

Shampoo.

Pour into hand, scrub.

Pour more into hand, scrub.

Aaaand pour more into hand. Scrub again.

Rinse. Rinse again. Keep rinsing.

My arms are already aching by the time I finish, and I glare at the conditioner.

My own personal nemesis.

This part takes the longest, and I manage to snap two teeth off my comb too. By the time I've found them, hidden amongst the soaking strands, my mood has plummeted.

The bathroom fills up with clouds of steam as I work. Taking my time, I wait until the very last bubble swirls away before I climb out and start squeezing the excess water out of my hair, watching the liquid escape down the drain.

I grab a clean white towel from the cupboard, wrapping it around myself and gathering up the heavy mass in my arms, carrying it out to my bedroom.

Dropping it to the ground with a solid thud, it drags along the carpet, leaving wet patches behind as I pull open the drawers on my dressing table. There are dozens of brushes, each one designed to help me wrangle the almost white-blonde hair that runs well past my feet, enough to wrap around my waist several times and *still* have miles left over.

Sighing, I take a seat and begin the arduous task of brushing it out. Starting from the bottom, I work out every single knot, wincing as I move through. Even with a boatload of conditioner, I still manage to find knots. Every. Single. Time.

Deep, emerald-green eyes peer back at me from the mirror, set against skin that stays a golden hue despite never seeing a hint of sun. My hair falls around me like a shield, and not for the first time, I wonder what I'd look like if I was able to cut it.

My fingers drum on the glass of my dressing table before I turn away.

Never gonna happen. Ethan would have a heart attack if I even mentioned it.

But the fluttering in my chest doesn't stop as I pull open the wardrobe and step back.

"Tell me," I ask out loud, tapping my lips. "What should I wear today? Green? Pink? A little neon?"

Row upon row of neatly pressed, identical white dresses stare back at me.

One has a slight crumple in the sleeve. Seizing it with a weird sense of satisfaction, I give the rest of the dresses a smug smile and slam the door closed.

Once I'm dressed, I wander into the wider apartment. My bedroom and bathroom is the only enclosed space in thousands of feet, the rest of the apartment completely open plan. Weaving my way between the various figures spread out across the vast space, I pause at one familiar face.

"Good morning, Dante." Tilting my head, I peer at the sculpture. Dante sits, his wrist balancing loosely on his knee as he stares back at me. A lock of hair curls over his eye.

"Good morning, Zella," I say in my deepest voice. "Did you sleep well?"

Nodding, I shift on my feet. "I did, thank you."

He stares back at me. Maybe he's not up for conversation this morning. Sometimes he talks for hours.

Or... maybe that's me.

Moving on, I work my way towards the kitchen, offering up greetings to a few of my other companions as I pass by. The coffee is running low, and I stare at the pot despondently as it dribbles the last little drop of liquid gold into my cup.

I hope Ethan remembers to bring some.

Taking my precious last cup, I wrap my fingers around the warmth and move across to my little sitting area. I've done my best to make it as cozy as I can, even with the lack of color. My fingers brush against my plant, my one piece of greenery, and I settle back into my leather chair, my eyes already turning towards the window. The little flip of daily excitement turns over in my stomach.

Any minute now.

The first, golden fingers of sunshine appear slowly, casting the white space around me in hues of rose and gold. My breath catches, the edges of my lips tilting up into a grin as I'm bathed in warmth.

The one time of day that my life is filled with color. Vibrant, beautiful color. It surrounds me, and I turn to see the statues I share my life with lit up like they could actually come to life and be the companions I pretend they are.

My chest aches as the sunrise moves on, settling smoothly into the early morning light that fills the apartment. I'll have to wait until tomorrow to see it again.

One day.

One day, I'll see it in person. Not from behind a wall of glass. I'll feel the wind on my face, flicking through my hair as I sit on grass in a pair of jeans, my fingers sinking into the mud.

That day is not today.

Hours stretch out in front of me, beckoning with emptiness.

Blinking heavily, I rub my fist against the pain in my chest and try to push back the selfish thoughts.

Here, I am cared for.

Here, I am *safe.*

Maybe it's not the most exciting life, but at least I'm warm, and fed.

To feel anything other than grateful feels like a betrayal to everything Ethan has done for me. Everything my parents did for me.

Brushing the dampness from my cheeks, I slap my hand down on my leg and push to my feet.

"Today is not the day for a pity party, Zella."

Placing my hands on my hips, I survey the room. The statues stare back at me, unblinking.

"Today," I announce, "will be a *busy* day."

Digging around under the sink, I pull out my supplies, laying them out across the marble counter like soldiers marching off to war. I start at the very end of the room, close to the elevator.

Every surface gets cleaned.

I carefully wipe over the pale metallic doors of the elevator, spraying them down to remove any sneaky non-existent finger marks, and do the same with the small keypad next to it. My hand pauses over the keys.

Cautiously, I lean forward, my finger gently pressing against a button as I hold my breath.

I wait. My breath quickens in short huffs, eyes flicking to the dark strip above the elevator that shows the lift rising.

But there's nothing. No lights ding. There's no sign of any life at all.

Safe.

I rip my hand away from the keypad. What is wrong with me today?

Turning my back on it, I work through my routine. Surface cleaning, vacuuming, mopping. Today I get down on my knees and carefully work my way down the room, cleaning each skirting board to make sure not a speck of dust exists.

When the main room is done, I turn to the statues.

Dante is first. Taking the fine, soft cloth in my hand, I gently press it over his hair, moving down in sweeping strokes. He stares straight ahead as I reach his stomach, my hands tracing over the hard edges and pausing.

"Talk to me, Dante," I whisper. It's almost a plea as I stare up at him, cold and unmoving.

But only silence responds.

Sometimes, I think I'm losing my mind.

And sometimes I think I've already lost it.

Getting to my feet, I turn my face away and move on, taking the liberty of approaching my favorites first. There's Maria, the archangel with the kind face whose wings take up more than their fair share of space. And then there's Psyche and Cupid, both of them curled around each other. They don't spare a look for anyone else.

"You're very lucky, you know that?" I tell Psyche softly as I run the cloth over her arms. "To have him."

Cupid ignores me, staring down at her. His arm curves around her protectively.

"Don't worry," I murmur. "I'm only cleaning her, Cupid."

I'm a little tempted to flick her nipple and see if his face changes, but Ethan would freak if I scratched her.

By the time lunch rolls around, the room is as spotless as it was this morning.

Sighing, I pull out the ingredients for my salad. Chicken, cherry tomatoes, lettuce, cucumber, bell pepper, a little ranch. Taking my time, I cut the vegetables carefully, laying them out on the plate and admiring the little burst of color before I take it over to the window to eat.

The skyline looks much the same as it always does. Rooftop after rooftop, bricks and cement and birds. Setting my plate down, I press my nose against the window and do my best to look down, but I'm too high up to see the people on the street below.

Giving up, I turn back to survey the room. It almost glints in the light.

I tilt my head.

I suppose my bathroom could do with a clean. And I could change my bed.

I mean, I did it yesterday, but there's nothing quite like the feel of clean bedding.

An hour later, I'm crouched in front of the little shelf in my corner. My fingers trace over the old, cracked spines almost reverently. Carefully, I pull out a tattered hardback copy of Pride and Prejudice.

"Hello, Mr. Darcy," I murmur absently, curling into my chair. I pull at my hair until it offers a cushion for my arm, opening the book to the ballroom scene.

"Such an ass," I mutter fondly.

My hand reaches out for caffeine-y goodness, but it only grasps empty air.

I *really* hope Ethan brings coffee. If I'm really lucky, he might bring a new book too. My eyes flick to the clock.

A few hours. Plenty of time.

Ryder

"God, you're sexy."

The dyed redhead – top *and* bottom – underneath me groans, her ass jiggling around my cock as I speed up, my hips pumping into her. My eyes aren't on the cougar giving her best *When Harry Met Sally* impression though.

Winking, I blow myself a kiss in the huge mirror the chick has hanging above her bed.

"Fucking gorgeous," I coo. Fuck knows I need the motivation to keep going. She moans loudly as I reach forward and casually tug on her nipple, flicking my fingers until she convulses around me with a strangled scream.

"So good, sweetheart," I praise easily, sliding my cock out and shoving it back into my pants, zipping up the denim before she can get a good look and realize that only one of us came until our knees were shaking.

Preening, she rolls onto her back, long painted talons plucking at her surgically enhanced tits as she grins at me. "Second round?"

"I would, but I think that filthy cunt has sucked me dry." Just as I knew she would, she groans at my words, her arms flopping to her sides.

"Close the door," she mumbles, but her eyes are already sliding shut.

I wait until a loud snore shakes the walls – and holy *shit*. No wonder our client doesn't hang around after his weekly fuck. This woman could be a weapon of mass destruction with the strength of her snoring.

Sliding off the bed, I casually make my way over to the painting hanging opposite. There's a little wooden sign in fancy curling calligraphy underneath announcing the prestigious artist, and I roll my eyes.

It's the work of a minute to swing the false door open, and I grin at the metal in front of me. You'd think, with all the expensive technology hanging around now, people would learn that a safe in the bedroom is *not* the best way to store expensive shit.

But it makes my life easier, and I whistle under my breath as I twist the tumblers. Gina was kind enough to share that today is her birthday, and it only takes a few quick guesses before it's opening smoothly and I can grab the little blue velvet bag that sits in the middle.

So. Fucking. Cliché.

As I head out, I spy a little notepad next to the still-snoring Gina. Grabbing the pen, I scribble a quick note before I sweep out, jiggling my prize in my hand.

You snore like an agitated hippo.

P.S. Your painting is a fake. A shit one.

Whistling, I exit Gina's West Side apartment block, sweeping straight past the concierge watching the game on his little screen. His beady little eyes don't even look up as I head through the double glass doors into the still busy New York street.

I merge into the crowd, just another faceless New Yorker as I stroll leisurely down the sidewalk. I wander for a few streets until I reach the bar where I charmed gaudy, snoring Gina out of her panties, ducking into a side alley to grab my bike.

Well. Technically, it's Enzo's bike.

Not my fault he didn't lock the door to his precious garage.

He might actually stab me for taking his one and only love on a little joyride into the city, but I can't say I care as I pull out, uncaring of the cop car on the corner as I shoot past. They've got bigger fish to fry than one guy on a bike going a little over the speed limit in this area.

Although they might be more interested if they knew I was carting around a ten-million dollar necklace.

I tilt my head back as I get out of the built-up area, enjoying the rush of the wind on my face as I fly towards the national park we call home.

Nobody batted an eyelid when we carved out a little land for ourselves, greasing palms and turning heads until our names vanished from the system and we had ourselves our own goddamn fairytale castle.

Maverick hates when I call it that, but it's the damn truth. The place still takes my breath away as I fly down the track, pausing only to enter the long-as-fuck security code into the heavy-set iron gates.

Mav is waiting for me when I pull in, his eyebrow raised as he takes in my mighty steed. "He's fucking furious, you know."

I give my little pony a loving stroke. Maybe I'll get one for myself, but there's something in knowing she belongs to someone else that makes her even better. "He'll forgive me," I coo. "Won't he, girl?"

"Ryder." Maverick's voice is the epitome of long-suffering, so I take pity and tug the pretty from my pocket, tossing it over to him.

"One diamond necklace. You owe me for that shit. I thought she was gonna chew my cock off."

"You'd probably enjoy it," he mutters.

Asshole. I have some taste.

Climbing off the bike, I stretch, popping the muscles at the top of my back. "I need a shower."

Possibly an STI test wouldn't go amiss either. I wrapped up, but she still managed to get her vacuum mouth on me before the main event.

Mav sighs. "Are you joining us for dinner?"

"Not hungry," I shoot over my shoulder. Leaving him behind to carry out his part of the job, I make my way through the side door connecting the garage to the main house. My feet tap out a pattern on the fancy wooden floorboards of our hall, echoing back in a weird muffled way as the sound bounces off the various paintings on the wall.

Unlike Gina's little pride and joy, every one of these babies is original.

I can confirm. The museums are still looking for them.

A little smug, I'm still internally crowing over my greatness when I step into the shower. Casually, I scrub off any leftover Gina particles, then I scrub again.

Once more. Maybe one more time, for good measure.

When I finally feel clean, my skin feeling almost raw from the abrasive sponge, I wrap a towel around my waist and walk into my room.

Enzo is perched on the edge of my bed like a creepy fucking gargoyle, and I give him a dirty look.

"Dude." I point at my sheets. "Those are twelve-hundred thread Egyptian cotton sheets. Get your skanky boots off them."

The knife flies past me, and I roll my eyes as I turn and yank it out of the wall. Another fucking hole to fill in.

Enzo doesn't say anything, the skull on his neck giving him an eerie vibe in the lamplight. If I was anyone else, I think I'd probably shit my pants.

Whipping my towel from around my waist, I fling it across the room, crowing when it lands on his head and he has to tug it off. He doesn't look half as scary with his head wrapped in damp toweling.

"The fuck is wrong with you?" he snarls when he's wrestled himself free.

I grin. "You trying to put the heebie-jeebies up me, Enzo? You can deal with a little dick towel."

He lobs it back at me. "You're fucking vile. And you *stole* my bike."

I shrug. "It needed a ride. It was lonely. I could tell."

I can *hear* his teeth grinding. Winding my brothers up – brothers in blood and carnage, at least – is one of my favorite activities. They know it, though, and I make a sad face when he doesn't bite.

I point the knife in my hand at him. "You're no fun anymore. You used to be savage, E."

He bares his teeth, and the scarlet caps he sometimes wears for his little sessions glow in the light. "Ask Antonio how much fun I am."

"He's still here?" I ask, yanking a drawer open and reaching for a shirt. Now I'm clean, I am actually a little hungry.

As if on cue, there's a high-pitched wail from underneath us. I turn to Enzo with a frown.

"Not cool. I don't want his screeching ass ruining my appetite."

He shrugs. "It'll stop soon. He's lost too much blood."

Sure enough, the sound cuts off with a garbled cry. Enzo gets to his feet. "If there's a single scratch on her, I will rip your fingernails off, Ryder."

I crook my sadly nail-less little finger at him in a little wave, wiggling my eyebrows. "Don't threaten me with a good time, Enzo baby. At least make it original if you wanna be a scary asshole."

He glowers at the reminder, stomping his way out of my room.

"You're still a petrifying little chicken," I call after him, and his cursing hits my ears like music.

Maverick

"You're late."

Ryder rolls his eyes as he swaggers across the room, collapsing dramatically into the seat at the end of the long wooden dining table. "I told you, I wasn't hungry."

I raise my eyebrows at him as he tugs a plate of roast lamb towards him, dragging half onto his plate. Thankfully the staff never take him at his word. The man is a black hole when it comes to food. I don't even know where he puts it.

"Blame Enzo," Ryder says. Or at least I think he does. His voice is a little muffled by the sheer amount of food he's shoveling into his mouth.

"For you being hungry?" I slide some meat onto my own plate, glancing at the door. There's no sign of him.

"For being late." Ryder sighs. "He was very dramatic over the whole bike issue. Did a bat impression on the end of my bed."

"I don't even know what to say to that."

He waves a lazy hand. "It's fine. I threw a dick towel at his face and that made him move."

The fondant potato I've just taken a bite of gets lodged in my throat, and I choke, grabbing my wine and taking a large swig. Swallowing the lump down painfully, I slump back in my chair. "Ryder."

"Maverick," he mimics. "Chill out. I'm here, aren't I? Enzo will be along shortly, once he finishes his little murder mission downstairs."

I frown into my plate. Enzo's little *missions*, as Ryder likes to call them, are becoming a more and more frequent occurrence. And as much as I understand his reasons... I worry.

Killing leaves a stain on your soul, whatever the motive behind it.

I should know.

And Enzo's soul was never the purest to begin with.

Parking that discussion until he's actually in the room, I focus on the day's events. "I called Benoit. I'll return the diamonds tomorrow night, at Parkers."

Ryder perks up immediately. "I might come with you."

I slant my head. "I'm not sure he'll appreciate our methods, so if you come, don't tell him exactly how you acquired it."

He shudders. "He should be thanking me. I have no idea what he saw in that woman."

"Clearly, enough to gift her a ten-million-dollar necklace."

He points his fork at me. "But not enough to let her keep it when his wife found out about his little tête-à-tête."

I acknowledge the truth in his words with a wave. "Still. A tidy profit for us, and we can focus on the Moore case now."

Ryder grimaces, his lips twisting in distaste. "John Martinez gives me the creeps, and Ethan Moore isn't any better. He's got a membership at Club X."

The city nightclub is notorious for catering to any and all tastes, including those of the illegal kind. "Try and get some footage. All Martinez wants is something to embarrass him. Should be plenty of material there."

A grimace twists Ryder's face. "Art dealers at war. I wonder what Moore did to fuck him over."

"Not our problem. He's paying the money, so we'll deliver the goods."

For a moment, I wonder what my father would think, if he could see his private investigation firm now. Our methods are darker now than when he first took me under his wing, teaching me everything he knew from his years in the police force and then with the FBI.

Ryder finishes his second plate with a heavy sigh. "Is Angela bringing dessert?"

I'm about to point out – again – that he said he didn't want any food at all and he's damned lucky that our housekeeper knows him well enough to cook a mountain of food anyway – when my phone buzzes with an unknown number.

Swiping it, I put it to my ear as I stand, gesturing to the door. Ryder shrugs, and as I walk out, he's already leaning in to help himself to yet another helping.

"Is this Brooks PI?"

My blood starts to fizz, adrenaline kicking in at the urgency in the man's voice as I make my way into my office and settle behind my desk, switching to the hands free and tugging my laptop towards me. "It is."

By the time we wrap things up an hour later, I'm feeling the same sense of urgency.

Ryder shoves his head around the door. "Do I detect a job?"

I nod, pushing the screen towards him as he steps inside. "Abby Millers. Disappeared three days ago. Her boyfriend had been causing some trouble – the father thinks he's a dealer and he's got her wrapped up in it. Name's Ed Sanderson."

Ryder grins, and it's a savage thing. "One for Enzo, then."

I hesitate. Another case to blacken his soul. He won't stop at finding the girl.

He won't stop until Ed Sanderson is split into so many pieces, even his ghost won't have a chance at finding peace.

Finally, I nod. We need him. And at least having this as an outlet stops him from looking elsewhere.

As I make my way downstairs, the desperate screaming I picked up on earlier has been replaced by a wet-sounding gurgle.

"Such a beautiful sound," a deep voice murmurs. "I wonder what would happen if—,"

Even I wince at the agony in the sound that follows, but Enzo only hums, a strange delight underscoring his muttered words.

"Shhhh," he's whispering as I walk into the room. He's crouched in front of a weeping male, his grip almost tender as he carves another letter into his face.

I know he knows I'm here, but he doesn't stop. Antonio's eyes flicker wildly between me, the open door, and his own death.

"There, now." Enzo stands up, admiring his handiwork. "It's important not to forget, don't you think?"

Antonio strains against the metal chains binding him to the tilted upright table as Enzo pulls the mirror across and holds it up. A wild scream breaks out from beneath the gag when he sees the shape of his face.

Enzo grabs his chin, forcing his face towards the glass. "Pretty faces get the pretty girls, Antonio. That's what you always said, wasn't it? Except Juliana wasn't quite as *pretty* as she used to be, not by the time you finished with her."

The man's eyes are locked onto his face as he continues screaming, tears mingling with the blood and slices marring olive skin.

I lean back against the wall, my arms crossed. I might have concerns about the impact this has on Enzo, but I have no qualms whatsoever about the men he brings below our home.

Not a single one of them is a victim.

My brother strolls to his cabinet. "She'll forget you, eventually, you know. The scarring will heal, and she'll adapt. She's strong, Juliana. Not like you."

He selects a small bottle painstakingly, giving it a little shake as he turns back to Antonio, who's watching him with a dawning terror as Enzo holds up the acid bottle.

"But you? You'll *never* forget."

When the screaming and sizzling of skin peeling from flesh has faded into the cold, gray silence that death leaves behind, I step out of the shadows. Enzo whistles as he scrubs his hands under the faucet.

"Come to watch the show?" His words bounce off the stainless steel walls around us, walls that are currently smattered with red but soon to be cleaned off, ready for a new victim. "Maybe one of these days you'll join in."

"Perhaps." We both know that I've been tempted. Some of the darkness Enzo faces... some would call him a vigilante. Others, a psychopath. Maybe both are true.

But it's undeniably justice, too, for the women and girls who slip under the radar of the emergency services, too overworked and underpaid to overly care when women from the wrong side of town get hurt.

Sometimes the streets police themselves, one of my old, tired colleagues said to me once over a beer.

Maybe they do. And sometimes, we do it for them.

I watch the muscles in Enzo's back ripple, the movement making the tattoos across his skin dance under the amber light from the single swinging lightbulb before my eyes move to the remains of what used to be Antonio.

All very dramatic.

I turn my gaze away. "Might have a new job."

Enzo stills, and I can almost taste his interest in the air. He knows I wouldn't bother coming down unless it was something where his particular skills could be of use.

I outline the brief Abby Millers' father gave to me, and Enzo grunts, throwing down the cloth he's using to wipe himself over. "Sounds pretty simple. Daughter runs off with loser boyfriend of her own free will and daddy doesn't like it."

I roll the words around my mouth before releasing them. Sometimes, I fucking hate the darkness of this world. "The last time he managed to track her down before they disappeared again, Sanderson had branded his name into her collarbone."

Enzo pauses, his lips pursing. "Well."

His interest is piqued. Job done, I open my phone and forward the email Millers sent after our discussion to both Enzo and Ryder. "Go through it. We'll look at the plan tomorrow."

He nods. His eyes aren't on me though. They're on the phone in my hand, and I close it off, turning the background image dark as I turn to go back upstairs. There's plenty of security cameras in that part of town I can start with.

"Mav." His voice stops me with one foot on the stairs. "You can't save them all, brother."

That's why he spends his days here, slowly cleansing the city of the scum that dwells beneath it. Justice for the ones we were too late to save.

My grip tightens on the phone in my hand. Silently, I continue up the steps.

Tell me something I don't know.

Zella

I manage to lose a few hours, sinking yet again into Darcy and Elizabeth Bennet's romance. My fingers only pause on the battered page when the light around me begins to dim, lazy afternoon settling into dusky evening.

Shifting to ease the tingling needles in the leg I've had tucked beneath me, I glance out of the window by habit, looking for any hint of the sun settling in for the night. But I never get to see the sun set. The apartment's wall of windows stretches right across, but only on one side.

The sunrise is beautiful, though.

Stretching, I put the book away and double check through the apartment, stopping off in my bedroom. Assessing myself in the mirror, my fingers smooth down the non-existent crinkles in my dress, shaking out the sleeves, and I just have time to brush out my hair one more time before the elevator dings.

Sixty seconds.

That's how much notice I get, every time Ethan makes his way up. When the doors slide open, I'm exactly where I'm supposed to be. Perfectly still, lined up alongside the statues, hands placed carefully in front of me.

I know the routine. Ethan has many little *quirks*. His aversion to touch being one. Just once, I wouldn't mind a hug, but I don't remember him ever touching anything but my hair. And, of course, there's his obsession with cleanliness.

Perfection, he calls it.

I glance around. Nothing is out of place, nothing that will make his face pull down into that particular frown that tells me how disappointed he is. I hate that frown.

Today though, his face is creased in a smile as he steps out, carrying a large brown bag. He's sharply dressed as usual, his gray suit buttoned neatly over a crimson shirt, the color a few shades darker than his hair. Although his hair has a few more strands of gray now than it used to.

The bag crinkles under his touch as he pauses, doing his customary sweep around the room. His smile widens, showing all of his teeth when he pauses on me. "Well, aren't you a sight for sore eyes."

Crossing to the counter, he sets the bag of groceries down before walking over to me, pausing a foot or so away as his hazel eyes sweep over my dress, my body, my hair.

"Perfect," he murmurs, and my muscles relax. "Your hair looks more beautiful every time I see you, Zella."

Smiling, I rock back on my heels. "Thank you. How was your trip?"

"Productive." He casts an assessing glance at the statues. "I may have another to join my collection soon."

My lips part. A new statue. He hasn't brought one for a long time, his frequent trips abroad as a renowned art dealer often unsuccessful. He's very particular in his tastes.

"We might need to make some space, though. It's looking a little busy in here." Ethan walks over to where Dante sits, and my heart pulses inside my chest.

"There's some space over there," I blurt out, waving my hand. "Next to Maria."

He tilts his head. "Hmmm. You may be right."

I bite my lip as relief fills me.

I can't lose Dante. Maybe it's a little strange to have a statue as your best friend, but beggars can't be choosers. And he's a good listener.

"Now, then," Ethan says briskly, turning to me. "Get those groceries packed away while I take a look around. There may be a little something in there for you."

"Really?" Excitement curls around me as I try to move elegantly towards the bag, despite wanting to run over and rip it open. "Thank you."

"You're welcome," he says distractedly, already moving towards my bedroom. "Get yourself together, and I'll be back."

As Ethan carries out his inspection, I keep my ear out for any disapproving sounds, but it's quiet. The whole apartment is spotless, my bed made, the bathroom back to its original clean state after the chaos of washing my hair earlier. Nothing for him to pick apart.

Unpacking the goods, I take a moment to thank the coffee gods when I spot a fresh bag of ground Italian coffee inside. A trophy from his recent trip.

Everything else gets packed away quickly, and I don't find what I'm looking for until I reach the bottom. My fingers graze the brown paper, and I tug out the rectangular parcel with a grin.

"I know what this is," I say delightedly to Ethan as he comes back in. Crossing his arms, he raises his graying eyebrows at me. His face looks more tanned than usual.

"You'd better open it then."

Despite my excitement, I take my time unwrapping it, savoring every moment as the pretty red and white cover is revealed, embossed with gold foil that spells out the title.

"Jane Eyre," I read out. Ethan nods.

"It's a classic. You'll enjoy it, I think."

"I'm sure I will. Thank you, Ethan." I add it to my shelf, and Ethan clears his throat. Taking the hint, I pull the small leather stool from the corner and set it up in front of my armchair. Ethan takes a seat as I head to my bedroom, taking out the special silver brush he brought me after a trip in Vienna several years ago.

When I'm seated, Ethan lifts his hands to my hair. I close my eyes, enjoying the feel of the brush moving through. So much nicer when my arms aren't aching from the weight of trying to do it myself.

He gently works his way through, always starting at the ends and moving upwards. I can almost feel his fingers brush my back, but he's careful to keep them away from me.

My hair is the only way he can touch me. We've never hugged, and as far as I know, he hasn't picked me up since I was old enough to walk.

For a second, I try to imagine Ethan with a crying baby. The image doesn't fit.

"Ethan?" I ask quietly. He hums an affirmative, so I take a breath. "How did you... look after me? When I was a baby, I mean. How did it work?"

His fingers pause in their work. I expect him to dismiss the question as he so often does, but he surprises me when he actually answers it. "I hired a nursemaid."

I whip my head around, shock widening my eyes. "You did?"

He's never *once* mentioned anybody else in our lives, not since my parents died. It's always just been us. Always.

He nods, and I sense his slight irritation, so I turn my head back around obediently, holding my breath as I wait for more information. "An older woman. Her name was Maria."

Maria. Like the statue, but I don't mention that. Ethan has never been a fan of me giving his art names. I wonder if there's a connection there that I never even realized. Maybe my subconscious was telling me the name was familiar.

I lapse into silence as Ethan describes his latest trip, the museums, the culture. "The *art*, Zella. You would have loved it. The statues are beyond comparison."

"Maybe one day I'll get to see them," I murmur, and then I bite my lip as Ethan pauses again. "Did you get any photos?"

He relaxes. "A few. I'll get some printed for you."

I sit quietly until he's satisfied and my hair falls in a silken sheet to the floor. "Exquisite," he murmurs. "What do we say, Zella?"

I consider his question. "One must give value to their existence by behaving as if one's very existence was a work of art."

He chuckles. "Nietzsche had it right. You are flawless, Zella. The crowning jewel in my collection."

I try to smile, but it feels a little forced, and he tilts his head.

"Art is difficult, Zella," he says quietly. "And as Dali said, a true artist is not one who is inspired, but one who inspires others. And you are nothing if not inspiring."

I glance down, thinking over his words. I have no wish to be a muse and nothing else. "Could it not be both?"

Thankfully, he laughs. "How is your sketching coming along?"

My smile becoming real, I pull out my sketchbook to show him. He glances through the pages, his eyebrows raising. "Not bad."

"If I had some color," I murmur, my eyes flicking to his face. "They could be better, I think."

He flips the book closed with a slight snap. "Perhaps for your birthday. It's coming up soon, I believe."

"It is?" Not for the first time, I wish I had a calendar, but Ethan always forgets to bring it when I ask him. I'll be twenty-three this year.

Twenty-three years of life. All of them lived within these walls.

My mouth opens, but Ethan is already standing, any potential moment for discussion quashed as he brushes himself off. "I'm sorry to leave so soon, but I have an event to attend this evening."

Disappointment curdles in my stomach as I nod, wrapping my arms around my waist as I follow him to the elevator. My hair slides across the floor behind me like a sheet, and I wince as it catches on the leg of the stool. "Of course. Perhaps next time, you could bring the photos?"

He nods. "I'll be back on Thursday."

When I stare at him blankly, he laughs, a little awkwardly. "In two days."

Right.

I suddenly feel uncomfortable, the weight of Ethan's stare heavy. I normally hate him leaving, despising the silent emptiness he leaves behind, but tonight I find myself craving the space.

"This to go?" He points at the small bag of trash, carefully double-bagged and placed by the door. At my nod, he grabs it, setting it down inside the elevator before he turns back to me.

"Two days, Zella," he reminds me. His eyes search my face, his irises darkening. "Are you sure you're alright?"

I half-shrug, and wave a hand. "Of course. I'll be... right here."

I can't stop the bitterness at the end of my words. Ethan's brows fly up, his mouth opening, but the doors slide closed before he can respond. I wait for a moment to see if they open again, but instead the sliding lights appear, showing him heading back down.

I bite my lip. I don't even know what *down* is. Does anyone else live in this building? Do I have people walking around underneath me?

The thought is comforting. I resolve myself to ask Ethan next time he comes, even though he won't like it. I went through a stage of asking a lot of questions in my teenage years, until Ethan lost his temper.

I stopped asking after that, but maybe it's time to ask again.

But thoughts of my birthday swirl inside my head as I make myself a coffee from the fresh supply, breathing in the familiar scent as I stare out of the window. There's nothing to see up here, only my own eyes staring back at me in the darkness.

I thought a hot drink might help settle my shaking fingers, but it's only getting worse.

Twenty-three. The thought of more years stretching out in front of me, lonely and cold in the vast expanse of this apartment, makes my throat close up.

A lifetime here. I may as well be one of the statues Ethan stores.

The tremor in my hands proves a little too much, and I cry out as the cup falls from my hands, smashing against the solid marble floor.

Hot coffee flies everywhere, hitting the wall, soaking into my dress, staining the floor. My hands continue to shake as I jump up to grab a cloth from the kitchen, frantically wiping and wiping until the only coffee left is the dark, damp stain spreading across the material I'm wearing.

Leaning back on my ankles, I realize my face is damp too. The tears come slowly, opening up into a flood as I bury my face in my hands.

I'm safe here. I'm *safe.* But I'm so lonely, too.

Zella

My mood is sour the next morning before my eyes even open, thanks to my sleepless night. I can almost feel the dark circles etched underneath my eyes, deep purple imperfections that I'll need to try and draw out with cold compresses before Ethan notices.

Everything about my usual routine irritates me. Washing my hair with almost frantic energy, I yank the comb through my hair roughly, uncaring of the snarls and knots and just working around them rather than working on them.

I can't face trying to dry it, so I sloppily drag it back into a messy braid, my fingers catching in tangles that make me wince. Tears spring to my eyes as I get caught on an especially stubborn blockage. I'm going to pay for this later when I try to brush it out.

Unease swirls inside my stomach as I tie the ends off. If Ethan saw my hair like this...

He won't know.

He's not even coming today.

Pulling my dress over my head, I force myself into the apartment rather than climbing back under my covers and hiding from the world.

All four walls of it.

"Enough of that," I mutter, reaching with relief for the new coffee. At least I have caffeine.

This morning's sunrise finally settles me, calming the frenetic energy that's filled me since I watched the doors close on Ethan last night.

I lean forward, coffee forgotten as I try and take in all of the color I can, my eyes flitting everywhere. Golden light rises up my arms, landing on my face as I tip it back, imagining how the morning air would feel on my skin.

When the little bird swoops past, so close I could touch it, I finally manage a smile. "Back again, are you?"

It glides back around, dancing back and forth as it flaps its wings before flying off to join the others.

The smile fades from my face.

Once the kitchen is clean, the coffee machine cleaned out and my cup dried and put away, I settle into my chair, opening the drawer of the table next to me and pulling out my sketchpad and pencils. Since Ethan won't be here until tomorrow, I can spend as much time as I like drawing today.

As soon as the graphite touches the page, I'm lost.

First, I sketch the sparrow, trying as best I can to capture the fluff in its wings, the markings along its back. Not for the first time, my fingers twitch, wanting color, but Ethan won't hear of it. He says that graphite sketches are cleaner.

When I turn to a blank page, my hand pauses, the graphite hovering over the white paper.

Just once, I wish I could draw something *new*. Something other than my immediate surroundings. But I don't have anything to reference.

It's hard to draw realistically when your entire world is contained to one place.

Closing my eyes, I think.

If only I had memories. Something from my childhood, before my parents died. But there's nothing, only a blank space and the echoes from this room.

I could draw Ethan. I've done it before, but I don't like those sketches. He looks harsh, and angry. And even though he's never said it, I don't think he liked them either. His face changed to match the sketch, and he didn't bring me anything nice for his next few visits.

I haven't drawn him since.

Chewing my lip, I press the graphite down, making a soft dent in the paper.

"Come on," I whisper. "Give me something."

The flicker takes me by surprise, and I almost drop my pencil. Grabbing for it, I run the tip over the page, soft and hard lines of gray making squiggles on the page until it begins to emerge.

A face.

A face like mine, but... older. Wide eyes, soft and happy. A gently sloping nose, high cheekbones with a blush, washed out by the gray I'm using. Framed with short curls, the exact same shade of blonde as mine.

In my mind, at least.

My fingers clench around the pencil so hard I hear a snap, but I don't care.

Because I'm staring down at something I've never seen before.

Shaking off the pencil pieces, my finger hovers over the sketch. I can almost see her in my mind, but it's fractured, little broken parts like the shattered pieces of a mirror. But the image in my hands is whole, unbroken.

A sound breaks me out of my stupor, and I glance up, my fingers tightening on the page. The afternoon light has darkened into early evening as I've sat here, and... the elevator is lifting.

My whole body locks up for a split second, and then I move.

Frantically, I shove the sketchbook back into the drawer, slamming it shut and jumping up. My hand flies to my braid, my throat closing up.

I'm a mess. My hair is barely dry and there's no way I can fix it before the doors open.

Fighting to keep my breathing normal, I take up my position opposite the elevator doors. My hand is shaking as I smooth down my dress, and I close it into a fist.

Pull yourself together, Zella.

This is ridiculous. Ethan's not going to care that much.

Maybe.

But it's too late to change anything now, as the metal doors slide open. Ethan steps into the apartment, somehow making it feel impossibly smaller as he sweeps a casual glance around. At least, it looks casual, but his eyes are assessing as he scans the statues. Hazel eyes turn to me.

My smile is weak. "Good evening, Ethan. I wasn't expecting you until tomorrow."

"Zella. I wanted to check on you. You didn't seem like yourself yesterday." His voice is smooth, not giving anything away. But the crease in his eyebrow deepens as he looks me up and down. "Busy day?"

I flush. "I... I lost track of time."

Thin lips purse in disapproval as he moves on to my hair. "I can see that. Your dress is dirty."

Breaking my carefully curated pose, I look down to see the gray smudges marking the white cotton. "It was clean this morning. I was sketching—,"

Ethan takes a few steps to stand in front of me, leaning down to look into my face. I can feel my lip wobbling as I avoid his eyes. "I'm sorry, Ethan."

My voice is barely a whisper as I wait, and he blows out a breath.

"Zella," he says softly. "What do we say?"

"Perfection," I mutter, still staring at the bright white flooring. Ethan hums, his breath ghosting across my cheek. He always smells of mint, a faint undertone of something chemical beneath.

Always perfectly put together. Almost like a statue himself.

"That's right. Perfection is possible, Zella. And you... you're perfect, sweetheart. And we have to maintain perfection, don't we?"

He raises a hand, his finger barely brushing my braid. "Why don't we sort this out, hmm?"

Nodding, I take a step back, my heart thundering. "Of course. I'll change."

He smiles, but there's a hint of steel behind it. "I think a shower is in order. Your hair looks awfully tangled."

I swallow down my protest, nodding as I back away. "I'll be back."

Ethan nods almost absently, his eyes already moving to the statues as his feet turn towards Maria. Pausing in the doorway of my bedroom, I glance over my shoulder, watching the way he circles around her, inspecting every inch for flaws.

Just like he does with me.

I struggle through the pain of washing my hair for the second time in a day, this time making sure that I take the time to comb it through, even as I watch the clock.

Ethan isn't the most patient of people. By the time I'm dressed in yet another white dress, this one without the gray smudges, and head back into the main apartment, he's standing by the window, watching the evening sky. His eyes lock with mine in the reflection of the glass.

"There we go," he says, turning to me with a smile. "Doesn't that feel better?"

Nodding, I shift uneasily on my feet. Our usual routine has been broken, and I'm not sure what to do. He makes a sound in the back of his throat.

"Get the brush, Zella. And sit down. We can talk then."

My lips twist. "Do you want a coffee first?"

He shakes his head. "I restocked the cupboards, but maybe we should cut down on the caffeine, hmm? I'm not sure it's doing you any favors if you're losing track of time."

His smile is easy, but his eyes are hard. He knows how much I love coffee. Proper, fresh coffee.

The back of my eyes starts to burn, but I bob my head in an imitation of a nod as I move over to my little living area. Dragging the leather stool across, I set it up in front of my armchair and pull the drawer open, taking out the ornate silver brush I didn't bother to put away last night. Handing it to Ethan, I make sure our fingers don't touch as he takes it from me.

Silently, I sink down onto the stool. The chair squeaks a little as he sinks into it. "Spine straight, Zella."

Tugging myself upright, I begin unwinding my braid from where it's wrapped around my waist. It's still wet.

I feel the slight tickle as he tugs away the band at the very end of my hair. His fingers start to undo the twists, and I try to stay still as he tugs and pulls. Tears spring to my eyes as he yanks one particularly gnarly patch. I didn't have time to work through all of the knots. "Ethan, please."

His hands pause in my hair, just for a second.

"This is why it's important to take care, Zella." His voice is low, even as he rips through another knot hard enough to make me whimper. "Perfection is achievable if we try hard enough. I'm not sure you're *trying* hard enough."

I bite back a sob as he does it again. "I'm sorry."

"I know." His tone is soothing. "Do I not give you everything you need, Zella? Am I not doing enough?"

I shake my head, wincing as it pulls against the brush. "No. I have everything I need."

My voice hitches on the last word, and Ethan pauses. "I can tell something is bothering you."

Squeezing my eyes closed, I take a breath. "I... I'd like to go outside, Ethan."

I can feel the way his body tenses behind me, and the words start tripping off my tongue chaotically. "Just for a little while. Just to feel the wind on my face, and maybe... maybe to see the people?"

I swear the temperature lowers, and I shrink into myself. My arms wrap around my waist, my shoulders tensing. But I can't bring myself to take it back. "Please."

It's a whisper, and I'm not sure he even hears me. But he pulls the brush free from my hair with a sigh. "We've talked about this."

"But I was younger then," I mumble. "I'm twenty-three now, Ethan. Surely... surely I have to leave at some point?"

The silence is somehow loud, loud enough to pound in my eardrums like a drum.

Ethan resumes his brushing, not responding. I wait silently, a small curl of hope wrapping itself around my heart.

"I have given you everything," he whispers finally. "And it's not enough for you."

I freeze. "No, Ethan. That's not... I know that."

"Then why?"

I turn around on my stool, and my cheek brushes against his fingers. My eyes widen as he flinches back, curling them into a fist. His face darkens.

"The world isn't safe." His words are dark, angry even, as I stare at him. "Do you want to end up like your parents, Zella? Your throat cut in an alleyway, your blood soaking into the stones, another victim of the city's darkness?"

I shake my head numbly. "Of course not. But other people *live*, Ethan. And I... I don't feel like I'm living, anymore. I'm just existing. I feel like a statue myself, some days. And every morning, I watch the sunrise and I just want to see it without the glass in my way. Just once, even. Please."

He's not listening. I can tell, the anger turning his pale eyes dark as he rips the brush out of my hair and tosses it aside. "I think it's time for me to leave."

I gather up my hair in a panic, jumping up and following him as he stands abruptly, heading towards the door. "Ethan, wait. Please!"

It's all gone so wrong. My breath seesaws out of me as I reach out desperately, my hand wrapping around his arm.

His whirls, his face a mask of anger and hand raised. "*Do not touch me!*"

Flinching back, I yank my hand away. "God – I – Ethan—,"

He stalks towards me, and I wonder for a moment if he might hit me. But something inside of me is pushing, pushing to make the most of this discussion before he shuts it down completely.

"You don't like to be touched," I force out, my voice trembling. "But that's all I want, Ethan!"

My voice raises, high and shaking. "You cannot keep me here!"

He stops, something flashing in his eyes. "I can, and I will. Someone has to protect you, Zella, and you're clearly not capable of making rational decisions."

I shake my head frantically. "I want to leave."

He crosses his arms. "Hate me if you have to, but I will keep you safe. You have no idea what it's like out there. People are evil, Zella. And they will look at you, and they will see how perfect you are, and they will want to destroy you for it."

My mouth feels dry as I stare at him. Ethan is the closest thing to family I have. Family, friends, all wrapped into one.

But at this moment, he feels like a stranger.

No, not a stranger. A keeper.

"That's my decision to make," I whisper. "Not yours."

His eyes tighten as he turns to press the button, the elevator zinging as it slides open. "I'll think about it. I want you to go to bed now, Zella."

His abrupt change takes me by surprise as I stare at him. "You... you'll think about it?"

He nods jerkily. "Clearly, you've been thinking about it a great deal."

The barb barely hits as euphoria fills me. "Thank you. I don't mean forever, Ethan. Just for a little while. An hour, even."

He walks into the small space, turning to face me. His eyes slide away, and I can see that I've hurt him.

"Wait," I say suddenly. "Don't go like this."

Ethan's hand catches the doors, holding them open as his eyes move back to mine. "Sleep, Zella," he says, more gently this time. "I think we're both a little tired. And when you wake up tomorrow, you'll understand."

Frowning, I watch the doors slide closed.

Understand what?

Taking Ethan's order for what it means, I curl up in bed, uncaring of the early hour.

What would be the point of staying up anyway?

What's the point of being alive, if I'm not truly living?

And Ethan may not like it, but I know he'll come around. He can't force me to stay here, after all.

Maybe he's right. Tomorrow is a new day.

Enzo

Ed Sanderson is perfect.

I watch him through hooded eyes from my perch on the fire escape. The alleyway is dark, broken only by the odd amber patch of streetlight. One of them is shining directly over his face.

I watch as it twists and contorts, almost demonic in its action as he pins his trembling victim to the wall by her throat, leaning in and snarling something in her face that makes her blanch. Her twisting movements double in effort, nails scrabbling for purchase in the skin of his wrist.

She can see death, this girl. I can tell by her eyes, by the frantic sounds coming from deep inside her chest, torn directly from that reservoir of strength you find when your oxygen is running out and your limbs begin to numb and you can feel the grim reaper hovering over you, ready and waiting.

It's a delicious sound, from the right throat.

But as my feet land soundlessly on the concrete and I stroll towards them, Abby Millers locks her gaze with mine. Her eyes widen even as her skin flushes with red from the vessels popping.

Sanderson is too far gone to notice if a truck came barrelling down the alley, too lost in bloodlust, a cocktail of drugs and the possibility of violence to notice me until I'm literally pressing against his back, my breath heated on his neck.

He freezes, his hand releasing the girl as he tries to turn, but my hand is already curled around his throat, the faintest line of the blade in my other hand drawing a sharp scarlet edge of blood from his skin.

Sanderson jerks, a curse flying from his mouth. "The fuck—,"

"Ed Sanderson," I whisper into his ear. It's almost a caress, if you remove the danger. But the threat is there, enough for Sanderson to start shaking against me as I lock eyes with Abby Millers.

"Go home, Abigail. Your father is waiting for you."

The burn on her collarbone stands out against the frailty of her body as she pushes herself against the wall, sliding out from our little gathering with rasping breaths.

I'm a little impressed when she turns to face me instead of running. "Will you kill him?"

"Look, man—,"

I cut Ed off with a little nudge of the knife against his trachea. "That depends," I tell her casually. "You think he deserves it?"

Her hands are on her throat, her fingers fitting into the bruising left behind by his hands as she stares at him. I wait. A serious question deserves serious consideration.

"Yes," she whispers finally. "He's done it to others."

There's something in her voice that tastes like shame, and I pull our boy a little closer to me, scenting the fear permeating his skin as he gasps. A fish in the shallows. He's completely out of his depth, and he knows it.

"Have you now, Eddy?" I murmur.

Looks like we might be bringing more than just Abby Millers home tonight. She pulls herself up even as she hesitates. "Look at the graves in the cemetery. They're recent enough so nobody notices the earth."

"Fucking skank," Eddy spits out, even as he trembles. "Talking to the cops."

"Oh," I breathe in delight, wiggling the blade a little until his chin is tilted high in the air as he works to avoid it. "I'm not a cop, Eddy boy."

I feel the jolt as he jerks against the needle I slide into the soft flesh of his stomach, a high-pitched grunt leaving his throat. "Who the hell are you, then?"

I love this part. Leaning in, I press my lips right against his ear.

"I'm Batman. Welcome to Gotham City, bitch."

He hits the ground with a thump, and I glance at Abby. She's shaking and pale, but she meets my gaze defiantly as her voice shakes. "You gonna kill me next?"

"Oh, he's not dead." I prod him with my boot, rolling him over until she can see his chest rising and falling. "Looks like he's got a little more to confess to the devil first."

She doesn't say anything, and I tilt my head, searching for a reason as to why she's still here and not running as far as possible from the stranger with the sharp knife. "Time to go home now, girl."

Her eyes slide to the side, and her fingers curl loosely at her throat again. "I don't think that's a good idea."

Something about her tone rubs me the wrong way. Crossing my arms, I stare at her. "Why not?"

She shrugs.

Testing a thought, I throw it into the air between us. "Seems like your dad is really missing you."

Bingo.

She locks up, her muscles tightening.

Fucks' sake. I'm not here to solve the world's problems. But I dig into my pocket anyway, yanking out the wedge of cash I carry around in case of... emergencies.

Like bribery. Or, as it currently seems, setting someone up to get away from their abusive father.

She watches me warily, but her arm shoots out quick enough, grabbing the stash when I toss it over and glancing down. Her eyes widen.

"There's enough there to get you settled somewhere cheap with a down payment and tide you over until you can get work. Got your ID?"

"I can get it," she whispers, touching the money before she flicks her eyes up at me. "I don't have to go back?"

I shrug. "No skin off my nose what you do. Go back, don't go back. Or you could grab your shit, head to the bus station and get yourself somewhere where people don't think they own you."

She touches the edge of the cash warily. "I don't know what to—,"

But I've already turned away. Leaning down, I grab Eddy and haul him over my shoulder. He'll be out for a while, so I turn away from her with a salute.

"Later, Abby Millers. Take care of yourself."

I'm whistling as I walk away.

Because I just added another name to my list.

Zella

Something feels different. *Off.*

Blinking up at the ceiling, I try to put my finger on it.

Maybe it's the dreams. I had another sleepless night, full of faces I didn't recognize, all of them trying desperately to talk to me with no sound coming out. Some of them were the statues – Maria, Dante, Seph.

Maybe I am losing my mind.

Last night plays through my mind on a horrible loop as I lay there, too agitated to start my morning routine.

I've never seen Ethan so cold. So angry.

All I want to do is leave for a little while. I'd even wear a disguise if he wanted me to. But he won't even open up a conversation about it.

My lips press together as I finally swing myself out of bed. I'd stay here longer, wallowing in my little pity party for one, but then I'd miss the sunrise.

I stumble out of my room in a hurry, pulling impatiently at my braid as I wind it around my waist, out of my way.

It takes me a moment to glance up and see the difference in the light.

The overhead lights are on. Frowning, I cross to the wall, hitting the switch with my hand, but nothing happens. Swivelling, I look to the windows, trying to judge the timing. The colors won't look right if the lights are switched on when the sun comes up.

My whole body locks up, the breath stolen from my lungs.

The *windows.*

My body feels heavy as I tread across the spotless floor, an iron taste in my mouth as my shaking fingers reach up to touch the steel covers. When they brush the cool metal, I recoil, a strangled scream working its way up my throat as I stagger back.

No.

He wouldn't do that. Ethan would never do this to me. He knows how much I love the light, how I wake up each and every morning to see the color in the sunrise.

But he has.

He's taken my light away from me.

Every window is covered with wide stainless-steel shutters, enclosing me inside a space that suddenly feels far too small for my body. My breathing gets louder as I back away, jolting when I hit the wall behind me.

It feels like the walls are closing in on me. A space that seemed just enough with wall to ceiling light now threatens to crush me with its shrinking size.

A sound I've never made before slips out of my mouth.

Darting to the elevator, I slap the keypad frantically, trying to guess the passcode.

But I don't know it.

His birthday, maybe? But I don't know that, either.

In a rush, it strikes me just how little information I truly have about the man who raised me.

And as fear seals off my ability to breathe, as my fingers dig into the shutters, yanking until bright, vibrant red dots spatter my ridiculous white dress, I finally understand what Ethan has been trying to tell me for the last twenty-three years.

"I will never leave," I whisper.

The words grow from a whisper to a scream. I scream until my throat is on fire with desperation, until my fingers are red with my own blood as I claw at the metal, until I can't see for the agony in my chest.

The statues watch my realization with pity in their empty gaze as I fight uselessly to get even a single glimpse of the day outside.

As I fail.

As I crawl backwards, my sobs ringing out into the lonely apartment as I curl up into a ball in the corner. A scared, lonely, useless girl.

And all the while, they stare at me, the statues.

As if I stay here long enough, maybe I'll become a statue too.

Ryder

Lingering in the shadows is definitely Enzo's thing.

I happen to find it boring as fuck.

So despite Daddy Mav's very clear, *do not pass go, do not collect $200, do not fuck this up* instructions, I scoop up a glass of champagne, smiling thankfully at the exhausted-looking waitress with the dark circles under her eyes and grubby pinch marks on her arms, and start to wind my way through the club.

Bass pounds a dull rhythm into the floor beneath my feet, the pulsing vibrations in line with the frantic activity happening around me.

Everywhere I look, people are fucking. Against walls, on the floor, strapped to machines. Groups of two, three, four, every type and shape and size, all of them voracious with their need to be consumed with the feel of a good, hard fuck.

A few people give me the eye, but I shake my head and move on, into a dark purple corridor dotted with lanterns. Against one wall are padded leather benches, most of them filled with moaning, lust-filled fuckery. The other wall is lined with one-way windows, each a voyeur's wet dream to watch the action happening inside the small rooms on the other side.

I wander down slowly, scanning each room and attempting to look even mildly interested in some of the depraved shit happening inside.

My hand curls around the glass in my hand until it threatens to snap. This is part of the darker side of Club X – that of pain, and blood, and fear.

And whilst I don't mind a little pain with my pleasure, I'm not a fan of forcing someone into my fantasies.

Muted cries echo out from the discreet headphones dotted strategically close to each window, all the better for the demons watching with slack mouths and evil eyes to hear the begging.

I keep moving, my eyes flitting across each offering and away as soon as I see their faces. One or two have masks, but none are the right build.

Ethan Moore.

He's supposed to be here, hence my little foray into depravity. But there's no sign of him.

Sighing, I toss back the remains of my champagne. Another circuit it is.

My eyes catch on the girl in the last room as I move to turn around. Her face is pushed down, hidden from view, her hair scraped back into one of those little nude swimming caps. She's strapped down, head facing me and her body spread-eagled on an x-style table.

As I pause, a man enters from a door in the back, fully dressed with fucking gloves on, despite the heat. I run through the description in my head. Six-one, slim, clipped auburn hair graying on the edges, squinty little eyes.

Bingo.

Ethan Moore strolls over to the girl, a bag in his hands that he sets down before he begins to stretch.

Spotting one of the security goons looking over, I give him a wink and settle myself into one of the benches, spreading out as though I'm watching a fucking show and making sure the tiny camera in my cufflink is facing the right way.

And Ethan Moore clearly enjoys a show. He pulls something out of the bag, and the girl tries to twist away as he presses something over her head, pushing her skull down harshly into the table. When he steps back, I lean in to get a closer look.

My fingers tap on the arm of the bench.

The girl's now wearing a long as fuck blonde wig.

Looks like someone's got a Rapunzel kink.

I try not to puke as Moore circles her, but I'm more interested in his body language. His gloves are still on, and he makes a big production of pulling them off, one finger at a time, before he presses his hands down into her skin. His head falls back, sick ecstasy written across it as he starts stroking himself.

I only watch for a moment or two more before the nausea threatens to overwhelm me. I've got what I needed – and if Moore is here, then his car will be outside.

When the fresh air hits my face, I take a minute to suck it in, clearing my mind of the vileness from inside and making my way across the darkened parking lot.

It only takes a few minutes to identify Moore's preferred transport. The cherry-red Lamborghini doesn't look out of place against the sea of high-end cars, but I glance around anyway as I dig the tracker from my pocket and casually bend down, attaching it.

Thirty seconds later, I nod to the valet doing a circuit. The cherry from his cigarette glows as he shifts uncomfortably, worried I'll call him out for smoking on duty. "Evening."

He nods back politely, and we continue on our merry way.

Tossing the barely touched cigarette I'm holding as a decoy, I pull out my phone and shoot a text to Mav.

Mission successful. Also, need bleach to wash my eyeballs.

His reply comes a moment later.

You needed that years ago.

Fair. Very fair. But something prickles across my shoulders as I glance back towards the dark doors of Club X. I don't want to leave those people there.

But I'm also not a one-man army and they have a fuckload of security, so I turn away reluctantly, heading back towards the pretty bike that I might've liberated, *again.*

Not a job for tonight. One day, Enzo will have a lot more people in his dungeon.

But it'll still never be enough

Zella

I'm not sure how long I stay there for.

Maybe hours.

Maybe days.

And then Ethan is there. His voice burrows into my head, his frantic words blurring against each other until clarity returns in a blinding bolt of pain.

My head spins to the side, and I blink, turning back to look at him. He's flexing his gloved hand, his face dark as his eyes scan mine.

"Zella – sweetheart," he murmurs. His brow is damp with sweat, his hair more unkempt than I've ever seen it as he stares at me. "I need you to get off the floor. It's dirty."

My eyes feel heavy. My heart feels heavier. "You took my windows."

Ethan presses his lips together. "They were a distraction, Zella."

It takes effort, but I turn my head to look slowly around the apartment. "Distraction from what?"

Ethan smiles, but it doesn't look real. It looks tight, and awkward. "From being who you need to be. Get up, now. I have a gift for you."

He stands up, staring down as I struggle to my feet. My legs feel numb, a prickling, burning pain spreading across them as they come back to life. Raising shaky fingers to my face, I trace the hot patch. “You hit me.”

Ethan closes his fingers into a fist. “I was scared, sweetheart. You weren’t responding to me. I’m sorry.”

I stare at him. He’s never touched me… but he slapped me. Even if he had his gloves on, it’s the most contact I’ve ever had with him.

And it *hurt.*

My whole body hurts as I silently sit on the stool he pushes out with his foot. His eyes flick over my dress, his face pressing into a fleeting frown, but he doesn’t mention it. I look down at the rusty spots marring the pristine white.

“Don’t worry,” he says quietly. “You have more. I’ll burn that one.”

I’m so tired, I don’t think before the words come out. “I wasn’t worried.”

His face twists, but he ignores my words, turning to a trolley by the door. “Look.”

I take it in dully. “A new statue.”

“Yes!” His previous ire all but forgotten, he rocks back on his heels with a bright smile. “It’s been a while, I know. We’ll need to be careful, the plaster is still drying out – but I couldn’t let her go, not once I saw her.”

Testing my balance, I slide off the stool and walk up to Ethan’s latest acquisition.

“She’s perfect,” he says wonderingly. “Isn’t she?”

Pausing, I look into her face. The churning in my stomach is spreading across my body, rising up my throat, the ache from my screaming subsiding in the face of brighter, fresher agony.

The statue stares blindly out, lips parted. She's pretty. But it's not her face I'm caught by.

It's the expression of sheer agony on her face.

I take a step back, pure reflex. I don't want to look at her face, don't want to see that level of pain, but at the same time, I can't look away from it.

"You see?" Ethan murmurs. He's close behind me as he sighs. "She's perfection."

My hands curl into fists, and I turn, nearly bumping into him before he steps back. Ethan frowns at me, distracted from the terrified statue behind me. "Zella, really. What has gotten into you?"

"Will you let me leave, Ethan?" I ask him baldly. "Am I allowed to leave here?"

He chuckles, but there's an edge to it as he glances at the windows. "Sweetheart, really. I thought we were past this."

I shake my head. "We're not. Can I go?"

He sighs, running a hand through his hair. "We talked about this. It isn't safe for you out there—,"

"That's my decision," I snap. "And I want to take the risk."

Holding up his hands placatingly, he moves a little closer, lifting up a lock of hair carefully.

"So perfect," he whispers. "So innocent, Zella. You have no idea what they would do to you out there. But I do. And I will keep you safe, even if you hate me for it."

My hair is a mess, my braid falling out everywhere, but I square my shoulders and look him in the eye.

"You have no right to keep me here," I tell him firmly. My voice rises with desperation, even as I fight to keep it level. "I'm old enough to make my own decisions."

"But you're behaving like a child," he snaps back. "I think you should go and get yourself cleaned up, and then an early night."

I can feel something pulsing in my head. "I am not a child that you can send to bed!"

He snaps. "If you will act like a child, then I will treat you like one. You're clearly not mentally capable of managing outside, Zella. Despise me if you want to, but you are not leaving this apartment. *Ever*."

I freeze. Ethan is breathing heavily, his eyes flitting to me and away. When he takes a step, I dart back, sudden fear grabbing my throat. "Stay away from me."

He frowns. "Really, this is ridiculous. I'm going to leave now, Zella. Perhaps the next time I come, you'll be feeling a little more like yourself."

"This is me being myself," I yell at him, throwing my hands out. "I will not change my mind, Ethan!"

"And how will you leave?" he challenges me. "Through the windows? The doors?"

He gestures angrily to the elevator. "It's locked to a code only I know. There is no way out of this apartment, Zella, not without my permission, and you do not have it."

Crossing my arms, I stare at him defiantly. "Then I'll wait until you leave, and watch you put the code in. You'll have to do it at some point."

The color in his face deepens to almost purple. "I'm disappointed in you, Zella. After everything I have sacrificed for you – after everything your *parents* sacrificed to give you a life, you would throw it back in our faces?"

My heart stutters, but I hold his eyes. "A life lived in a cage is no life at all."

And I refuse to believe that this is what my parents would have wanted, whatever Ethan thinks.

When he begins to nod, the tiniest fizzle of hope sparks to life inside my chest. Maybe he's finally starting to see.

Ethan spins on his heel, moving towards the storage cupboard he keeps locked up next to my bedroom door. Staying where I am, I watch him warily. His back is to me as he rummages around. The silence is deafening, the rift between us widening with every moment.

A weird clinking noise rings out as he kneels, the metallic chime making me take a step back. "Ethan," I whisper through suddenly dry lips. "What are you doing?"

He shakes his head as he stands up and turns to face me. The bottom drops out of my stomach as I take in what he's holding in his hands.

"I didn't want to do this, Zella," he says in a low voice. He takes a step, and I back away. There's pity in his face, real, genuine pity.

Even as he advances on me with a chain in his hands.

I stumble back, horror clawing up my spine as he moves towards me.

"Come, now," he urges. "Don't make this any harder than it has to be, sweetheart."

"You can't chain me," I breathe in horror. "I'm not an animal, Ethan."

My back hits the far wall, next to my little reading nook, and I dart around the chair, trying to put space between us. He actually smiles at me as he reaches down, and I stare at what he's holding in his hands.

My hair.

Slowly, he starts to wind it around his arm, and my hair begins to tug at my scalp, into pain that sends tears into my ears as he begins to drag me closer.

"Stop," I beg him. Tears start to spill out, soaking my face as I grab my hair and try to pull it away from him, but his grip is too tight. He drags me in, his fist firm and wrapped in my hair as he tows me across the open space, closer to the steel pipework decorating the wall.

My hands try to push him away, and for once he doesn't seem to care that I'm touching him, shoving and scratching as he forces me down. I barely recognise my own voice as it rises.

"Get it off me," I cry, as his gloved fingers brush my skin. "Ethan! I'm sorry!"

I'm sobbing brokenly as the shackle clicks into place, a heavy grip around my ankle. Ethan pauses, his face close to mine and yet so unfamiliar. This Ethan... I don't know him.

Flinching, I push back against the wall as he strokes my hair back, my scalp burning from the bruising force of his grip.

"There, now," he murmurs, his voice low. "I know it all seems strange now, Zella. But you'll get used to it, in time. And you can still reach everything you need to, I made sure of that. This is for your protection, sweetheart."

"Don't touch me," I force out. Something I've always wished for now feels like a violation. My voice shakes so badly I'm not sure he even hears the words, but he drops his hand with a frustrated tut.

"You'll see, soon. This is for your own good."

I can't stop staring at the iron shackle. Ethan's footsteps sound through the apartment, and I jerk my head up to see him moving towards the elevator.

"I'll be back soon," he calls over his shoulder. "A few days for you to think this through, and you'll see that I'm right, Zella."

Desperately, I claw myself upright, using the pipe for balance before I follow him. My balance is off, and I stagger across the white marble, trying to get to the doors, to where Ethan is typing in the security code.

But the chain at my ankles pulls taut before I reach him, and I land heavily on my knees with a cry of pain. "Wait. Don't do this. Ethan—,"

But the doors are sliding closed without another word.

Enzo

"Why am I here?" I mutter irritably.

Ryder elbows me. "Because this place gives me the willies, and I want to go in."

I purse my lips, taking in the dilapidated warehouse. It looks abandoned. "Why?"

Ryder checks his phone. "Because Moore spends a fuck load of time here, and I want to see what he's up to."

"Storage," I suggest. Breaking away from the wall, we make our way to the entrance we saw Moore slinking out of a few minutes ago, his eyes shifting around him before he slid into his car and pulled off. "He's an art collector."

Seems fairly simple to me, but Ryder shakes his head. "Building's not registered under his name," he points out. "No record of any leasing arrangement. I checked and it's linked to an overseas company that doesn't actually exist."

I look upwards with a little more interest. "So he's hiding something."

"Maybe." Ryder shrugs. "I ran it past Maverick, and he told me to check. So here we are. Can you hold my hand?"

"Fuck off." I sling my bag over my shoulder as we push the doors open. They screech as if disused, but the handle is clean, the entrance clear of dust and debris as we walk in and Ryder flicks a torch on.

"Empty," I deadpan, as the light flashes around the bare walls. Peeling plaster and old wooden floorboards. How exciting. "I'm so glad I came."

"Will you shut up?" Ryder pokes at a rickety chair, left lying against the wall. Ahead of us are boxes piled up in a makeshift sleeping area, but it's covered with dust.

We split up silently, moving around the edges of the open space to check we haven't missed anything. I'm about to call it when I glance down.

Ryder pops up from nowhere, peering over my shoulder. "What is it?"

I poke the floor with my shoe. "There's dust everywhere," I observe, shining the light of my own torch to make sure. "Except this path."

We follow it, and Ryder whistles. "A wall. Nice."

But I lean in, inspecting it and scanning the floor. "This isn't a wall. Not a proper one, anyway."

It's clearly fake, the height not tall enough to reach the ceiling. Stretching up, I grab the edges and pull it. Ryder grabs the other side, and we manage to push it out of the way.

"Jackpot," he breathes, sliding me a sly look from under his lashes. "And you thought this was going to be boring."

I grunt. "He's probably one of those paranoid fuckers who hides their art stuff."

Ryder prods at the shiny, dust-free buttons on the gleaming metal elevator. A light comes on, but nothing happens.

"It's locked."

"Thank you, Captain Obvious." He pulls out his phone, checking something before he types a number in. The light on the elevator flashes green, the creaking of pulleys and metal announcing its arrival. "See? Not just a pretty face. It was his birthday."

"You got lucky," I point out drily. Nine times out of ten, a code or password is obvious as fuck. Our faces reflect back at us as the doors slide open.

Ryder sweeps his arm out. "After you, dearest."

Zella

I slam the drawer closed with a frustrated cry.

There's nothing here. Nothing that will help me undo the solid iron that connects me to the steel bars of this building, like I'm becoming part of its fabric, piece by piece.

Slumping back against the kitchen cabinet, I stare at the band around my ankle. It feels tight, almost itchy, and I try to dig my finger in, but there's not enough space to scratch.

Irritating.

I'm trying not to panic. Ethan is clearly angry, but he can't keep me in chains forever.

Why not? He's kept you here forever.

Smacking away the terrifyingly negative thoughts invading my head with a slap to my forehead, I debate just going to bed.

Tomorrow is another day. I can keep trying. There must be something here that will help me get into the lock. Or if I can get into the cupboard where Ethan was keeping it, I might even find a spare key.

This feels like a plan. Exhausted, I roll onto my knees, wincing a little at the bruising I received earlier, courtesy of the marble.

The elevator dings, and I flinch, sudden fear flooding my mouth.

He's back. He told me he wouldn't be back for a while... but we haven't exactly been keeping to routine, lately.

Maybe he's changed his mind, but he was so angry earlier.

Maybe he's back for something else.

Slowly, I press myself back against the cabinet. It won't do any good, but I feel better feeling that there's something hiding me, even if it's temporary. And if he's expecting me to be in my usual spot, waiting obediently like a little lapdog, then he doesn't really know me at all.

I think I'm done following Ethan's instructions.

I hear the elevator open, footsteps tapping.

Footsteps. Too *many* footsteps. Heavy ones.

I suck in a breath and hold it.

I don't think this is Ethan. He'd never bring someone else here.

A new type of fear locks inside my chest.

Straining my ears, I let out a shaky breath and try to keep them even and quiet. I scooch forward an inch, but the sound of a male voice freezes me to the spot.

"I'll tell you now, Moore has some weird as fuck fetishes."

There's another person inside the apartment. Someone who definitely isn't Ethan.

A second voice sounds, but this one only grunts.

"I mean, look at this shit. If you looked up *creepy fucker* in the dictionary, his picture would be a full-page spread."

Another grunt. "He's an art collector."

"I feel like they're going to come to life and suck out my soul."

"They wouldn't want your soul."

"Well, that's rude." The voice sounds affronted, and I use the raised voice to slide open the door behind me. I don't want to risk moving around anymore, so I wrap my fingers around the handle of the first thing I feel.

Glancing down as I lift it out, I bite my lip.

A wok. Very dangerous.

But I still feel better as I close the door gently and lean back against it, the cool wooden handle held firmly in both hands. The footsteps continue winding their way through the room.

They're going to see me. They'll see the chain, or my—

Oh, no.

My *hair.*

Frantically, I look down to where it's spread out in a long, tangled mess that extends out way past my hiding place behind the cabinet, into the apartment. Slowly, I take one hand off my weapon and drag it towards me, inch by perilous inch.

"Stop." The second voice cuts off the ranting of the first, and silence cuts through. I drop the hair like my fingers are on fire.

The footsteps get closer, and I huddle in, squeezing my wok for dear life.

Oh god. Oh god. Oh—

Feet appear in front of me, and I glance up… and up.

The man's face is shadowed, but I see the shape of his lips, the way they part in surprise. "Holy shit."

He leans down, and I do the first thing I can think of.

I smack him with the wok as hard as I possibly can.

He stumbles back with a shocked shout, and I watch in disbelief as he staggers, before crashing to the ground.

Wow. Hopefully he isn't dead, but I'm a little impressed by the capacity of the wok. Glancing down, I give it a thankful pat before warm fingers wrap around my arm and lift me as though my weight is nothing, dropping me to my feet.

Struggling, I try to get in a second whack, but the man wraps his hand around my wrist, his grip firm but not painful as he holds my hand to the side.

My breathing feels harsh in the silence, but he makes no sound at all as he presses into me. Staring up, I catch a glimpse of dark eyes. There's no color to them at all, the irises swallowed in black. But his face...

Beautiful.

No. He's a burglar. I should not be thinking he's pretty.

But full lips, a strong, square jawline and elegantly shaped nose... he could easily be one of my statues. Except he's too alive. I can feel his heartbeat. Swirls of color run out of the neckline of his shirt and over his throat, a perfectly rendered skull.

He has art on his skin.

Full lips tilt into a faintly mocking grin as his full weight presses against me. "Who are you, little prey?"

He's so warm, even as his eyes are stone cold. A contradiction. My breathing is heavy as I take him in. I'd love to draw him.

A squeak escapes me as a hand curves around my neck and he leans in, his breath warm against my ear. "I asked you a question."

A little bit of sanity returns as a groan sounds from behind him. The man's eyes don't move from mine as his companion stirs, and I let out a small sigh of relief. His eyebrow quirks up in a clear question.

"I didn't want to kill him," I mumble, my cheeks flushing.

His fingers tighten around my nape, his thumb stroking the soft hairs gently. "What did you want to do to him?" he asks softly. Leaning in, he presses his nose against my neck, and I lose every piece of air from my lungs as he inhales.

"You broke in," I choke out. "I was... defending myself."

"Mmm. And now?" There's enjoyment in his voice as he runs his nose down the column of my throat. "What would you call this?"

Blinking, I try to move away, but I'm pinned to the counter as he towers over me. For the first time, a hint of true fear sneaks in.

"There it is," he mutters into my throat. "Delicious."

I jerk in his hold as he darts out his tongue and *licks* me.

Is that what people normally do?

"Okay... ew." I mutter the words to the ceiling, but there's a choked laugh in front of me, and the first man pops back into view. His eyes widen as he takes me in, his eyes moving to his friend and the way he has me pinned down.

His cheeks crease in a smile.

And woah. If his friend wasn't devastating enough, this one is enough to have my mouth hanging open. Even the rapidly darkening egg on his forehead doesn't take away from his looks.

Floppy brown hair curls charmingly over his forehead as he winks at me.

"Well, hello there," he murmurs. Deep brown eyes rake over me. "Name's Ryder. What's your name, princess?"

Frowning, I give his friend a dirty look as he finally pulls his head back, although he keeps me where I am. He watches me unrepentantly, his face expressionless. "Your name, little prey," he coaxes, when I don't answer.

I wet my lips. "Doesn't feel like the kind of thing I should tell people who break into my home."

The brown-haired man, Ryder, raises his eyebrows. "You live here? In a warehouse?"

My eyes widen at this new information. "This is a warehouse?"

Not an apartment block, then. Both of them frown, exchanging glances. Tattooed guy steps back, keeping my wrist in his hand as he takes me in, his dark eyes moving down and landing on the iron gripping my ankle.

The growl that rolls out of him makes me flinch, and his fingers squeeze my wrist. Reassurance or threat, I don't know. "Ryder."

Ryder drops into a crouch, reaching out for my foot. "What's this, princess?"

"Don't touch it," I snap, and aim a kick at him with my unshackled right foot for good measure. He staggers back with his hand against his nose. "Shit!"

Strong hands wrap around my arms again, and I struggle against the tattooed man's grip. His voice echoes in my ear. "Stop. Moving."

"Make. Me," I hiss back, and I swear a low laugh escapes him before I'm turned. My face is pressed into the cold marble of the kitchen counter, my hands held behind my back. A firm leg presses between mine, pushing until I'm up on my tiptoes.

My breath catches in my throat on a strangled gasp.

I… can't move.

"You were saying?" he taunts, and I close my eyes against the embarrassment.

"Let me go, please."

"You're awfully polite," Ryder mutters from behind me. His voice sounds nasally, like he's pinching his nose. "For a little savage with a wok and a strong right leg."

A hand winds into my hair, tugging it just enough to make my back arch. Wincing, I yank away from his touch, my scalp still sore from earlier.

"What's with all the hair?" the tattooed man murmurs into my ear.

I wriggle uselessly. "None of your business. What do you want?"

Both of them pause.

"Enzo," Ryder murmurs, and now I have a name for the tattooed psycho who's having far too much fun positioning me however the heck he wants. "We seem to have an unexpected development."

"Is it the thing pressing against my leg?" I mutter irritably. "Because it's definitely developing."

I had a biology textbook once. I know exactly what that is. It had diagrams and everything.

There's a moment of silence before a bellow of laughter rings out behind me, followed by a smacking sound.

"Oh," Ryder says finally, his voice filled with amusement as he catches his breath. "I like you. Can we keep you?"

"Enough," Enzo snaps before I can respond. "Call Maverick."

"Um. Yeah, hard pass. He'll tell us we fucked up, and we did." Ryder's face appears next to mine on the counter. "How do you know Ethan Moore, princess?"

I've never understood the expression about blood draining from the face, until now. Ryder watches me closely, a knowing glint in his eyes as I lick suddenly dry lips. "Never heard of him."

A hand wraps around my throat, and I gag as it squeezes lightly. "I don't like liars, little prey," Enzo warns behind me.

"Hey, now," Ryder says, without moving his eyes. "No need for that. Is there, sweetheart? Tell me – did Moore put that restraint on your ankle?"

My hesitation is answer enough, and Ryder and I watch each other silently, assessing the other.

Finally, I break the silence. "I don't understand what you're doing here," I whisper. "Do you want the statues? There's nothing else worth taking."

It's clearly not me, given the surprise on their faces when I popped up with my wok.

Ryder grins. "We were just having a little look around. But we seem to have found something much more interesting than a few statues."

He straightens. "Anyway, I think we've got what we need. Enzo. Time to shoot, brother."

Both Enzo and I freeze. "What?" we both ask at the same time.

Craning my head, I see Ryder shrug. "Like I said, we just wanted a little look, and we got one. So now we're leaving."

"Ryder," Enzo growls. There's a moment of silence as Ryder moves out of view, and Enzo's weight moves off me. Shoving myself upright, I push my hair back and turn to them.

They're already heading towards the elevator, without a backward look.

Crossing my arms, I call out, a hint of smugness in my voice. "There's a code on that door."

"Is there?" Ryder calls back airily. I watch with growing agitation as they fiddle around with the key code, and the doors slide open.

My mouth dries. They're... leaving.

Just like that?

The doors begin to close. Enzo's eyes burn into mine.

"Wait!" I cry out. I dart towards the door, banging my hip against the counter on my way. "Please!"

The doors close as the chain jerks my ankle, pulling me to a stop.

No.

That could have been my only chance.

I'm still staring at the closed doors when the little bell rings. And just like that, they're sliding open again.

Ryder steps out, arms crossed, and eyes raised. Enzo follows behind him, a silent, threatening shadow as they both come to a stop in front of me.

Ryder grins. "Knew you'd miss us. Time to start talking, princess."

I narrow my eyes at them, mildly irritated at their little game. But mostly... I'm just relieved they came back.

And that's the only explanation I have for what falls out of my mouth.

"Take me with you."

Ryder opens his mouth, but Enzo interrupts him. He steps forward, his hands curling into fists. "Your name."

He doesn't look like he's messing around this time.

I swallow. "Zella."

"Hmmm." Ryder says consideringly while Enzo stares me down. "Interesting choice."

"What does that mean?" I ask, moving my eyes to him.

He gestures nonchalantly towards my head. "The hair, of course. Rapunzel? In the tower?"

When I stare at him, uncomprehending, he frowns. "Exactly how long have you been in here?"

I take a breath. "Always. My whole life. I'm twenty-three."

Well, soon, but close enough. It's not like I know the exact date.

They both stare at me, mouths slightly agape, and I shift on my feet. "What?" I ask, a little defensively.

"A real-life fucking princess," Ryder mutters. "I'll be damned."

Before I can delve into that little tidbit, he moves on, wandering around the apartment as he calls back to me. "You said you wanted us to take you with us. Is that what you want, or do you want to be free? Two options, princess. Pick."

"I—," I stop. He's right. Those are two very different things.

Enzo is still close, still watching me. His presence feels all consuming, his eyes a brand. Like the world around us could be on fire, and he still wouldn't take his eyes from me.

"Choose carefully, little prey," he murmurs, without looking away.

It's a little disconcerting. And that's the only reason I give myself as I press my hands to my cheeks and head to the kitchen for a glass of water. He watches me silently as I drink, his eyes tracking the way my throat flexes. I hold up the glass. "You want some?"

I meant a new glass, but I gulp as his hand wraps around my hold, lips pressing over the exact same place as mine as he steals the last of my water.

Ryder breaks the weird standoff, appearing on the other side of the counter. "So?" he asks cheerfully. "Which is it, princess?"

I wet my lips. "I wouldn't know where to start on my own. So, I guess I'm asking... to stay with you."

He laughs, but there's a definite edge to it that I can't work out. "You always ask to stay with random strangers?"

I shrug, a little embarrassed. "No. But you're the first people I've ever met."

"Apart from Ethan Moore." I jump at the sound of Enzo's voice. "He keeps you here."

Carefully, I nod. I don't want to get Ethan in trouble. I just want to leave. And now it might actually be possible, my heart is pounding inside my chest, so loud in my eardrums I wonder if they might be able to hear it.

"That doesn't matter. He thinks it's for the right reasons. But I need to get out of here."

"It matters," Ryder mutters. His eyes slide to the shackle. "Right reasons, huh?"

I glance down, chewing at my lip. "We had a disagreement."

It feels like more has happened today than in my entire life. My windows, Ethan, the iron around my ankle... and now this.

A frisson skitters down my spine, but I steel myself to look them both in the eyes. "So can we leave now?"

Please. Before I lose my nerve.

It's Enzo who steps towards me. Standing my ground, I stay still as he moves closer, until his breath is warm against my lips as he looks down at me, our bodies almost brushing.

"You're giving yourself over to strangers," he says, almost wonderingly. "Just like that."

Doubt creeps into the back of my mind, but I swallow it down.

A chance. This is a *chance*. I might never get another one.

And as I said to Ethan... a life in a cage is no life at all.

Holding his eyes, I dip my head into a nod. "You won't chop me into little pieces or anything, right?"

My voice jumps at the end, and his face remains expressionless. "A little late to be worrying about that, don't you think?"

My audible swallow feels a little like surrender. "I could change my mind."

Enzo smiles, and it's ice cold. "Could you?"

Ryder interjects, nudging himself between us. "Okay, let's try to dial down the psychopath vibes for a minute. Pack your shit, princess. Time to get out of your tower."

My heart pounds. I'm leaving.

I'm getting out of here.

I take a step back, and Enzo keeps staring at me, that handsome face empty enough that he fits right in amongst the statues.

Or he would, if it wasn't for the burning in his eyes. He watches me move backwards, my fingers feeling for the handle. The chain jingles, and I glance down. "The chain—,"

"We'll take it off," he says shortly. Then he tilts his head. "For now, at least."

Swallowing, I duck inside my bedroom, not responding to his words as I push the door closed as much as I can with the chain in the way. My breathing feels choppy, loud in the quiet space, and I force it back as I press my ear to the door.

Nothing. I can't hear anything.

I peek through the gap, and the squeal that escapes my throat could probably shatter glass. Enzo's dark, burning eyes are *right there*, staring back at me, and I jump back as Ryder calls out cheerfully.

"Don't mind him! He doesn't get out much."

Swallowing, I back away from the door.

Clearly.

Enzo

Ryder yanks me away from the door, his hand gripping my shoulder as the girl skitters backwards with a startled yelp.

"Will you stop?" he hisses. "She's going to think we're serial killers."

"I am a serial killer," I point out, and he throws up his hands.

"You know what I mean."

Not really, but I step away from the door. My feet sound loud in the silence of the vast space, and I decide to do a little digging into our new houseguest.

Ryder is already digging into the cupboards in the kitchen, investigating the contents of the refrigerator with a disgusted sigh.

"Not a bag of chips in sight," he mutters. "No wonder she's so small."

My fingers flex, remembering the frailty of her small wrist under my grip. I could have broken it so easily, just by squeezing.

I pause in front of a statue, taking in the petrified look on its face. Hardly one for a museum. Ryder stands next to me, and he leans in to get a closer look.

"What?" I ask. His face is creased in a frown.

"Nothing... doesn't matter."

Shaking his head, he turns to me and tips his head in the direction of the bedroom. I can hear little rustling sounds, like a mouse is scurrying around inside.

Little prey.

That's exactly what she looked like, when I lifted her up and pressed her into the counter. All wide green eyes, plump pink lips and *hair*.

So much fucking hair. It almost drowns her, the blonde so light it's nearly white.

"So," Ry whispers loudly. "On a scale of one to seventeen hundred, how pissed is Maverick going to be?"

I give him a dead stare. "With you? Off the scale."

He actually pouts at me. "Unfair. What are we supposed to do, leave her here?"

Turning, I take in the wide space. There's a little nook crammed into the corner, out of place in the sterile environment with its chair and little bookshelf. Something catches my eye, and I cross to the space where the windows should be. The shutters rattle when I tug on them.

Locked.

"Motherfucker," Ryder curses. "This isn't a home, it's a fucking prison."

I'm inclined to agree. But given how little we know about Moore, and how trusting his little pet seems, my senses are tingling.

I don't trust her.

I don't trust anyone. Much easier that way.

"What are the chances?" I ask Ryder quietly. "That we just happen to come across her, and she's so desperate to leave?"

And that she feels so fucking perfect under my hands?

He rolls his eyes at me. "My god, you see conspiracy everywhere. You wouldn't want to leave, if he was keeping you here? What exactly is the big evil plan supposed to be?"

Turning, I survey the room again. "I don't know. But I don't like it."

He elbows me as he struts past, throwing himself down into the chair that faces the closed shutters. "Live a little, Enzo. This is the most exciting thing to happen on a case in years."

Before I can answer, there's a creak as the door opens. Our little prey emerges, eyes still wide as fuck as she edges into the room.

"Is that a pillowcase?" Ryder asks. She nods.

"I don't have a bag," she explains quietly.

My eyes slide to the cotton she's hugging to her chest. "Looks a little empty," I note.

She freezes as I walk up to her, grabbing the case to look inside. "What – what are you doing?" she asks, her voice high.

Ignoring her, I stare at the contents. A hairbrush, a replica of the shapeless sack she's wearing, and a toothbrush.

"Hey!" A small hand jabs into my stomach. "That's private!"

I frown. "Where's the rest of it?"

She rolls her eyes, pointing behind me. "In here."

Taking a step back, she brushes past me and heads to where Ryder is watching, his hands locked behind his head as he lounges in her chair. She pulls two books from the shelf and slides them into her makeshift bag before pulling open the little drawer in the side table and lifting out a sketchpad and what looks like pencils.

"Okay," she whispers. Her golden cheeks are flushed with pink when she looks around at us. "I'm ready."

"Great." Ryder jumps up, but I'm still caught on the packing situation.

"Clothes?" I point out drily. "Underwear?"

She grimaces. "I only have white dresses. A spare is enough."

"And the underwear?" Ryder asks curiously. Her face flushes deeper.

"I don't... I don't own any."

An awkward silence descends as I stare at her and she looks anywhere but at me. Her whole face is a bright scarlet.

"Look," she mutters finally. "I get it. I'm a strange girl with long hair stuck in an apartment and voluntarily choosing to leave with men who I'm pretty sure might actually kill me. It's weird."

Bright green eyes lock with mine as she swallows.

"I just want to be free," she whispers, pushing white-gold strands away from her flushed face. "I want to see what's outside these walls. I need to feel the wind on my face. I don't feel... like I'm human, here. It's like I'm a thing. A possession."

Ryder's face softens, but my body locks up at her words.

It's not that I don't know what she means. It's that I know exactly what she means.

And that's the fucking problem.

She's too perfect. Too trusting. Too soft.

Too... *much.*

Sliding my hand into my pocket, my fingers brush the syringe. I always carry a fresh one. You never know when you might need it.

"Let's take that chain off," I mutter, turning away from the innocent fucking hope in her expression before it makes me lose what little control I have left.

She inhales sharply as I crouch down at her feet, my eyes on the thick metal band with the padlock wrapped around her ankle. Her hair falls like a curtain around us, and her ankle twitches beneath my grasp as I grip the smooth skin and pull the knife from my pocket.

"You carry a knife in your pocket?" she asks, and I chance another glance up at her.

"You never know when you might need it." I push the sharp edge into the lock, wriggling it. It's an older lock, one she wouldn't have a clue how to break but one I could snap in my sleep, and it takes a few seconds at most before it clicks. Moore isn't the criminal mastermind he thinks he is. Pulling off the padlock, I push the metal open, and it clatters to the floor.

Her foot circles in my grasp as she rotates it, the relief clear in her sigh. "Thank you."

"I wouldn't thank me just yet." Getting to my feet, I don't give an inch, our bodies pressing together as she looks up at me with wide, uncertain eyes.

"Why not?"

Her lips part as my hand circles her neck and I lean in.

"Because we're not the good guys, little prey."

She gasps, her neck pushing against my grip as I push the edge of the syringe in, depressing it and watching those vibrant green hues dull as her body slumps against me.

Ryder shouts in surprise as I catch her. "For fuck- *Enzo*!"

Turning, I shrug off his outrage. "It's better this way. Safer."

He growls, shoving his finger into my face. "We should've talked about this."

"Please." I scoff. "You're already gaga for her."

He might not see it, but I do.

There's no softness in Ryder's expression when he looks at women. Heat? Lust? Wanton promise? That, he's a pro at. He was taught well, and he uses his charm as a weapon.

But that's not how he looked at *her*.

No, he looked at her like he might find redemption in her pretty green eyes.

Zella. The word rolls itself around my tongue. It doesn't fit properly.

Ryder presses his fingers against her neck, feeling for a pulse.

"Fuck off," I mutter, turning towards the door. "I haven't killed her."

Yet.

But I won't hesitate if she turns out to be a liar.

I don't like liars.

He picks up her sad little bag and follows, holding up the scanner to the keypad with irritated, jerking movements. "You're insane."

I don't respond. Some things don't need confirmation.

The doors slide open, and Ryder carries on, ranting about *Maverick's going to kill us* and *chivalry is dead* and *what kind of weirdo carries sedatives in their pocket* and all of the shit that I don't give a flying fuck about as we head down to the car. Luckily I emptied the trunk after my little trip with Ed Sanderson.

As I stare down at the unconscious girl in my arms, I don't feel a shred of regret, even as my arms hold her firmly against my chest.

She could be a weakness.

But I don't fold to my weaknesses.

I annihilate them.

Maverick

"Where the fuck have you been?"

My bellowed words make Ryder jump as he tries to sneak past the open door, but I'm past caring.

"You've been fucking hours," I snap. "No contact. Radio fucking silence. So where the *fuck* have you been?"

There's no sign of Enzo, and it tells me all I need to know. "Did you bring Moore back with you?"

I swear to God, if he's downstairs in the dungeon—

"No!" Ryder slides his hand to the back of his neck, squeezing. He looks... sheepish.

Ryder doesn't do sheepish. Petulant, yes. Dramatic, absolutely.

But *sheepish*?

I cross my arms, waiting for an explanation and fucking hating the way he shifts on his feet. I'm not his fucking father – I'm nowhere near old enough. But damn if it doesn't feel that way sometimes. Between Ryder and Enzo, it's no wonder my hair is greying at the ripe old age of fucking thirty.

But damn it to hell, someone has to keep order in this house. And as much as I hate that it has to be me, I hate the idea of them both spiraling even more.

I tip my chin at him. "Talk. Now."

He starts to sidle towards the lounge, and I stalk after him. "A conversation like this is probably best with wine."

"You hate wine," I snap.

He shrugs helplessly. "Maybe I've developed a taste for it?"

Crossing to the bar, he pours a large glass and holds it out to me. Blinking, I stare at it. It's nearly overflowing.

They've definitely killed someone they shouldn't have.

"Just tell me," I grit, snatching the glass and throwing back a large gulp, sucking down at least two hundred dollars' worth of vintage merlot in one fortifying swallow. "Who's dead?"

Ryder laughs nervously. "Er – no one."

Raising my eyebrows at him, I wait. He squirms, not sitting down. Just standing there looking awkward as hell. "Where is Enzo?"

His shoulders slump. "Downstairs?"

I take another sip, not much smaller than the first, with the strong feeling that I'm going to need it. "Ryder. Just spit it out."

He rotates his shoulders, drawing in a big breath. "*Westoleagirl*."

Blinking, it takes me a moment to decipher the garbled words. Then a good thirty seconds of trying to work out what he means, and then praying that it doesn't mean exactly what I think it fucking means.

Another sip, as he watches me warily. "Say that again. A little slower."

His teeth sink into his lip. "We... stole a girl?"

Carefully, I place the wine down on the table next to me. "See, I thought you might have said that. Except, then I realized that couldn't possibly be true. There's no way that you and Enzo would be stupid enough to kidnap a girl off the street. So, I must have misheard. Yes?"

"It wasn't off the street," he nearly shouts. "She was in the warehouse."

My hand reaches out for my wine again. "In the warehouse."

A headache is starting to form behind my right temple as I watch him twitch. "For Christ's sake," I snap finally. "Sit the fuck down and tell me exactly what happened."

He sits.

And I try to take in the information he's throwing at me, my hackles rising as I fight to keep my breath even.

"Let me get this straight," I begin, sitting forward and holding up a hand to cut off the flow of absolute shite spouting out of his mouth. "You broke into the warehouse."

Ryder nods, his hair flopping over his forehead. "Well, the main doors were open, but there was a false wall..."

He trails off as he gets a look at my face. "Yes. Yes we did."

"And you found a girl, chained to the wall."

He nods again. "With really long hair. Proper Rapunzel in the tower shit. And her name is Zella."

More wine needed.

"And instead of calling the authorities," I begin slowly, massaging my temple as I get up to refill my glass, "you made a bargain... to bring her here."

He shrugs. "She didn't want to be on her own. She was right, too. No way she would have survived if we'd just let her run off."

I stare at the dark liquid inside my glass. "So you made a deal with her to bring her here, broke the chains off her ankle, and then... Enzo knocked her out."

Ryder looks obstinate when I turn to him. "I didn't agree with that."

I think I've run out of words.

"And... she's where, now?"

I think I already know the answer to this. Ryder drops his head. "In the dungeon."

My fingers trace the edges of the glass. "So you kidnapped a girl who would have come willingly, and then took her into a torture dungeon."

Ryder grimaces. "I mean, when you put it like that, it doesn't sound like the best idea. Enzo was pretty insistent, though."

My mouth dries.

Maybe this... this is it.

The moment I've been watching for, dreading, for years. Where we lose him to the darkness completely, lose him to the shadows covering his soul and I can't bring him back, can't fix up the tears in his psyche with the blood of evil men.

The pain in my head explodes into a full-blown rage.

I'm not losing him. Not to this. I won't let the shadows have him.

We've fought too hard to let him slip away now.

The glass smashes into the floor as I spin and head out of the lounge. Ryder follows me as I stride to the door covering the inside entrance to the dungeon, the one we rarely use.

"She's fine. He won't hurt her, Mav."

Fuck, I hope that's true.

Zella

Awareness slowly crawls into my consciousness.

I feel full of cotton wool and candy floss, like the sweet fluff Ethan brought me once, before he took it away in case I rotted my teeth.

That's what's inside my head.

Drowsily, I roll my face from side to side, attempting to shake it off. Maybe I'm getting sick. It doesn't happen often, but the last time, I thought I was on fire.

I don't feel that way now though. In fact, I almost feel cold. The cool brush of air against my skin makes me shiver.

I pause. I shouldn't feel air.

And the bed – it's too hard. Solid and cool against my back.

I force my eyes open, blinking lazily before my sight sharpens into terrifyingly clear focus.

Because this isn't my bedroom.

Clarity returns like a slap to the face. In a rush, I remember. My windows. The chain, cold metal against my ankle. And... the break in.

Ryder and Enzo.

I swallow, but there's a desert in my throat, and I cough.

A hand slides around the back of my neck, lifting me up as the kiss of cool water touches my lips and I drink it down desperately before it's taken away too soon.

"More," I rasp. Blearily, I turn my aching head and flinch.

Enzo leans over me, his mouth the barest inch away from my face. Those black eyes bore into me as a shocked sound erupts from my still-dry throat.

Trying to calm my racing heart, I nod at him. "Hello."

When he doesn't respond, I tilt my head to look around. Disappointment hits me hard in the chest at the steel walls, the bright lighting above me making me squint and driving the lingering ache in my head. Wherever I am, there are no windows here either.

Oh, Zella. You might've messed up here.

"Too bright," I choke. The lights dim instantly, and I let out a breath as I continue my assessment.

I'm lying on some sort of hard table. It feels cool against my fingertips, and I twitch them experimentally, surprised when they move without restriction. Fingers encircle my wrist, and I glance up at Enzo with a swallow.

This is his space. I can feel it in the way he watches me, intense but relaxed. Not like in the apartment, where every movement set him on edge.

Here, he feels comfortable. His presence fills the room, almost visible in its overwhelming feel.

And I... do not feel particularly comfortable.

"I thought you weren't going to chop me up," I mutter, and dark brows pull down into a frown. He stares like he's waiting for something. "What?"

He blinks, something like confusion swirling in his gaze. "Aren't you wondering where you are?"

I look around the room again. My heart starts to flutter when I spot the manacles under the wall, and his fingers tense on my wrist.

"What a fast pulse you suddenly have, little prey," he whispers. "Are you scared?"

Surprisingly, I'm not. At least, nowhere near as much as I probably should be. Instead, I sigh, and my shoulders slump.

I so wanted to see the outside. Instead, it seems like I might have landed somewhere worse. But it's not the white walls of the apartment, and even though my heart is thrumming like a little bird, it's enough.

"You haven't hurt me yet," I say softly, and his grip on my wrist jerks as he drops it like it's burnt him.

"I could hurt you," he murmurs. "So easily."

Closing my eyes, I try not to panic. Ryder must be here somewhere. He seemed a little more... normal. Less serial-killer, more charming rogue. "Why would you want to hurt me? I haven't done anything to you."

My breath catches as I open my eyes and find his face directly above mine. His breath brushes my lips. "Yet."

When he backs away, I turn my head to watch him. "This feels a little like a stalemate."

"It's not." I watch him select something from the various items on the table. My heartbeat stutters when he turns around and moves towards me.

How can someone so angelic look so demonic?

My imagination is clearly running away from me, but I can almost see the brush of white and black feathers against his shoulders, see the battle for light and dark and how it would play out under my hand as I draw him.

I would give *anything* to draw him.

My eyes skitter down his body. The black shirt he wears hides most of the art decorating his skin, but the sleeves are pushed up past his elbows, and I can see the intricate work, layer upon layer of shapes, words, *art*.

Not a single one has any color. The possibility makes my heart hurt.

"Can I color in your tattoos?" The words burst out of my chest, and he stops in surprise.

"Absolutely fucking not. Do I look like a damn coloring book to you?"

I nod honestly. "A little, yeah."

My hands grip the sides of the metal table when he lifts his knee, pressing it between mine as he climbs up on top of me. His legs settle on either side of mine as he leans down, and I close my eyes against the sensation of another person being so close to me.

The air that escapes my lips is somewhere between a sigh and a shudder. When I open them again, he's watching me, running something between his fingers.

"You're not normal," he says quietly. It doesn't feel like an insult.

I tilt my head. "I spent twenty-three years locked in an apartment. What's your excuse?"

We watch each other in silence, the atmosphere ratcheting up until the tension feels heavy on my tongue at our standoff.

And all the while, he plays with the tool in his hand. It looks heavy.

"Got any plans for that?" I ask him boldly, and he looks down almost as if he'd forgotten all about it.

"I can't decide." His face looks tortured in the dim lighting, his weight pressing me down into the table. "If I want to kill you."

I hold my breath, watching him and letting it out when his eyes move to mine. "Is there another option?" I whisper.

Please let there be another option.

He raises the tool and I flinch, but he lays it down, so it presses flat against my chest. The long handle nestles between my breasts, and I suddenly become aware of my own body as the white material pulls tightly across them, pulled taut by the weight.

Swallowing, I whisper. "It's heavy."

My hands raise as if to move it, but Enzo grips them, pushing them over my head as he follows, his weight pressing down against my chest, my hips, his legs tangling with mine as the tool pushes into me.

He's everywhere, wrapped around me, and I can't stop the groan that falls from my lips as I tilt my head back. Maybe I shouldn't feel like this, shouldn't like the weight of him on top of me, but I do.

Maybe I'm broken.

But I want more.

He stares down into my face. The mask is flickering, confusion and something darker hiding behind it. "There is another option."

His hands slide up to my neck, curling around it and pressing gently as he leans down, his mouth touching mine. I open for him, my lips trembling as they part. But he doesn't move, doesn't do anything, doesn't touch me like I suddenly, desperately want him to.

"You respond to touch like a flower to the light," he murmurs against me. "Who are you?"

I swallow around the light grip on my neck. "Zella."

But he shakes his head firmly. "No, you're not."

"I...," My eyebrows draw together. "That's my name."

But he only smirks, his lip tilting upwards in a way that turns him from handsome to devastating. "Little prey suits you better."

Before I can respond, his lips press against mine, warm and firm as his hands weave into my hair. My whimper is lost to him, and he growls against my mouth as he presses every inch of him against me like a brand.

Tears fill my eyes as he holds me for him, kissing and sucking my lips until I feel swollen and heavy, my eyes lazy as he lifts his face from mine.

"The options," he says roughly, and I swear I can see a spark of light in his eyes, a single, solitary star against the soulless dark night.

But there's a crash, and his weight disappears from on top of me as I cry out in shock.

Scrambling upright and fighting off the lingering dizziness, I stare down at where Enzo is sprawled across the floor. There's a sound, and I realize he's laughing up at the man who stands over him with fists clenched.

"The *fuck* are you doing, Enzo?" The man roars, and I flinch back at the unfamiliar shout.

Enzo is still laughing, but the man looks really angry, and I throw myself off the table, staggering slightly before I push in front of him. "Leave him alone!"

Enzo's laugh cuts off abruptly behind me as I stare down the very large man.

I swallow as he stares right back at me, his own eyes widening.

God. Is everyone on the outside this attractive?

There's a choked sound from the side of me, and Ryder laughs as he slides into view, wiggling his hand at me in a wave. "Not everyone, princess. We're just lucky fuckers."

He sounds amused, and the blood rushes to my face as I realize I said that out loud.

Crossing my arms, I frown at the handsome, tall man. "Stop shouting at him. He wasn't doing anything."

He just stares at me. Dark hair with the faintest thread of gray curls around a strong, olive face, light blue eyes crinkled at the corners. "Did he hurt you?"

I shake my head, my eyes sliding to the tool that clattered to the floor when I jumped up. I quickly look back to him in case he spots it too. "Nope."

Enzo sucks in a breath behind me, and Ryder lets out a breathless laugh. "See, Mav? All fine."

Mav – who I'm guessing is the man staring at me like he's never seen a girl before – turns to glare at him before his eyes return to mine. He scans my face with a frown.

"Have we met?" he says abruptly. Startled, I shake my head.

"Ah... no. That would be unlikely."

"Maverick," Ryder says slowly. "Did you miss the part about her being locked in an apartment for twenty years?"

Maverick frowns again. His arms are like trunks, and I gulp as he folds them, a disapproving look entering his eyes as he scans us before he sighs.

"Zella, I assume?"

I stare at the hand he holds out, before reaching out to grasp it and dropping down to the floor. He looks a bit confused as I bob back up, and I bite my lip. Maybe I did it wrong.

"Did... did you just curtsey?" Ryder asks in a slightly strangled tone. When I glance at him, his shoulders are shaking.

"Um." Clearing my throat, I take a step back, and a hand curls around my ankle. Enzo stares up at me as I wave a hand. "Just ignore that I did that."

Clearly, I shouldn't rely on Jane Austen to provide accurate descriptions of current social behaviors.

But Maverick steps forward, and my lips part in surprise when he leans down into a flawless bow. My stomach does a little flip in excitement.

Even Darcy couldn't have done that any better.

Maverick watches me closely as he straightens, and I give him a little wave before I tuck my hair back behind my ear. The braid around my waist is unraveling, and I can feel Enzo's hands playing with it where he's still sat on the floor.

"Anyway." I smile at him. "Zella. That would be me."

Enzo tugs on a loose piece of hair, and I try to discreetly step on his hand without Maverick seeing. He feels like the one in charge, and I casually try to straighten my dress as I give him my best smile. He looks a bit shell shocked.

Shaking it off, he offers me a nod before his eyes slide down to Enzo. "Get up. We need to talk about what we're going to do with her."

As he turns, I dart forward. "Wait! What do you mean?"

What does he mean, *do* with me? I'm not a vase. Or a chair.

Maverick's eyes drop to where I'm clutching his arm, and I let it go with a gulp. "Sorry. Do you have touch issues too?"

Oh, dear. It looks like a little vein has popped up on his forehead. "No."

"Oh. That's good." I give him another smile, and he takes a step back. "Thank you for having me. I promise I won't get in your way."

I get a side eye and a grunted sound before he turns away from me and heads up a flight of stairs in the corner.

"Enzo. Ryder." His voice echoes behind him, deep and rumbling and just a little masterful. I try not to shiver. Maybe the Darcy bow got to me, just a little. "Dinner is in an hour."

I think Ryder groans, but dinner sounds *really* good. I'm starving. I haven't eaten anything since yesterday.

Bouncing on my feet, I clear my throat loudly in a very casual, *I-know-you're-not-about-to-have-a-yummy-meal-and-not-invite-me* way, and a sigh sinks into the air.

"You too, Zella."

"Looking forward to it!" I call cheerfully, and spin to where Ryder and Enzo are both staring at me.

"He seems nice," I say happily. Now that the awkward introductions are out of the way and it seems that Enzo is probably not going to kill me, I feel much better.

Enzo's hand is still wrapped around my ankle, and I yelp when he tugs it sharply. He drags me down until I'm sitting in his lap, my legs swung out to the side and his hand around my throat. He doesn't squeeze, holding me firmly in place.

"You have no sense of self-preservation," he snaps in my face. "Why did you stand in front of me?"

"Hey." Grumbling, I push his hand away. Or try to, at least. It's like trying to move a boulder. "I didn't know who he was, and he was shouting at you."

Enzo leans in and makes a growling sound in his throat. "You do *not* put yourself in between a fight. Ever."

My shoulders square mutinously. "But you didn't do anything wrong! And there wasn't a fight. I just... wanted to clear up any confusion."

"Why?" he demands. "Why would you do that?"

I shrug, trying to look away, but he grabs my chin, forcing me to look at him. "Tell me."

He looks furious, his eyes black as night again. The little hint of stars I thought I saw has disappeared, swallowed by darkness.

"I didn't want you to get hurt," I admit in a whisper.

Although right now I'm starting to regret it. Enzo is giving me a funny look that's making my stomach flip, and Ryder clears his throat.

"All right, then. So, that was Maverick, the last of our merry trio. I'm sure you'll get to know us better at dinner, Zella."

Wiggling, I nudge Enzo's fingers away from my face and scramble to my feet, grimacing at my tangled nest of hair as I trip over it. I can't go to dinner looking like this.

"Could someone show me where I'm sleeping?" I ask. "And did you bring my pillowcase?"

Zella

"Princess."

Ryder sounds a little desperate, and I turn to him with a sniffle. He hands over another box of tissues, and I tug one out and blow my nose loudly, the honking sound echoing around the large room.

"Sorry," I cough out, turning to him with a wobbly smile. He shrugs, but there's a frown crinkling the middle of his handsome forehead.

"So, you like the view?"

Nodding, I turn back to the view that stole the breath from my lungs and had me sobbing like a baby for the last twenty minutes.

"Yes," I whisper. My fingers raise to touch the clear, floor to ceiling glass. "I like it."

There's a shift in the air as Ryder steps up next to me, both of us looking outside. Miles upon miles of greenery sweep away from us, hills and trees and even what looks like mountains in the distance.

And there's so much *color*. Brilliant oranges, reds and yellows mix in between, a paint palette I've never seen before.

"Is this autumn?" I ask Ryder, bouncing on my feet as I press both hands against the glass, getting my face as close as I can. "It looks like autumn."

"It is. October. You know the seasons?"

I know the seasons. Despite my limited upbringing, Ethan at least taught me something – mathematics, biology, physics, literature, languages, *art*.

"He taught me plenty," I mutter. "Just never anything about the actual world outside."

Nothing about history, unless it's directly connected to books or art. I have no idea how the world works, governance structures, politics. They're all hazy terms to me.

My lips tighten, but I can't find any anger in my heart.

"How could anyone be unhappy with a view like this?" I whisper, my voice full of awe. "If I'd had a view like this, maybe I would never have wanted to leave."

Ryder's weight brushes against me, the touch unexpectedly warm, comforting.

"I think," he murmurs, "that the limited world you inhabited could never have been enough for you, Zella. Anyone with half a brain could see that."

Tearing my eyes away – just for a second – I look up at him. Chocolate-colored hair falls lazily over his face, and he doesn't bother pushing it back. His eyes flicker as he glances down at me, the warm hues not out of place with the world outside this window, almost amber in the fading afternoon light. The darkest hint of stubble lingers at his jaw. "What do you mean?"

He grimaces. "That place... it was one of the coldest places I've ever set foot in. Not in temperature, but in feeling. It would have sucked the life from you, Zella. And that would be a tragedy."

"It would?" I ask softly.

He turns, giving me his full attention, and his lips quirk. "You're the most vibrant person I've ever met. You don't belong in that cold place, princess."

I half-smile, suddenly a little flustered by the look in his eyes. Swallowing, I spin to stare back out of the window. "I don't belong anywhere, really."

It's a confession, a tiny piece of truth in the air between us.

Ryder is right. I didn't belong there.

I know that. I can feel it with every beat of my heart, every pulse of relief that I'm not trapped within those walls any longer.

But I don't belong here, either.

I begged them to take me with them, and they did.

But they have their own lives. This isn't forever.

Swallowing back the burn in my throat, I step away from the window, my hands hugging my elbows. "I should get ready for dinner."

My hair alone will take forever, and I don't have a lot of time.

Ryder doesn't move immediately, his eyes tracking me, lips parting as though he's not finished with our conversation. But eventually he nods, stepping back and heading towards the door. "I'll be back to get you in thirty minutes. Don't leave this room until then."

The large wooden door slides closed behind him, and I glance around the ornate room. Ryder seems to enjoy calling me Princess, and this room makes me feel like one. An ornate, four-poster bed with soft golden sheets takes up most of the middle of the room, with an equally detailed armoire and dressing table at one side.

Taking my pillowcase, I pull out the items I brought.

My hairbrush is placed carefully on the table.

My dress is hung up in the empty armoire.

My sketchbook is placed next to my bed.

Toothbrush and toothpaste in hand, I pull open the door in the corner, my eyes rounding at the pretty bathroom.

There's a bathtub, a gigantic, clawed thing with pretty golden feet that looks like it might swallow me up if I tried to lay down in it.

I am in love.

I know what I'm doing later.

But now I'm really late. I scrub my teeth frantically, splashing water on my face and hustle back to the bedroom.

My hair is a lost cause, but I still try to wrestle with it, dragging the strands into a new braid that I'm still looping when Ryder knocks on my door again.

"Coming!" I call. I look like I've been asleep for ten hours and I have hair sticking out everywhere, but it'll have to do. I don't want to waste my one dress on dinner, not until I know how I can wash clothes here.

My breathing is a little fast as I pull the door open, and the sight of Ryder leaning against the door doesn't help in the slightest. Dressed in an olive shirt and dark trousers, the shirtsleeves hug his arms, showing the muscle underneath.

His eyes sweep over me. "Princess. You look ravishing."

I scoff, just a little. I'm the last thing from ravishing.

And why do I suddenly wish I had something prettier to wear? Next to Ryder, I feel like a sack.

I don't even have any shoes, I realize, as his smart black shoes tap against the oiled wooden floorboards. My bare feet pad along next to him as he leads me down the hall, and I glance around at the paintings on display. My feet trip as I recognize some of them.

"Is that a Monet?" I gasp, when Ryder grabs me to stop me from falling on my face for the third time.

He grins. "It is."

I crane my neck to look up at it. "It's an original?"

When I turn to look at Ryder, there's a dull flush of deepening red spreading along his cheekbone. "How'd you know?"

"I wouldn't say I'm certain, not without examining it more closely. But that looks like original canvas, and I can see the texture."

Craning my head, I look up and down the hall. More familiar art jumps out at me, and my eyebrows fly up.

Ethan would love this.

My throat dries up. I wonder if he knows I'm gone, yet.

What he'll do.

Pushing the thoughts away, I turn back to Ryder. "Quite the collection."

He throws out a hand carelessly. "I enjoy acquiring art. It's a process."

I know, probably more than he realizes. Ethan would be away for weeks sometimes to work on building his collection. I never even saw most of it, a lot stored in the gallery he always told me about. But he always talked about the *process*.

Ryder nudges me, offering his arm. "Come on, princess. Maverick hates lateness. He's a bit of a stickler for the rules."

Taking his arm, we make our way down a beautiful double staircase and into a large, open room with a long dinner table. Candles flicker, the light coming from the large windows throwing golden light across the white tablecloth. I crane my head, taking in the new angle of the trees outside.

Maverick is seated at the end of the table. He stands when we enter, moving to a chair next to him.

"Zella. Why don't you sit here."

It's not a question. His voice is so deep I can feel it, a faint vibration inside my chest. Swallowing, I step away from Ryder and walk around, sliding in with a whispered thanks as Maverick pushes the chair in until I'm tucked under the table.

He sits back down, completely focused on me. I look down.

There's something about Maverick that ties my tongue into knots.

"Well, this is very formal," Ryder drawls. He throws himself into a chair opposite me, on Maverick's other side, and reaches for a glass. "You drink wine, princess?"

"Um. Sure."

I have never, in fact, drank wine. Or any alcohol. But I don't tell Ryder that as he pours me a large glass and passes it to me. I can feel Maverick's eyes on the side of my face as I take a sip.

"Good?" he asks in a low tone. When I turn to him, his blue eyes are completely focused on my face. Heat suffuses my cheeks.

"Lovely," I murmur. The rich taste takes a little getting used to, so I take another small sip and place it down. "Will Enzo be joining us?"

Ryder laughs. "I very much doubt it."

But the door bangs on the edge of his words, and Enzo stalks in. His tattoos are hidden beneath another black shirt as he pulls open the chair at the furthest end of the table, dropping into it and glaring at us like we've personally dragged him in and tied him up.

The lump in my throat intensifies when he stares at me, his brows drawing down.

He doesn't say anything.

The silence stretches out for a few minutes, until two black-clad people enter, setting down trays on the table. My eyes round at all the food, and I nearly bounce in my seat.

I'm so hungry.

"Thank you," I say with a smile to one of them, and he slides wide eyes to me before his head dips in a nod. When he lingers, a deep voice rumbles from the end of the table.

"Remove your eyes from her, before I do it for you."

It takes a second for the words to register in my head. The man pales, backing away with a fumbling apology and disappearing out of the door as I frown down towards Enzo. All he does is stare back at me, his face expressionless.

The delicious smells soon distract me, and I take a deep breath.

"Hungry?" Maverick asks, and when I nod, he stands up. "Allow me."

Wide-eyed, I watch as he makes his way around the table, adding food to the plate in his hand. He towers over me as he comes to a stop beside me, and I stare up at him.

"Open up, Zella," he murmurs. Electric blue eyes don't move, and my mouth opens without thinking. He lifts a fork to my mouth, sliding it in slowly, and my lips wrap around it, taking in the offering.

I barely taste it as I chew, my eyes still on him.

"Good girl," he murmurs. My stomach flutters. I jump at a slamming sound, but when I look down the table, Enzo is digging into a plate of food, not looking at us.

Ryder is watching us with a strange expression, but he doesn't say anything as Maverick sits back down with my plate in his hand. I inhale sharply as his hand reaches out, dragging my chair closer to his.

He holds up another forkful. "More."

It's not a question.

Maybe this is how they treat all their guests?

Obediently, I lean forward, taking the food he offers. It melts in my mouth, some type of meat and sauce, and Maverick leans forward.

His thumb slides across my bottom lip, dragging it down, and my breath tangles in my throat as he pulls away.

Maybe.

Maverick

I can feel the stares from Enzo and Ryder, the silent question in the air as they stare and I pick up another piece of chicken with my fork.

What the fuck are you doing?

What the fuck *am* I doing?

I don't know.

I don't know why I insisted Zella sit next to me. Why I made her a plate up rather than allowing her to serve herself, why I insisted she take food from my hand.

But as those plump lips close obediently around the fork once more, green eyes wide on mine, I can't tear my eyes away.

After storming from the dungeon, I spent the last hour stalking up and down this room, fists clenched as I tried to resist the urge to storm upstairs and bring her down to me immediately.

Tried to push down the feeling in my chest. The darkness.

But as I watch her, I know I'm going to fail.

Maybe it was never Enzo I needed to worry about.

Maybe it was me all along.

Because all I want to do is *own* her.

My eyes trace her face, taking in the expressions she makes with every bite. What draws out that little crease between those gorgeous eyes, what makes her lips twist up in pleasure.

I want to know everything about this girl.

Who she is.

Where she came from.

Doesn't matter, a voice whispers. *She's here now.*

And most of all, I want to know how she looks pinned beneath me, her head thrown back in ecstasy as my cock sinks into her.

The battle rages on inside my head as I nudge her glass towards her. "Drink."

Her throat looks so delicate as it flexes, swallowing down a gulp of wine.

Ryder taps his fingers on the table, and I tear my eyes away to look at him. His head is tilted towards me, but he's watching her. Enzo, too. I'm amazed he even showed up to this dinner, but maybe I shouldn't be.

I would have showed up for her, too.

I continue feeding her until she shakes her head, a small, protesting sound coming from her throat. "You need to eat too. I think I'm full."

I scowl down at the plate. She's barely eaten a third.

That's going to change, but I'll let it go for tonight.

Ignoring my own plate, I settle back in my chair. Zella shifts, her fingers clutching her glass like it's her own personal comfort blanket. Her braid trails over the back of the tall chair, pooling onto the floor in a messy rope.

My hands ache to touch it, to unravel it and see the full glorious length, but I hold myself back.

I need to control myself.

Enzo has no such compunction. Standing up, he makes his way around the table and throws himself into the seat next to Zella, his hand whipping out to wrap around the back of her neck.

Ryder and I stiffen. Leaning forward, I'm about to rip into him when I see Zella relax, tension leaking out of her body as she leans back into his touch.

He gives me a knowing smirk, but his fingers move, rubbing her neck as she nestles back with a quiet sigh.

She wouldn't look so relaxed if she knew how easily he could snap it.

Forcing myself to look away, I drum my fingers on the table. "So."

Three sets of eyes focus on me.

"Zella." I allow myself to focus on her completely. "What are we going to do with you?"

Zella shifts as if to lean forward, but Enzo keeps her exactly where she is, his fingers squeezing in light warning. A little huff slips out, but she stays still. Her mouth opens, and then closes again.

"I don't know," she responds finally. There's a little shake in her face as her eyes stare down at the table. "I don't exactly have a plan here."

The touch of sass in her voice lifts the edges of my lips, but I straighten them, leaning forward. "You have no family? Friends?"

She looks at me, all eyes and hair. "I don't have anyone."

Her voice is even now, even as sadness bleeds into the air.

Enzo growls, but he stops when I glare at him. I can't work out exactly where his head's at, so he doesn't get a fucking say in this.

Ryder smiles languidly. "Not entirely true, princess."

He waves a hand around the table towards us, and I frown.

She's already gotten under our defenses. Invading our space. And if she stays, then it'll only get worse.

I don't know if I'll be able to let her go.

"We can give you money," I bite. The words feel like they burn on my tongue, and she pales.

"You're making me leave?"

I swipe a hand over my face. She's so fucking naïve, I can't work out if I want to shake her or pin her down and show her exactly why she shouldn't have volunteered to come home with men who *broke into her fucking apartment*.

Jesus. If I make her leave, she'll be a prime target for any asshole on the street. One look at her and she screams *victim*.

If I allow her to stay, she might become one anyway.

But she'd be ours, the voice whispers.

She stares at me beseechingly, and behind her, Enzo pins me with a hard stare. "She stays."

Zella turns to him, relief flitting across her face. "Really?"

Straightening, I reach out and turn her face towards me, my fingers gripping her chin.

"He's not the one you have to convince, Zella."

Even her bones feel fragile, breakable under my hand as her soft puffs of breath fall against my skin.

It would be so easy to break her. And easier for us than most.

She wets her lips. "Please," she asks quietly. "Please, Maverick."

Fuck if her words don't make my cock harden like a damn rock. The choked sound next to me tells me Ryder feels the same way.

My fingers rub her cheek. "If you stay... there are rules."

Her eyes brighten immediately, and she nods enthusiastically. "I can do that. I'm good at following orders."

Ryder lets out a strangled groan. "Princess."

"What?" She tries to look at him, but I won't let her.

I need her to see the risk she's taking.

"We are not good men, Zella," I tell her quietly.

Ryder and I are fifty shades of fucking grey. And Enzo is ninety-nine per cent dark.

But she nods anyway. A small hint of what looks like hesitation enters her eyes. "You're talking about the room downstairs, right? Where I woke up?"

Enzo stiffens next to her.

"You don't go down there," I say firmly. "Not unless one of us is with you."

She nods eagerly. "What else?"

"No going outside." At my words, her face crumples.

"At all?" she whispers. "Not even the garden?"

"Same rules apply. With one of us only."

She blows out a shuddery breath. "Okay."

Her acquiescence does fucking things to my insides.

The last rule slides out too easily. "Finally, you do exactly as you're told."

To keep her safe. And keep her here.

"Okay," she whispers. "I understand, Maverick."

When I release her, trembling fingers rise up to massage her face.

Maybe she's not so unaware after all.

But she agreed anyway.

My chest hums with satisfaction as I sink back in my chair and raise a glass. "Then you can stay."

It feels like a net is closing, predators circling a blissfully unaware lamb.

Ours.

Zella

Sighing, I let my head fall back against the edge of the bathtub.

Bliss.

This... this is perfection.

Mentally thanking whoever thought to add bubbles to the stocked cupboard I found when I investigated the pretty bathroom more closely, I wiggle my toes with happiness. Not that I can see them. I think I might have added a little too much of the strawberry scented liquid.

I wish I'd had a bath in the apartment. I had no idea what I was missing out on.

Slowly, the fizzy happiness in my stomach fades away. My toes clench.

I wonder if Ethan knows I'm gone yet. If he's walked into the apartment, expecting me to be there.

And what he'll do when he realizes I'm not.

Sinking down until the water brushes the edge of my nose, I shiver.

The Ethan I saw last time wasn't the Ethan I know. And that Ethan... I don't want to think about what he might do.

I wait for the guilt to settle in. He's the closest thing to a parent I've ever had. He raised me, cared for me, looked after me.

Except... did he, though?

The more time I spend away from the place I used to call home, the darker the thoughts inside my head. He told me it was to keep me safe. Repeated it over and over again, until I didn't even think of not believing him because it was the framework for my entire *life*.

I rub at my chest, trying to sweep away the stab of pain.

And if none of it was true... what does that mean?

The walls start to squeeze smaller, like they're closing in on me. My breathing seesaws again, the sharp stabbing in my chest fading to a dull pounding that isn't going away.

Sitting up with a gasp, I curl over and squeeze my eyes shut.

It doesn't help. It only makes the feeling worse, the space around me shrinking until there's not enough air. I pull myself out of the water, sending droplets and bubbles sliding across the tiled floor as I grab a towel and wrap it around myself.

Staggering into the bedroom, I make for the window and press my hand against it, staring desperately out into the night. But there's no light out there, the moon too hidden and the area too dark for me to see.

The sob cracks in my throat.

As I lean in further, pressing my face against the glass to try to *see* something, there's a click, and I stagger.

Pushing myself back, I look down. The window... is not, in fact, a window.

It's a *door*.

My fingers curl around the edge of the glass, and I pull it gently towards me, not daring to hope until a soft breeze dances over my exposed skin.

I jump back, my hand flying to my throat.

Air. *Fresh* air.

I've never felt fresh air on my skin.

Taking a tentative step forward, I worry at my bottom lip with my teeth. Sudden trepidation fills me.

This is what I wanted, but I'm suddenly scared.

Walls are comforting.

Walls are safe.

The air that dances over my fingers when I hold them out... there's a big world out there. No walls to be seen.

My shoulders firm.

I will not be afraid.

This is all I ever wanted. Freedom. And it's right there for me to take.

I'm taking it.

I yank the door wide open. It clatters back against the wall with an ominous clash, but I don't pay it any attention.

I'm leaning out over the small set of bars built into the wall, and all I can do is breathe in. The breeze flits around me, playing with my hair, tickling my nose and making me sneeze.

My hands shake on the bars as my eyes blur, the limited darkness fading into an incoherent mass as the tears start to fall.

It's better than I ever imagined. Inhaling deeply, I take in the fresh scent I didn't expect. It feels brisk, a little sharp, and all I want to do is suck it down and expand my lungs with it, fill myself up so nobody can ever take this feeling away from me.

Why do people even have windows? What's the point when they could have *this*?

The soft carpet under my feet suddenly feels too itchy. Leaning out, I stare down into the dark garden. A criss-crossing piece of wood winds up the wall beneath me, curling around my window, fading blooms offering the promise of flowers in summer. A petal crunches in my hand as I gently pull it off, curling my fingers around it.

The sudden, desperate urge has me staring at the wood.

I'm not that far from the ground, not really.

I could do it.

Holding my breath, I swing my leg up before I realize I've got no actual clothes on. The towel slips with my movement, slithering down to the floor as I stare down at it and then back to the garden.

It's really dark. Who's going to see me?

Just for a few minutes, and then I'll climb back up.

The thought of stopping for even a second, of turning my back on this and worrying about clothes makes my chest hurt more.

I need to get down there.

So I swing my leg over, and it's only when I'm precariously balanced on the other side of the bars, facing the bedroom, that I remember my promise to Maverick.

I told him I wouldn't leave without one of them.

Pursing my lips, I hover on the edge and debate the options. The ground is right there. My toes could be sinking into the cool grass right now.

Instead, the breeze is blowing directly against my ass, making me shiver. Swallowing down the nagging sense of disloyalty, I start to gingerly make my way down, testing the weight of the wooden slats to make sure they'll take my weight.

He probably meant away from the house. He wouldn't mean the gardens. There's nobody around, that's clear from the lack of lights.

He won't even know.

The anxiety dancing in my stomach ratchets up as I climb down, and by the time I pause, hovering just above the ground, I'm drowning in guilt. Pressing my face into the back of my hands where they grip the wood, I take a deep breath.

I'm reading way too much into this. He's not going to care.

My stomach doesn't agree with me, but I swallow the unease down. I only get to experience this moment once, and I want to make the most of it.

Softly, I press my toe into the ground. It feels cool beneath my toes, a little damp, and my breath catches as I scrunch up my toes, digging them into the moist earth.

The smile spreads across my face until I'm grinning, and I set my other foot down, savoring the feel of the ground sinking slightly beneath my feet.

"Freedom," I whisper, tasting the word on my tongue. As I stare out into the dark, a delighted laugh erupts from my throat.

A moment later, I'm sprawled on the ground. Little sticks and stones dig into my stomach, my legs, but I don't care. Pressing my cheek into the ground, I take great, gasping breaths, breathing in the earthy fragrance.

My heart is singing.

"I'm so glad I left," I whisper. My confession fades away into the dark.

No matter what. Even if I went back tomorrow, I will never, ever forget this moment, not if I lived in that place for another twenty-three years.

I don't care how angry Ethan is right now. This is all I wanted, and I'm going to make the most of it.

My hair trails along the ground as I climb to my feet, twisting my feet to feel every piece of dirt as I start to move.

I have no idea where I'm going. My pace picks up slowly until I'm almost running, and my hair flies out behind me as I run as fast as I can, laughing breathlessly at the sensation. I need to go back, but five minutes won't hurt.

Just five more minutes.

Ryder

Maverick is lurking in his study when I pop my head around the door, his usual position. The screen of his laptop lights up his face in the dark room, and I bend down to flick on a lamp.

"That will never not be creepy," I tell him when he looks up, his face ghostly against the bright light. "Do you have to sit in the dark like that?"

Maverick sighs. "What do you want, Ryder?"

Shrugging, I move over to stare at the wall. Notes, photographs, maps are scattered everywhere. A face looks out at me, bright curls surrounding a laughing face. The baby in the woman's arms waves chubby fists. The photo is old now, curling around the edges, but he's never taken it down.

To Maverick, it's evidence of his failure. Every case we have, he pushes harder.

Turning away from the image, I survey him. For once, he won't meet my eye, staring stubbornly at his screen with his jaw set.

"Mav," I ask him outright. "What was that?"

I don't know what I expected from dinner, but it sure as fuck wasn't Maverick going full-blown caveman on us. Enzo, I would have expected. But our esteemed leader-slash father figure - even though he hates it - is very clearly enamored with our new guest.

He ignores me, but I push his screen down with a click, and he mutters a curse. "Leave it alone, Ry."

"Nope." I pop the 'p'. "Don't think I will. You *like* her."

He rolls his eyes. "We're not in school, Ryder. I'm not about to pull her pigtails on the fucking playground. Besides, it's none of your business."

I settle down into the chair opposite his desk, pushing my feet against the ground so it swirls from side to side. "Just curious, is all. Enzo likes her too."

He frowns. "We need to watch him with her."

Folding my arms, I glance at him coyly. "I'm not worried about him *hurting* her."

Well. Only a tiny bit.

A dull flush colors his cheekbones. "Then what exactly are you worried about?" he asks irritably. "Why are you here?"

I frown. I'm not entirely sure.

Except the idea of Maverick or Enzo laying some sort of claim to the girl upstairs... I'm not sure I like it.

"She's innocent," I force out around the sudden dryness in my throat. "That's all. We can't overwhelm her."

Maverick scowls. "I'm aware of that. It's not me who needs the warning, Ryder. I'll speak to Enzo."

"Are you?" I challenge, holding up my fingers and pressing them together. "Because you were *this* close to dragging her onto your lap earlier. And as much as I appreciate your masterful ways, I'm not sure she's ready for it."

Maverick's patience snaps. Getting up, he moves to the door and holds it open. "We're done here."

Standing, I pause in front of him, suddenly uncertain. Maverick's been a constant in my life for ten years. I don't want us to fall out over this.

Swallowing, I try to articulate the weird feelings inside my chest. "Look... if you want her, Maverick, and she wants you, then go for it. Same with Enzo. Just take it easy, that's all I'm saying."

He looks confused. Hell, so am I. "And you?"

Shaking my head, I slide past him.

"I'm not for her." My words are abrupt as I head down the hall.

But that little truth doesn't stop thoughts of her from invading my brain as I move outside and into the trees, breathing in the familiar scents. The small forest on our grounds is perfect for testing my movements. Forests are noisy places. Insects, birds, branches, twigs - endless opportunities to reveal your presence.

If you can move silently through a forest, blend in with the natural sounds, then anywhere else becomes ridiculously simple.

The perfect exercise for a thief. And a good way to empty thoughts from your mind until your sole focus is the world around you.

Losing myself in the forest, I push away any thoughts of the girl we stole from a warehouse.

As I lift my foot to cross over a broken branch, a noise filters through that doesn't fit. Pausing, I lift my head and listen.

I hear her well before I see her. Excited, almost harsh feminine breathing, the snap of twigs under her feet, the scattering of rocks and bending of branches. Her feet smack into the ground as if she's running.

The forest silences, aware of the intruder in its midst.

My head turns in her direction.

She's running.

From us?

Absolutely fucking not.

I might not be able to have her, but I'm not about to let her go, either. Besides, she made a promise to Maverick to stay safely inside, and our little princess has clearly forgotten. I'm more than happy to remind her.

It's easy enough to make my way through the forest and wait as Zella crashes towards me. She's completely unaware of my presence as she pelts past where I'm standing, but the view throws me off balance, my mouth drying. Swiping a hand over my face, I lean out to watch as she darts ahead. Her skin shimmers, moonlight crossed with gold.

And that fucking hair trails behind her like she's some sort of damn forest nymph.

Groaning, I dig my palms into my eyes, swallowing down the sudden rush of arousal that's shot straight to my dick.

Why the ever living fuck is she running through the forest naked?

I think it's safe to assume that she's probably not running away unless she's got the urge to join a nudist colony, so I follow her from a distance, doing my best to keep my eyes up even as my chest tightens with every step she takes.

What the hell is she doing out here?

A shockingly husky laugh rings out as she reaches a clearing and throws herself down, rubbing her hands into the dirt. Swallowing, I watch as she rolls over and then over again, her hair wrapping around her as she comes to a slow halt, throwing her arms out wide. A delighted grin spread across those plush lips as she wriggles, sighing contentedly.

My fingers curl with need.

The urge to stride in, to push her legs open, see the shocked surprise in those pretty green eyes change to arousal when my fingers push through the pale thatch of curls I can see hinted at between her creamy thighs, to drag my tongue over her clit and roll it until it's nice and swollen for me, the better to graze my teeth over until she's shaking and begging against me.

Zella shuddering, crying out into the forest as I steal her pleasure from her and make it mine.

Make *her* mine.

Fuck, it would be so easy. She closes her eyes, stretching her arms over her head and breathing deeply. Completely relaxed.

Completely innocent.

I force the thoughts back, locking them down.

But there's one thing I can teach her, if only for her to think twice the next time she decides to run at night with not a fucking stitch on.

My strides are slow and lazy as I walk up to her. She's completely clueless, a soft smile on her face as I lean over her.

Her hands curl into the ground, her fingers toying with the dirt.

Her skin fucking gleams, almost angelic in the faint strands of moonlight filtering through the trees.

I ease down silently, my elbows on either side of her face. Her eyes fly open as she registers the danger a little too late, but my body is already pressed against hers, my hand over her mouth as I grip her wrist and hold it up.

She wriggles, green eyes wide and panicked noises coming from her throat as I hold her.

Leaning down, I turn her face to the side and run my nose along her neck, up to her ear.

"You," I murmur, "have been a *very bad princess*."

If her sense of self-preservation wasn't already fucked, she relaxes as she recognises my voice. Zella's body softens as I sink against her, jean-clad hips pressing into her bare skin. My cock hardens, and I wonder if she can feel it. If she even knows what it means.

She grumbles something into my hand, and I take just one more second to breathe in the faint, flowery scent of her skin, the mix of fresh earth and warmth. Wishing I could take more.

But angels like her aren't for the darkness of devils like me.

So I free her lips instead of catching them with mine, watching the way the plump lines turn up. She smiles at me, even as her breathing shakes. "Ryder," she whispers. "What are you doing?"

Her hands are still gripped in mine, and I lean down to rub my nose against hers. She *laughs*.

Zero self-fucking preservation.

"Stalking you through the forest," I raise an eyebrow. "Why are you not wearing any clothes, princess?"

At the reminder, her cheeks flush a deep color, the red spreading up and over her chest. I don't look down. I won't have any self-control if I do.

I need a fucking award for this shit. And a cold shower.

She wriggles underneath me, and I squeeze her wrists in light warning. "Did you not promise Maverick you wouldn't leave the house without one of us?"

Her mouth opens, then closes again. "You're right here, though?"

Her hopeful tone draws a small laugh from my chest. Sneaky. I can get on board with that, and my own lips lift in response.

"Looks like you've got yourself an out," I say. She wriggles, her face flushing as my hips shift against hers.

"We should go back," she says, and the first hint of trepidation enters her eyes when I don't move. "R-Ryder?"

Leaning down, I brush her mouth with mine, just once, inhaling the shaky sound that comes from her lips. "And if I don't want to let you go? What would you do then, princess?"

I watch the realization hit, the way her breathing changes as she pushes against me. I don't move.

"The world is a bad place, Zella," I say quietly. "Moore got that right, at least. And while you're safe on our land, I wouldn't recommend running at night anywhere else. You understand?"

She nods, her eyes flickering between my face and the forest behind me. Her face softens, the fear sliding away.

"I've never been outside," she whispers shakily. "It's so beautiful out here, Ryder."

I swallow as I shift back. At this point, I wouldn't have a clue if it was all burning to the ground around us.

The only thing I see is her.

Clambering up, I hold a hand out, her small hand swallowed inside mine as I lift her up. She winces as she stands, and I glance down to her bare feet.

"Have you cut yourself?" I demand. My words come out more harshly than I meant, and she shifts uncomfortably. "I don't care. It was worth it. I– ak!"

She flails in my grasp as I turn and stride for the house. She's all soft curves and warm female in my arms, my arm reaching under her thighs and hand gripping the curve of her bare hip.

She tries to protest, and I growl. "Enough, Zella."

"But—"

"*No,*" I snap irritably. Turns out I do actually have a line, and it's Zella hurting herself. For fucks' sake. She looks up at me, and that fucking lower lip of hers is trembling.

"I'll take you back out tomorrow," I grit out. Anything to make her stop looking like someone drowned her puppy. "*After* we've found you some fucking shoes."

The smile she gifts me with in return lights up my entire chest.

Ignoring her protests, I carry her through the main doors, taking the stairs two at a time until we reach my room. Zella looks around curiously as I carry her through into my bathroom. "This isn't my bedroom."

"No, it's not." Lifting her to sit on the vanity, I yank open drawers until I find a first aid kit. She watches me silently as I run a clean cloth under the water until it warms and drop to my knees.

Taking her ankle in my hand and making a valiant effort to not look at the fucking heaven tempting me mere inches away, I wipe away the dirt as gently as I can, pausing every time she winces. My fingers rub her ankle, reassuring her.

"A few scratches. Not too serious," I note, smoothing some cream over her foot that makes her hiss. Her skin is ridiculously soft.

"I didn't think about that," she admits ruefully. "I just wanted to run."

Her hair trails next to us, and a glance tells me it's full of mud and sticks from the forest floor. That's a problem for tomorrow. Getting to my feet, I hold up my hand and motion her to wait, ducking back into the bedroom.

When I walk back in, Zella glances up at me shyly. Her arms are crossed over her chest, and that delicious flush is fucking everywhere.

She looks edible.

Swallowing, I step closer. "Arms up, princess."

When she raises them, I slide her arms into the soft material, tugging it down until she's covered. Gently, I thread her hair through the top until the full length is out, as she watches me.

She jumps when I wrap my hands around her, hitching her legs around my waist and carrying her back into the bedroom, hair dragging behind us like a rope. "What are we doing?"

"Sleeping," I say drily. Tugging back the cover on my bed, I place her on the side closest to the window, pulling the covers back over her and dragging her hair up so it's not pulling on the floor. "God knows what trouble you'll get into on your own."

"In my sleep?" she grumbles lightly. But her breathing softens as I move around the room, collecting what I need to get changed in the bathroom.

Before I head in, I move over to the window. It's cool but the lingering summer air is still around and I unlatch it, pulling it out so she can sleep with it open.

"Ryder," she murmurs as I walk past. "Thank you."

Breath hitching, I swallow. "You're welcome, princess."

Watching her eyes slide closed, I wait until her breathing evens out before diving into the bathroom.

Ice cold fucking shower.

Zella

I wake to an extremely angry bear hovering over me.

Jumping about a mile with a squeal lodged in the back of my throat, I dislodge the warm leg pushed between mine. Heat rises in my face as Maverick stares down at the shirt I'm wearing. Ryder grumbles, his arms tightening around me as he buries his face into my neck. "Go back to sleep, princess."

I avoid Maverick's gaze as I carefully disentangle myself.

Waking up to a very large, very male body tangled with mine in the middle of the night was a bit of a shock, but Ryder was so warm that I didn't wake him. Kind of regretting it now, with Maverick glaring like he's about to yank me out of bed altogether.

Oh, boy. Blowing out a breath, I lift my chin to face the music. Maverick looks furious, hands curled into fists at his side as he looks down at us.

"Could you... not sneak up on me while I'm sleeping, please?" My voice is almost a whisper, not wanting to wake Ryder, but I frown at him. "It's not very polite."

Maverick makes a weird choking sound in the back of his throat, but his face darkens as he looks away. Leaning down, he picks up the edge of my braid where it trails over the end of the bed. His face clears, expressionless as he rubs the ends between his fingers.

"Why aren't you in your own room, Zella?" he murmurs. Swallowing, I try to think of a reasonable excuse for being in a different room when he took me to mine last night and told me, very clearly, not to leave. Preferably an excuse that doesn't tell him I went for a little run outside.

Although that plan falls apart pretty quickly when he pulls out a tangled stick from my braid.

He holds it up, one eyebrow quirked in a clear question.

When I do nothing but chew on my lip, his hand smooths along my braid, feeling it between his fingers. I watch him cautiously as his hands move up until his fingers are precariously close to my neck.

"Maverick," I try to explain, but his hand slides into the back of my hair, and my words cut off as he turns my head, leaning down.

"You broke your promise."

He sounds *extremely* displeased, and I fight to maintain eye contact, even as a small amount of guilt trickles into my stomach. "Um."

Ryder shifts, and I seize on the reminder. "Ryder took me. I... I asked him. It's not his fault."

One teensy little white lie won't hurt, right?

Maverick doesn't say anything as the silence stretches out, and I lick my lips. "I should probably get up."

He releases me suddenly, so much so that my body tilts a little, and I scramble out of bed. Ryder just mutters something and rolls over, and I blush again as a large, muscular leg wraps around the covers where I was a moment ago.

Maverick's eyes trail over me, leaving little licks of fire wherever they land. He seems particularly focused on my bare legs, and I shift awkwardly. Blue eyes fly up to my face, and his voice comes out gritty and low.

"Come down for breakfast. Five minutes."

"O-okay." I look at Ryder, and a finger lifts my chin.

"Just you and me this morning, Zella," he says. "We have some things to discuss."

My gulp is audible, and I stare after him as he leaves.

Breakfast with Maverick.

This is fine.

As I stumble down the stairs a few minutes later, my stomach swirls with uncertainty. Something about Maverick puts me on edge. It's almost like he has a switch. Sometimes, he comes across as incredibly polite and distant, and others...

He makes me more nervous than Enzo.

Something is definitely wrong with me. I woke up in a *dungeon* with Enzo leaning over me, and I didn't feel as nervous as I do now.

Maverick is sitting in the same seat as yesterday when I sidle through the door, and we follow the same routine as he stands and pulls out a chair. As soon as I'm sat, a silent signal triggers the arrival of breakfast dishes. I watch as steaming plates of eggs, toast, meats, and fruit are laid out in a sumptuous banquet. The staff disappear as quickly as they did last night, and I turn to Maverick. "Where do they live? Those people?"

He glances at the door. "Mostly in the city. They work in shifts. If you're worried they'll tell anyone you're here, don't be. We pay very well for their silence, and they know it."

Brushing that aside, he picks up a plate and again selects a variety of foods before laying it in front of me.

"Are you going to feed me again?" My voice comes out a little more breathlessly than I intended, and his fingers tighten on the black ceramic.

"Not today," he murmurs. "Eat."

I lift the cutlery perfectly set out in front of me. Maverick moves over to the wall, and when he turns, I gasp at the delicious scent that wafts over. "Coffee!"

His lips twitch as he places the cup next to me, and I scoop it up, inhaling the fresh scent greedily.

"You enjoy coffee?" he asks, taking a seat with his own cup as I nod.

"Very much." Staring down into the dark liquid, a flash of Ethan holding it over me slides into my mind, and my fingers shake. Carefully, I place it down before I spill it.

Maverick watches, but he doesn't say anything. After a moment, he pulls a notebook towards him.

"I didn't want to overwhelm you last night," he says as I take a mouthful of fluffy eggs, "but I'd like to know more about your background, Zella. Specifically, your life in the apartment and your relationship with Ethan Moore."

Any appetite I had flees out the door. The food in my mouth turns to dust, and I force myself to swallow it down. Of course, they want to know about Ethan. That's why Ryder and Enzo were there, in the apartment.

I was just an unexpected bonus.

Maverick is waiting for a response, so I reach for my coffee and take a slow sip, trying to buy time. Whatever is between Ethan and I… I don't want to betray him.

Any more than I already have.

"Zella?" Maverick pulls me out of my own thoughts, and I smile at him awkwardly.

"Sorry," I offer. "It's just… I don't know what you want with him."

He tilts his head. "You're not worried about yourself, being here with us, but you're worried about him?"

I shrug, my finger tracing circles in the white tablecloth. "I'm responsible for my own actions. I asked to leave, so whatever happens, that's on me. But Ethan… I don't want my words to bring him harm."

"Even though he had you locked up, with an iron band around your ankle?" Maverick's words hit like bullets, and I hunch in on myself.

"It wasn't like that," I whisper, before I look up at him. He looks disbelieving, and I shake my head. I need him to understand.

"He raised me," I tell him. "Since I was a baby. He's the only parent I've ever had, really."

"What about your real parents?" Maverick presses, his tone even. "Where are they?"

"Dead. They died when I was a baby, and Ethan ran with me to keep me safe."

Now Maverick leans forward, his expression falling into a frown. "From what?"

I shrug helplessly. "That's what I've been wondering since Ryder and Enzo brought me here."

What if there wasn't anything? What if he just stole me?

Did he even know my parents at all?

"What if they're not really dead?" I whisper brokenly. "My whole life might have been a lie, and I was too stupid to realize it."

I'm lost in my own thoughts, and I jerk when a hand curls around mine. Maverick squeezes, and his blue eyes are deep as I look up at him.

"I can help you find out," he says calmly. "We run an investigative company here. Well, I do. Ryder and Enzo have their own skills, and they help out when I need them."

My head spins at the possibility he's laying before me, so I focus on the easiest question. "What kind of skills?"

Maverick's face shutters. "Nothing you need to concern yourself with."

My teeth sink into my lip. Having woken in Enzo's dungeon, I have an idea that some of their work might be a little messy. Maybe it's naive of me, but the suggestion doesn't overly bother me.

He could have hurt me, and he didn't.

Instead, he told me there were *options*. And then he kissed me.

I haven't forgotten our interrupted discussion, and my cheeks flush at the memory. Maverick raises a quizzical brow, but I shake my head, forcing myself to think about the possibility that my whole life might not have been what I thought it was. "Could you do that? Look into it, I mean?"

He leans back in his seat. "I'll need you to give me everything you know. Even then... not all cases get solved, Zella. This isn't a guarantee."

His voice sounds strange, and he looks away from me.

"I understand." Straightening, I think back to what would be useful, and begin relaying my life to Maverick's notebook. His hand is steady and sure as he scrawls notes in handwriting I can't actually read, throwing out questions I can't answer.

After a few minutes, the back of my throat aches with the urge to cry. It's becoming increasingly clear that I know *nothing*.

"Hey," he says firmly. "None of that. It's not your fault if you don't have all of the answers, Zella."

I push my palms into my eyes, trying to shove away the emotional riot happening in my chest. "But why don't I know? Why was Ethan so secretive?"

My voice breaks on the last word, and Maverick pushes his chair back. "Come here."

I hesitate, a hiccup rattling in my chest as he beckons me. The white shirt he's wearing stands out against his olive skin, and he tilts his head at me. "You promised to obey."

There's a dark reminder in his voice, and I hug my arms as I stand, shifting over to him and yelping when he pulls me into his lap. A large, warm hand smooths up and down my back, and I gradually relax into his touch.

His voice rumbles, soaking into me. "Talk to me."

I swallow, not looking at him. "I feel so stupid."

"What could you have done differently?" he asks me. "First you were a child. Then you were locked in. When you challenged him, he tied you up. What more could you have possibly done to make your situation better, Zella?"

"I don't know," I murmur. "But something."

"Sometimes the only thing we can do is survive. You seem to have done a pretty good job of that." Maverick clears his throat. "Did Ethan... did he ever hurt you?"

I shift on his lap, turning to face him. "What do you mean? He didn't hit me."

Maverick lifts his hand, brushing his fingers across my face. His works are low, an undercurrent of something that makes me shiver in his voice. "If he didn't hit you, why is your cheek swollen?"

My fingers rise to cover his, the memory rushing back in. "I panicked. When he blocked off the windows. I couldn't breathe properly, and he slapped me. I think that was the first time he's ever actually touched me."

"Because he had a... sensitivity to touch."

I look at Maverick. His face is twisted with something. "What?"

For the first time, he looks away from me, his voice strained when he responds. "Zella... Ethan didn't have an aversion to touch."

I frown. "Yes, he did. He never touched me. Only my hair. And anytime I got close, he would freak out. He even had gloves on when he put the iron around my ankle."

A lifetime of isolation, of being told no when I asked for a hug, of bandaging my own scrapes and bruises.

Maverick clears his throat. "Zella," he says carefully, almost slowly. "We've been following him. He definitely doesn't have any issues with touching. Ryder witnessed it many times."

I yank my head back, staring at him with disbelief. "That's not true."

This is the one thing I know with certainty. There's no way.

"You must have the wrong person," I shrug. "I promise you, he does."

Maverick's lips thin. "Maybe. Don't worry about it for now, though."

He looks back down, his eyes scanning the page. "You spent your whole life in the apartment? You didn't live anywhere else when you were a child?"

Shaking my head, I take a breath, inhaling the faint musky scent of his skin. His arms are around me as he makes more notes, the warmth of his skin soaking into mine through his shirt. "No. I mean, I can't remember when I was a baby, obviously, but all of my memories are in the apartment."

"What are your earliest memories?" he presses. "How old were you?"

Frowning, I try to think. "Maybe... six? Seven? I'm not sure."

He makes a considering noise. "And nothing before that."

I try to think harder, even scrunching up my face as though that will magically create a full set of memories inside my head, but all I feel is blankness and an ache forming behind my eyes. "No."

He sighs, leaning back and running a hand down my braid. "Okay. I think that's all I need for now."

"What will you do?"

He grimaces. "Ryder and Enzo left a camera behind in the apartment, and there's a tracker on his car, so we'll know when he comes back. We tracked him to the airport, so he was telling the truth about going on a trip. When he gets back, we'll re-assess."

They're tracking his car.

"Is that allowed?" I ask curiously. "To just... follow someone around like that?"

Maverick's lips tilt up, and his hand comes up to cup my neck. "Everything is allowed, as long as you don't get caught."

I press back against him, soaking in the contact. After a lifetime without it, I'm cherishing every touch they choose to give me. When he pulls his hand away, I can feel my face drop.

"I have to work," Maverick murmurs. "You'll be with Enzo today."

He sounds a little hesitant, but my pulse spikes, a flip of excitement inside my chest. "I am?"

His eyes scan my face, his shoulders relaxing. "You don't mind?"

Mind? I'm nearly bouncing in place, and I scramble off his lap with a smile. "I don't mind. Where?"

"You can go to the dungeon for today. He knows you're coming. But remember–,"

"No going down without permission or on my own. Got it." I nod vigorously, my feet already turning towards the door.

"Zella?" Maverick calls me as I pull the handle, and I turn back to him.

"Be careful." His words are soft, but intentional. "Enzo... he's not like us."

My mind skitters over my last dungeon experience, and a furnace simmers to life inside my stomach. Maverick is right. Enzo's energy is what I imagine a trapped animal would feel like - temporarily contained, but always dangerous.

Not something to turn your back on, unless you want to feel their teeth in your neck.

Swallowing, I nod, and then dart from the room.

Why does that visual make the furnace hotter?

Enzo

I'm wiping down the walls when I hear the soft pad of footsteps on the stairs. The girl's light breathing sounds a little fast, and she pauses, her feet shifting from side to side when I don't turn around.

"Enzo?" Her voice is tentative, on edge.

My lips pull up as I continue in my work, my image reflected back at me in the metal. Zella makes her way over to me, and I watch as her reflection gets clearer.

"Maverick told me to come down here?"

The words are uncertain, and it sends a rush of enjoyment through my veins. I like her being on edge around me. I spent a sleepless night tossing and turning, tormented with images of her.

A little fear in return is only fair.

I'm not expecting soft fingers to land against my back, and I flinch away from the touch instinctively. With a growl, I spin, my fingers shooting out and wrapping around her slim neck.

She chokes in my grasp. The entertainment I felt a moment ago has disappeared, and I drag her closer to snarl in her face. "Never touch my back."

Her face has darkened, the choking breaths an apology I don't give a flying fuck about as I loosen my hold and she backs away from me.

"I'm sorry–"

"I don't care." Cutting her garbled words off, I go back to my task. Dipping the cloth into the bucket, I run it over a patch I've already done, my flash of temper ebbing away as quickly as it came.

Still. Better she learn now than later.

When I finally turn to her, I expect her face to be filled with fear, for her to flinch away from me. But she's silent, her eyes distant as she stares at the far wall. She doesn't respond to my movements at all.

Frowning, I take a step closer. "What's wrong with you?"

It takes a moment, but she blinks, turning to me. A red ring of finger marks already rings her neck, and I pause.

It looks like a collar.

I expect fear, but she responds calmly enough. "Where do you want me?"

Her innocent question sends my eyes flying to the table. She looked perfect on there.

I've never had a female on my table before. Perhaps it's something I should consider. Expand my horizons, so to speak. Evil doesn't only exist in the men of the world.

But the only person I can imagine there right now is my little prey, who's watching me with wide eyes.

Fuck, does she know how ripe she is? Just waiting for someone to come along and destroy her innocence.

I want to destroy it.

Fire blazes in my veins, but I force it down. Ignoring her, I stalk over to the desk I have set up in the corner, sitting down and reaching for my paperwork.

She follows me. "So… what are we doing?"

The battered leather chair creaks as I swivel around, villain-style.

Maybe I should get a cat.

Although blood would be hard to clean from the fur. Maybe not.

Irrationally disappointed in my non-existent cat, I snap at her. "You're going to sit here and say nothing. I need to work."

Her eyes follow my pointing finger. "You want me to sit on the floor?"

"Did I stutter?" I ask coolly. "Feel free to go back upstairs if not."

I'm expecting her to kick off, maybe to storm out, but she surprises me when I see her settling down on her knees out of the corner of my eye. The floor is solid concrete and her legs are bare under that ridiculous white dress, but she doesn't murmur as she sets her hands in her lap.

I ignore the way my cock hardens at the sight of her.

She wants to sit there instead of going back upstairs? Fine.

I spend the next hour working through camera footage of the city. John Millers is a typical blue-collar male. He goes to work in his car garage at the same time every day, returning home by six sharp every evening. Man likes routine. I can appreciate that.

Shame he's a perverted son of a bitch. Abby Millers isn't the only girl he's hurt.

It doesn't take me long to realize that this might be the easiest run I've ever done, and my jaw locks in disappointment. I was hoping for more of a chase than this podgy fucker's going to give me.

But the look in Abby Millers' eyes tells me he's earned his spot on my table, so a quick one will have to do.

I calculate a rough plan in my head and lean back, stretching my arms up and pulling out a knot in my back. The space around me is silent, and my eyes move to the girl.

She's in exactly the same position she was an hour ago, her breathing too quiet for me to pick up and her eyes closed. There's no sign of the fire I saw before, no trace of the quiet strength she showed with my hands around her neck.

No sign of life whatsoever.

It annoys the fuck out of me.

"Why are you so quiet?" I demand. My voice echoes off the walls, and she jumps. Her eyes slide open, the bright green turning to me in question.

"I thought you wanted me to be quiet?"

Surveying her, I tap my fingers on the chair. "Nobody is that quiet."

It's true. It's almost impossible for someone to be truly silent for that length of time. People shift, stretch, cough, sneeze, pick their fucking nose, scratch their ass.

She's silent. Those golden cheeks develop a hint of color as we watch each other. Finally, she swallows, pushing back a stray piece of hair from her face.

"I'm used to it," she murmurs. "Ethan used to make me sit for hours, and I had to be still."

Her breath hitches when she says that fucker's name, and my fingers tap harder.

I think Ethan Moore will be on my table soon.

"I don't like it," I grunt. "Say something."

A hint of challenge enters her eyes. "What do you want me to say?"

Is she baiting me intentionally? Her head tilts to the side, all fucking innocence, but I'm not buying it.

She's fucking perfect. Nobody is this perfect.

It's not *right.*

I want to see her lose control. I want to see her scream, see her skin leech of color as terror steals the breath from her lungs.

Even at the apartment, she showed no fear.

How the fuck is she going to survive when she can't recognise a predator even if he's staring her in the face?

My hand wraps around the top of her arm. She finally jerks, her body twitching as she tries to pull away from me.

My lips curl into an amused smile. It's cute.

Like a kitten pulling away from a tiger.

Lifting her is easy, and her hands bat at me ineffectively as I pull her across the room. "What are you doing?"

She tries to hold her ground, pushing her feet into the floor, but there's no grip to be found.

"I've decided this is what we're doing today." My grin is still lingering as I push her onto the table and she scoots back, her bare feet sliding up the metal. Rolling my eyes, I grip her ankles and tug her forward. She slides down with a shocked cry, but I'm already winding the leather around her lower legs, entangling her as I pull it tightly. Her legs jerk, parting for me like the fucking red sea, toes twitching like she's dangling from a damn rope as she tries to pull them free.

I pinch one, just to see what she does, and she curls them in like I'm about to cut one off.

"I don't understand." Her voice is raised now as I place my hand directly into her chest and push her down firmly, until her back is flat against the metal. Her heart thunders under my palm as I push up her arm, getting the straps in place and doing the same to the other. Her head whips from side to side as she watches me, and I breathe in deeply. I'm expecting the familiar tangy, slightly sour scent of fear, a mix of sweat and heavy breathing, but all I can scent is her. She smells like fucking flowers, like the forest.

Leaning back, I watch her. Her breathing has quickened, pushing up her breasts in a regular rise and fall. The white cotton is stretched, showing me a hint of peaked brown nipples shadowed against the cloth every time she breathes in. her face framed in white-gold wisps of hair that have escaped from her braid.

She looks like prey.

She looks like a goddess.

She looks like *mine.*

Zella

I can barely breathe as Enzo moves out of sight. I feel fingers tugging at the edge of my braid, the strands unraveling into his hands as he untangles them inch by inch.

The fire in my stomach that began in Maverick's arms earlier feels like a blazing inferno now, my stomach clenching and twisting with something that draws the air from my lungs, my forehead damp with sweat as I strain to look behind me and see what Enzo is doing.

But the restraints are too firm, my wrists and ankles locked into place. The faded dark leather doesn't give an inch when I tug on it.

My nerves are on a knife edge, every single part of me aware of the man behind me, his hands buried in my hair as he gently releases the braid. His fingers dig into my skull, rubbing at my scalp, and my eyes slide closed at the sensation.

"So prim and proper," he murmurs. My eyelids flutter open, and my lips part on a gasp when his eyes appear. His face is barely an inch away, his mouth close to mine.

"Breathe, little prey," he coaxes, and I suck precious air into my lungs.

"Good," he murmurs. "Don't want you passing out and missing the show."

My tongue darts out, and I wet my lips nervously. "What show? What are you doing?"

Instead of answering, he reaches behind and pulls my hair forward in two sections, each one passing over my shoulder and down until it's on display alongside me, the ends reaching beyond the edge of the table past my ankles. Enzo hums as he smooths it out, stepping back to view his work.

"So perfect," he purrs. But his eyes are dark again as his fingers stroke the skin of my ankle.

"Are you going to hurt me?" I ask.

He turns those black orbs to me. "You chose to run to the monsters, princess. Are you regretting it now?"

He doesn't understand.

"I chose to run from one," I whisper. "I don't think you're going to hurt me, Enzo."

Brave words, but his hands are gentle on my skin. His body pauses, his fingers lifting.

"Don't trust me," he whispers. "I could break you so easily, little prey."

Maybe he could, and maybe I'm as naive as they imagine... but I'm not sure he's going to.

I don't want him to stop touching me.

"Don't stop."

He jerks. "You think pretty words are going to save you?"

I shake my head. "I don't care. Just... don't stop."

He sets his hands against my legs, one on each side, and moves them upwards in sweeping strokes over my skin. The movement pushes my dress up, and I'm dangerously close to him seeing my most intimate parts.

I hold my breath, watching his inked hands caress my skin. His skin tone is paler than mine, his hands big and warm as his fingers brush the edges of my dress.

He looks up at me. "I'm not nearly done with you yet, little prey."

His fingers push up my dress, inch by tortuous inch, and my legs tremble as his eyes follow.

A cry falls from my lips when his hand cups me suddenly, right *there.*

My body feels too sensitive under his grip, and I truly thrash against the restraints for the first time, bucking as he holds me. He pulls his hand away, and I shake as he moves over, grabbing the stool and pulling it over as he settles himself on it, his knees spread.

"What..." My words cut off as he pushes my legs open even further.

"Stop moving," he says sharply. "I want to look at you."

It takes me a second too long and he raises his hand. His palm connects with my hot flesh, the slapping sound echoing around us. I still, panting.

He reaches forward, his fingers pulling apart my folds as he looks at me. The light shines above us, and I squeeze my eyes shut, too overcome with embarrassment and something deeper, hotter, to watch.

The protest dies on my tongue, unspoken as he traces his fingers over me, right *there.*

"So pretty and pink and plump," Enzo murmurs. His hand strokes across me and I make a noise in the back of my throat. "All these pretty curls are hiding you from me, little prey."

He pulls on one. "Stay still."

I open my eyes, staring down at where he balances a knife in his fingers. Holding the handle, he leans forward, and I bite my lip as I feel a soft scrape against my skin. My cheeks flush even brighter, heating my face as Enzo cuts away the curls that cover my genitals, laying them out one by one on my stomach. It flexes under his light touch, and he squeezes my hip. "Still."

When he's finished, I can't look at him for the embarrassment heating my body from the inside out. One hand grips the inside of my thighs, and he squeezes. "Open your eyes, prey."

Slowly, I crack them open. The knife is still in his other hand, and he flips it so the blade is held in his grip.

"Have you ever had a cock inside you?"

His words are low and dark, and they make my heart thump inside my chest. "N-no?"

I know the basics. The anatomy of the human body. The differences between us, and that the pieces... fit together. But Ethan confiscated the textbook that taught me even that small amount.

And this feels nothing like the cold impracticality of those images. This is fire, and heat, as though I'm going to burn up into ash under Enzo's touch.

"Good," he murmurs. "Ours will be the last."

Shock renders me immobile. "O-ours?" I manage to croak.

His eyes meet mine. "Mine. Ryder's. Maverick's."

The handle of the knife slides up my center and back down, a warm and solid weight. He pauses it right at my entrance, and I suck in my breath as he moves it in a circle.

All of them? They all want to do... this?

I won't survive it.

I'm not sure I'll survive this.

"Nobody else touches what's ours." His eyes are still on mine, and I lift my hips, chasing the promise in the gentle touches. "I will kill them, prey. I will kill them slowly, and then I'll fuck you on top of their corpse. Tell me you understand."

My nod feels frantic. "I do. I understand."

He rewards me with the push of the knife handle *inside*, and I throw my head back in a quiet moan at the feel of it pushing inside me. It feels so big, and Enzo laughs darkly when I gasp it out loud.

"This is nothing," he promises. "My finger alone is twice the size, prey. I'm going to split you in half on my cock, and you're going to beg me for more."

He slides the knife in and out, my hips settling into a rhythm as I try to settle the clawing need in my belly. It's like nothing I've ever felt. "Enzo, please."

He hums. "So fucking needy."

But he spreads his hand out, his fingers moving over me, rolling and flicking a specific spot that makes stars burst in my eyes.

"You like me playing with your clit," he observes. "Look at me. Watch me, prey."

When I stare at him dazedly, he leans down, and I try to pull away from the overload of sensation as his mouth seals over me, licking and circling until the clawing changes into fireworks and my back bows off the bed. Something releases inside me, a burst of fireworks that shatter as I scream. Enzo keeps going even after I beg him to stop, my breath rasping out of my lungs in hoarse pants as he plays with me until my panting changes to a broken sob.

"Please," I cry. "Enough. For now."

When Enzo pulls back, his face is damp, the dark curls everywhere as he stands and moves closer to me. His lips hover over mine. "Maybe

I'll carry on," he whispers against my mouth. "You taste like my own personal hell, little prey."

Sudden embarrassment heats my cheeks. "That doesn't sound good."

Instead of answering, he presses his mouth against mine, his tongue sweeping inside and tangling with mine as he pushes my taste onto me. There's a hint of sweetness and something almost musky about it, and I'm not sure which part is me and which is him.

Enzo's breathing is almost as harsh as mine when he pulls back, and we stare at each other in silence. I'm bare from the waist down, Ryder's shirt rucked up, hair trailing everywhere, and the look in his eyes as they slowly look me up and down makes my breath catch.

"Ours," he growls. "Don't forget."

I shake my head as a voice calls out from behind me.

"Princess, I think we should – what the fuck?"

Ryder

Speechlessness isn't something I'm particularly familiar with, but my mouth is dry as I take in the sight of Zella sprawled across Enzo's fucking *torture table*.

The breath disappears from my chest as my steps eat up the space between us.

"Zella?" Shoving Enzo aside, I lean over her frantically, checking for signs of impending death and undoing the leather straps holding her in place. She blinks up at me lazily, her cheeks flushed with color.

"Hi, Ryder."

Her whisper is almost shy, and the panic tightening my chest recedes as I take in the situation that's entirely different to my first dark thoughts. My eyes drop to where her toes are curled inwards, following the trail of golden skin up to the curls I saw last night.

Except... they're not there anymore.

Sucking in a breath, I turn to Enzo. He's leaning against the wall nonchalantly, twirling a knife between his fingers in that irritating way he likes.

"I told you before to stop doing that," I snap. "You're gonna lose a finger."

The smirk he gives me in return is dangerous. "Only idiots chop their own fingers off."

My eyes slide to Zella in a clear question. "Care to explain?"

Instead of answering, he shrugs and waves the knife at me. "I like to see my food."

Mother*fucker*.

Zella scrambles off the table, hastily yanking the edges of my fucking shirt down. "Ryder," she says breathlessly. "We were just... um..."

Well, this should be good.

"Tell me, princess," I say shortly. I have an indescribable urge to pinch the bridge of my nose in exasperation, closely followed by a flash of terror that I might actually be morphing into Maverick.

Something's really fucked up when *I'm* the responsible person in the room.

Shaking off the shiver, I stalk towards her. She nibbles nervously on her lip, watching me as I approach and lean down, making her meet my eyes as I push her hair back.

"Why," I murmur, "do I keep seeing you naked?"

Fuck, but her skin is glorious. She can't hide her emotions from us, not when she doesn't just wear them on her face but in the way her skin rapidly changes, flushing with color.

"I wasn't naked!" she says, a touch too indignantly given the picture I seem to have stumbled on. "I still have your shirt on."

"For now," Enzo murmurs behind me. Both Zella and I turn to frown at him, and he raises an eyebrow. "Are we not all consenting adults here? I don't see an issue."

Spinning back to Zella, I pin her with a look. "Princess. I feel like we're corrupting you."

Enzo's choked laugh rings out, but I ignore him.

This feels important.

"We're not normal, Zella," I tell her softly. "None of us. Our lives aren't like other people's. You might feel like you've stepped into the light, but all you've done is take another step closer to the dark. You need to be more careful."

"Ryder." Enzo growls behind me, but she needs to understand. First, it was the forest, and now this?

Zero self-preservation. And if I have to play the damn fucking good cop role to make sure she stays safe, then I will.

"You," I whisper, "are far too good for scoundrels like us."

The little crease between her eyes gets deeper. "You want me to leave?"

Her voice is flat, the spark in her eyes fading as she looks away. "You don't want me... like that."

"That's not even a question," I say quietly. "I can't have you, Zella."

When you fuck for a living, the job absorbs you, until it covers you entirely. I walk around every day with a film of filth covering my skin that nobody else can see.

I don't want to sully her with my dirt.

And the longer she spends with us, the more the darkness will touch her.

We all wear our darkness, in one way or another.

"That's enough," Enzo snarls. "Go upstairs, little prey. Ryder and I need to have a chat."

She slides out, avoiding both of us as she quietly gathers up her hair and walks out, her bare footsteps padding out of sight. As soon as she's disappeared, Enzo is on me with a snarl, yanking me around to face him. "What the fuck is wrong with you?"

I stare at him. "With me? What the fuck is wrong with *you*? She's not for us, Enzo."

When I try to push him off, he shakes my arm, getting into my face.

"Says who?" His vehemence takes me by surprise. "You think we haven't earned something a little good in our fucking lives, Ryder? You think we haven't *suffered* enough?"

"This isn't about us," I snap. "It's about her."

He barks a sarcastic laugh. "Like fuck it's not. You're letting your own demons get in the way."

Squaring up to him, I push him. "I have no demons, Enzo. I know exactly who I am. Have you forgotten?"

He points a finger on me. "I *never* forget. Not for a single fucking second in every fucking day do I forget where I came from."

I stare at him. "So what? We're just going to keep her here? She hasn't seen a single part of the world - you want to keep her here so she doesn't have the chance to choose something else!"

His skin flushes. "She might choose us. You're not giving that girl nearly enough fucking credit."

I bury my palms into my eyes, pushing into the skin. "If she chooses us, then she's crazy. You had her tied to a fucking table!"

"So?" he shoots back. "She loved every single fucking second of it, Ryder. Your mistake is thinking she's normal. She's not. She's got her own fucking demons, and if you're letting her little innocent act fool you, don't. She just came all over my hand after I fucked her with the handle of the knife I used to shave her fucking pussy."

"You what?"

"And she loved it," he throws back at me. His eyes gleam. "She's ours, and I'm taking her. Pull your head out of your ass, Ryder. She was fucking made for us, and I'm not letting her go. I don't give a flying fuck what you and Maverick have to say about it."

He shoves past me towards the door. "Or her, come to think of it. None of you get a fucking say in this. Pick her or don't, but I've made my choice. She's not going anywhere."

He leaves me to stew on his words in the dungeon. Infuriated, I kick the chair with a roar, watching as it hits the wall with a loud bang.

I finally found something worth doing the right thing for, and now he's telling me I'm wrong?

Fuck him.

Maverick

Who are you, Zella?

The words bounce around in my brain as I scour missing person records from the approximate time of her birth. It would help if she knew the exact date, but I'm working across a two-year window, just in case.

Nothing of note so far. One or two possibilities, but nothing that genuinely feels like a lead.

After working through each file, I have four left to do some follow-up checks on, but dissatisfaction is thrumming as I stretch. I don't think any of them will lead to Zella.

Grabbing my phone, I pull up the app we use to track our camera locations and click through to Zella's apartment. A brief glimpse is enough to tell me it's still untouched. No sign of Ethan Moore.

Although from what Zella told me, that's not unusual. By the sounds of it, he used to leave her for days at a time.

Sometimes her food would run low, and she'd have to ration it.

Irritation turns to anger, and I throw my phone down. Moore will get what's coming to him, whatever Zella thinks. I've seen the other side of him, thanks to Ryder and his trailing.

Asshole's a sick bastard. That he hasn't abused Zella physically, or fucking sexually, is both a miracle and a mystery I need to unravel.

Given his other activities... why not?

My pen taps on an empty page.

Maybe he genuinely cared for her. But his actions don't stack up with that.

When my phone lights up again, I reach for it with a curse. "Martinez."

The man who started all of this doesn't waste any time. "I expected to hear from you earlier."

"My apologies," I say coolly. "I wasn't aware we were working to a timescale."

John Martinez huffs but doesn't push. "Is there any news?"

Hesitating, I stare at the wall in front of me. Martinez hired us to look for dirt on Ethan Moore, and we've got it in spades. Photos of him at Club X, video footage from the subtle pin camera attached to Ryder's cufflink.

And then there's Zella.

"Nothing yet," I tell him shortly. "We're close."

Martinez grunts. "I hired you because I heard you're the best, Brooks. Don't let me down."

I grit my teeth, wondering why the fuck I took this job in the first place. The man's an asshole.

But if we didn't, we wouldn't have found Zella.

"We are the best," I say simply. It's the truth. We get shit done, and the powerful across the city know it. And the money they're happy to hand over from their dirty pockets funds the main focus of our work – helping those who need it.

Like the girl who's somehow managed to work her way inside my thoughts.

Ending the call, I scan the images in front of me. My eyes move across the wall, to the case that never comes down.

Every person in law enforcement has that one case. The one that never came home. It fuels them, colors their perceptions, their decision making. It makes them better.

But sometimes it consumes them.

Digging into my pocket, I pull out the picture. I don't know why I still carry it around. Maybe it's a fucking punishment, like Ryder says. A little self-immolation every time I see the innocent, smiling face, the mother and daughter.

I couldn't save them.

Taking a breath, I put it away, carefully folding the edges and sliding it back into my pocket. Maybe I couldn't save them, but Zella is right here.

And I want to give her answers, help her fill the gaps that might otherwise consume her, once her excitement wears off and the reality of her life so far sets in.

A few hours later, I check the camera again. I'm not expecting to see anything as I pull the apartment up, the clear images of the statues coming into view on my phone.

But there's an addition that makes me bolt upright, staring at the screen.

Because Ethan Moore is back in town.

And he's fucking *furious.*

Zella

My feet slap against stone as I run up the steps and into the hall, not pausing until I'm pushing open the door to my bedroom. My throat aches, my body shaking to try and hold back the tears.

I don't understand why Ryder looked so disappointed. And Enzo... he sent me away.

What did I do wrong?

Splashing water on my face in the bathroom, I stare at my blotchy face and watch as my vision blurs, tears plopping into the basin.

Everything on the outside is so complicated.

Maybe Ryder is right. Maybe I don't know enough about this world to make the right choices. But what happened with Enzo didn't feel wrong.

I throw more water on my face, trying to dampen the fire I can feel on my cheeks. The way he moved over me, tasting me, *shaving* me.

When I first started reading the few books Ethan would bring me, I always imagined how it would feel to be introduced to a man, like Elizabeth Bennet and Mr. Darcy, or Heathcliff and Cathy. As I grew older and learned more about my own body, I would trace my hands across my skin in bed, trying to imagine someone else's hands in their place.

The reality is beyond my own imagination.

I never expected this. I never expected *them.*

My face is still scarlet when I turn away from the glass. Collecting my sketchbook from the side, I make my way downstairs, searching for a space I can use to clear my head. Sketching always helps when my head feels too full. Like the chaos inside finds its way out onto the page.

My fingers pluck at the edges of Ryder's shirt as I peer cautiously around one of the many doors in the house. Some rooms are completely empty. Others have furniture inside, white covers thrown over them in a way that reminds me of the apartment, making me back out quickly and close the door.

Finally, I find a little room with a dark blue couch and settle down, opening my book. I've always had to search for inspiration, but today my pencil begins to fly almost as soon as it touches the page.

Chaotic strokes shape into a familiar face. Enzo's face appears, looking straight at me, his eyes burning with dozens of stars. I try to draw the skull covering his neck, but my fingers falter. I need to spend more time studying it.

For the first time, I don't wish for more color. Enzo's likeness stands out on the page, bold in shades of black and white, so similar to the real him that it makes my breath catch.

Flipping the page, I move on to Ryder. His curls flop over his forehead as he smiles, full lips coming to life under my hand. He's standing next to a window, his hand curled towards me as if in invitation. And then there's Maverick. His eyes pierce the page as he lifts a glass, his brow quirked in silent demand.

My fingers trace over the three sketches.

Three men.

Enzo told me I would be theirs.

Ryder told me I wouldn't be.

I wonder if anyone plans to ask me what I want.

The quiet knock on the open door makes me jerk, my sketchbook sliding to the floor. Maverick leans down to pick it up, his eyes glancing down as he hands it back to me. "You have a gift for art."

The words draw a smile to my face. "Really?"

"You didn't know?" He settles down on the couch next to me. Maverick is impossibly large, his shoulders taking up most of the empty space as I slide closer to him. He lays his arm along the back of the blue leather, fingers brushing my shoulder. "I mean it. That sketch is amazing."

I glance down at the picture of Enzo. "Thank you. It would be better with some color, I think. I used to ask Ethan for paints all the time, but he always forgot to bring them."

Maverick's lips are pressed together, a frown in his eyes when I look at him.

"Zella... Ethan is back in the city."

My whole body goes numb.

He's back.

The buzzing in my head grows to a roar, and my breathing stutters and dies. Maverick's face appears in front of me. He's on his knees, talking, his face urgent, but I can't hear him.

I'm barely aware as I'm lifted and settled against something warm.

"He's coming for me," I whisper. Soon, I'll be back in that cold place. Prison or home, it won't make a difference when those doors close behind me. Sound finally penetrates as Maverick swears.

"No, sweetheart," he says firmly. His hands are roaming up and down my back, smooth, firm strokes that help reduce the noise inside my head. "He's not coming. He doesn't know where you are."

Images of the elevator opening, Ethan stepping inside.

To face an empty space.

"He's going to be so angry with me." I twist my head to face Maverick. His body is curled around mine protectively, those wide shoulders a reassurance that I cling on to as he keeps rubbing my back.

"Listen to me," he says firmly. "We're not going to let him near you, Zella. You don't have to go back there. Not now. Not ever. We will keep you safe."

The words don't reassure me. When I glance away, fingers lift my chin.

"Tell me." It's an order, given in deep, rumbling tones.

"What if I'm not here? And he finds me?" I ask carefully, and his head jerks back.

"Are you planning on leaving?"

I manage to shake my head and shrug my shoulders at the same time. "I... I don't know. Ryder said—,"

"What did Ryder say?" Velvet over steel, something cold in his voice. "I told you that you could stay, Zella, and I meant it."

His words loosen something inside my chest, and I take a deep breath. "Okay. That's... that's good."

"Tell me what's bothering you. Apart from the obvious, that is."

I don't want to admit that I'm having a meltdown over Ryder not wanting me, and I'm definitely not about to explain how I spent my morning, so I shake my head. "It's nothing. Ethan... has he been to the apartment?"

Maverick's hands pause in their stroking for a moment. "He has."

Deep breath, Zella.

"Okay," I whisper. "So he knows I'm gone, then."

A throat clears. "Zella...," Maverick's voice is gentler than I've heard it before. "I wasn't going to show you this. But I think you deserve to know."

Phantom prickles linger at my neck. "What do you mean?"

Instead of responding, Maverick pulls something out of his pocket. My eyes widen as he taps the screen and it lights up. "What is that? Is that a phone?"

Maverick pauses, and he lets out a low laugh. "I keep forgetting that you wouldn't have seen a lot of this stuff. I think we need to introduce you to technology, Zella. Yes, this is a phone."

He shows me how he unlocks it with his fingerprint, and he presses buttons on the screen until a little film pops up. My mouth is open.

I thought you used a phone to call people, like a radio. This is insane.

My attention is drawn when he presses the screen, and I see the apartment. The bright white space looks too bright, the lights on throwing shadows from the statues across the floor. Confused, I look at Maverick. "How can you see this?"

"The guys put up a camera before they left. Watch." At his urging, I look back to the screen, flinching when a figure appears. It's unmistakeably Ethan, the picture crystal clear as he moves across the floor.

My whole body flinches involuntarily, and I swallow the surge of fear down when Maverick looks at me, staring down at the images instead of meeting his eyes. This is ridiculous. I shouldn't be this scared of Ethan.

He saved my life when I was a baby, raised me, looked after me. The last few weeks with him weren't great, but there's no reason for the chill invading my body as I look at him.

But as the images change, I lean in closer. "What... what's he doing?"

"Nothing good," Maverick says grimly. The little screen version of Ethan moves around the apartment, his mouth opening and his head turning from side to side. He disappears out of view for a few minutes, and when he comes back, he has something in his hands.

The chain from my ankle.

I jump when he lifts it, smashing it into the kitchen side. His arm sweeps away my few kitchen items, and my coffee machine smashes to the floor. His feet move over the broken parts, and my breathing speeds up as the camera follows him to my little reading nook.

The table is thrown. My little bookcase is picked up and thrown against the wall, my chair tipped over.

Maverick rubs my back again. "Breathe, Zella."

But I can't, my chest constricting as Ethan leaves again. "Is that it?" I ask Maverick, trying to keep my voice level. "Has he gone now?"

"No." Maverick's voice is lower now, softer. "He comes back."

He presses something, and the film jumps to Ethan in the apartment again. He's throwing something in his hands, tipping it everywhere. Frowning, I lean closer as if I can get a better look. "Is that water?"

Maverick's hand pauses. "No."

A gasp slips out as he throws the liquid over Maria. "I don't understand."

He's always been so set on preserving the statues, on taking care of them, making sure they had no *imperfections*. Why would he risk ruining them?

My anxiety ratchets up as he moves between each of my favorite statues. Psyche and Cupid are next, Ethan's movements jerking as he throws more of whatever liquid in his hands on to them. My hands start to shake as he moves over to Dante. Awareness is starting to trickle through in crawling fingers up my spine, the knowledge that something terrible is going to happen.

"Stop it," I whisper, staring at the screen. "Ethan."

But he can't hear me. My nails dig into my knees as I watch him carefully cover Dante in the liquid. He moves on to the wider apartment, creating a trail back to the elevator and stopping a few feet before it.

He gets into the elevator, and I hold my breath.

But just before the doors close, he tosses something out. And a small flicker appears on the floor, following the line he drew in a trail of color I've never seen before inside that space.

Orange. Yellow. Red. Flickering flames appear, climbing into a fiery monster that devours.

My face crumples as it reaches Psyche and Cupid first, swarming over them, burying them in fire before it moves on to Maria. The first sob falls out, my arms reaching around me to hug myself as it spreads over her, until her tall frame is engulfed.

"Zella." Maverick is murmuring, but I can't hear him over the sound of my own sobbing. I frantically scrub the blurriness from my eyes, watching as the fire moves closer to Dante. It takes over the apartment, spreading to my nook, my chair, my furniture.

Everything I had is burning.

"Dante!" I'm sobbing now, watching as his handsome face, the one I spoke to every morning, talked to when I was lonely, the one silent friend I had my entire life is hidden under licks of flame.

I watch as it takes everything, creeping closer to the screen until it eventually turns black.

"Zella," Maverick turns me to face him, his hand cupping my cheek. "I'm so sorry, sweetheart. I didn't know it would upset you this much."

"That was my home," I choke. "My home, Maverick. They were my... my friends."

Maverick doesn't point out the absurdity in my words. Instead, he pulls me close, murmuring soothing words in my ear that I barely hear as I bury my face into his chest and let the tears free. My whole body shakes in his embrace, his shirt growing damp beneath me as I grieve for them.

All my life, I asked for color. And Ethan gave it to me, in brutal vibrancy.

"Why did he do that?" I croak. "Why did he destroy them?"

"I suspect he thought people might come looking," Maverick murmurs. "Everything in that apartment is evidence, Zella. Evidence that he was keeping you there. I think it's safe to say that what he told you probably wasn't the real story."

I can't stop crying.

Everything I ever had just went up in smoke.

And now I'm truly alone. There's no going back.

And as much as I didn't want to, there's a ball of grief in my chest, cutting off my air.

It feels like the final nail in the coffin. I'm not sure what I'm grieving for – the loss of my home, my friends, my family.

Maverick sits quietly, his arms tight around me. But even this isn't final. Ryder pretty much confirmed it.

Finally, I pull myself together, pulling back. Maverick's arms loosen gradually, until I'm able to scramble up and onto my feet. I can't look at him.

"I'm sorry," I force out, staring at the floor. If I look at him, I might lean on him again, and I can't do that.

I can't lean on anyone.

I can feel his eyes on me. Before he can say anything, I turn, rushing out of the room. Maverick's voice calls after me, large footsteps striding across the floor as he follows, but I can't be around him.

I need to be alone.

I need to get used to it.

But as I dart through the hallway, running for my room, a shadow emerges from the wall and I collide with it blindly. Enzo folds his arms as I stagger back, his eyes bleeding into darkness.

"What happened?" he demands. I can't look at him either. Ryder emerges from the dungeon, his handsome face looking more serious than I've ever seen it. I glance at him and his expression changes, concern filling it as he takes a step towards me.

Maverick comes up behind me, filling the rest of the space with his energy as the three of them crowd me. They're all saying things, and it's too *loud*. My head is pounding, and I feel dizzy.

Too much.

Enzo reaches for me, but I dart under his arm.

I just need space.

Enzo snarls something at Maverick as I reach the top of the stairs, and I glance behind me. They all look so angry. Maverick mutters something too low for me to hear, and Enzo stalks out. The crash of a door sounds in the distance, and I flinch.

I'm bringing trouble to their home. Making them fight amongst themselves.

Maybe... maybe I should never have left.

When I reach my room, I climb under the cozy covers on my bed, hauling them until they cover my head and my breathing heats the small space in muffled pants. I don't want to look outside. I don't want to do anything at all.

The pounding of my heartbeat gradually settles inside my chest. Curling up into a ball, I fall into a restless doze.

The slamming of the door jerks me awake, and the covers are ripped away.

Flinching, I glance up at Enzo. His eyes are still black.

"You're angry," I whisper, and his head jerks back. He tilts it to the side, examining me.

"And you're sad. Why are you hiding?"

I half shrug, my arms still wrapped around me. "It makes me feel better. Why are you mad?"

Instead of answering, his hands reach out and roll me over. I stay still as he climbs into the bed next to me, pulling me back against him until my back rests against the warm cotton of his black shirt. "What are you doing?"

"Hush," he mutters. "You're cold."

I am, I realize. His arms wrap around me, chasing away the icy sensation in my limbs as I gradually relax into him, the tension leaking away from my muscles as we lay in silence.

"I'm sorry," I say quietly into the silent room.

His breath huffs against my hair. "Why are you sorry?"

"For earlier. You didn't enjoy it."

I squeak as I'm rolled again, and Enzo appears over me. Dark hair falls over his forehead as he leans in, our noses almost touching.

"Who told you that?" he snaps. Swallowing, I glance to the side, but his fingers trap my jaw. "Prey."

The demand in his voice brings out that curling, twisting sensation in my stomach.

"I thought... you sent me away." Avoiding his eyes, I stare determinedly at the carved wooden table next to my bed. "And Ryder was disappointed."

"Not in *you*," he murmurs. "He thinks I'm corrupting you."

He lifts a stray strand of hair, curling it around my finger. "I am corrupting you. But I don't care."

His body presses down into mine, and his fingers grip my cheek. "I told you, you're mine, little prey. And you'll be theirs too, even if they don't realize it yet. But I do. You were always meant to be ours."

My hand shakes as I lift it up, carefully tracing the edge of his cheek. The faintest edge of stubble tickles my fingers. "Do I happen to get a choice in this?"

Enzo growls, his face dropping down. "Not particularly. Did you want one?"

Slowly, I nod. "That doesn't mean I wouldn't choose the same thing. But I don't want to go from one prison to another, Enzo."

His jaw clenches. "You think I'm like him?"

"No," I whisper. "I don't think so."

The words seem to soothe him, and he pushes himself away from me in a sudden movement that tilts me to the side. Righting myself, I sit up as he strides across the room, picking something up from the sideboard. "I got you something."

His voice is gruff, and he clears his throat as he drops something in my lap. "Here."

It takes me a second to understand, and I turn the packet over in my fingers. A little thrum of excitement begins to build in my chest. "You brought me paint?"

He shrugs, and for the first time, a little flash of red tints the top of his defined cheekbones. "You said you wanted to color in my tattoos."

I'm still staring down at the paint, blinking rapidly as I fight not to cry.

Enzo brought me *color*.

He's not looking at me when I look up. His brow is furrowed as he stares at the floor.

"Ryder was right. I am not a good man," he says slowly. "I don't think I'm an evil one, but I'm not a good one, little prey. I can't be. Not even for you."

Climbing to the edge of the bed, I reach out and take his hand in mine, pulling him closer. "What do you mean?"

He stares at me, and his hand pulls away from mine as he slowly unbuttons the front of his shirt. I hold my breath as he tugs it off, revealing a body that would rival any of the statues at the apartment. Dark hair trails down his chest, ending at the edge of his dark jeans.

But then he turns around.

I'm not sure what noise I make. Horror, maybe. Some kind of groan as I take in the damage that's been done to his flawless skin. His tattoos extend over his back, thick black wings with whirls and symbols covering its entirety. But they don't quite cover the thick raised edges that criss-cross his skin, pale scars upon scars that collect on his body in sickening clarity.

"Enzo...," I choke. My hand reaches out, but he spins, grabbing my wrist in a gentle grip.

"I told you not to touch me, before," he tells me. "But you're the only person I'll ever allow to get this close, little prey."

Taking my fingers, he reaches around, placing them against his damaged skin.

"The only one allowed to feel these scars is you."

The low, harsh words make my eyes burn, implicit understanding of the gift he's offering.

"When I woke up downstairs," I say softly, "I thought you seemed like a dark angel. And you have the wings to prove it."

He snorts as he turns. "I'm the furthest thing from an angel you could possibly imagine, prey."

Nudging me over, he settles down on his stomach, tilting his head to look back at me and nodding at the pens in my hand. "You gonna do your thing or what?"

My fingers squeeze against the plastic, and I glance at his torn up back hesitantly. "It won't hurt you, right?"

He shakes his head, a small smile curling his upper lip. "Nothing you do could hurt me."

He watches me patiently, his head to the side as I carefully open the packaging and lay out the pens. He's brought me special ones, suitable for painting skin.

"I can't believe you remembered," I say reverently, stroking my fingers across the rainbow of color. "That I wanted to color them in."

"I don't forget anything where you're concerned," he murmurs. His eyes follow me as I sit up on my knees, hesitating. "Climb over me. Sit that ass right here."

He reaches behind him and pats his lower back. Shuffling on my knees, I lift up my leg and crawl over him, huffing as I push myself into position. My fingers skitter across his back, and I take a second to trace the edges of his scars softly. He inhales underneath me.

"I didn't think I had much sensation left," he mutters. "But your fingers feel like a damn brand."

I snatch them away quickly, and he makes a complaining noise. "I told you, you won't hurt me. It feels... nice."

A smile curls my mouth. "Okay. I'm going to get started now."

He stays still, his body a little tense as I lift the first pen up. I know exactly what I want to do, and as the first edges of bright, glittering gold sink into his skin, I bounce accidentally in excitement. "Sorry!"

"Do that again," he says in a muffled voice. "And we'll have to take a break."

I immediately stop, not wanting him to pull me away just yet. After a few minutes, I fall into the art in front of me as just as I do in my sketchbook, the pens gliding across Enzo's skin as easily as my pencil on a page. Slowly, his body relaxes underneath me.

As I finish the first wing and sit back to admire it, I summon the courage to ask the question in the back of my head. "What happened?"

When he doesn't answer, I take the hint and carry on. It's a few minutes later before his voice filters through, softer than I've ever heard it.

"You're not the only one who was kept in a cage, little prey."

My fingers nearly smudge the glittering gray, but I yank them back just in time, a lump appearing in my throat as I glance down at the scars. I don't want to push too much, but something tells me that Enzo's captivity was much more brutal than mine ever was.

"How did you escape?" I ask quietly.

"Maverick."

Of course. Their set-up makes a little more sense to me now. Maverick feels older than Enzo and Ryder, even though he doesn't look it. Like he's the leader. "He helped you, and you stayed with him."

Enzo shifts underneath me. "He saved my life. I owe him mine in return."

I want to ask more, but there's a warning note in his words that tells me not to push further, and I settle back to continue my work.

This is enough, for now.

And as I reach for the lilac, my fingers happily dancing over the set, Enzo's hand reaches back and curls around my leg.

It's more than enough.

Ryder

I reach for the leftover lasagne, pulling it out and settling in at the kitchen counter. Thank fuck for housekeepers. Ours makes sure we're well stocked, even when the staff have left for the evening. None of us are chefs.

I barely glance up when Maverick enters, grunting a hello through my food. He ignores me, setting up the coffee before he slides into a stool opposite me.

I stare resolutely down at the table. I don't want to go over our discussion earlier again. He's already hauled me over the coals for making Zella feel unwanted, and I feel shitty enough about the whole thing.

That was never my intention.

He gives me a minute, and when I continue ignoring him, he reaches forward and yanks the plate away from me. "Hey!"

"Have you spoken to Zella?" he asks calmly instead, and I glare at him.

"She's with Enzo upstairs," I point out. "And you told me to trust him."

Maverick's lips tighten. We both know what Enzo's capable of. But he treats our little stowaway with a gentleness I haven't seen from him before, even if it's edged with his own personal brand of psycho. "You will, though."

It's not a question, and I give him a salute, my fingers bouncing off the side of my head flippantly. "Aye aye, captain."

A flicker of hurt enters his eyes, and I hate myself for it. He despises any reference to him being our leader, even though it's the fucking truth. God knows where Enzo and I would be without him.

The lasagne turns to ash in my mouth, and I swallow it down in a tasteless lump. "I'll speak to her. Is that all?"

He sighs, but his fingers drum out a rhythm on the counter, a sure sign that there's something else. "John Martinez called earlier. He wanted an update on Moore."

I straighten. "You didn't tell him—,"

"Of course not," he snaps. "Jesus, Ryder, give me a little credit. I don't want to give him anything that might put him on Zella's trail. But we've got our own reasons to follow Moore right now, and I could use something else to add to the recordings from Club X."

Sudden queasiness turns over in my stomach, and I experience some regret about the lasagne. "You want me to follow him again."

He nods. "We need to know where he is and what he's doing. He dumped his car and torched it, so we don't have the tracker anymore."

Which means we're working blind, and we need to retrace his steps. It means I'm heading back to Club X.

"Ryder..." Maverick starts. His voice is more gentle this time. "If you—,"

I cut him off. "It's fine. I'll go."

The club doesn't open until midnight, so I have a few hours to kill. As I'm contemplating my options, footsteps sound, and we both turn to see Enzo saunter in.

Both Maverick and I stiffen in surprise as he walks to the refrigerator. His typical black shirt is nowhere to be seen, and as he turns his back on us, his scars are on full display.

Full, colorful, shimmering display.

The wings covering them have been painted in painstaking detail. One side is vibrant color – gold, red, orange, a mix of fire and flame that gives him the look of an avenging angel.

The other is darker. Grays, deep purple, shot through with slivers of silver.

Light and dark.

It's a perfect mix for him, and as he turns, he graces us both with a sardonic smile. "Enjoying the view?"

My eyes narrow. "That's a nice addition to your tattoos."

"It needs to dry." All of our heads spin around to where Zella lingers awkwardly in the kitchen door. Maverick and I both stand instinctively, and Enzo crosses the room, drawing her in with his hand at the back of her neck.

"Are you hungry?" he demands. "Thirsty?"

She shakes her head, but her eyes move to the coffee pot. Maverick gets there first, so I just lean against the counter and try to act like my half-sprint across the kitchen was for nothing more than a bit of light exercise. Maverick nudges me out of the way with his shoulder as he reaches for a cup, and I not so casually shove him back.

We've officially regressed to teenagers, and Enzo's snort tells me he hasn't missed it.

Zella is thankfully oblivious. Enzo leads her to the table, and she gives Maverick a soft smile when he places the cup in front of her. "Thank you."

We're all trying not to stare as she takes a sip, her soft lips opening in satisfaction.

Jesus.

Swallowing, I blurt out the first thing that enters my head. "Clothes."

Everyone turns to me, and I try to form a coherent sentence. "Zella. I thought we could look online, get you some new things to wear."

I see her eyes light up, although she looks confused. "What's online?"

"Like my phone," Mav reminds her. "You can use different things to find what you need and have it delivered here. It's a good idea."

She looks dubious. "Like... clothes? Through the screen?"

Everything is so damn *new* to her. Considering I'm so jaded about just about everything in life, Zella is a breath of fresh air in comparison.

Yet another reminder that we're worlds apart, whatever Enzo thinks.

I head to grab my laptop from my room, bringing it back and opening it up on the counter. Zella's eyes widen as the screen comes on. "It's so bright!"

I glance at the generic beach background. "I guess so."

It only takes a few strokes to bring up a search for a large department store. Zella's eyes get bigger by the second as I start scrolling through, showing her the different styles and types. "You can get all of this... on the line?"

"Online," I correct her, biting my lip to hide my smile. "It's called the internet."

"Wow," she whispers. "I only knew about phone calls. Not all of this."

I wave my hand at the screen. "You can choose whatever you want."

She takes a hesitant step forward and touches the pad, her hand making a tiny movement that doubles the screen size and makes her jump back, snatching her hand away. "I don't think it likes me."

"You just need to get used to it." Sitting next to her and breathing in that flowery scent, I open up the section for tops and slowly scroll through, watching her face. When it changes, I stop. "You like this one?"

Maverick chokes. It's a bright gold silky-looking halter neck with large, dangling sequins. Mildly aghast, I flick my eyes to Zella. She's practically got hearts in her eyes as she stares at it. "I could wear that?"

"Please no," Maverick mutters, and I shoot him a glare. If Zella wants to wear feathers and tar, then she damn well can. Taking a guess at her size, I put it in the basket.

It takes a few more minutes of coaxing, but we all sit back and watch as Zella hunches over the screen, feverishly flicking through the pages and crowing with increasing joy when she spots something she likes. Everything she likes is on the vibrant side.

"Uh...princess?" I offer, when she lingers over a particularly hideous bright purple and green playsuit with orange lightning stripes. "Maybe we should get you some basics, too."

She glances around, her eyes taking in the decidedly *not* rainbow colors we're all wearing, and her shoulders slump. "Oh. Yes, probably."

God fucking damn it. I add the playsuit to the basket too.

Maverick gives me a death glare. Enzo ignores us all, working his way through his third bowl of cereal as he watches Zella like she's going to vanish if he takes his eyes off her for a single second.

When I check the time, I'm disappointed at how much time has passed. "Sorry, princess. I need to head out for a little while. Rain check?"

She nods, and Maverick seizes the opportunity to snag the laptop. "Why don't we grab some of those basics now?"

Before I leave, Zella reaches out, touching my arm. Her fingers close over my skin, warm through the end of my bottle green shirt. "You're going to work?"

I give her an easy smile, not letting my disgust at the task ahead of me seep through. "That's the plan. Try not to miss me too much. Maybe these two will put on a movie if you ask them nicely."

Enzo looks like I've just proposed a tooth extraction, but Zella bounces in her chair with excitement, so he stops short of telling us all exactly what he thinks of that idea. She doesn't let go of me, though, and I glance down. "Mind if I have my arm back, princess?"

She blushes, but her fingers release my sleeve. "Just... be careful. Please?"

She has no idea what I'm going to be doing, but her concern makes something flip over in my chest. "Always am."

With a final wink, I slip away. Leaving them to their cozy evening, I liberate Enzo's bike again and hit the road, speeding into the city.

I hit my first road bump when I knock on the door at Club X. The bouncer gives me a closer look than he did before, the search much more thorough this time around. They still manage to miss the little camera built into my cufflinks, and I tidy them as I stroll through the club.

Something is definitely off. The staff look a little more wary this time, some of the serving girls a little too pale as they grit their teeth against the wandering hands and plaster too-tight smiles across their faces.

When I try to wander down to the underground level where I saw Moore before, I'm stopped again.

"This section's closed," the security guard grunts. Summoning a glare, I gesture around.

"Look, man, the rest of the club is a washout. I just wanna get to the good stuff, you know?"

Leaning in, I flick a piece of non-existent lint from his shoulder, clapping him on the back. The pig-faced guard squints at me, clearly not used to anyone being nice to him. "Uh. Sorry?"

Sighing dramatically, I lean against the wall. "All the good shit gets closed down. Why'd they close it, anyway?"

He leans in, clearly not used to any of the patrons talking to him as ruddy cheeks gleam in excitement. "One of the girls... she went missing. Reckon one of the punters got a little too excited. You know what I mean?"

I don't have to force the grimace that appears on my face as my stomach begins to churn. "I don't like playing with my food. What happened?"

The guard shrugs. "Dunno. But someone reckons the bosses were paid off not to say anythin'."

Nodding, I slip a crisp, hundred-dollar bill into his hand under the guise of a handshake. His huge hand clamps over it greedily. "Fair enough. Guess I'll give my club a try instead."

Dropping Maverick a message to let him know, I decide to make good on my words and head to our club in the city. We don't spend a huge amount of time there thanks to the overabundance of wealthy assholes, but we've picked up our fair share of jobs thanks to a little networking.

I ignore the nudge to go back home, to curl up next to Zella and watch her face as she sees her first ever movie in full fucking high-definition in our very own custom theatre. Those assholes better have picked a good one.

But my place is here, among the lowlifes and reprobates that make up the worst of city society. As I enter the club and push my hair back, I glance around. One hand up to the barman gets me a whiskey to curl my hand around as I wander, picking up the snippets of gossip that only tell me who's fucking who and not much else.

A hand on my elbow stops me. "Croft."

Fucking fabulous. My already sour mood takes a further nosedive. "Can I help you?"

The portly man in the insanely expensive suit smiles around the lit edges of the cigar. "Reckon you already are. John Martinez."

Nodding slowly, I give him a once-over. So this is the man who started it all, who contacted Maverick to look into Ethan Moore and kick started this whole fucking chain of events. "Pleasure. How can I help?"

Martinez leans in. Man's got a face like a rat, all beady dark eyes and narrow chin with a few whiskers hanging off. Not exactly an oil painting.

On second thoughts, I take it back. That's a fucking insult to rats.

Even his voice is oily. "I've been waiting patiently for an update on our arrangement. I'm afraid that Maverick hasn't been especially forthcoming."

Bored, I flick at the end of my sleeves. "Well, these things do take time. I'm actually doing some research tonight."

"Interesting," Martinez almost purrs. "And I'm glad to hear it, given that the man of the hour is right over there."

I force myself to turn slowly.

"He doesn't look quite himself," Martinez muses. He sounds delighted, and it's true. Moore looks... untidy, to say the least. Maybe even a little dirty. Hunched over the end of the bar, he's a far cry from the pristine man I saw at Club X. Gloves are still on, though, I note with disgust. Even his hair looks like it could do with a wash.

"No," I murmur. "He doesn't, does he? If you'll excuse me, Martinez, I have work to do. I'll ensure Maverick updates you tomorrow."

I don't hear what he says as I move closer, before sliding into an empty stool two along from where Moore sits, staring into his glass. His head turns slowly, taking me in with bleary eyes, but I ignore him as I pull the leather evening menu towards me.

"You," he slurs. "I know you."

I grace him with a disapproving flicker over his appearance, and my lip curls. "The pleasure isn't mutual, I'm afraid."

The lie rolls off my tongue like honey, and his face darkens. Stumbling off the stool, he makes his way towards me. The bartender glances over with a frown, and I unobtrusively hold up a hand, warning him off.

Ethan Moore slides into the stool next to me, nearly falling off the other side. Wrinkling my nose, I take a sip of my own drink. I can smell how many he's had already, the fumes wafting off him in waves.

When he's finally settled, he turns back to me. "You're from that company. The one that *finds* things."

This close, I can see the little pock marks in his skin, the way he's styled his hair to try and cover the increasing baldness, the sheen of sweat on his brow.

The idea of Zella anywhere near this man makes me want to do things that would make Enzo look like a choir boy.

When I don't respond, he pokes my arm with his gloves. "'M talkin' to you."

Slowly, I slide my arm away, glancing over. "I wasn't aware you had asked a question."

I take a little enjoyment in the way his face reddens, but it rapidly drains away at the reminder that this is what Zella saw when he wrapped that fucking chain around her ankle.

"I need help," he slurs. "I've lost something."

My whole body tightens, and I force it to relax. "Oh?"

I pitch my tone at just the right mix of inviting and disinterested, and he falls for it. Hook, line, fucking sinker.

Spinning and nearly toppling off, he rights himself before he looks around. I try to hold my breath when he leans in.

"I've lost something, and I need it back," he mutters feverishly. "I can't... I can't work without it."

I can't look at him. Instead, I lift my glass and take a healthy sip. "I can't help if I don't know what it is."

I want to see how he'll describe her, if he'll just front right up and announce that he's been keeping a girl prisoner in a city warehouse for more than two fucking decades. But he hasn't held her for that long by blabbing to every man on a barstool. He shakes his head. "I'd need a contract first. Non-disclosure."

Weighing up the possible advantages of signing some meaningless piece of paper to get more information out of him, I decide against it. Even the thought of pretending to work with him makes me feel sick to my stomach.

Getting up, I offer him an easy smile. "Sorry, man. We're fully booked at the moment. If anything comes up, I'll let you know through the club. What's your name?"

He narrows his eyes somewhere in my general vicinity. "Ethan Moore."

"Great." Draining my glass, I push it back over to the bartender and sign the slip he holds out to bill our tab. "Perhaps we'll meet again."

I can feel eyes on me as I walk out – Moore or Martinez – but I don't stop, starting the bike up and pulling out of the lot. The tension in my body doesn't relax until I catch sight of our gates.

Instead of heading to the home theater, I go straight upstairs and get in the shower. It feels like a thin layer of oil is covering my skin after the interactions I've had this evening.

By the time I'm finished and head back down in a pair of gray sweatpants, it's late. I'm not expecting anyone to be up, so I jolt when I walk into Maverick in the hall.

"Everything okay?" he asks quietly, and I nod.

"Everyone else in bed?"

He tips his head towards the kitchen door.

"She wanted to wait for you," he says in a low voice. "Was worried about you being out so late."

I stare in the direction of the kitchen. "Oh."

"Yeah." He claps me on the shoulder. "I'm glad you're home. Make sure she gets to bed."

With a final look over his shoulder, he heads upstairs. Staying where I am, I stare uselessly at the kitchen door.

She waited up for me.

When I push the door open, Zella is cradling a coffee in her hands as she stares out of the double windows into the dark night. She glances absent-mindedly over her shoulder, a soft smile on her lips, but it grows when she spots me.

"You're back," she says quietly. "I... I wanted to make sure before I went to bed."

Swallowing, I force a nod. Her eyes slide down, taking in my bare chest with a flicker of heat in her eyes. Fighting back the irrational urge to cross my arms over my chest like I'm shy – because come on, I'm a fucking whore – I cross the room and pour my own cup of coffee, moving up beside her with a gap between us. Zella stands quietly, but I can feel her eyes on me as I move around the room.

When I settle next to her, she blows out a breath, but stays silent, her eyes on the darkness outside. Guilt twists in my stomach. I promised I'd take her back outside today, and I didn't.

Truthfully, I don't think I can be this close to her and not touch her. My body is fucking vibrating from the effort.

"Ryder?"

I choke back the thoughts clouding my head. "Yes, princess?"

"Why don't you... why don't you want me here?" She turns to me, those fucking green eyes pools of sadness that I can't even look at. Her words finally register, and I frown.

"Why would you think that?"

She shifts in place, her eyes dropping to her drink. "You said... earlier. In the dungeon. You said you didn't want me. I thought – well. It doesn't matter now."

Fuck. *Fuck.* I knew she was upset – Maverick told me to pull my head out of my ass, but I thought he was being dramatic.

"Listen to me," I say firmly, turning to her. Her hair trails behind her as she peeks up, her expression crestfallen. My hand physically aches with the urge to reach out, to push the loose strands away, all the better to see her face. "Zella... I do not want you to leave."

Her expression stutters. "I don't... I'm sorry. I don't understand."

I keep forgetting that this is all fucking new to her. Groaning, I press my hands into my eyes. I'm fucking this up. I know I am.

"Look," I say finally. She waits patiently. "You're welcome here, Zella. I mean it. Our home feels brighter for you being part of it, and I don't want you to leave."

She half smiles. "But...,"

"But," I emphasize quietly. "I can't give you what Enzo... and maybe Maverick can. Not like that."

"Because you don't want me," she emphasizes, and I throw my hands up.

"I do want you," I blurt out. "I just... I *can't*, Zella."

"You want me," she whispers. She sucks in a breath, and fuck if her face doesn't look hopeful. "Then why—,"

"I am not good enough for you," I say, and my voice is harsher this time. "You need to understand, Zella. Whatever you have with Enzo and Maverick – I cannot be part of that. Do you understand?"

Her face falls. "Why would you say you're not good enough?"

Jesus. I'm no good at this emotional shit. I turn away from her, not wanting to look at those damn doe eyes for another second. Then I spin back.

"Is this what you want, then?" I ask roughly. Setting my cup down on the side with a bang, I move towards her, my body pushing her backwards until she's pressed against the refrigerator door, our hips pressed together so she can feel exactly how hard I am. "You want my cock, Zella?"

Just like everyone else.

She swallows, and then she tries to push me back, but I'm not budging. "You wanted it, princess," I breathe. "I'm at your disposal."

Now she looks like she's going to cry. "Stop it."

"No," I push out, my throat dry. "This is what you wanted, right?"

She shakes her head, white-gold curls flying everywhere. "Not like this. Not when you're so cold."

I feel cold. Ice-cold, as I lean down and whisper in her ear. "I am cold, Zella. Don't mistake me for anything else. I want you to stay, but I can't give you whatever it is that you think you want. Whatever you see when you look at me... I am not that man."

I thrust my hips against hers, once, and then pull back, shoving my hand into my air and turning away as I stalk across the kitchen. She doesn't let me get more than a few steps away before she's on me, her finger poking into my back. "Don't walk away."

"What?" I bark, spinning around. "*What*, Zella? This is what I do. Do you understand that, at least? This is *all I can fucking do*. I am a *whore*, princess. I fuck people to get what I need from them."

Her jaw tenses, nostrils flaring. She looks angrier than I've ever seen her. "Don't talk about yourself like that!"

"Why not?" I challenge. "This is the truth, Zella. You want to hear about my last job? I fucked a woman to get back the necklace her lover gave her because he wanted it back. I have fucked hundreds, if not *thousands*, of people."

"I don't care!" She's shouting now, her face red and her lips trembling. "Did you want to?"

My laugh is rusty and sarcastic, torn from my chest. "Like that matters."

"It matters," she whispers. "It matters, Ryder."

"What, you want my sob story? You want to know about how little Ryder helped to pay his mother's debts by fucking anyone and everyone? How they'd parade me around like a fucking trophy?"

Zella's sob breaks the silence. "Ryder..."

"And when she couldn't get any more from me," I whisper, "she sold me to a bad man, and he squeezed out every last drop. There is nothing left of me to give you, Zella. All I am is empty on the inside, and filthy on the out. That is who I am."

I crowd her again. "I shouldn't even touch you," I murmur, "but you're so damn bright, little thief."

My head jerks back when she throws herself at me, her arms wrapping around my waist. "That is not who you are, Ryder."

Whatever is left of my shriveled heart cracks wide open. "So tell me," I say heavily. "Who am I, if I'm not him?"

She doesn't let me go as she talks into my chest, her lips over my heart like she's trying to breathe some fucking life into it. "You saved me when you didn't have to. You brought me here. You watched over me, in the forest, and when I hurt myself you carried me inside and helped me. You opened the window for me so I could sleep with fresh air against my face."

My eyes close. "None of that means anything, princess."

Her fingers grip my sides. "Well, it meant something to me. Or do my feelings mean nothing to you?"

When I stay silent, she pulls her head back to look into my face. "Tell me, Ryder. Tell me right now that this doesn't mean anything to you, that my feelings don't mean anything, and I'll let it go."

My hand reaches up, tracing over her cheek, barely brushing the skin. "I'm a liar by trade, princess. A liar, a thief and a whore. You can't trust anything I say."

"But I do," she says firmly, her eyes on mine. "Lie to everyone else if it makes you feel better. But don't lie to me."

"I can't be what you need." I try to tell her, try to give her the unbroken truth, but she doesn't listen, shaking her head.

"I spent my entire life with someone telling me what I needed," she says quietly. "It's my turn now. And I won't let anyone else tell me what I need, Ryder, not even you. This is the time for me to make my own choices."

"Shitty choices," I mutter, and she pokes me in the chest.

"We'll see," she says softly. "But stop hiding from me, Ryder. Don't say that you want me, and then tell me I don't have the right to choose whether or not I want you."

"Even when it's for your own good?" I mutter, and she nods.

"Even then."

Finally, she lets me go. I've reached my limit. Heavily, I hold the door open, and she rinses her cup out and mine, stacking them both to dry before ducking under my arm and into the hallway.

"Sometimes," I murmur, and she stops, her back to me. "I feel so filthy that no amount of washing will clean it off. I don't want that to touch you, princess."

She stays silent for a moment. "I believe that we are more than the sum of the people who made us, Ryder. We're every interaction, every relationship, a perfect patchwork of memories. No single person can shape who we are, not if we choose otherwise. So choose, Ryder. Choose Maverick, and Enzo. Choose the people who love you instead of the ones who wanted to destroy you."

She swallows. "And maybe you could choose me, too."

Zella

I wake up alone.

Stirring, my eyes blink open to the clean white ceiling overhead. I turn my face to the side, but there's no one there. Ryder escorted me to my room last night, refusing to engage further after our argument in the kitchen and nudging me into my bedroom with a clipped 'goodnight'.

I did not, in fact, have a good night. I had a sleepless one, tossing and turning mixed with nightmares. I saw Ethan, reaching out for me with his hands on fire. Ryder, small and frightened in a dark room as people advanced on him. Dante, his smooth face twisted and tortured as if he could feel the fire crawling over him as his face melted into grotesque shapes.

My whole body aches as I try to roll out of bed, but I'm stopped by a sharp and sudden pain in my abdomen that makes my body hunch over. It lasts a few seconds, enough for me to realize exactly what this is. My eyes squeeze closed just as I feel the wetness between my legs.

Oh, no.

Ripping the covers off, I let out a mortified squeak at the drops of red covering the clean white bedding, frantically counting days in my head until I come to the inevitable conclusion that yes, this is that time of the month already. Just in time for me to fold over at the second spike of agony that drags across my lower half, reverberating up into my back.

It spreads down to my thighs, and I stumble into the bathroom, holding onto myself so I don't make any more of a mess than I already have. It takes me a few tries to work out the shower, and my hair trails out as I yank off my dress and climb in, letting the water wash over my stomach and thighs. When the pain hits again, this time working up my upper thighs, I can't hold back my groan.

I sit down on the floor of the shower, and the water flows over me as I contemplate my options. The pain continues until tears track down my face, washing away in the spray of the shower when I tilt it up.

Finally, the water begins to run cold, and I climb out. I'm shivering all over, the pain starting to increase in waves of agony that make my eyes blur as I grab my dress from the floor and try to tie it around myself. I don't have any packs here to help.

"Stupid," I groan as I stumble back to my bed. "Stupid, Zella."

I fold over from the pain radiating from my abdomen, losing track of time until there's a banging at the door. "Zella?"

Maverick sounds worried. I didn't come down for breakfast. Weakly, I raise my head. "Don't come in!"

"Why?" he calls out. "What's the matter?"

I'm too embarrassed to answer him, burying my head into the pillows instead.

The banging intensifies. Much to my mortification, I can hear Ryder and Enzo out there too, demanding to know why the door is locked and calling my name.

"Please!" I shout out, and they quiet. "Just... leave me alone!"

The agony spikes, and I curl over with an audible groan. Silence comes from behind the door, and I silently pray that they've left me alone.

But then there's a thud.

Another thud.

And I choke out a shocked cry as the door flies open, splinters of wood everywhere. Maverick storms in, followed by the others, and his eyes find me immediately, scanning over me in the bed and filling with concern.

"Zella?"

I can't stop the agonized whimper that falls from my lips as he strides over, his hand feeling my forehead. "Are you sick?" he asks softly, his brow creased in worry. Ryder and Enzo crowd the space around us, all three of them staring down at me.

Humiliation heats my entire body. "Please... I'm fine. Just leave me alone."

"You're not fine," Enzo says shortly. Ryder scans me in silence, his brows lowering. "Tell us what the matter is, little prey. Now."

I shake my head mutinously. I just need them to leave me alone.

"It happens every month. Just leave it alone, please." My words sound wobbly, and Ryder nudges Maverick aside.

"Princess," he says firmly. "We need to know what's wrong. If you're sick, you need a doctor."

"I'm not sick!" I say feebly. "I'm just... not feeling myself."

"That's sick," Enzo points out drily. "Let us see, prey."

Mutinous, I shake my head. "No. Absolutely not."

There's absolutely no way I'm showing them. I'll clean the bedding... somehow. I just need to work out how they wash their own clothes.

My hands clutch on the bedding when Enzo reaches out. He peels off my fingers with ease, lifting my arms up as I stare at him in horror. "Ryder."

Ryder drags down the bedding before I can do more than wriggle, and my moan of dismay is swallowed by the frantic activity that follows.

"Fuck." Enzo swears, his hands dropping down. "She's bleeding."

His hands move down as if to move my makeshift dressing, and I slap them away feebly, stopping when another wave of pain ripples through my stomach. He stares down at me in horror. "She needs a doctor."

"I don't," I whisper. "I'm sorry about the bedding. I'll fix it."

"Zella," Ryder pushes Enzo out of the way and kneels next to me, putting his hand out and squeezing mine as I avoid his eyes. "This is completely normal, sweetheart."

I pause. "It is?"

My voice sounds tiny, and he actually smiles as he pushes my hair back. "You didn't know? Happens every month, right?"

Enzo makes a noise, and I glance at him. He's still glowering down at the stained bedding, and shame tangles my chest.

"I'm sorry I made a mess," I apologize quietly. "I can clean it up."

Ryder strokes my hair back, and it feels so nice I have to close my eyes. "Don't be silly. We'll do that."

They pop back open. "What?" My voice is a yelp. "You can't!"

Ryder gives me a firm look. "Princess. You think we're going to just leave you here, in pain and alone, when we can help?"

I manage an embarrassed smile. "See?" I whisper. "There you go again."

A dull flush stains his cheeks, but he still turns, hissing instructions to Enzo and Maverick that have them moving around me. The pain returns, and Ryder strokes my hair as I curl into myself with a groan. "We're getting you some painkillers, sweetheart. But... I can help with the pain, if you're comfortable with that."

At this point I'm about as embarrassed as I can get, so I nod. But I regret it immediately when he shifts, nudging at my closed knees. "Open."

"What?" I yelp. I immediately press my legs closed. "No!"

Enzo's face appears over Ryder's shoulder. "Do as he says, prey, or we'll do it for you."

Ryder's finger rubs soothing circles on the outside of my bare knees. "You think we're going to sit around while you're in pain? Let me help, Zella."

His voice dips lower. "You wanted me to choose. This is me choosing."

The bed dips on my other side, and I glance up at Maverick. His jaw is tight, but he gives me a comforting smile as he takes over from Ryder, stroking my hair across my head. "Do as he says. Remember your promise."

The slight teasing tone makes me half-smile, before another cramp doubles down in my stomach. Ryder seizes my momentary weakness, wedging himself between my thighs and unwrapping the clumsy knot I tied to try and keep the dress around my hips.

My cheeks flush in mortification, and I scrunch my eyes closed as he pulls it away gently. "I promise you, sweetheart. None of this is embarrassing for us. We just want to help."

"Hurry up about it," Enzo snaps behind him. "She's hurting."

"Painkillers first," Ryder snaps back over his shoulder. Maverick lifts a little white button up to my mouth, a glass of water in his hand. "Have you ever taken these, Zella?"

I frown. "I think I did, once. I had a fever."

He makes me take two, holding the back of my neck as I choke down the cool water. Enzo gives Ryder a cloth, and I moan as he presses the warm material against me right there, moving the cloth over me in firm strokes.

"Does that feel good?" he asks me softly, and I nod. I can't look, so I bury my face into Maverick's side instead. He smells amazing, a little musky, and although he stiffens, he keeps stroking my hair as I hide from the fact that they're looking at me and touching me down *there*.

Ryder takes the cloth away, and I inhale as his fingers stroke up and down, barely brushing my slit. "There, now," he murmurs. "This will help you until the painkillers kick in, princess."

He pushes my lips apart, spreading me open with one hand as his fingers press down, moving in a circular motion that makes my hips buck. Everything feels more sensitive, my body swollen as he rubs his fingers back and forth, scraping the same place over and over until the agonizing pain in my stomach feels less than the sensation he's drawing from me.

"Ryder." I try to say his name but it comes out on a garbled moan, my face still pressed against Maverick's chest.

"Shhh," he soothes me, still playing, not letting up for a moment. "Let it happen, Zella."

My hand reaches down, and I jerk when a hand closes over my wrist. Enzo settles in on my other side, lifting my arm and pinning it in place. My legs are spread, my hands held, and I can't move, can't pull myself away as Ryder continues his slow assault that brings a slow licking of flame, the pain muting in the face of something much stronger.

"Use your tongue," Enzo prompts, and I gasp as his hand reaches down, cupping my breast. He rolls my nipple between his fingers, tugging and pulling softly. "She tastes like honey."

Ryder's face looks almost tortured as he glances up, and our eyes lock. The ghosts of our last conversation are in his gaze, and I hold it. "Ryder," I croak. "Please."

I'm not sure what I'm asking for. I don't know if I want him to stop, or if I never want him to stop as the flames curl at the base of my spine. He hesitates, his hand pausing where he presses into me before he dips his head.

The first swipe of his tongue lifts my back from the bed. Maverick and Enzo press me back down, and my eyes lock on to Maverick as he cups my cheek. He looks hungry, his blue eyes traveling across my face, tracing my features as Ryder groans. The sound vibrates against me, and I cry as his hands move under me, lifting me and holding me to his face like an offering.

The pressure builds, and builds, the pain almost forgotten as Ryder's tongue dances over me. His teeth graze, just a little, and the precipice feels so close I start to sob.

"Hush, Zella," Maverick murmurs. His eyes flicker down the bed, and they're full of heat as he turns back to me. "This is about pleasure."

I can't speak, my mouth open in a silent scream as Ryder gently bites down on my most sensitive area and Enzo pulls on my nipples, twisting them as I spiral into an abyss of feeling. Wave after wave of pure ecstasy wash through me and they never stop moving, their hands constantly on me until I sink back into the bedding with a depleted gasp.

Ryder pulls back, and Enzo releases my nipple with a final graze as I sag into the covers.

"How do you feel?" Maverick asks me, and I blink.

"I think I'm dead." Ryder's lips curl into a small smile as I stare down at him, and he shakes his head.

"Oh, little thief. If anyone is dead here, it's me."

Ryder

Maybe I'm not dead, but I'm going to hell.

Because *fuck*, if Enzo wasn't right. Zella tastes like heaven, and his face is smug as he follows me into the bathroom. I rinse out the washcloth, setting it to the side, and he props his hip against the sink like we're about to have some juicy gossip session and finish it off with BFF friendship bracelets.

"Don't," I mutter before he can say anything. I'm not in the mood.

He clicks his tongue. "She was in pain. We helped. Don't get your little martyred ass in a twist over it."

Pressing my lips together, I scrub at my hands. Enzo mercifully shuts the fuck up, but it only lasts for a minute before he starts again. I swear to God, he's spoken more in the last week than he has in the past fucking decade.

She's changing all of us.

"Why are you fighting this so hard?" he murmurs. When I flick my eyes to him, he's staring at me in the mirror. "We've never been ones to take the moral high ground."

Shrugging, I reach for the small towel to dry myself off. "Never a bad time to start."

"Bullshit." When I try to leave, he gets in front of me, shoving me back. "You feel clean yet?"

My head jerks back like he's slapped me. "What?"

He nods at my hands. When I glance down, they're bright red. "You use any more hot water, you're gonna take your skin off. It's giving me ideas, but probably not healthy."

I didn't even notice the temperature of the water. I'm so used to washing with it as hot as possible. "Drop it."

"No." He pushes me back again. "This will work. But it needs all of us."

I swallow. "No, it doesn't. Four's a crowd, Enzo. Normal relationships—,"

He barks a sarcastic laugh. "You serious? None of us are fucking *normal*, Ry. You. Me. Maverick. And not her, either. Conventional isn't in our fucking vocabulary. And she needs you."

"Sure she does," I say drily. "I bring so much to the table."

He leans in close. "You want a fucking comparison? I'm a *psychopath*, Ry. I've made my peace with it. Ain't never gonna change. I can't do any of that mushy shit. Wouldn't even know where to start."

He jerks a thumb over his shoulder, and I shrug. "Maverick—,"

"—can't do it either. He's focused on keeping her safe and making sure she's fed, but he doesn't have what you have. Neither of us do. We need *you*. So get on the fucking boat, Ryder. And if you're that torn up over the fucking day job, pack it in and become a damn nun."

With a final push, he turns and leaves, and I stare at his retreating back.

That was the *worst* pep talk I've ever heard.

Hesitantly, I make my way back into the bedroom. Zella is curled up in the corner chair fiddling with her hair, watching Maverick remake the bed with wide eyes. "You really don't have to do this."

"Yes, we do." He says the words softly, his eyes locking with mine as he straightens.

Avoiding his gaze, I try to smile at Zella. "How are you feeling?"

"Better. I think the little buttons helped?"

"Those are pills. Painkillers." Taking up the spot next to her, we watch Maverick fuss over the bedding like an old woman in silence.

Finally, he turns. "Arms up."

Zella raises her arms obediently and he lifts her from the bed, carrying her across the room and tucking her back in. She looks smaller as she curls back up, even her hair tucked away under the covers. Maverick leans over, testing the temperature of her forehead. "One of us will stay with you."

"This is silly." Her muffled voice protests before her head pops out of the covers, looking adorably mussed. "I'm used to doing this on my own. And if it's so normal, why is everyone fussing?"

I stay back as Maverick sits beside her. "It might be normal," he says gently. "But this – this is new to all of us, Zella. We're all learning as we go. And none of us like the idea of you being in pain."

"I don't mind," Enzo drawls, "but I'd rather be the one in charge of it."

Maverick pins him with a disapproving stare, before stroking his fingers across Zella's cheek. "Enzo and I have work to do. We'll come and check on you later."

Well... I guess I'm first up.

After they've left, we linger in awkward silence. I stay against the wall, and Zella disappears back under the covers. I hear her grumbling, and the covers jiggle as she moves herself around until her head pops back up with a frustrated huff.

"I feel fine now," she says grumpily. "I can get up."

I waggle my finger at her. "Nuh-uh. Maverick gives the orders around here, princess. I think he might blow a gasket if you jump up straight away. Maybe in an hour or so."

She flops back against the pillows with a huff. "Will you at least come over here? Or are you so determined to avoid me?"

My brows fly up. "I... ah. I'm not avoiding you."

Vivid green eyes pin me with an accusing stare. "I might be... naïve, but I'm not an imbecile, Ryder. You're avoiding me because of last night, and then what just happened."

I swallow down the urge to pinch my nose. I really am turning into Daddy Mav. "You're very direct, you know."

She shrugs. "Will you come over here? Please?"

My feet are moving before my brain can give the direction, and I hover over her. "What's wrong?"

She frowns at me. "Nothing. Will you lay down? You're making my neck crick."

When I hesitate, she crosses her arms. "You did it before, after the forest. Why is now any different?"

Because it feels like more now.

But I lay down beside her anyway, on top of the covers with my hands folded over my stomach. Zella wriggles until both of us are staring at the ceiling, the sound of soft breathing filling the space between us.

Her hand creeps across the covers. When I flip my hand over, her fingers entwine with mine, and she sighs.

"I'll never get used to that. You're so warm."

I turn my head on the pillow, watching the way her brows draw together as she watches the empty ceiling above us. Her face looks... shadowed. Like she's not in the room. "What do you mean?"

"When you have a lifetime without touch... you learn to live without it. But I never knew what I was missing."

Her fingers squeeze mine. "I don't know how I lived without it," she whispers. "I don't know how I existed in that apartment, Ryder. I think I'd lose my mind if I went back."

She huffs a short laugh, but it's tinged with pain. "Not that I can. But I couldn't live like that again. Not now that I know."

I absorb her words quietly. "He never touched you? Ever?"

She shakes her head. "I asked him once... before I met you. He told me I had a nursemaid when I was a baby, but I don't remember her. And then when I was old enough... never. Not as far as I remember."

It's a blessing, considering the sick shit I watched at Club X. I contemplate telling her, for a moment. But she doesn't need those nightmares in her head.

"He never tucked me in," she whispers. "He never changed my bed when I was sick or brought me the painkiller buttons. I think he might have once, when I had a bad fever. But he didn't like doing it. He said it wasn't a good thing to have inside my body."

I stiffen. "So what did you do? When you were sick? Or when you had your period?"

"I managed. Not always well, though. I had to bag everything up, and Ethan would burn it and bring me fresh things. He's obsessed with things being clean, fresh, bright. He wouldn't even talk about it, just collected the bags and brought new ones."

For twenty years, she lived alone. Images of a younger Zella, sick or worried and trying to make the best of a shitty situation fill my mind. I squeeze her hand back, clearing my throat.

It feels only fair to offer up a little part of me, in exchange for a little part of her.

"My mother was a junkie," I murmur.

She turns her head to mine with a frown. "What's that?"

"An addict," I try to clarify. "She was addicted to drugs. They'd make her act strange. Sometimes slow and sleepy, but sometimes she'd be wide awake and full of energy, but not the good kind."

The kind that would blow all of our rent money on an impromptu shopping spree, or make her decide to decorate our shitty trailer, buying expensive paint and throwing it everywhere. The kind that scratched at her skin until it bled, scabs on top of needle tracks until she was unrecognizable.

"We never had any money," I say quietly. "And when I got a bit older, I wanted to help. So I lied about my age, got a job working for cash at this little bar in the city."

Zella smiles a little. "You wanted to help your mom. That's sweet."

I swallow. "Yeah. But it wasn't enough."

My voice sounds rough, and Zella picks up on it, squeezing my hand. "What happened?"

"I came home one night," I start slowly. "And her dealer – the person who she bought the drugs from – he was there. She owed him a lot of money, and he was hitting her."

Her hand tightens in mine.

"He kept hurting her," I whisper, "and I couldn't get him off. But then he stopped, and he turned to me. He told me if I went and worked for him, he'd leave her alone. Her debts would be paid off."

"Ryder," she whispers. "What did your mom say?"

"She asked me to do it." My throat feels thick. "She begged me. And she was all bruised, and she was so thin. So I told him that I would, if he stopped her supply. And he agreed."

Zella inhales sharply. "I'm so sorry. Did he stop?"

"Yeah." I turn her hand over in mine, drawing patterns in her palm. "But she found someone else pretty quick. Died a few weeks later of an overdose. But he told me I'd signed a deal, and it wasn't his fault she didn't know how to stop. Didn't have much of a choice, then."

I can feel her looking at me, feel the sorrow in her gaze, the sympathy.

"How long?" she asks softly. "How long did you do that?"

"Years," I confess, the words feeling like jagged, broken glass in my throat. Years of unfamiliar hands, rough touches, harsh laughter. Being passed from person to person like I was nothing more than a thing.

"Lots of people started doing drugs, to get them through. But I… I never wanted that."

But it meant I remembered. Every little, horrible part of it.

"How did you get out?"

Blowing out a breath, I pull myself back into the room. "Maverick. He was on a job with his father, and I gave him some information that he needed. We just… clicked. And the next thing I knew, he'd spoken to Antonio and… he bought me out."

My stomach flips over. Zella gapes.

"He bought you?" she asks in horror. "Like a possession?"

I shake my head. "No. Not like that. He had to pay them to get me out of there. It's never been like that between us."

Even if it still feels like an invisible noose around my neck.

"So I came to work for him and his dad," I say with a smile to cover up the aching in my chest. "Then Enzo joined us a few years later, and here we are, the merry band of reprobates you see today."

"What about Maverick's dad?" Zella asks curiously.

"He died." Sorrow builds in my chest. "Robert was a good man. Better than all of us, really."

"I don't believe that," she says softly. "Thank you for telling me."

We're facing each other, and I poke her gently, over her heart. "A piece for a piece."

Her lashes cast feathery shadows on her cheeks as she tries to smile. "A piece of my heart for a piece of yours?"

"Yep," I murmur. "Seems fair."

"Does that mean...," she stops, and chews on her lip. "Are you choosing?"

"I'm not sure you were ever a choice, little thief," I say quietly. "I think you were always going to be inevitable."

I think I knew it the second I locked eyes with her in that apartment and she knocked me out with a damn wok.

"Does it feel like this for everyone?" she asks me, and I give her a questioning look. She presses her fingers against my heart, and then against hers. "So... consuming?"

I shake my head. "No. Not for everyone."

"Then I feel very lucky," she murmurs. "That it was you and Enzo that found me."

Lifting her hand, I twist her wrist lightly, baring the soft skin and pressing my lips against it.

"I think we were the lucky ones, Zella."

She gives me a soft, sweet smile, and then she rolls over. "Come here," she says, looking over her shoulder. "Please?"

I shift closer, wrapping my arms around her and pulling her back against me. She shifts, settling into the crook of my arms like she's always belonged there.

Maybe she has.

"In an hour," she mumbles after a few minutes. "I'm getting up."

I smile into her hair. "Sounds like a plan to me. I do have a promise to keep."

And a whole world to show her.

Maybe I'm not a good man. But maybe I could be a better one.

For her.

Zella

"Your clothes have arrived."

I glance up at Maverick's words. He's been quiet through dinner, almost distant, but his words send a thrill of excitement through my stomach. "They have?"

I'd almost forgotten, but I'm tired of wearing these dresses. And as much as I enjoy wearing a combination of the guy's clothes, it'll be nice to have something of my own to wear.

He smiles, but it's distant. "They have. I'll bring them to your room after dinner, and you can try them on."

Trying to hide my frown, I nod and stare back down at my plate.

I wish Ryder was here, but he's out this evening, working.

My throat tightens. He promised there was nothing for me to worry about, but how can I not?

I sneak a glance at Maverick, but he's staring out of the window, his lips pursed.

"Maverick?" His name slips out almost before I'm ready, and he glances at me. His eyes seem especially pale today, much paler than the color I gave them when I was sketching this afternoon. I've nearly worked my way through the pens Enzo bought already.

"Yes, Zella?" he prompts, and I focus.

"Sorry." I can't meet his eyes, so I stare down at my plate again, my emotions churning in my chest.

It's been a few days since Ryder told me about his story, and the unfairness of it has burrowed into my chest. On top of that, Enzo has disappeared, not coming to meals, and Maverick has been cooler too.

"Zella," he says my name again, and this time, he's completely focused on me when I look up hesitantly. "What's wrong?"

"You can't let Ryder do that any more," I blurt out. As soon as I say it, I want to kick myself. But the anger simmering inside me isn't going away.

"I'm sorry?" He looks confused, but I plough on.

"Please," I ask quietly. "Don't make him... have sex. For work, I mean. Surely there must be other ways?"

When I dare to look up, Maverick is frozen. His throat flexes as he swallows.

"Ryder told you that I make him... have sex? For his work?"

He sounds horrified, and a flicker of doubt appears in my chest. "You don't?"

"Zella." Maverick gets up, moving over to me. I flinch, but he kneels in front of me, turning my chair around. His finger lifts up my chin.

"Is this why you've been avoiding me?" he asks softly. My nod is hesitant, and he sighs.

"Ryder," he says, and it's almost a groan. "Sweetheart, I swear to you that I do not ask Ryder to have sex as part of his work. He's always seen it as something he's good at, something he can do, so he's done it – even when I have begged him not to."

My mouth rounds. "O-oh."

Maverick surveys me, and I shrink back, embarrassment heating my insides. He looks... tired.

This is why I shouldn't get involved.

"I'm sorry," I whisper. "I'm really sorry, Maverick. He told me about his background, and I just thought..."

"I can imagine," he says heavily. "Self-flagellation is one of his many talents. I promise you, Zella, it's not something he has to do. I would never force either of them to do something they didn't want to do. Ryder has always believed he doesn't have anything else worth giving, and he is wrong."

I nod. "I shouldn't have said anything."

"No," he says quietly. "You should. I wondered what I had done wrong, to make you look at me the way you have."

I pick at the end of my dress. "I just... it didn't match up with what I thought of you. And then I realized that I don't know much at all, and it just... got to me."

I'm dreading his reaction, but when I look at him, he's smiling.

"I'm relieved," he says before I can question him. "I thought maybe... maybe you'd changed your mind about being here. I didn't want to push you, so I stayed away rather than force myself on you."

I flush. "Oh. No, I haven't. Changed my mind, I mean."

"I'm very glad to hear it," he says softly. "I missed having you next to me at meals."

I don't have to force the smile that blooms, relief filling me that the only issue here is my own stupid assumptions. "I missed you next to me, too."

"Well, we can rectify that." A gasp catches in my throat as he scoops me up, and I blow it out when I'm settled in his lap. He stares down at me, a smile curving his lips. "Much better."

"I feel like a parcel," I say lightly, but I'm fighting back a stupid giggle. "I do have legs, you know."

"I know," he says, reaching out and picking up a roasted carrot with his fork. He lifts it to my lips, and I take it, wrapping my lips around the tines. "But I very much enjoy taking care of you, Zella."

I swallow down the food before I respond. "It seems like you take care of everyone. Me. Ryder. Enzo."

When I mention Enzo's name, the brightness in his gaze dims. "I suppose so. Just the way things worked out."

"Will you tell me? Not about their stories," I say hastily when he looks hesitant. "But about you. Your story. Ryder said you worked with your dad?"

"I did." He offers me some more food, and I take it. Everything tastes better when he feeds it to me. "My dad worked in law enforcement for years. He was a well-respected senior cop, and then he moved to the FBI. He retired early, but he got bored, so he set up an investigative agency."

"And you helped?" I ask. I try to imagine a little Maverick, toddling after his dad, and the image makes me grin. He's such a giant, the image of him smaller than anyone is hard to imagine.

"I did. Never wanted to do anything else," he admits ruefully. "My dad taught me everything he knew. I did join the force for a few years to get some field experience, but I ended up back where I started. Too many rules there. We're a little more... flexible, in how we do things."

"And that's how you met Ryder and Enzo."

He nods. "I knew I couldn't leave them where they were. They both deserved better than the shitty hand they were dealt in life, and I could help with that."

"You're a good person," I say, and he snorts.

"I believe good people deserve good things, and bad people deserve everything bad," he says quietly. "Life isn't always fair, but we try to even out the scales a little. It's why I left the police. Too many bad people getting away with it, and too many of the good ones losing out."

I sigh. "The world seems like an awfully complicated place."

He laughs. "It is. I'm sorry you haven't seen a lot of it yet, but I'm conscious that Moore is still around."

I nod. It makes sense. "After so many years, this feels like a lot of freedom to me."

Maverick frowns. "I don't want to overwhelm you, but I promise things will change. In fact... there's a street fair next week in the city. Maybe you'd like to come? If all of us go, we can take turns keeping an eye out. I think you'd enjoy it."

My hands start to tremble. A street fair.

"Do you mean it?" I ask him eagerly, and he laughs, a low rumble that I can feel against my side.

"I never say anything I don't mean," he says, and I grin, the smile stretching from ear to ear.

"I'd love to go," I tell him earnestly. "With all of you."

"Good."

He continues feeding me in silence, until I begin to fidget. "Where's Enzo?" I ask, and he looks away from me.

"He's busy, Zella," Maverick says gently. "He won't be around much for the next day or so."

The high of anticipation fades beneath disappointment, but I swallow it back down. "Okay."

I slide off Maverick's lap. His arms tighten before he lets go, almost as if he's reluctant. "Where are you going?"

I shrug. "I think I'll get an early night. See you tomorrow?"

He nods, his blue eyes examining my face a little more closely than I'd like, so I offer him a quick smile and sidle out of the room.

The hallway has darkened in the time we've spent at dinner, and I jump as I catch a pale glimpse of my own reflection in the ornate mirror. Hurrying past it, I'm lost in my own thoughts when something jars me.

Frowning, I look around at the strange noise. A moment later, it comes again.

A low, groaning sound echoes, and I stop where I am, swiveling on my heel and looking up and down the hallway.

It doesn't sound right. The hairs stand up on the back of my neck, and I debate going back to the dining room. But then I hear it again, and my eyes are drawn to the dungeon door.

It's ajar, the edge balancing against the frame, and I take a step as the sound comes once more, this time deeper and more agitated.

"Enzo?" I whisper, but I don't hear anything else.

What if he's hurt himself?

My head turns back to the dining room. I should go and tell Maverick.

But then you won't know what's going on.

Maverick's caginess, Enzo's absence. Something is going on.

Curiosity overtakes me, and I reach for the handle.

Just a little peek, I reason. Just enough to make sure that he's alright, and then I'll leave him alone until he's ready to talk.

The handle opens smoothly under my touch, and I pull the door open silently, staring down. The stairwell is pitch black, but I can see a small flicker of light just beyond the turn in the stairs. Gingerly, I place my feet down on the cool concrete, pausing when the groan travels up. It sounds worse this time, and my feet move, taking me around the corner. The weight of trepidation settles in my stomach as I descend, and I let out a relieved breath when I hear the low murmur of Enzo's voice.

He's fine. Nothing to be worried about.

I'll just take one peek and sneak out. Just enough to reassure myself. He won't even know.

My nose twitches as my foot reaches the bottom step, my mouth twisting in distaste. It smells funny down here, almost metallic. I don't know how Enzo can stand it.

Bracing myself, I peek around the corner.

But as my eyes settle on the reason Enzo's been hiding away, fear hits me like sharp, jagged shards of glass fluttering inside my chest.

He looks up, dark eyes locking on mine.

Not a single star to be seen.

And underneath him, on the table he tied me to, is... something unrecognizable.

Zella

At first glimpse, it looks like an animal.

But then it *moves*, and the same groan that drew me down here travels out of its throat, filling the air around us with pain.

My breathing stutters to a stop. I take a step back as Enzo raises his hands in the air, slowly.

He takes a step away from the thing he's working on, a step closer to me.

When I back up, my heels hitting a concrete step, he pauses.

"Oh, little prey," he breathes. "Why did you have to come down here?"

The air is locked inside my chest, my head swimming. When he takes another step, I shake my head frantically, my eyes darting between him and the table.

"W-why?" I choke out. Instead of answering me, he moves closer, and a terrified noise erupts from my throat. "Stay away!"

He tilts his head. "I can't do that."

His voice is low, intimate, as he takes steps that eat up the distance between us. I can't not look at him, my hands gripping the rail desperately as I try to back up before he reaches me.

His hand shoots out, gripping my wrist and pulling me closer. When I thrash, pulling my other hand up to try and push him away, he grabs that too, yanking me closer to him and dragging me down the steps, carrying me into the dungeon with calm efficiency.

"Look at him," he snarls, and I shake my head desperately. I don't want to look at the piece of meat that used to be human, the way its head turns slowly from side to side, with desperate, gurgling sounds coming from its throat.

"I can't," I sob. "I don't want to."

"But you wanted to know," Enzo breathes in my ear. "You wanted to see, little prey. You didn't do as you were told, and now you're here. What do I do with you now?"

"I'm sorry," I gasp. "Let me go. I'll go back upstairs—," He buries his face in my neck, inhaling, and I flinch. He rips himself away with a snarl, and I lose my balance. My hands shoot out to stop me tipping onto the table, and I moan in horror at the wetness under my hands.

"Why are you doing this?" I ask him, my voice shaking as I stare down. "What did he ever do to you?"

What could any human do to deserve this?

All of Ethan's warnings run through my mind.

The world is full of evil, Zella.

And I walked straight into it. Ran to it, my arms wide open.

Enzo is silent behind me, and I suck in a rasping breath, steeling myself to turn around.

"Am I next?" I ask, waving my hand at the scene behind me. My voice shakes, but I refuse to let myself cry. "Was this all a game to you? Will you carve me up like this, Enzo?"

His fists clench. "So quick to judge, little prey," he snaps out. The tendons on his neck stand up in harsh lines under the bulb overhead. "When you have no idea."

I have nowhere to go when he stalks me, pushing me until my hips are pressed into the hard metal of the trolley behind us.

"You have no idea," he murmurs, his eyes a bare inch from mine. "You think this is evil? This is what he *deserves*. He deserves everything he is feeling and more."

He. I feel sick, and I swallow it down. "I don't understand."

He grabs me, spinning me around and sliding his hand around my neck in that familiar way, pushing me down so I'm facing the man on the table.

His breathing is warm against my ear. "John Millers. Fifty-seven years old. Mechanic. Every day, he gets up and goes to work. He's a hard worker, this one. Works long days, comes home, has a beer in front of the telly. A real stand-up guy. Quiet, keeps to himself, but nice enough. Everyone knows John."

My eyes feel wet as I stare down, looking into the clouded brown eyes of the thing that used to be John Millers.

Enzo rubs his hands up and down my arms. "Breathe, prey."

I take a gasping breath, my stomach roiling. "Why, then?"

Enzo presses against me. "Angelina Burrows," he murmurs. "Seventeen. She was hitchhiking when John picked her up one night. It was an icy December. He was so worried she'd be cold, he wrapped her up in an old duvet when he was finished with her. She was snug as a bug when he buried her a few hundred yards from the highway."

He presses his lips to my shoulder. "Sherileen Jacobs." I shake my head, but he doesn't stop. "Fourteen years old," he whispers. "She was looking for her dog when he called her over. Told her he'd help her look, and then he *buried* her, prey. He buried her so deep, her family never had a chance at finding her."

My face crumples, my head bowing. "Enzo."

"Abby Millers," he says quietly. "Aged seven, when it started. Her mama couldn't live with him, so she tried to run, and he buried her for it, just like the others. Abby grew up a sad, sweet little girl, and everyone said how *kind* John was to care for her so when her cruel mother ran off and left her. He was so devoted, he never even looked at another woman. Why would he when he was such a *loving father*?"

His voice is harder now, and he looks over my shoulder.

"He owes the devil, Zella," he murmurs. "And I'm right here, collecting my dues."

"How do you know all this?" My lips feel dry, my mouth like a desert as I look down at what's left of John Millers.

"There's always a trail," he murmurs. "Men like him, they like to revisit the good old times. John here wasn't particularly smart. Had all of his recordings lined up like trophies. Didn't you, John?"

There's no response.

"He can't hear us," Enzo says softly. "Can't see us, either. He's already in hell, little prey."

His words are so casual, even as he plays with the edges of my braid. Tearing my eyes away, I turn around, Enzo giving me the barest amount of space before he pushes back against me.

"Are you scared?" he whispers. "You should be, prey. I told you I wasn't a good man. I don't tell lies."

My head is spinning. "Do you do this... a lot?"

He tilts his head. "Depends. There's a lot of bad people out there. So many sins to atone for."

He searches my face for a response, so I nod mutely. His hands reach up, cupping my face.

My lips part. I need to understand why he does this. "Where were you?" I ask quietly. "Before you came here?"

His fingers stroke my cheeks gently. "In a cage," he murmurs. "Such a small little cage, prey. They tried to contain me, but they let me out when they needed me. And they always seemed to need me. Always someone to be punished."

I try to breathe, try to work through what he's telling me. "Do you mean... a real cage?"

"Metal bars and everything," he whispers. "They'd parade me like an animal in a zoo, their little pet demon on a leash. Except they didn't find me quite so entertaining when I went back for them, that last time."

"You hurt them?" I ask. Something cold curdles in my stomach. The image of Enzo trapped inside an actual cage. When he nods, I take a breath.

"I'm glad," I whisper, and his eyes shoot to mine. "I'm glad you hurt them."

"They were the first on my table," he motions behind us. "And I thought that would be it. But the burning didn't stop, prey. They opened something up when they made me, and I can't put it back. But this... this stops the burning."

"But it's only the bad ones?" I ask, my eyes searching this. "You're sure?"

He nods. "Maverick keeps me in line."

"But....," Swallowing, I turn and glance at the table, avoiding the man who deserves everything he's getting, if what Enzo is telling me is true. "You put me on that table," I whisper, and I look at him. "You tied me to it."

His hands move from my face to my neck, gripping it as I hold my breath.

"When I saw you," he whispers. "The burning was so bright, little prey. Brighter than it's ever been. And I thought it meant you needed to be on my table. So I put you there, and then I realized."

His lips are closer to mine now. "What?" I whisper back.

"It's just you. *You* make me burn, little prey. You're like acid in my veins, a knife inside my chest."

My body trembles as he leans in closer, until his lips press against mine.

"You are my hell, and you are my redemption. And I will never let you go, prey. If you run, I will bring you back," he murmurs into my mouth. I suck in his words like oxygen, my lungs inflating with air.

When he suddenly steps back, I stagger, the removal of his weight against me making my body feel light as a feather.

"Run now," he says quietly, looking away. "And decide if this is something you can live with."

My head feels too full. "I thought—," His laugh is dark and rich. "You don't get a choice? But you do. You can come to me by choice. Or you can try to get away, but I will chase you, prey. That's the only choice I'm willing to give you, and I'm only giving it once."

He nods towards the stairs. "Go."

My legs feel unsteady underneath me as I move past him, his gaze heated on my back as I start up the stairs. By the time I hit the door at the top, I'm running, the little breath left in my lungs burning as I race into the main house and up to my room, slamming the door behind me and backing up as though he'll make good on his promise right now and burst through the door, ready to drag me back downstairs to his table.

The room feels too small, and my fingers fumble at the latch as I yank the little door open, breathing in the fresh air.

As the shaking in my limbs starts to subside, I pull in a great, shuddering breath.

The evening air is peaceful, the leaves from the trees rustling softly and the scent of autumn in the air. While below me, a man lies on a table with his skin carved apart, careful slices reducing him to nothing more than meat.

I retch over the railing, my dinner threatening to make a reappearance as I force it back down.

My skin feels too hot, but my hands feel ice cold as I press them to my burning cheeks. Enzo's words play on a loop inside my head, and something Maverick said comes back to me, in his deep, reassuring voice.

Good people deserve good things, and bad people deserve everything bad.

When my stomach stops swirling, I slowly step away from the window.

Maverick

Tipping my face up into the shower spray, I let the heat of the water wash away the filth I feel after a day spent working on identifying the exact locations of John Miller's victims.

The heaviness continues to press down on my shoulders as I turn it off, reaching for a towel and wrapping it around my waist as I head back into the bedroom.

As tired as I feel, my body still feels too wired to sleep. I'm very aware of the fact that Enzo is working out his demons on John downstairs right now, whilst Zella is sleeping, blissfully unaware of the torture taking place right under her nose.

Ryder pokes his head around the door, coming in when he sees me sat on the edge of my bed. "You too?"

I nod. We both feel it, when the end of a case like this one draws near. We know what we have to do. "You want to go tonight? Get it over with?"

"Yeah." He sighs heavily, taking a seat next to me. "What about Zella? I don't want to leave her on her own."

I frown into my hands. It's a good point. Enzo is not someone to be reasoned with when he's in this mood. We'll be lucky if we see him anytime in the next two days.

A creak on the floorboards outside pulls me from my thoughts, and Ryder and I pause as Zella appears in the open doorway. "Sweetheart?"

It takes me a bare moment to notice the shivers racking her frame. She's shaking violently, and as I jump up and move towards her, I notice the paleness of her skin.

Ryder is close behind as I take her hand and gently draw her inside. I nudge her to sit on the end of the bed and she folds her fingers in her lap, her eyes darting everywhere like a wild animal.

A thought occurs to me, and I share a look with Ryder. Comprehension dawns on his face, and he drops down, putting his hands on her knees and rubbing them as though her skin is cold to the touch.

"Princess," he coaxes softly. "What's the matter?"

But it's me she searches out when she looks up. "I didn't... I didn't realize."

She wets her lips with the tip of her tongue. "You told me not to go downstairs."

Fuck. Icy fingers wrap around my heart as I kneel next to Ryder. Her eyes look dazed, her forehead clammy when I press my fingers against it.

"I should have listened," she whispers. "Why didn't I listen?"

My lips press together. I know exactly what she would have seen. "Zella, listen to me. That man downstairs... he's not a good man, sweetheart. I know that probably doesn't help, but he's a murderer."

He's a sick son of a bitch, in fact. But I don't think the gory details will help her right now.

She looks at me bleakly. "But so is Enzo."

I hesitate. The line between black and white, that sharp edge of good and evil, has never seemed as thin as it does right now, with Zella staring at me blankly.

"Yes," I admit finally. "Yes, he is."

She nods slowly, and I sit back on my heels, contemplating our next steps. Finally, I pull myself up to sit next to her. Her eyes glance at my bare chest, a hint of awareness filtering in as her golden skin darkens in a blush. "I didn't mean to barge in."

I clear my throat. "Don't worry. Will you tell us what you're thinking?"

Her shoulders sag, and she sighs. Her tone is defeated when she speaks. "I'm thinking… I don't know. My whole life, Ethan would tell me these things about the world, and it turns out they were all true."

"No. Not all of them," Ryder says softly. "There's a lot of good in the world, princess."

"But not here," she murmurs.

Ryder and I share a concerned look. "Zella," I ask delicately, trying to swallow down the sudden pounding in my chest. "Do you not want to stay here anymore?"

She shakes her head, and the dread tightens my throat, only to relax a moment later. "I want to stay," she whispers, almost too quietly for us to hear. "I think I'm panicking because… I thought it would bother me more. But… it doesn't, really."

She turns her eyes to mine, a question in them. "What does that say about me? If I don't care?"

She looks so desolate that I wrap my arm around her shoulders, pulling her into me. She comes willingly, and I breathe out a sigh of relief as her head tucks into my side. "Enzo isn't evil, Zella. At least, I don't believe so. He likes to pretend he is. Maybe he even believes it.

But he only goes after the bad guys. I've never seen him hurt someone who didn't completely deserve it."

"But why him?" She challenges me. "Why does it have to be him?"

"I... he needs it. I don't know how to explain it."

Ryder shrugs when I glance at him for help. "He was brought up in shitty circumstances, princess. Something is broken inside him."

"Has he ever tried to stop?"

I nod. "Once."

He lasted three months. Three months before we had to sedate him to make him sleep, the nightmares inside him crawling out, making him a danger to everyone.

"It didn't go well," I tell her. "And given our line of work, we were able to work out a way for him to get what he needed."

"By killing people. Bad people." Her face is unreadable when I glance down.

"Yes. You asked what it says about you, if you don't care. None of us care about the people on his table, Zella. They deserve everything they get, and then some."

I turn her to face me, cradling her cheek.

"What I do care about," I say firmly, "is my family. There is *nothing* I won't do to keep my family together, Zella. Even if we have to hunt down murderers to do it."

She takes a deep breath. "So you just... look for people to give him?"

"Not quite." Letting her go, I stand up and move to the closet, pulling out fresh clothes in preparation for our trip tonight. When I turn around, she's watching me, and her eyes drop down a little too late. "We identify cases where we can help people get out of bad situations, and we try to help them, where we can."

"Sometimes we're too late," Ryder tells her. "Sometimes the bad guys win, princess."

"So Enzo makes sure they pay for it." I duck inside the closet, pulling up the jeans and buckling them. "And then Ryder and I finish the job."

"What does that mean?" she calls out, and I tug the hoodie over my head before I head back into the bedroom. "Why don't you come with us, and see?"

Ryder makes a concerned noise in the back of his throat, but I hold out my hand to Zella.

There's a faint challenge in my silent question.

How much is too much?

If she can stomach what we do... then perhaps this is possible, after all.

She looks up at me uncertainly, but her hand reaches out, her fingers curling around mine as I lift her up. "Where?"

"You'll see." I nod to the parcels stacked up against the wall, the deliveries I was planning on giving to her this evening. "You'll need shoes, and something a little warmer than that shirt."

Ryder stands, making his way over to the packages and rummaging through them. "I don't think the gold sequins will cut it this evening, princess," he says, turning with some dark material in his hands. "But Maverick ordered you some plainer things too."

She takes the clothes slowly, hugging them to her chest. "I've never worn anything apart from white," she murmurs, looking down at them. "They don't feel plain to me."

"Get dressed," I order softly. "We'll be leaving in thirty minutes."

She nods. "What about... is Enzo coming?"

Shaking my head, I place my hand on her back as I lead her to the door. "No. He won't appear for a little while."

I jerk my head, and Ryder follows her out, pausing beside me.

"I'll keep an eye on her," he says under his breath as we watch her make her careful way down the hall. "She's very calm."

Too calm, considering what she might have seen.

"We're in this now," I say to him just as quietly. "It was going to happen sooner or later, if she's staying."

Even if it's happening much sooner than I would have chosen.

Zella

My hand keeps running over the soft material covering my legs as I sit in the back of the thing they call a car. There's a rumbling beneath me, and my body vibrates as Maverick does something and the car comes to life beneath me. Ryder's hand covers mine and I glance down briefly, distracted by the warmth.

I'm so *cold.*

But my eyes are huge, glued to the glass window as Maverick drives us out of the garage. I can't see much, and Ryder leans across me, pressing something that makes the glass slide down.

"Thank you." With the glass down, I still can't see much. It's pitch-black outside, the only light coming from the lights of the car. As I crane my head, I catch glimpses of the trees I ran through on my first night.

"Whoa there, princess." Ryder tugs me back as I stick my whole head out of the window in my enthusiasm to see. "You won't see much if you fall out."

As the car picks up speed and I try to get used to the sensation of moving so quickly, nausea flips in my stomach and I pull my head back, leaning it against the back of my seat and closing my eyes.

"You okay?" Ryder asks softly. His fingers trace shapes on the back of my hand. "It's been a strange day."

My nod feels absent, and I keep my eyes closed as I try to process how I'm feeling. I'm not entirely sure that the churning in my stomach is just from the car.

"Where are we going again?" I ask, my eyelids cracking open in time to catch Maverick's eye in the little front mirror.

"You'll see."

Hmmm.

"Is this where you kill me and bury me so nobody will find out your secrets?" I ask absently.

Ryder and I tip to the side as the car jerks, but Maverick pulls it back. "Shit!"

Ryder steadies me. "You okay, princess? Jesus, Maverick."

"Sorry," Maverick says shortly. He waits until I look up and meet his eyes to respond. "Zella, we are not going to hurt you. Not now, not ever. We're just... showing you something."

I swallow back the small ball of relief. Not that I seriously thought they would hurt me... but then, I didn't actually think Enzo was a serial killer who carves up evil men in a dungeon underneath their house.

I'm pretty sure I shouldn't trust my own instincts at this point.

They seem to be broken.

"What are you showing me?" I ask, leaning forward. Maverick snaps his eyes up.

"Sit back," he says firmly. "We're showing you the other part of our work, Zella. What happens at the end."

At the end?

I turn the words over in my head, sitting quietly with my own thoughts as we drive into the night. I press my face against the window as I see a sea of lights in the distance, rising high into the sky. "What's that?"

"New York," Ryder says softly. His hand plays with the edge of my braid, pulling it between his fingers. "That's where your apartment is."

Was.

"Right," I whisper. New York looks gigantic to me. I can't believe I've spent so much of my life there, and yet it feels so unfamiliar.

The lights disappear as Maverick continues to drive. Ryder settles in next to me, and my head leans against his arm. When the car finally stops, I blink, half asleep as I lift my head up. "Are we here?"

"We are," Maverick confirms. When I look out of the window, there's a row of houses opposite us. Lights are on in a few, and my eyes are drawn to a little flickering light in a dark window. A single candle, the little flame bright.

Maverick turns around in his seat. His light eyes look dark, purple shadows underneath.

"Where are we?" I ask softly, my eyes still on the little orange light.

Maverick draws in a breath. "This is where Sherileen Jacobs lived."

It takes me a second.

"Sherileen Jacobs. Fourteen years old. She was looking for her dog when he called her over. Told her he'd help her look, and then he buried her, prey. He buried her so deep, her family never had a chance at finding her."

My mouth dries, and I look between them. "I don't... I'm sorry. I don't understand."

"Sherileen's parents are Roger and Sandra Jacobs," Ryder says from next to me. His eyes are on the candle too. "They lost their daughter ten years ago, when she went missing on a dog walk and never came home. Every night, Roger and Sandra light a candle in their window."

"We've been watching them, Zella," Maverick murmurs. His face looks sorrowful when I turn to him, my heart starting to twist inside my chest. "They know that their little girl isn't coming home, but their pain is eating them alive. They have no idea what happened to her, and it torments them."

I turn back to the light, to that little beacon. "You're going to tell them," I breathe, looking back to them. Something cracks inside my chest when Maverick nods.

"They deserve to have closure, sweetheart." He reaches out, catching something on my cheek. When I touch my fingers to the same place, my cheeks are wet. "They deserve to know why their daughter never came home, and we can give them that."

It hurts. Inside my chest, something twists and breaks, as I imagine Sherileen's parents waiting for an answer that never came.

I swallow heavily, sniffing. "Can I come?"

Maverick blinks as if surprised. Ryder stiffens next to me when he nods. "Mav."

"Let her see, Ryder," Maverick says softly. He doesn't move his eyes from mine. "This will not be easy, Zella. Brace yourself."

The air feels cold, biting on my face. I shiver inside the sweatshirt Ryder pushed over my head before we left, grateful for the warmth as I silently follow Maverick up the tidy wooden steps. The house is dark, but Maverick knocks anyway. I hold my breath, but a bright light flickers on within seconds, and the sounds of feet pounding echoes through the door a second before the door is thrown open.

An older man, gray-haired and tired looking, clutches the edges of the door as he peers out. I see the second the light fades in his eyes, the way the little piece of hope is snuffed out, and it breaks my heart.

A woman comes up behind him, patting her hair with shaking hands. "Roger?"

"Can I help you?" he asks. His eyes flit between the three of us, and he takes a step back.

Maverick steps forward, holding out his hand. "Mr. Jacobs. My name is Maverick Brooks, and I'm a private investigator."

I fight to keep my composure as Roger Jacobs shakes his head. "If you're selling, we already tried that route. They didn't find anything."

His wife places a hand on his arm. "Don't you think we've tried everything?" she asks, her voice shaking. "We can't afford any more. We've *tried*. I'm sorry, but you've wasted your time."

"We're not selling," Maverick says quietly, and they both silence. "I know what happened to Sherileen, Mr. and Mrs. Jacobs."

Mr. Jacobs drops like a stone to his knees, his wife grabbing his shoulders as he curls himself inward. "She's dead, isn't she?"

He looks up at us with wet eyes. "We know she is. We just want to know where she is, Mr. Brooks."

His wife is crying, and I watch with a closed throat as Maverick kneels in front of Sherileen's father. His words are firm, enough that they focus on him as he speaks.

He tells them that their daughter is dead. Their grief is a tangible, dark thing, hovering in the air around us. But there's relief, too. Relief that the ax hanging over their head has finally dropped.

"Every day," Mrs. Jacobs whispers shakily. "Every day I'd wake up, and it would take me a second to remember."

She looks at me desperately, and I swallow. "I'm so sorry."

She nods vacantly. "But we know now. I didn't think we'd ever know."

"She's coming home?" her father says, and the tears on his face shine in the little light from the porch.

"Yes," Maverick tells them. "Your daughter is coming home."

I manage to hold on to my tears until we're back in the car. And then Ryder lifts me, pulling me across the seat and drawing me into his chest as I choke on my tears and sob into his chest. Maverick makes a call from the front, talking into the earpiece about search areas.

"It's so unfair," I gasp. "They waited all that time."

"The world isn't fair," Ryder says softly. "But they know now, Zella. They know what happened to their little girl. They'll be able to bury her, visit her. It's better than the agony of not knowing."

I don't think I could have understood that without seeing their reaction. The pain, the agony, but the relief too. Relief that so many questions left unanswered are now solved.

"Closure is the only thing we can give them," Ryder whispers.

Closure.

"Not the only thing," I whisper, and he makes a noise of acknowledgement.

It burns in my chest, the injustice that Sherileen will come home to her family in a box because of the actions of one man.

But there's a dark satisfaction curling in my stomach, too, satisfaction that the man responsible is suffering for his evil. A poetic justice that he will die in agony, that he will writhe and scream for mercy that doesn't come, just like they did.

I don't know what happens after we die. But I hope that whatever the afterlife looks like, John Millers spends it in as much pain as he is experiencing right now, for eternity.

My heartbeat thuds loudly in my chest.

"Take me home, please," I say into Ryder's chest. "I'm ready to go home now."

Maverick finishes up his call, and we pull away from the Jacobs's home.

And behind us in the window, the little light is blown out.

Enzo

I shove the last of John Millers into the furnace, latching the door shut with an irritated sigh.

I normally feel more settled after a table session. More *stable.*

But not this time. No, this time I still feel on edge. The itch underneath my skin, the prickling electrifying my nerve endings is still very much there, poking and prodding at me.

It isn't *satisfied.*

I set upon the rest of the room with grim determination, scrubbing away the last traces of Millers until the room gleams once again, the floors hosed down, the last traces of evil trickling into the drains at the edge of the slightly sloping floor.

But the itching is still there.

With a frustrated roar, I throw the steel brush into the sink, knocking off bottles as they clatter into the metal opening.

"Enzo?"

Breath heaving, I spin around. I didn't hear her footsteps on the stairs, and I don't know whether it's because my head is spinning or because my little prey is learning to temper her footsteps, to tread quietly when the monsters are in sight.

And it all pisses me the hell off.

"I told you to run," I snarl at her, and she takes a step forward. She's not wearing that fucking hideous sack of a white dress anymore, the shapeless material replaced with dark jeans that hug the fucking curves of her legs like hands gripping her skin. The dark green sweatshirt clings to her, and the sneakers on her feet tell me why I didn't pick up on her steps.

I've become used to her tread.

I'm caught up in staring at her, so much that I flinch back when I focus and she's closer to me. Her green eyes are dark, her pouty little mouth set in a frown as she crosses her arms.

"No," she says shortly.

Trying to regain some fucking sense of equilibrium, I step back, putting the table between us.

"I told you." My voice rises, ringing off the walls between us, "To fucking run, little prey."

Is she so fucking willing to be an active participant in her own demise?

Does she not fucking understand?

She slams her hands down on the clean metal, the slap ringing out. Her breathing is just as harsh as mine, as though she's run back to this fucking room instead of as far away as she can possibly get.

My head swivels, looking for Maverick or Ryder, waiting for them to come storming in, but she snaps her fingers in my damn face.

"Look at me."

My head turns slowly back to her. Her fucking hair is trailing everywhere, like she's been running her hands through it. Or more likely, Ryder has. He can't keep his fucking hands off it when she's around.

"You told me to decide if this is something I can live with, Enzo." Her words are soft, just like the rest of her.

Too fucking soft.

I choke down the burning ball of pain in my throat. "And?"

"You told me I had a choice." She spreads her arms out wide, her face full of challenge.

"I've made my choice," she whispers. "I choose this."

I bark a half-strangled laugh. "No, you don't."

Her head snaps back, and her eyes are full of green fire when she stares at me challengingly. "Don't tell me I have a choice and then try to take it away. I have chosen, Enzo. And I choose this."

She moves around the table, and I stay exactly where I am. I don't even breathe as she moves closer, as her hands lift and cup my cheeks as if I'm something breakable.

Something fucking *precious.*

"You act like the villain," she murmurs. "And maybe you are. But you're not evil, Enzo."

My snort is scathing. "What qualifies you to make that decision, prey? You've met, what, five people in your entire life?"

She half-smiles. "Seven, actually. That I remember, at least. You want to know who I met tonight?"

My lips press together. They fucking took her with them.

"I saw the candle in Sherileen's parents window," she whispers. "I saw the agony of not knowing in their faces, and the agony of grief. But I also saw relief, Enzo. Relief that Sherileen is coming home to them. You freed them from that agony."

"Don't paint me as a hero, prey," I say quietly. "You'll be disappointed."

She tilts her head. "Ryder told me that you give them closure. But you also give them vengeance, Enzo. *Justice.* Poetic justice, and that doesn't make you evil."

"Enough." I push her fingers away from my skin, embracing the cold that rushes in. "I kill people, prey. Rip them apart. Carve them up in as many inventive ways as I can think of. And I enjoy every damn second of it."

"But only the ones who deserve it," she whispers. "Have you ever killed anyone who didn't?"

The memories flash like a brutal assault in my mind. "I don't know."

"Because of the cage?"

"Yes." I can't look at her anymore. She looks so fucking hopeful, and it's catching, like a little light is coming to life inside my chest. So I turn around, taking a breath when soft hands land on my shoulders.

"Whatever you did inside that cage wasn't your choice," she murmurs. "It's what you did outside of it that counts. Have you killed anyone that didn't deserve it *outside* of that cage?"

I press my lips together, refusing to answer, and her hands tighten before her fingers trace down my skin, gently tracing my tattoos.

I lean back into her touch, unable to help myself. "Why did you come back?"

She presses her lips against the marks on my back. "I told you," she says, almost chidingly. "Because I choose you, Enzo. All of you. I've made my decision."

I sigh. "You haven't seen what else is outside of these walls, Zella."

She hums against my skin. "You'll show me."

"You have so much faith in me," I mutter.

"Someone has to," she says quietly. "Since you have none in yourself."

I've had enough. Turning, I take in her face a split second before I lift her, carrying her over to my table. She doesn't flinch when I lay her down, her face open and too fucking trusting for her own good.

Leaning down, I breathe in the fresh scent of her neck. "Fine, then. No more running, little prey."

I gave her a chance. I gave her the space that I could.

No more.

Zella

The cold of the table presses into my back, making me shiver. Enzo hovers above me, his eyes black and narrowing. "You're cold."

"I'm fine." But he ignores my protests, lifting me again and striding to a door I've never noticed before. He kicks it open, and I take a deep breath.

The dungeon smells metallic, cold almost. But this room is all Enzo, dark walls, dark bedding. He sets me down on the soft sheets, and I inhale, giving in to the urge to stretch out like a cat.

This room is like a little piece of him. It even smells like him, a little spicy, and I prop myself up to watch him as he unbuttons his jeans. He leaves them on with the top button undone as he climbs onto the bed, and I suck in a breath as he covers me, pressing me down into the covers with his chest bare.

"Oh, little prey," he murmurs. Leaning down, he presses his lips to my neck, and I arch against him, gasping when he drags his teeth over the delicate skin. "No escape now."

I don't want to escape. I want to burn up in this feeling that has my abdomen clenching as his hands slide beneath my sweatshirt, pushing it over my head.

Enzo pauses, my arms still tangled as he takes in my bare skin. My cheeks flush with heat.

"I haven't worked out the underwear yet," I admit with a breathless laugh, but it dies as his hands close over my breasts.

He's not gentle, gripping them and pushing them up. My nipples tighten under his eyes, and I struggle to free myself from the tangled shirt as he leans down and seals his mouth over one.

He sucks hard, and my back arches on a gasp as he pulls me into him, his hands sliding under my back and lifting me up to him. My panting fills the air between us as he switches from one to the other, tugging and twisting and drawing until I shove the sweatshirt away and tangle my hands in his dark hair.

"Enzo," I choke out, and he briefly glances up at me.

"Prey."

It's almost a purr, and he returns to my breasts, capturing one nipple gently between his teeth and tugging at it until the pleasure borders on exquisite pain.

When he releases me, I seize the opportunity and pull myself up using his neck, his hands leaving my back as I press my lips against his. They part underneath mine, our breathing mingling as he growls in the back of his throat and pushes me down. His lips don't leave mine as he plunders my mouth, his tongue tasting every part of me and his hand curling around my throat, holding me in place. His hips push down against mine, and I can feel the hardness there even through our clothes.

I push my hips up in silent question, and he spends another few seconds kissing me before he pulls away. My stomach flexes as he pushes hard, almost bruising kisses against it, sucking at the skin and leaving a trail of little marks behind him until he reaches my jeans and flicks them open, tugging them down my legs.

He leaves them tangled at my ankles, and I cry out as he slides his hand between my legs, pushing at the sensitive flesh and separating it, his thumb moving over the hard bud that sends jolts of pleasure down my spine like liquid lightning.

He alternates between hard strokes and gentle flicks, over and over again, until his hand pressing into my abdomen is the only thing keeping me in place.

My moan is wordless, certain that he's torturing me as he keeps me carefully balanced on a knife edge. Every time the fire twisting my insides starts to crest, he loosens his touch just enough. "What are you waiting for?" I half snap, half sob.

"He's waiting for us, princess."

My head snaps up, my mouth falling open in a gasp as Ryder meets my gaze, his brown eyes hungry as they skate down my body. "W-what are you doing here?"

He raises his eyebrows at me, his tone mischievous but his face hungry as he approaches the bed. "We work as a team, little thief. Choose one, choose all."

I can barely breathe, my attention split between Enzo, Ryder, and the silent shadow that leans against the wall. A flash of icy blue glints in the low light given off by the lamp. "Maverick?"

His voice is low and gruff. "I don't like to share, Zella. I like to watch, though."

I stare with wide eyes as he settles into a chair, and Ryder shucks off his shirt, climbing onto the bed. "You look a little hot and bothered, baby."

Enzo pulls back again, and I snap my teeth in frustration, pushing my hips upward.

"He's torturing me," I groan, and Ryder chuckles.

"That's what he does best," he chides. His mouth covers mine, his tongue sweeping along the seam of my lips until I open for him.

"Good girl," he purrs when he pulls back. "Is she doing as she's told, Enzo?"

He grunts, and I bite back a cry as his finger dips, circling me somewhere new. "Didn't have much of a choice."

Ryder strokes my hair back from my face. "I think you could be such a good girl for us, princess," he murmurs. My eyes flicker down, to where he's undoing his trousers. "I think I want to see exactly how good you can be."

I'm on fire. Flames lick along my arms, my legs, twisting me up into a feverish mess as Enzo pushes a thick finger inside me, and Ryder unzips his trousers. My toes curl as I groan, trying to close my legs against the sweet agony of Enzo pushing up inside me. He shoves my knees open, using his shoulders to stop me from closing them.

"Little prey," he chides, before he presses his lips to the soft inside of my thigh. His teeth flash, and he bites down gently. "Stay."

When I still, my chest rising and falling in rasps, he rewards me by sliding his finger in and out, pushing a little more with each small thrust.

The next feels fuller, and my back bows.

"It's too big," I choke, and Enzo laughs darkly.

"You'll get used to it, little prey," he promises darkly. "Need to get you ready. Ryder."

My eyes flicker to Ryder. He's kneeling next to me, his hand inside his trousers. When he smiles, it's not a smile I've seen before. This one is darker – more animalistic.

He pulls his hand out, and I choke at his size. "Nope," I hiss, bucking when Enzo thrusts a little harder, "definitely not going to fit."

Ryder laughs. "It's not going in your pussy, princess. I think one cock is all you can take for your first time."

My face falls, and he clicks his tongue. "We'll see."

He taps the side of my cheek. "Open up, princess."

My mouth drops open in shock, and he presses the edge of his cock past my lips. It feels bigger than I expected, wider, with a unique taste that feels like Ryder. My eyes feel like saucers as they flash up to his face, and he grins down at me savagely. "More."

On that demand, he pushes inside me, sliding past my lips inch by inch as Enzo adds yet another finger and I feel myself stretching around him.

Too much. Too full.

A gentle hand grips my throat, and I stare hazily up at Ryder.

"Swallow, sweetheart," he coaxes. His fingers massage my throat. "Let me feel you swallowing my cock. I can feel you flexing around me."

My eyes start to water, and Enzo slides his fingers free with a wet squelch. "I think you're ready now, little prey."

I try to shake my head in protest. His face appears in my hazy vision, his lips on my cheek as I try to take in the sheer width of Ryder, finding a rhythm and sucking and licking the top of his head, bolstered by his quiet praise in my ear.

Enzo breathes into my ear. "This is what it means to be ours, prey."

I moan around Ryder's cock as something much bigger than fingers pushes against my entrance. Enzo spreads my hips, pushing me wide as he sinks in a single inch, then another. His chest presses against mine, warm and possessive as he presses me down into the bed, his fingers sinking into my hip as he presses himself inside.

It hurts, but the slight burning sensation is minimal compared to the flickering, burning embers twisting my insides. Enzo sits up, his hands sliding under my thighs and lifting my legs into the air as he pushes impossibly deeper, stretching me for him as Ryder pushes into my mouth.

Just as I start to feel impossibly full, like it's a little too much, they start to move in an unspoken rhythm, pushing in and out with me held between them. The air is filled with the jagged sounds of our breathing, my muffled moans, their soft praise as they fill me over and over again.

It's nothing like I imagined, alone in the apartment with my hand between my legs and an impossible gap in my knowledge. I could never imagine *this*.

Ryder grunts, his hand threading into my hair. "Fuck, princess, you take me so fucking well. Like you were made to fit me."

Enzo squeezes my thighs as Ryder picks up his pace, thrusting into my mouth and stilling with a groan as something pushes into my mouth, tangy and hot and a little salty.

"Swallow," Enzo orders, leaning forward and plucking at my nipple. "Swallow him down, little prey."

Ryder pulls himself free from my mouth. "Perfect," he praises, and my skin flushes in appreciation as I do as I'm told. He leans down, and his kiss is gentle against my lips, so at odds with the way he thrust himself into my mouth. "So fucking perfect, princess."

"It was good?" I ask hesitantly, and he groans, pressing his lips against mine.

"You've ruined me," he tells me, dropping soft, pecking kisses across my face. "Gonna need that every day for the rest of our lives."

I could do that. He stares at me like I'm powerful, and I revel in it, twisting my hips a little to nudge Enzo into moving. When I glance over, my eyes hooded, Maverick is watching us with a clenched jaw, his hands curled around the arms of the chair.

"Any regrets, Mav?" Ryder calls, and there's a hint of playful laughter in his voice. Maverick shakes his head.

"Just storing up ideas," he grunts, and I squirm when his eyes land on me, traveling across my breasts, taking in the light sheen of sweat on my skin. "So many ideas, Zella."

As Ryder pulls himself away, I try to catch my breath, only to lose it in a shocked cry as I'm suddenly airborne. Enzo flips me effortlessly, and I land with a muted thud on my front. He pushes my knees up and apart, and I moan with my face pressed into the sheets as he thrusts into me, impossibly deep.

"Too much," I groan. "Too deep."

Instead of responding, his hand slaps against the soft, fleshy part of my ass, and I feel a tugging on my braid as he pulls my head backwards until I'm almost facing the ceiling, but all I see are stars across my vision. I can feel him pressed up against me, my head back against his shoulder as he pushes in and out.

"Look at me," he hisses in my ear. "Look at who you belong to, Zella."

I push my head back to try to see his face. His hair falls over his forehead, but it's his eyes that catch my attention. They're brighter than I've ever seen.

"Stars," I half-moan, and he wraps his arm around my waist, one hand still tangled in my hair as he increases his pace.

"Ours," he grunts. Ryder crawls onto the bed in front of me and I'm caught between them, captured by their fingers and their hands, Enzo's cock holding me in place as Ryder licks his way down my front. He spreads me apart, and I almost close my eyes.

Almost.

He glances up at me. "Look at this swollen pussy, baby."

He rubs me right there, and I lean my hands on his shoulders as his head dips down and he swipes his tongue through my folds. It's enough to tease the fire right to the edge, and I buck in their hold as it grows, deeper and hotter.

"That's it," Enzo purrs in my ear. "Come for us, little prey. Let me feel you flex those muscles around my cock, and you'll feel my cum filling you up."

He sinks his teeth into my neck, and I scream out, the fire ripping through me in an inferno. They don't stop touching me, and Enzo roars into my skin as he floods me, hot fluid pushing out of me and dripping down my thighs.

My legs begin to shake as he eases out of me, and he and Ryder lay me down on the bedding in a boneless pile. Little aftershocks of flame are still flickering through me as I'm turned over, and Ryder presses a warm washcloth against me.

"Feels good," I mumble, and he strokes it through again before he presses a kiss to what's left of the curls covering me.

I'm lifted into warm arms, and I burrow my head sleepily into someone's chest.

"She's staying with me," Enzo snaps, and Ryder mutters about a bigger bed before I'm tucked into soft covers. Enzo gets in behind me, his arm wrapping around me like a band as he pulls me against him.

"Prey," he says sharply, and I frown at him over my shoulder.

"No shouting."

His eyes are still full of stars, and one side curves up as he leans in and kisses my mouth roughly. "You're out of choices now."

"Don't need them," I yawn. I'm so tired. Exhaustion weighs down my eyelids as I mumble out the thought in my head. I'm not even sure if it's legible, but Enzo goes still behind me, before I feel his lips in my hair.

And then I sleep.

Zella

"I think we should go out this evening."

My heart skips a beat at Ryder's announcement, and I glance up at Maverick. He's working his way around the dinner table, carefully selecting food for my plate as normal. He frowns, his hand hovering over a bowl of vegetables. "I'm not sure that's a good idea."

I can almost feel my body deflating.

It's not that I'm not happy here. But the urge to see more, experience *more*, is starting to pull at me now more than ever. I don't feel as enclosed here as I did in the apartment – not with the gardens open to me. But I'm starting to feel the tug for something else, something different.

When I glance at Enzo, his eyes are on my face. Biting my lip, I duck my head, reaching out for my wine glass and taking a slightly too big sip that almost makes me choke.

I nearly miss his next words over my cough. "Little prey wants to go out."

Everybody's attention turns to me, and I shrug awkwardly. "I... wouldn't mind. But I know we're still watching for Ethan."

With every day that passes, my time with Ethan begins to feel more like a memory. My time in the apartment feels faded when I think of it, almost muted. Life outside is so *vibrant* in comparison.

Ryder senses Maverick's hesitation and leans forward, tapping his fingers on the tablecloth. "Come on, Mav. He's not suddenly going to pop up in the middle of Victrola."

"What's Victrola?" I ask, and Maverick runs a hand down his face.

"We're not taking her there," he snaps at Ryder. "What the hell are you thinking?"

"We can book the private area," Ryder points out. "Dress her up so she's harder to recognise. The only person who would is Moore, and he's disappeared off the face of the earth."

Maverick places my plate down in front of me as I frown. They've been tracking Ethan's car, but he hasn't used it for days. My chest tightens at the thought that something bad may have happened to him. "Do you think he's okay?"

Maverick settles in next to me. "I'm sure he's fine, Zella. But until we know exactly where he is, I think I'd feel more comfortable with you staying here."

My nod feels heavy, but Ryder interjects before I can respond.

"Hold on a second, Mav. She didn't leave that place only to become a prisoner somewhere else."

Maverick narrows his eyes. "I'm trying to protect her."

"But so was Ethan," I whisper. Maverick pales, and I instantly feel a stab of guilt. "Zella... this isn't the same."

"No," Ryder says softly. His eyes are on Maverick. "Because you're not a prisoner here, Zella. So what do *you* want to do?"

I look between Maverick and Ryder. Both of them are staring at each other, and Maverick's jaw is clenched. Eventually, he nods.

"Ryder is right," he acknowledges, looking down at me with an apology in his eyes. "I don't want to trap you here, Zella. If you want to go, we'll make it work."

"I... I'd like to go." I avoid his eyes. "But what's... Victrola?"

Ryder's eyes gleam when he leans forward. "It's a place where you can wear your gold sequins, princess."

Oooh.

***

I'm drying my last section of hair when the bedroom door knocks. After dinner, we all split up to get ready for tonight.

At an actual club. With *dancing.*

I'm trying to keep my excitement under wraps, but the nerves flip flopping in my stomach are doing the job for me.

What if I embarrass them?

I can't dance. I've never danced in my life.

I'm on the verge of passing out when I rip the door open and my eyes widen.

Ryder lounges against my door frame, and if I thought he was handsome before, it's nothing compared to how he looks right now. A silky dark green shirt hugs his chest, tucked into smart trousers with black shoes. His hair is slicked back, and the slow smile on his face tapers off when he gets a good look at my face.

"Hey, now," he chides, stepping into my room. "What's the matter, princess?"

Huffing, I pick my hairbrush back up. "It's nothing. I'm looking forward to it."

His hand closes over mine, gently wrestling the brush from me as he turns me around by my shoulders. "Then why do you look like someone died?"

I turn to glare at him, but he taps the back of my head with the brush and begins pulling my hair through it with long, firm strokes. "It's not that. I am looking forward to it. It's just... I'm a little nervous, that's all."

"Makes sense," he murmurs. "It's a whole new experience for you. Lots of people, and lots of noise. But we've got our own private area, so you can get used to it slowly. And if you don't like it, we can leave."

"I don't want to ruin everyone's night." I chew on my lip, and Ryder laughs.

"I think Daddy Mav would be delighted. He's more nervous than you are."

My lips twist up. "Daddy Mav?"

Ryder smirks. "Because he fusses over us like a dad."

I have the feeling Maverick would hate that nickname, but it does make me laugh. Ryder starts playing with my hair. "I'll braid this for you, keep it off the ground."

My head twists. "You can do that?"

I always loop it around my waist, but Ryder nods. "When I was working in some of the clubs, I used to do the girls' hair sometimes, when they were in a rush. Got pretty good at it too."

I stay silent for a few minutes as he works, forcing down the yawning pit of envy that's opened up in my stomach.

Don't be stupid, I tell myself firmly. Ryder hated that time. I know that.

It takes him a while to work though, but he finally sets his hand on my shoulders and turns me towards the mirror. "What do you think?"

My hand raises up, tracing the layers he's woven into my braid, layer upon layer of hair that runs down my back and ends just below my thighs. "Wow. You weren't kidding."

"I have magic hands." Yawning, he throws himself down onto my bed, propping his head on his hand. "Time to get dressed, princess. The others will be waiting for us."

"Right." I move over to the closet, pulling it open and inspecting the contents like the right outfit is magically going to appear. I pull out the gold sequin top, since Ryder mentioned it earlier. And then... I stare at the rest.

Warm hands slide around my waist, and I jump. "Need some help?" Ryder murmurs, and I nod.

"I feel very underprepared for this," I admit. He leans in, pulling open a drawer and fishing around until he pulls out some underwear.

"Pop these on," he tells me, pointing to the top. "That goes over the top. I'll find you shoes."

I stare down at the very small piece of material. "What about the bottom?"

I swear he hides a smile as he kneels down, inspecting the shoes they ordered for me. "That's a dress, princess."

My eyes widen. "This is *not* a dress."

Despite my misgivings, I duck into the bathroom. I'm still awkward about changing in front of Ryder, even though he's seen every part of me.

When I look in the mirror, my cheeks flush a deep red. He's going to be seeing most of me tonight too, judging by the length of this top.

"This is definitely not a dress," I announce, stepping out of the bathroom. Ryder makes a choking sound, and I watch with interest as the tips of his ears turn red.

"My mistake," he says quickly. "Here, I'll find you something else."

He throws himself into the closet. "Maybe a snowsuit," he mutters.

I glance down at the length of leg on show. Maybe I should wear this. I want to see if Enzo and Maverick look at me the same way Ryder did.

"Actually, I like this one," I announce. "What shoes should I wear?"

Ryder groans. "Princess."

"Ryder," I say, mimicking him. "Come on. I don't want to be late."

He reappears, looking flustered with a pair of gold strappy shoes in his hands. "Sandals," he says, passing them over. "I don't think you're quite ready for heels yet."

As I bend over to slip them on and tie the long ribbons around my legs, I think I hear a groan, and I bite my lip in a smile.

This is going to be fun.

Ryder

Enzo is still stewing as we pull up to the club. His hand flexes on Zella's thigh, and she gives him a *look*.

It's not a look I've seen from her before. Half pissed, half flirtatious.

"It's a dress," she tells him patiently for the fiftieth time since we dragged him out of the house, and he snarls.

"That's not a dress. It's a fucking band-aid."

When I snicker, he turns his gaze on me, his jaw flexing. "This is your fault."

"Enough," Maverick snaps from the front seat. "Or we're going home."

Zella gives Enzo pleading eyes, and he relents. She leans forward to press her face against the window, taking in the queue winding down the block with wide eyes. "There's so many people!"

"Definitely going to kill someone," Enzo mutters, and she elbows him.

"Now now, children," I say lightly. "Tonight is about fun. Letting our hair down."

Zella winces. "Here?"

"It's just an expression." Maverick pulls to a stop outside the main entrance, and I climb out. The crowd is noisy, dozens of chattering women and men who all crane their necks to have a look as I help Zella out. She steadies herself against my arm, looking up at Victrola with a dubious expression. "This is a place for dancing?"

"Wait and see." I offer her my arm as Enzo stomps up behind us and Maverick hands the valet his keys. I keep watching her face as the doors are pulled open, and it doesn't disappoint.

As we walk through, we're hit with the pounding bass. It reverberates in my chest, and Zella puts her hand over her heart. "I can feel it here."

Leaning in, I murmur in her ear so she can hear me. "Means you've got music in your soul, princess."

I lead her through the ground floor of Victrola, keeping to the outskirts as Enzo follows, snarling menacingly at everyone who dares to get within a foot of us.

Not many do.

The scarlet walls are lit with sconces, highlighting the artwork on display. Zella cranes her neck to stare at them as we pass by, swiveling to take in the black marble bar, the hundreds of bottles on display, the huge golden chandeliers overhead that light up the dancers moving in perfect chaos. "It's so beautiful!"

We make our way up the winding gold staircase, and she peers over the edge to the dancers on the stage below, craning her head until I have to tug her gently back before she tips over. Her eyes are huge, her smile even bigger when she turns to me. "This is amazing, Ryder."

"Glad you like it," I say as we reach the section we've reserved for tonight. Maverick murmurs in the ear of a security guard as he unclips a black velvet rope to let us inside.

"They'll send someone up for drinks orders," he says. Zella spins, taking in the space. Comfortable, deep wine-colored couches line the back wall, a large table with an ice-cold champagne bucket ready and waiting. Directly opposite us is floor to ceiling thick glass, designed to offer the experience of the club without the peasants in the crowd pushing and shoving. Zella makes a beeline for it immediately, pressing her hands against the glass as she stares down.

Enzo settles himself against the far wall, arms crossed and a glower on his face as Maverick reaches for the champagne. All of us are unashamedly watching Zella, taking in the way her hips shift underneath that ridiculous excuse for a dress in time with the music, the way the ribbons of her sandals wind up her calves, gold upon gold.

She's so beautiful, she makes my fucking chest ache.

Maverick calls her in a low voice, and her face lights up when she sees the champagne, a delighted laugh spilling from her lips when the cork pops and Maverick catches the spillage in a tall, fluted glass, handing it to her.

Sniffing the bubbles, she takes a tentative sip before turning to watch the crowd again. Unable to help myself, I take a few steps, slipping my arms around her waist and pulling her back against me. "Happy?" I murmur in her ear, and she hums.

"There's so much," she says softly. The music is slightly muted in here, with speakers to help us control the volume. Easier for Zella's ears, since she hasn't been anywhere as loud as this before. "I don't know where to look."

I press my lips against her neck. "We've got all night, princess. Take your time."

We sway together, and Zella leans her head back against me as she sips her drink and watches the dancers on stage. Maverick murmurs behind us, and I turn my head to see him giving our main drinks order to a waitress at the door.

I frown. She looks familiar, but she ducks out before I can get a good look at her face.

A new song begins and Zella wriggles in my arms. Pushing away any thought of the waitress, I lean in, pressing my fingers lightly into her hips. "Dance with me, princess."

She turns under my touch, facing me with a self-conscious smile. "I don't know how."

"I'll teach you," I say without thinking. But as soon as we start moving, as soon as I start coaxing Zella to move her hips in time with mine, her body pressed against me, I realize that this was very much a mistake.

She sucks in a breath as she feels the outline of my cock pressed against her. "Ryder?"

I cup the back of her neck, pressing her into me as we move. "You feel that?" I breathe in her ear. "That's all for you, Zella. You and your little gold top."

I feel her laughter in my chest. In my fucking soul. "It's a *dress.*"

"Hmmm." We dance, and I feel the moment the music pours into the room, as Enzo flicks the speakers up and Zella throws her head back, her arms raising in the air as she sways. We move across the floor until her back presses into the glass of the window, and I swoop down, capturing her lips with mine.

Soft, sweet, she matches my movements until we're tangled together, her leg wrapped around my waist when I tear my mouth away. She's breathing just as heavily as I am, but she grins when I look down at her. "Can people see us up here?" she asks, craning her head to look behind her at the crowd below.

It gives me ideas. Probably bad ones, but I've never been known for good judgment.

She gasps when I spin her, my hands sliding up her arms and pressing her palms into the glass. "Would it bother you?" I murmur into her neck. "To have all these people watching you, princess?"

She tilts her head, silently asking for more, and I sink my teeth into her skin, gently nipping until I reach her ear. She jolts when my hands slide up and inside her dress, reaching inside the lacy excuse for a brasserie she's wearing and cupping her bare breasts. "Ryder!"

"Shhhh," I murmur. My hands squeeze her plump mounds, my finger flicking over her nipples as she hardens beneath my touch. "They're not paying attention to you, little thief."

I glance over my shoulder. Enzo is solely focused on us, and he moves over to the door, casually settling himself against it so nobody can interrupt. Maverick's jaw is tight, but he sits back, his eyebrow flying up in silent challenge.

"Play with me, Zella," I whisper, tugging her nipples until she drops her head back against me, silently pushing into my palms for more. She stiffens when I move my hand to the back of her sequinned dress, slowly undoing the laces. "What are you doing?"

"Trust me," I murmur, leaning in and kissing her shoulder. "Will you?"

At her slow nod, I pull the halter free, letting it slide down her body until she's left in the lace set I picked out for her earlier. Reaching forward, I slide my fingers around the lace covering her breasts, tugging it down until the lace pushes them up, her nipples stiff in the strobe lighting that streaks over us in patterns.

"Fucking gorgeous," I whisper reverently, and she shudders. She tries to glance over her shoulder, but I nudge her head forward. "Eyes up front, princess. See how many eyes are drawn up here to those pretty tits."

I press my hand into her back, pushing her forward until she's pressed against the glass, her hips pushed out. An offering I don't intend to waste.

She jumps when I kneel behind her, peeling away the pale pink lace covering her.

"Are you wet for me, baby?" I say slowly. She moans when I press my face between her legs, my tongue flicking out for a small taste. She tastes like the finest whiskey on my tongue, and I pull her hips back, settling her against me as I stroke my tongue up and down her folds.

"Ryder!" Zella cries my name as I devour her, her legs trembling against my grip as I push her onto my face.

"Gotta get you ready for my cock, princess," I rasp when I manage to pull myself away. I'm almost painfully hard, my cock pressing against my slacks, and my groan rings out as I pull myself free, my head already weeping for want of her.

Enzo and Maverick are silent behind me. I can feel their eyes on her, and so can she.

"Please." She pushes herself back, and I push two fingers slowly into her channel, stretching her out for me and adding a third.

"Are you still sore here?" I ask, and she shakes her head frantically. "N-no. More."

I slide my hands up the soft skin of her legs as I stand, drawing a line down her spine with my fingers that makes her tremble against me. "Please."

"Fuck, I love it when you beg, baby." I notch the head of my cock against her entrance, pushing in a bare inch and feeling her tighten around me. "Breathe, princess."

When she relaxes, I push in another inch, and then another, slowly entering her as she shudders against the glass. She's fucking dripping, and I kiss her shoulder, relishing in the idea of a little exhibitionism.

"Look at them," I murmur. "Can you feel their eyes on you, Zella? Wanting you?"

When she only moans in return, I thrust the rest of the way in, filling her and bottoming out as she cries out, her breath fogging up the glass.

"They can look," I rasp, pulling out and thrusting in again. "But they can't touch, princess. Nobody touches what belongs to us. You understand?"

She makes me feel feral, and I reach around, grabbing her pussy as I push into her, my finger finding the swollen nub of her clit and pinching it between my fingers. She writhes under me, and I move my other hand to the front of her neck, pulling her back until she's flush against me. The little sobbing sounds falling from her lips feel like fucking music of their own, and I fuck her to the rhythm of them, the sounds of our fucking obscene in the otherwise silent room.

"Enzo and Maverick are watching you," I growl in her ear. "Watching you be such a good little slut for me."

She fucking melts against me, her pussy tightening on my cock. "Oh, God!"

"There's no god here, princess," I say roughly, pushing her forward. "Whose cock is inside you?"

"Yours," She sobs, as my thrusts increase in speed. "Yours, Ryder!"

"That's it," I grunt. I can feel my release tightening at the base of my spine, and the way she's pulsing around me tells me she's nearly at that cliff. "The only fucking names you say with our cocks inside you are ours, princess. Because you belong to *us*."

Her shriek rings out as I pull her back against me, reaching around and slapping her pussy, feeling the quivers of her release beginning. I bury my face in her neck, roaring into her damp skin as I empty myself inside her with a guttural curse.

She gasps for breath, her fingers curling against the glass as I press my skin against hers, my lips tracing the side of her head. I can feel the moment embarrassment starts to set in, the way her body stiffens beneath mine as she looks down. "Ryder...,"

"Little thief." I kiss the damp skin below her ear, breathing her in. "You think I'd let anyone else see what belongs to us?"

Reaching out, I tap my knuckles against the thick glass. "It's one-sided. We can see out, but nobody can see in."

She sags in my grip as I carefully withdraw from her. Enzo tosses me some napkins, and I clean her up, throwing the cloths into the trash and carefully redoing the knot of her halter as she leans into the window.

Her legs shake when she tries to step away, so I lift her, carrying her across the room and settling her between me and Maverick on the sofa. He presses a glass into her hand, and she takes a greedy gulp, avoiding our eyes.

My hand traces circles on the bare golden skin of her shoulder. "None of that," I murmur in her ear, and she glances up at me shyly. "No embarrassment here, princess."

Zella

Easier said than done.

I burrow myself between Maverick and Ryder, sipping on my drink as the door opens and a woman wheels in a cart. I can feel Maverick's eyes boring into the side of my head, but I ignore him in favor of drinking as much champagne as I can until my head starts to swim.

Maybe I've had a *little* too much.

Ryder's hand tightens on my leg, and I shiver. My eyes flick over to the window, and I let out a mortified squeak. Two very obviously Zella-shaped handprints are imprinted on the glass.

I can't even look at the circles underneath.

I can't bring myself to regret it, though. A little aftershock flutters in my stomach, and I swallow.

I'm so lost in my thoughts that it takes me a moment to pick up on the chatter around me. When Ryder's hand tightens on my leg, I glance up, and immediately regret it.

"God, it's so good to see you! I thought I saw you come in, so I thought I'd come and say hello."

The woman beaming at Ryder looks like a goddess. Her hair is cut just below her shoulders, razor sharp edges and raven black in color. She flashes a smile at Ryder. "I missed you, baby. Maybe we can catch up later? Like old times?"

The pain in my chest takes me by surprise, and I flinch back. Ryder looks down at me, and I frown. He doesn't look happy to see her. In fact, he doesn't look happy at all.

He looks... empty.

He doesn't respond, and the woman laughs, reaching down and curling her hand around his wrist. "Playing hard to get? Nothing new there."

I barely register the way my hand shoots out, wrapping around her wrist. She jerks under my grip as I pull her wrist back, shoving it away from Ryder. She staggers awkwardly, letting out an uncomfortable laugh. "Someone's possessive."

"Don't touch him," I say quietly. "He doesn't like it."

She scoffs. "Trust me, honey, he likes it plenty."

Ryder is still beside me, his face pale. For a second, I don't recognise the hot feeling in my throat, the way my palms start to itch.

But when she reaches for him again, I recognise it for exactly what it is. Anger.

This time, I grab her wrist before she gets anywhere near him. "I said, don't *touch* him."

When she moves to shake me off, Maverick leans forward. "I would be *very* careful about your next move," he says softly.

The woman looks between us, her lip curling. "Jesus. I'm not that bothered. Keep your little fuck toy."

She steps back, but Enzo is there, and she squeaks as they collide. "What did you just call him?" he asks softly, and she blanches.

"Do you even know who I am?" She takes a step away from him, backing up towards the door. "He's not worth the trouble, you know. He's not that good of a fuck."

I lunge, and glass flies everywhere as Maverick wraps his arms around me and pulls me back. "Zella. Enough."

He looks at the woman. "If you don't leave immediately, I will throw you out. Consider it a first and final warning."

The woman slides out of the door, and I watch as Enzo sidles after her. He glances back at me with a question in his eyes, and I shake my head.

As horrible as she was, I don't think she's a candidate for his table.

Unfortunately.

Maverick releases me, and I spin around, my hands landing on either side of Ryder's face. He swallows, his jaw flexing. "Why did you do that?" he asks quietly. "Why did you grab her wrist?"

"Because you didn't want her to touch you," I say slowly. He blinks, scrubbing his hands down his face with a harsh laugh.

"Sorry, princess. There's no getting away from it sometimes."

"Hey." I lean in until he focuses on my face. "You said that I belong to you. Well, you belong to me too, Ryder. It doesn't matter what that woman said."

He sighs. "More than the sum of the people who made us, right?"

I nod. "She does not define you, Ryder. None of them get to decide who you are. Only you."

He cracks a smile. "You're like a little mini Yoda, you know."

My brows crease. "What's a yoda?"

He leans forward, resting his forehead against mine. "So many things to show you, little thief."

"Little thief," I whisper. "Why do you call me that?"

My heart flips over in my chest. I like it.

He presses his lips against mine, a soft caress. "One thief recognises another. You stole my heart the first time I saw you, Zella. You and that damn wok."

"It was the only thing I had," I protest weakly, but my heart is singing. "And I apologized!"

His laugh shakes his whole body. "Never apologize. I'm putting a wok in every room. Those things are lethal."

He pulls away from me slowly, giving me a reassuring smile as he stands. "I'll be back."

I take another sip from my champagne, and glance around. Enzo is still hovering in the back, and Maverick is sitting silently across from us, his eyes on the dancefloor and his hand wrapped around a glass of amber liquid.

He looks over when I shift. "Do you need anything?"

Silently, I shake my head, pressing my knees together and gripping them. "You don't like it here, do you?"

He holds out his hand, and I glance at it questioningly. "Come here, Zella," he says softly.

I'm on my feet before my brain fully catches up, and as I reach him, he tugs me down into his lap, setting his glass down and curling his hand around my thigh. "I don't hate it. What makes you say that?"

I study the long, fluted glass in my hands. "I can tell. You don't look as comfortable here as you do at home."

He captures my chin, turning me to face him so I can't hide my face. "Is that how you think of the house? As home?"

I shift my eyes away. "Um... I don't know. Maybe. Is that bad?"

"No," he breathes, and my gaze flicks back to him. He looks tired, dark circles under his eyes, and I press my finger against them.

"You need to take better care of yourself," I say quietly. "Always looking out for everyone else, Maverick."

Even here he's on edge, looking around, watching over us all.

He half smiles, the lines at the edges of his eyes crinkling. "I've never been very good at that."

He's really not. I've never seen him let go. He's always so controlled, so aware.

"Dance with me," I say. The words fall from my lips but as I say it, I realize how much I do want to dance with him. I want to know how he'll feel against me, how his hands will feel against my skin.

I want to see him lose control.

He stands up with me still in his arms, letting me slide down slowly. He keeps his arms around me as he walks me backwards, his hands sliding down to grip my hips.

The music changes, the pound of the bass becoming something slower, more sultry. I suck in a breath as his hand finds my back, pulling me against him as his hips shift in time to the music. His other hand captures mine, entwining our fingers together as we move.

His grin is unexpected, almost bashful. "You didn't expect me to be able to dance, did you?"

I bury my answering smile in his chest. "Well, I definitely can't dance, so we could have been a perfect pair."

His laugh feels like a victory, so deep in his chest I can feel it in my own. "I wouldn't say that. Just because you've never done something doesn't mean you never could."

I gasp as I fall backward, his arm banding across my lower back as he slowly pulls me back up. "Now you're just showing off," I say breathlessly, and he smirks at me, his blue eyes bright even in the dim light of the room.

"Oh," he teases. "You haven't seen anything yet."

I laugh as we move around the room, only stopping when I protest half-heartedly that I need a drink. Maverick keeps his arm around me as he leads me back to the table, handing me a bottle of water from the bucket and watching me drink it down.

"Stay with me tonight," he murmurs, pushing back damp hair from my forehead and wrapping his hand around the back of my neck.

The room feels warmer than it did a moment ago, and as our eyes meet, I nod silently.

"Yes," I whisper. "I'll stay with you."

"Good," he murmurs, and my throat flexes under his fingers as he slides them to the throat, rubbing his thumb over the fluttering pulse in my neck. "Because I've been watching, Zella. And I have a lot of plans to work through with you."

His voice drops, low and intimate in the tiny amount of space between our mouths. "All sorts of plans."

My heart thunders in my chest.

I have a feeling his plans might finish me off completely.

Maverick

The ride home is quiet. Zella sits in the front with me, my hand gripping her knee as she dozes with her head against my shoulder. Enzo and Ryder talk quietly in the back as I pull up to the house.

When I switch off the engine, they both silence, and I clear my throat.

"She's mine tonight," I murmur. "No interruptions."

Ryder snorts. "Have you got your ropes ready?"

I don't respond. I don't need ropes tonight. I have everything I need in the sleeping girl that I carry from the truck. Zella curls herself into me, so trusting as she grumbles incoherently into my chest. Her heavy breathing is the only noise as I carry her up the stairs, my feet pressing softly on the floor as I shoulder open my door and carefully lay her down in my bed and kick off my shoes.

Fuck, she looks good there. Her eyelashes cast shadows on her cheeks as I turn on the lamp next to my bed, her braid catching my eye as I pick it up and begin unraveling it.

I'm so tired. Tired of always being the one to do the right thing, tired of holding back from what I want. And I know exactly what I want.

I want her. The others have claimed her, and tonight is my turn.

Enzo warned her that he wouldn't let her leave us. I kept my own counsel, but silence in this house is tacit agreement. Tonight, she's going to find out exactly how true that is.

Zella continues to breathe deeply as I roll her onto her front, loosening the braid and separating it into four sections. My hands are steady as they weave through the white-gold strands, drawing them into simple, tight braids that will work perfectly for what I have in mind. By the time I'm done, the braids fall past her ankles. Simple. Perfect.

Tonight isn't about showing off. Tonight is showing her what it means to be owned by us.

A smile tugs at my lips as she lets out a snuffling sound, burying her face into my pillow. I tug at the thin straps holding her dress around her neck, watching them unravel and fall away from her skin like a perfectly unwrapped gift.

"Zella." I say her name in a low voice, sliding my finger down the delicate curve of her spine. When she doesn't respond, I slowly roll her over onto her back. My fingers curl into the edges of the sequinned dress and I peel it down, until her breasts and stomach are revealed to me. Her chest rises and falls in time with her soft breathing as I pull the dress down and past her ankles, tossing it over my shoulder.

Fuck. I never thought I'd have a somno kink, but fuck if she doesn't make my mouth water. I change my mind about waking her up, wanting to see how instinctively comfortable she is to stay asleep as I work. Lifting her head, I work the braids free until I'm left with white-gold ropes to play with.

Holding her right ankle in my hand, I bend her knee up and lift her wrist, quickly tying a two-column tie that binds the two together with the first braid. I follow the same movements with her left leg, until she's bound and open to me. Her pussy is wide open, vulnerable, and my cock's so hard I have to take a deep breath to control myself, like I'm some fucking teenager on his first time.

I eye the final two braids. I have plans for those, but I need her awake.

Shucking the rest of my clothes, I climb onto the bed, settling my shoulders between her bound thighs. This close, I can see the slight puffiness of her slit from her adventure at the club. I stroke my finger softly down her center, and she twitches.

"Zella," I murmur. Leaning in, I press my lips against her, savoring the tang of her and suppressing my groan in my chest. "Time to wake up."

Final warning.

I drag my tongue through her folds, once, twice, and again. Then again, until I feel her stir under my hands. The gasping sound she makes as consciousness invades, as realization slowly sinks in, sounds like music.

Pausing, I sit up, running my hands up her legs and over the bindings. Zella's eyes blink open, widening when she sees me.

"Maverick," she whispers. She moves to sit up, only succeeding in rocking back and forth, and her eyes clear as she tugs at the hair tying her in place. "What... what are you doing?"

Taking my time, I climb up her body. Her breasts press against my chest as I lean in and capture her plump power lip between my teeth, tugging it softly. Her lips open under my silent demand, and I kiss her deeply, the way I've wanted to for fucking days.

It feels like coming home, like she was made to fit me, soft edges against jagged tears. She moans into my mouth, and I drink it down before I release her.

She takes a shuddering breath. "When you asked me to stay with you," she whispers, "I thought you meant sleep."

I brush my nose against hers, rewarded when she smiles. "I trust you no longer have those thoughts."

"No," she whispers, tugging at the bindings again. She looks down, following the trail of hair, and I have a moment of sheer, pure satisfaction as her whole body flushes, from her cheeks down to her breasts. "My hair!"

"Very useful," I murmur, and she gapes at me. "I have a particular love for something called shibari, Zella. Have you heard of it?"

She shakes her head, and I smile. "I didn't think so. Shibari is a form of rope play. It has many uses. Meditation. Relaxation...," I pause, sliding my hand down her side and cupping her as her breath stutters. "Pleasure."

"But my hair—,"

"Is perfect," I say softly. "I knew it would be. But I'm not quite finished with it yet."

She audibly swallows. "There's more?"

"There is."

She twitches when my hands slide under her armpits, letting out a breathless laugh when I pull her upright and she nearly topples over. When I pick up the ends of the final two braids, she glances at them and then gives me a look that Enzo would be proud of, if I was of a mind to let him in here to see it.

Which I'm not. Tonight is mine.

"Did you... braid my hair while I was asleep?" she enquires. A smile lifts the corners of her lips. "I didn't know you could braid."

Taking the hair, I criss-cross the braids over her shoulders, looping them underneath her breasts and tugging hard enough to make her gasp. "It's a useful skill," I whisper in her ear. "As you'll find out."

I can't do a typical chest harness when my rope is attached to Zella's head, so I improvise. Positioning the bight at the center of her back, I draw the working ends through and wind them around her, moving in the opposite direction. When I reach her back again, I draw the ends up through the loop and bring them around one more time, this time above her chest, wrapping the ends underneath the rope stem I've created to lie vertically against her spine.

She presses her face into my chest as I work. "You smell really good."

"Thank you." I create the half hitch, making a loop in the ends and bringing the rope over the stem and back, tugging it to tighten and wrapping the last piece of her braid around it, making sure it's secure.

When I sit back, I have to run a hand over my mouth. "Well," I say roughly. "Shibari suits you, Zella."

She smiles up at me shyly, tied up with her own fucking hair and open for my touch. "I think so, too." She wriggles. "It's surprisingly comfortable."

I run a teasing finger down the arch of her foot, and she squeals, unable to move away. "This is about pleasure for both of us," I say quietly. "I want you to think of a word. One you'll use if you want me to stop. If you say it, I'll stop immediately, Zella. I'll untie you straight away. Do you understand?"

She nods, and I can see her thinking. "Rodin," she blurts out finally, and I blink.

The laugh catches in my chest. "An erotic sculptor for your safe word. Appropriate."

She manages to shrug, even as that perfect blush makes its way over her face again. "It seemed appropriate."

Her words trail into a soft moan as I press my head against her entrance, sinking in slowly as she watches our joining with hooded eyes. I slide out, slowly, keeping up the movements until she's twisting within her bindings. "*More.*"

Her mewled demand draws a smile to my lips. "As my lady commands."

Her laugh cuts off in a choke as I thrust, hard, pinning her back to the bed and fucking her with every inch of the lust that's consumed me ever since I saw her in that fucking dungeon.

She tries to speak, but all that comes out is jolted sounds, jagged and needy, torn from her throat as I bury myself inside her.

"Your tight little pussy feels like heaven," I tell her roughly. My hands land on either side of her shoulders as our hips slap together, the rough sound of our breathing and the wetness of our movements filling the room with savage desire. She moans and I pull back, my fingers finding her clit and pinching it. Her hips buck wildly, and I tweak her clit again, just to hear that noise pulled deep from her throat.

"Maverick," she gasps, and the sound of my name on her lips does something to me, drives me to thrust deeper, faster, until she's convulsing around my cock, her cries rasping as I empty myself inside her with a bellow. My release sends white lights across my eyes, and I look down, half expecting to see her stomach swollen with all the fucking cum I've just pumped into her.

Also... fuck.

"Birth control," I say hoarsely as I reluctantly pull out of her. My release trickles from her opening and I gather it up with my fingers, pushing it inside.

Tomorrow. Definitely tomorrow.

Zella twitches, and I shift to untie the makeshift ropes. Her limbs flop down to the bed as she's released, and she watches me through half-closed eyes as I grab a pot from my bedside drawer. "What's that?"

"Cream." I dip my fingers in and begin massaging it into her reddened skin, drinking down the little noises she makes as my fingers knead her muscles. "You'll be sore tomorrow."

"Worth it," she whispers, and I press a kiss against her lips. "When can we do it again?"

I give her a stern look. "When the marks have gone down."

She gives me a full-blown pout that she's clearly learned from Ryder, and I smirk. "Plenty of other things we can do."

She stumbles sleepily to the bathroom and I quickly swap the sheets for clean ones. When she wraps her arms around me from behind, I turn, and she smiles at me.

I wrap my hand around her hair, tilting her face up to mine.

"Why don't I have a nickname?" she asks me. "Enzo calls me little prey. Ryder calls me princess, or little thief. But you... you don't call me anything."

My hand slides around her throat, cupping her possessively. As I grip her throat and breathe her in, her legs buckle and I drag her closer.

"You have one," I breathe. "Mine."

She flushes scarlet, but a grin lights up her face as I nudge her into bed and tug the covers over us. As I settle her against me and sink my face into her neck, she turns, her lips brushing mine. "Night, Daddy Mav," she whispers.

I choke.

I'm going to fucking *murder* Ryder.

Zella

Stretching out in the late afternoon sun, I turn my face up to the light. It feels warm against my skin, even through the hooded sweatshirt Maverick insisted I wear when he caught me sneaking out of the front door, sketchbook and pens in hand.

The weather is getting colder now, but I relish in every shiver as the cool breeze passes over my body. I'll never get tired of this sensation.

Closing my eyes, I take in the orange light left by the sun through my eyelids. A shadow falls over it, and my lips twist into a grin as warm lips seal over mine.

Ryder cups my cheeks as he presses me back into the sun lounger, his tongue sliding between my lips in a way that mimics exactly what we were doing this morning.

I'm breathless when he pulls away, his brown eyes warm as he kneels in front of me and slides his hands up my legs. "How are your bruises, little thief?"

I roll my eyes. They barely even count as bruises, whatever Maverick muttered as he was rubbing cream into them the other day.

"Fine." I tug up the dress I'm wearing, showing him the slight yellow marks that still dot my skin. "They're almost gone."

And I'm about ready for some new ones. It's been a whole *week*. I think I'll sleep with Maverick tonight. I've spent the last week bouncing from room to room.

Frowning, I glance down at the sketch in my hand. Maverick, Enzo, and Ryder, all of them covered by a small amount of bedsheet and nothing else. Ryder gently tugs the book from me, and I blanch, trying to grab it back.

He whistles. Is it possible for my face to actually catch on fire? "Holy fuck, princess. You have a *very* vivid imagination."

I'm not sure what the noise is that erupts from my throat, but Ryder throws his head back in a laugh, taking pity and giving me back the sketchbook. Flipping it closed before I can get myself into more trouble, I reluctantly stand up and make to head inside.

His hand grips my wrist, and I turn my head away. "Princess. Hey, look at me."

I slide my eyes to him, and he rubs his thumb over the pulse in my wrist. "Nothing to be embarrassed about. In fact, this feels like a good time to show you something we've been working on."

He slides his hand down, entwining our fingers together as he tugs me along in his enthusiasm. Curiosity pulls at me as we walk into the house and he stops, pulling open the dungeon door and yelling down. "I'm showing her!"

We wait for a second, and then there's a response. "Don't you fucking dare!"

I blink. "I don't think Enzo wants me to see...whatever this is."

Considering how open he was to me discovering his little torture-murder secret, I'm starting to get a bit worried about what exactly *this* is.

Maverick yanks open his study door. "Did I hear shouting?"

By this time, I'm chewing my lip. Enzo comes bounding up the stairs, a snarl on his face. "It's not ready," he snaps at Ryder, and he shrugs.

"Close enough."

Maverick sighs. "Enzo is right. We talked about this, Ry."

Ryder ignores them, tugging me towards the stairs as they follow. "Well, our timeline got moved up. Our little princess is getting itchy feet."

I swivel my head between them. "What does that mean?"

"You'll find out," Ryder promises. Maverick and Enzo overtake us as we reach the top of the stairs, and Ryder shouts after them as they disappear. "Chop chop, ladies! Thirty second warning."

"The more you open your mouth, the more worried I'm getting," I mutter, and he spins around, caging me against the wall.

"Good surprise," he promises, pressing a quick kiss to my cheek. "I swear."

I'm withholding judgment. Yesterday, he made me sit through hours of a movie about little furry creatures, men in white dresses and aliens that go to war against each other with shiny light sticks, swearing that it was the best movie ever made. I fell asleep after the first one, and he didn't even notice.

We wait until there's a shout, and then Ryder nudges me forward. "Close those pretty eyes for me, little thief. I want to see your face when you see it."

"See what?" I ask, but his hands are already sliding over my eyes and he's guiding me forward. I put my hands out, taking stumbling steps until cool hands slip into mine.

"Easy, prey," Enzo's low voice murmurs. "Wouldn't want any more bruises on that pretty skin of yours."

I shiver as his breath ghosts my ear. "At least, not unless you're screaming my name when I put them there."

"Enough," Maverick says from nearby. "Let her go."

It takes a second for my eyes to adjust as the room comes into view. My body turns slowly as I take it in, my eyes widening. The bed in front of me is *huge*.

"Plenty of space for all of us," Ryder murmurs as he props his head on my shoulder. "Guess those sketches of yours weren't so far off after all."

"What sketches?" Enzo demands, and I clear my throat, taking a few steps forward.

"Wow. That's... impressive."

"We figured you wouldn't want to keep bed hopping forever." Maverick rubs his hand over one of the wooden posts at each corner. They have vines and leaves carved into them, reaching up to a pale canopy of material that hangs above the bed, creating a little cocoon. "What do you think?"

"This is my new room?" I ask, and they all nod. "I love it."

"And that's not everything!" Ryder bursts out. Maverick and Enzo both break into matching scowls.

"For the love of fuck," Enzo groans. "Somebody needs to fucking gag you."

"Sorry." Ryder doesn't sound sorry at all as he bounces in place. "I just get too excited."

"Wait until you see him at Christmas," Maverick says with exasperation. "No gift is safe."

Christmas?

"What's... Christmas?" I ask. The room suddenly silences. You could hear a pin drop.

"You... you don't know what Christmas is?" Ryder sounds horrified. "That *asshole*."

"Ryder," Maverick snaps, before he turns to me. "It's a holiday we celebrate once a year. You give presents, put up a tree and decorate it."

My eyes round. "Inside the house?"

When he nods, I immediately make a note to look up Christmas on the laptop Ryder gave me. The googirl will know. She knows *everything*.

"God, I can't wait for Christmas this year," Ryder says, and Enzo snorts. Ryder points a finger at him. "Shut the fuck up, Mr. Grinch. Guess who's getting coal in his stocking this year. *Again*."

"I like coal," Enzo says smoothly. "I use it to light the fires of hell."

I have zero idea what's happening right now, but my shoulders start to shake anyway.

Maverick pinches his nose, exhaling softly. "Alright, Satan. Can we just put a pin in this conversation for a minute? Since Ryder can't keep a damn secret to save his life, I think we should probably show Zella the other thing."

"My idea," Enzo interrupts. He's glaring at Ryder. "I get to show her."

Ryder throws up his hands. I think he's poking out his bottom lip, too, and I bite back my smile. "Fine. Have it your way, Saint Dickolas."

Enzo ignores him, holding out his hand. "Little prey."

This time, we go downstairs. "This is a lot of surprises," I say softly, and he squeezes my hand.

"We would have spread them out," he says coolly. "If it wasn't for people with *big fucking mouths*."

He says this over his shoulder, and Ryder yelps. When I turn to look, he's rubbing the back of his head. Maverick is walking behind him, his face expressionless, but he winks at me.

Enzo doesn't cover my eyes this time, but he turns to look at me as he pushes open a set of wooden double doors with stained glass windows. I haven't been in this room before, and my breathing stops altogether as I walk in and stop dead.

There's so much light in this room. The sun beams in through the floor to ceiling windows that surround us, highlighting the easels set up in different spaces across the room. Each easel holds an empty canvas. Across from me is an empty space with shiny flooring, and I cross it as I move to the far wall. Dark wooden shelves are stacked with various items, and my hand shakes as I pick one up, turning it over in my hands. Oils.

Behind me, Maverick clears his throat. "We tried to get as much as we could, but if there's something missing, we can get that too."

My eyes lift up, taking in the sheer number of art materials in front of me. Some of them I don't even recognise.

"You made this for me?" I ask softly. "All of this... is mine?"

"All yours, little prey," Enzo murmurs. When I turn to him, he's half-smiling, this tiny movement that transforms his entire face into something gentler. "The space in the middle is for sculpting, if you wanted to do that."

The lump inside my throat gets bigger, cutting off my thoughts before I can even voice them.

They made me my own art studio.

"No tears," Enzo says immediately when the first one falls down my cheek. His hands are there, wiping them away as he frowns down at me. "I don't like them."

"Happy tears," I assure him in a choked-up voice, and he makes a look of disgust.

"Happy tears," he mutters. "That's a first."

"Stop." With a half-laugh, I bury my face in his chest, breathing him in. "I love it, Enzo. Thank you."

He doesn't say anything, but his arms close around me.

Maverick

We're all waiting in the hall when Zella comes bouncing down the stairs.

"I'm ready!" she announces brightly. "Does this look okay?"

When I turn, my automatic *yes* catches in my throat. Ryder chokes, his usual charm deserting him. For once, it's Enzo who steps up. Dressed in his usual black clothing, they look like night and day next to each other.

"Prey," he breathes. "You look edible."

She beams at him, and I finally pull my head out of my ass, moving to her side. "I agree," I murmur, and she turns to grin at me.

"It's not too bright?"

"Absolutely not," I assure her. Ryder's cough sounds suspiciously like a laugh, but he steps up alongside me. Zella smooths her hands down her vibrant metallic blue strappy dress, pointing to the little black heeled boots on her feet.

"Do these shoes work?" she asks Ryder, and he gives her a thumbs up.

"You look perfect, princess," he reassures her. "Excited?"

She bounces on her feet. "I can't wait. I've been looking forward to this for days."

Guilt swamps me at the enthusiasm in her voice. I know she wants to get out, to see more of the world that's been hidden from her for so long, but I'm not convinced that Ethan Moore isn't going to slither out of the cracks like the snake he is.

Nobody puts that much effort into stealing a child and keeping her locked away for so many years, only to give up.

Ryder escorts Zella past us, and my chest tugs at her delighted laugh as he pulls the door to the garage open with a sweeping bow. Enzo pauses next to me.

"His dominoes are crashing down," he murmurs. "We need to watch, but I doubt he's focused on her now."

Not with his whole life crumbling in ruins. The videos I handed over to John Martinez have mysteriously found their way into the hands of the royalty of the art world. Ethan Moore, renowned art collector and respected businessman, is done, the depravity in the videos enough to condemn him in the eyes of his peers.

I wonder what they'd think of us. We're not the same, but a lot of people see the world as purely black and white. Normally the people who are privileged enough to not need to think about it any more than that.

I nod in response to Enzo's words. "We still need to find him."

Zella needs answers, and I'm determined to find them for her. Not to mention Moore's taste for violence against young girls.

Enzo is grinning when I look at him. It's not a smile I'd want to be faced with. It's the smile of a predator on the hunt.

"We'll find him," he says in a low tone, sweeping past me. "Have faith."

I swipe a hand down my face, wondering if the circles under my eyes are as deep as they feel. Exhaustion weighs me down as I follow them to the truck. Ryder slides into the driver's seat, and I seize the opportunity to settle next to Zella. Enzo positions himself on her other side.

She glances at the window, chewing her lip. It's the most natural thing in the world to lift her, to pull her onto my lap, and she presses her lips to my cheek in thanks before she leans forward, lowering the window so she can look out.

Enzo gives me a disgruntled look. Lazily, I play with the end of Zella's braid.

"Have you ever thought about cutting it?" I ask, and she turns to me with a slight frown.

"Often," she admits. "Ethan was always so focused on it, though. He would never have allowed it."

"But you're not with him anymore, prey." Enzo's voice is low. "So what do you want to do?"

She pulls the braid into her lap. I have to admire Ryder's craftsmanship. He's woven little flowers from the garden all the way down. She looks like a modern-day fairy princess in her blue dress as she fiddles with it, her lips twisting into a wry smile.

"It sounds stupid," she says with a wry smile. "But it feels like part of me. And everything's changed so much... I do want to cut it, eventually. It's not practical to have hair like this. Just... not now?"

"It's your choice," I say firmly, closing my hand over her hip. "It'll be busy tonight. Stay close to us."

I'm a little concerned about taking her somewhere so busy. The annual street festival is a chaotic event, and even at the nightclub, we were separated from the crowds.

As soon as we manage to find a space in one of the side streets, I take her hand in mine. Ryder and Enzo fall into step behind us, scanning the crowd as we reach the busier main street.

It gives me the breathing space to watch her. I want to see her face.

Worth it.

Her lips part as we merge with the crowd, the three of us spreading out in an attempt to prevent her from being jostled. All around us, people spin and twirl and dance to the beat of the drum music from a local group up ahead. Everyone is dressed to impress, with costumes ranging from animals to mythology. The crowd splits, merging around a street performer acting as Medusa. She twists to look at us, a small smile twisting her lips as snakes hiss, dozens of them coiled around her. Zella takes a step back, bumping into me, and I steady her with my hands on her waist.

When she reaches out a hand, I snag it hastily. "Careful. They might bite."

She turns to me with wide eyes as we pass. "She had snakes on her head!"

Her wonder only grows as we explore. Any initial uncertainty about the crowds soon drains away, and soon we're focusing on keeping up with her as she dashes from stall to stall, laughing at the many performers, gaping at the dancers on stilts who move slowly through the teeming mass of people. All around us, music and laughter ring out, and our arms slowly fill with packages. Not all of them paid for.

"Ryder," I hiss. He gives me an angelic look as he swipes a cake from a stall, handing it to Zella with a charming grin as she squeals over the intricate decoration. I glare at him until he rolls his eyes, holding up a wad of cash and pulling a note out, handing it over to the bemused stall owner.

"Consider me reformed," he says, sauntering over to me as Enzo practically curves himself over Zella. She pushes the cupcake into his face, and he blinks. Yellow frosting drips off his nose, and both Ryder and I can't hide our snickers as he levels us with a glare.

Doesn't stop him tasting it, though.

"Excellent choice," Ryder acknowledges. "She loves it, Mav."

My answering smile is smug as fuck. Because Zella is almost incandescent with joy, her face lighting up at each new experience as she tries to take in as much as possible.

When we reach a courtyard, she darts forward, stumbling to a stop as she takes in the dancers. "Oh," she breathes. Above us, dozens and dozens of lanterns string from light to light, casting everything in a warm golden glow. Fiddles start up next to us, and she spins in place as people start to move onto the cobbles, partners embracing each other as they spin across the stones to the lively folk music. When the singers begin, the folk music filling the space, I step forward and offer her my hand.

"Dance with me, Zella," I urge, and she stares at me, desire warring with indecision on her face.

"In front of all these people? I don't know how!"

"Doesn't matter." I pull her into the dancers, swirling us in circles and listening to the sound of her laughter as she tries to keep up. She picks up the rhythm quickly enough and then we're flying, around and around in circles until we come to a rapid stop, both of us pressed together as the crowd cheers wildly around us.

Zella looks flushed, her eyes bright under the lanterns as she grins. "I could do that again."

Cupping her cheeks, I draw her into a long, lingering kiss, ignoring the few extra cheers that come our way from a few rowdy revelers next to us. "We will."

As we cross the yard back to where Enzo and Ryder are waiting, I notice a burly, particularly bleary-eyed drinker who looks the worse for wear lurch towards us, his eyes on the girl in front of me. A thick hand reaches for her, and a second later, there's a snapping sound and a scream as the man staggers back. Everyone turns, Zella and I with them, and she gives me a questioning glance.

I shrug, nudging her back to Ryder and Enzo. Enzo gives me a congratulatory nod as Ryder pulls Zella to yet another stall, this one selling tiny pocket-sized watercolors that she exclaims over with glee. "Excellent technique."

"Shut up," I mutter, and he snorts.

"Don't stress it. She has a habit of bringing out the murderer in me too." A middle-aged couple next to us blanch, quickly moving away, and I have to laugh.

Zella

Bright lights, music, people. *Happiness.*

It's everywhere, so visceral I can almost see it. My fingers twitch for my sketchbook, desperate to capture everything I can see, to keep it close to me in case it never happens again.

I've never been as deliriously happy as I am right now, here with them.

Ryder tips another handful of pretty watercolors into my hands, and I cradle them carefully. "I don't want to lose any!"

He nudges me over to the next stall, filled with silky bags in bright colors.

Well. It would be rude not to.

When I'm loaded down with more than I could possibly carry, Ryder confiscates my new bright pink bag, carrying it with complete confidence over his shoulder as we rejoin Enzo and Maverick. They've got their heads together, breaking apart as we stop next to them.

Maverick cups my cheek. "We have one more stop to make," he says softly. "If you don't mind?"

If I don't *mind*?

"All the stops," I mutter, a tad feverishly. "I want to see them all!"

He laughs. "I think we've seen most of the stalls, but my friend has his own gallery just down from here. Want to go and see?"

I'm already pressing forward in my enthusiasm, and he grabs my shoulders, spinning me around and placing his hand in the middle of my back. "This way."

The lively music fades as we move away from the main festival, pausing at the top of a little alleyway. My breath catches at the thousands of tiny candles flickering in the darkness, lighting a path, and I turn to Maverick. "It's down here?"

When he nods, I take careful steps into the light, making my way down the path with them close behind me. I follow the little lights, enthralled, until we reach a brightly lit building. The candles reach all the way to the glass double doors, and Maverick pulls them open for me.

As we walk inside, I tilt my head to hear the music. More candles flicker everywhere, making the bright space warmer and more inviting. Only a few people move around the open space, their voices muted, and my chest tightens at the sad, somber notes playing. Dozens of canvases fill the white walls, each one lit with a soft light.

And they all show the same two people.

"Maverick!" An older man calls out, and I turn with interest as Maverick steps forward. The man excuses himself from the woman he's talking to, squeezing her hand and moving over to us with his arms open. "I'm so happy to see you," he murmurs, as he wraps his hands around Maverick and squeezes. To my surprise, Maverick squeezes back. His face is twisted with emotion, and he clears his throat as he steps back.

"Emerson," he says hoarsely. "You know Ryder, and Enzo."

"I do," the man says, with a welcoming smile. He turns to me with an enquiring smile. "And who might you be?"

"I'm Zella," I say softly. Emerson holds out his hand, and I take it. He cups his hands around mine, not shaking them.

"Zella...," he says softly. Almost sadly. "It's very nice to meet you."

"You too." He takes another second before breaking our contact, but his eyes flick back to me as he smiles at Maverick. "I wasn't expecting you."

But Maverick is watching me too, his face settling into a slight frown as he shrugs. "I thought it was time. Zella enjoys art, and we came to the street festival. I didn't want to leave without saying hello."

"You do?" Emerson says brightly. He offers me his arm. "Please. Let me escort you around."

When I look at Maverick, he nods reassuringly. "Emerson knows everything there is to know about art," he tells me. "I think you'll enjoy each other's company. We'll be here."

Intrigued, I take Emerson's arm, and he leads me to the first of the paintings. A woman in shades of green, yellow and blue, her face shadowed, cradles her stomach as she sits looking out of a window.

Emerson waits quietly as I take it in. "It's beautiful," I murmur. "You painted all of these?"

"I did." We move on to the second painting. In this one, the woman cradles her child to her chest. It's intimate, so much so that my chest tightens looking at it. "This is your family."

Emerson pauses next to me. "You're very astute. How did you guess?"

"The emotion," I murmur. "There's so much... hope. Joy, maybe? I can feel it. You're very talented."

Emerson doesn't speak for a minute. When he does, I almost miss the catch in his voice. "Thank you."

We move around the room, and I absorb the journey of his daughter as she progresses to a toddler, then to a little girl. Every stage of her life is carefully preserved in art, and the sheer love embedded in each painting makes my eyes glisten as we reach the final image.

This one... is different.

Hesitating, I turn to Emerson. He's staring at the painting, but he's not looking at it. He looks far away.

"What happened?" I whisper. He swallows.

"There was a fire," he murmurs. Carefully, he reaches forward and traces his fingers softly over the face of the woman. She's on her knees, her arms wrapped tightly around her child, her back bowed. "My wife did not survive."

My own chest burns in sympathy, thumping, painful heartbeats. "I'm... I'm so sorry."

He turns to me, a sad smile on his lips. "It was a long time ago," he assures me. But now that I know, I can see it in the way he carries himself. Emerson carries his pain with him, etched into his heart, into every smile.

I wet my lips. "And... your daughter?"

"Both of them," he says quietly. "My Aria too."

Stepping back, I take in the room with new eyes. A journey, one brutally cut short. There are no more paintings after this one, no more memories to record painstakingly on canvas.

"It's funny," Emerson says quietly, and I turn to him in question, swallowing back my tears. "You have very similar eyes. Aria... she had such vibrant green eyes, too."

He pulls a crumpled photograph from his pocket, smoothing it out before handing it to me. I take it carefully, looking down at the pale-haired little girl with the green eyes and toothy smile. Emerson is holding her, his face beaming and his arm wrapped around his wife.

My hands clench on the photograph.

A hand lands on my arm as I wobble. "Zella?" Emerson asks in concern. "Are you all right?"

Taking a deep breath, I nod, handing the photograph back. "She was beautiful."

I try to smile, but it feels stiff on my face. When I turn, looking for my men, Enzo appears in an instant. "Prey? What's the matter?"

They're talking around me, and my head hurts. I hear Emerson's apologies, and I want to tell him not to apologize, but the words are stuck in my throat, my thoughts on a panicked loop inside my head that I can't quite catch.

"I'm sorry," I whisper. "I need... I need to go."

Enzo lifts me, and then we're moving away from the gallery with rapid steps. Maverick stays behind a moment, his legs eating up the distance between us as he catches up with Enzo's rapid steps.

Maverick looks down at me with concern, blocking my view of the gallery as it disappears behind us. "I'm okay," I force out. "You can put me down."

"No." Enzo keeps walking, and I tap his shoulder.

"Please," I say quietly. "I can walk."

He humphs, but slides me slowly down his body, holding onto me. I suck in the crisp night air, letting it expand my lungs as they surround me.

"Zella," Maverick pushes. "What happened?"

Forcing a smile, I shake my head slowly. "I think... I just felt a little hot."

Maverick feels my forehead, his own creasing. "We'll take you home."

"I'm sorry," I whisper, my voice cracking. "I had such a lovely evening, Maverick."

His thumb brushes my cheek. "There will always be more nights like this, Zella. I promise."

Ryder

I cradle Zella in my arms, carrying her up the stairs.

"Put her in the new room," Maverick murmurs behind me, and I nod. I don't think any of us want to leave her tonight. Enzo yanks the bedding back as I place her into the bed. Her breathing stutters, and another small sob slips out.

We all exchange looks. She's been crying in her sleep since she fell asleep a few minutes into the ride home.

Maverick flicks on the lamp as I carefully take her dress off, Enzo handing me one of the soft shirts we bought for her to sleep in. She doesn't twitch as we change her, lifting the blankets over her and settling into the chairs dotted across the room.

None of us leave.

"Maverick." He looks up when I say his name, the shadows in his face even more pronounced under the light. "What do you think?"

He sighs. "I don't know, Ry."

“Show me,” I demand quietly, and he pulls the photograph he always carries out of his pocket. Reaching for it, I unfold the familiar image, taking in the beaming little girl, Emerson, and his wife, Maria. My eyes flicker between Aria and Zella. “You don’t think…?”

“She recognized something,” Enzo says, his voice cautious. “We all saw it. Her face went pale as soon as she looked at it.”

Maverick’s jaw ticks. “Twenty years,” he says hoarsely.

He doesn’t say any more. He doesn’t have to. We’re all very aware that the girl in the bed could very well be the key to solving the case that we all thought was unsolvable.

The silence ticks on, and we all wait.

“If it’s her,” Maverick says finally. He looks almost ill when I look at him, the guilt carved into his face. “Then I missed something.”

I shake my head. “Your father searched for eleven years, and found nothing,” I remind him. “Give yourself a break, Mav. Even if it is her, you couldn’t have known.”

He doesn’t say anything. We settle down in the seats, unspoken agreement that none of us feel like sleeping tonight.

And we wait.

Zella

I wake up soaked in my own sweat, terror bleeding out of my pores as I gasp voicelessly and pull myself upright.

The nightmares linger on the edge of my consciousness, just out of reach as I look around, trying to catch my breath. Maverick and Ryder are both asleep on chairs at the end of my bed, but there's no sign of Enzo.

Slipping out from under the covers, I quietly open the door and head down to my old room. I need to wash off the fear that still coats my skin.

I also need to acknowledge the thoughts lurking in the back of my head, but I'm not quite ready for that just yet. So I hit the shower, trying my best to not get my hair wet as I duck under and rinse off the sweat.

Slipping into a long yellow woolen dress sweater and a pair of thick tights, my feet pad down the steps as I make my way towards the dungeon. A dull, thudding sound reaches my ears, and my mouth dries as I reach the bottom stair.

Directly ahead of me, Enzo smashes his fists into a tall bag that hangs from the ceiling. Music plays loudly, enough that he can't hear me as I linger where I am to watch him. Sweat trickles in rivulets down his back as his muscles flex, over and over again as he punches the bag like it's his own personal nemesis.

Taking a seat on the stairs, I wait for him to finish, pulling my sweater down to cover my knees and rubbing them with shaking hands in the cool air. It takes a few minutes before he notices me, and he flicks the music off.

"Little prey." Dropping down to his haunches in front of me, he studies my face. "What do you need?"

I try to take a full breath, but it hurts. My breathing turns to short, stuttering gasps, and I fold over, hitting my chest with my hand. "Can't—,"

"Stop." Enzo's voice is steady, his hands on either side of my face warm in comparison to the ice sweeping over my body. "Stop this. Now."

When I struggle to pull away, he holds me tightly. "Breathe," he says, a little softer as I look up at him beseechingly. "Breathe for me, little prey. In, out. Slowly. Follow my lead."

I struggle to copy him as he takes a deep breath, but he doesn't stop, and the pain starts to settle into a dull ache as my lungs open back up. Each of us is watching the other, and Enzo's eyes widen as the first tear spills down my face.

I grapple with the words, trying to explain. "I... I can't. Need something else."

Something to distract me. Something to take my mind away from the awful, sneaking possibility that's crept into my head and is sitting there, waiting for me to acknowledge it.

"Please," I breathe. I don't even know what I'm asking for.

But he does.

Strong arms slide underneath me, lifting me from the cool step. "Wrap your legs around me, little prey."

Wordlessly, I do as he asks. My arms are around his neck, and I bury my face in his skin as he carries me back up the stairs. I focus on breathing, on sucking down his warm scent.

Cool air hits my back, Ryder's braiding skills enough to still have my hair in place even after I've slept. I lift my head enough to take in the garage. "Where are we going?"

My voice is a whisper, and Enzo's hands tighten on me before he places me down on a small table. "Breathe. No talking."

I concentrate on keeping my breathing even as he moves around the vehicles. He takes a black jacket from the wall, shrugging it on over his bare chest and walking over with another one. He threads my arms into it silently, tucking my hair into it and drawing the braid around my waist like padding.

His fingers brush my cheek after he finishes zipping it up, and he picks me up again. We head across the space, approaching a sleek metal machine I haven't seen before. Enzo shifts me in his arms, lifting his leg and settling us across it like a seat.

"What's this?" I ask. Curiosity bleeds into my voice, and he raises his eyebrow at me.

"Freedom, little prey," he murmurs. I'm sitting astride him, my legs dangling free, and he leans down to press my foot against a bar. "Keep them here."

My toes curl into the metal. "Do I need shoes?"

Enzo silently watches me for a moment before he shakes his head in response. I'm pressed so closely to him that I can see every one of his long eyelashes. He blinks. "What?"

"You have pretty eyes," I murmur, and he makes a scoffing noise at the back of his throat, looking away from me. I jerk as his hands move down, sliding up my tights and beneath my dress. His thumb stretches the material, and my eyes fly to his as he reaches the apex between my thighs. "What—,"

A ripping sound tears through the air, and I gape at him. "Did you just *rip* my tights?"

I *liked* these tights.

His hand pushes through the hole he's created, his fingers tracing my underwear as I shift on his lap. His other hand squeezes my leg as he ignores my words. "Stay still."

An impossible task as his fingers trace me, over and over again until I feel dampness pooling, soaking the thin silk. Enzo tsks, pulling his hand free and rubbing his damp finger across my lips. "Your little cunt is soaking, prey."

I dart out my tongue, licking his finger, and he takes it further, pushing two of his fingers into my mouth. "Suck."

I do as I'm told, and his other hand slides back to my underwear, tugging and pulling until the material snaps against my skin. His fingers slide from my mouth with a wet pop, and my protest catches on a strangled groan in my throat as he pushes them inside me.

He pins me until I feel thick bars pressing into my back, the top of my body curving as he slides his fingers in and out of me, the noise almost obscene in the small space.

"Do you think," Enzo murmurs, almost conversationally, "that I would let anyone take you from me, prey?"

My eyes feel lazy as I blink slowly, taking a minute to register his words. "N-no."

"Good." He moves his hands faster, and I whimper at the curling, burning sensation that winds its way through my body as he plays me like an instrument. "Do you think that we would let anything happen to you?"

When I don't respond, he pushes his fingers further inside me, his palm grinding against my sensitive skin as my body bucks in his grip. "Answer me."

"No!" My cry echoes around the room as he moves faster, the familiar wave building in my core.

When he abruptly stops, pulling his hand free just as I'm on the crest, I groan. His wet fingers move to my throat, cupping the skin as he leisurely rubs my own scent into me, marking me.

"Believe in us," he whispers against my lips. "Whatever hardships lie ahead, little prey. We will face them together. You're not alone in this."

His words are fierce, and a lump appears in my throat as I nod.

I don't feel alone, not with Enzo wrapped around me, his hands on my skin and his promises in my ear.

"Take me somewhere," I say. "Anywhere."

He smirks, and it's almost devilish. "What did you think we were doing on this bike?"

I hear a zip crackle in the quiet, and Enzo pulls me forward. The head of his cock rubs against me, warm and demanding, and he catches my cry with his lips as he pushes inside me, stretching me until I'm completely seated on him. The slight burn is a welcome one, and he taps my legs. "Keep your feet where I showed you."

My feet tap around, until I feel the edges with my toes. "Is this safe?" I ask him breathlessly. I have a feeling that Maverick will not be happy.

"If you wanted safe," he drawls in my ear, "you would have run from us at the first opportunity, little prey. You don't want *safe*. You want lightning in your blood and electricity in your veins."

His hands reach around me. "Hold on to me. Don't let go."

The machine rumbles to life underneath me, sending vibrations rolling through my body as I press my knees against Enzo and tighten my hold on his neck. He turns his head, pressing his lips to my ear.

"The only thing I want you thinking about," he growls, "is the feel of me inside you. This body is ours, little prey. Remember who you belong to."

Any response I might have given is lost in the rush of wind as the bike darts forward. My hands tighten around Enzo as I gasp, but he doesn't flinch, his chest strong and steady beneath me as I squeeze my eyes shut, my head tucked into the crook between his head and shoulders.

The bike gathers speed, and I crack my eyes open as the house starts to get smaller and smaller behind us. We're flying down the main road, and I take in the trees on either side, blurs of orange and green and brown that bleed into each other in the early morning light.

Air rushes past me, wind pressing against my back, pushing me further into Enzo as we move faster than I ever thought was possible.

My eyes open wider and wider, the exhilaration of pure freedom bleeding through me as I laugh in delight, my head tipping back.

This... this is everything.

I keep my eyes firmly open, not wanting to miss a thing as we drive down a smooth road. Enzo slows the bike to a stop, and I twist around to take in the sight of the tall gates sliding open.

"You ready?" he asks, and I grin. The fear curdling inside my mind is pushed away, shoved into a dark corner, still there but not overpowering.

"Yes," I call. My throat tightens with excitement as the engine makes a roaring noise, and then we're soaring past the gates, pulling onto a main road dotted with other vehicles. I lose myself in the sensation of flying, the way we weave in and out of the moving cars.

The world moves around us, impossibly big but *right there*, close enough for me to reach out my hand and entangle myself.

Enzo was right. This is what freedom tastes like.

***

When we finally stop, my heart is full, my body on edge with the motion of the bike combined with the feel of Enzo inside me. I soften against him, my hands stroking the tuft of hair at the nape of his neck as he turns off the engine. "Welcome to Queensbridge Park, little prey."

"That was... everything." My eyes are wide as I lean back to stare at him, then around us. "Can we do that every day?"

His hands drop to my hips, his voice low. "We can do it for the rest of our lives. If you want to."

My breath hitches. The rest of our lives.

My thoughts snap off as Enzo twists his hips, the motion making him rotate inside me and bringing me right back to the here and now.

"Oh," I gasp. He pushes me back into the bars, his fingers rubbing over my slit as my back arches. The fire builds again, slow molten lava in my abdomen growing as he holds me in place and thrusts his hips against mine.

He keeps his movements slow and rhythmic, and I lose myself in the feeling of him pushing inside me, over and over again.

His hand finds my throat, the loose collar a comfort as he strokes the skin in time with his thrusts. "Tell me what you feel, little prey."

My eyes feel lazy and languid as I blink at him. "I feel... you inside me."

He half smiles. "As you should." He encompasses his words with a push that brings a moan to my lips, and he kisses it away. "What else?"

My head lolls to the side, and my lips part.

A river rushes next to us, turbulent liquid glass that glitters with the bright light of the morning sunshine. Above us is a huge gray metal structure, twisting in columns up into the air and reaching across the river, bringing the faint sound of cars to my ears. On the other side of the riverbank, the city stretches out, thousands of people going about their lives with certainty. They know what their life looks like. They have a routine, a family, a *plan*.

Enzo twists my chin back to face him, slowing his movements. "Tell me."

"I feel like I'm on the edge of something." The words are almost soundless, a confession pulled straight from my chest. "Like everything is going to be different now. A whole life stretches out in front of me and I don't know what it's going to look like."

He shifts. "None of us know what our lives will look like, little prey," he says, almost gently. "All we can do is adapt to the changes that come. And they come for everyone."

I nod, slowly. "I don't want to lose this," I tell him pleadingly. "Whatever happens, Enzo."

"I won't let that happen," he whispers back to me. "I promise, prey. I told you that you're ours, and I meant it. For all our days, from now until hell takes us."

He moves inside me, and it's so gentle it brings tears to my eyes.

"It would take Lucifer himself to tear me away from you."

My release is a slow, smoldering pleasure that tips me over the edge of a waterfall, sweeping me out to sea. My hands grip Enzo, holding his shoulders tightly.

"You won't leave me."

A belief.

"Never, prey. Never."

A vow.

When the small aftershocks have drained from my body, Enzo lifts my lethargic body off the bike, ignoring my protests, and carries me over to a bench overlooking the river. Tugging my sweater down to cover me, he settles down with me in his lap.

His hands run over my arms, the tops of my legs, slow and reassuring as I stare out over the water. The slight tang of the river fills my nose, and I wrinkle it.

When I mention it to Enzo, he snorts. "Nothing in this world does as much damage as humanity, prey. Every one of us is toxic to the ground we walk on."

I poke his arm. "There's good out there too, you know."

"I know," he says. He's not looking at me. "I'm holding it."

Oh. A warmth infuses my chest, and I lean back against him. "Enzo?"

"Mmm?"

"The man from the gallery. Emerson. I think... I don't think his daughter died in a fire."

"No," he says, and his voice is gentle. "Are you ready to go back?"

The unspoken words hang in the air.

But I need to face this. If I'm right, then everything will change.

And not even Enzo can stop it.

Maverick

I'm pacing back and forth in the hall like a caged animal when I finally hear the noise from Enzo's bike.

Ryder's footsteps pound down the stairs. "Are they back?"

My nod is short. It takes everything I have not to rush into the garage, but I hold myself back until the door swings open and Enzo saunters out, his hand on Zella's back as she walks in, her fingers tugging at the sleeve of her dress.

I'm not sure what to expect, but when she sees me, she darts forward, burying her face in my chest. "Maverick."

Exhaling, I wrap my arms around her, my hand cupping the back of her head. "Are you alright?"

She nods into my shirt. "Enzo took me for... some fresh air."

I bet he did. I narrow my eyes at him, and he shrugs.

"It helped." Zella swallows as she shifts back, pushing her hair away from her face. Her braid is coming undone, long tendrils of gold falling past her shoulders as she looks between us all. Her face creases in hesitation, but she straightens her shoulders. "I think... I think we need to talk."

"Okay," I say softly. "Whatever you need."

Her feet move, and she glances back as we start to follow. "I just need to get something. Will you wait for me? In the sitting room?"

"Of course." Ryder, Enzo and I filter into the room as she darts up the stairs, returning a few minutes later and glancing at where we're all sat. She comes to sit next to me on the couch, curling herself into a corner and taking a deep breath.

Silence stretches into minutes as we wait, all three of us still as Zella's expression barely flickers. Finally, she looks up at us, and the forlorn expression on her face makes my chest ache. "Zella."

I reach for her, but she shakes her head, holding her hand up. "No, I'm alright. I just... needed to work through some of the thoughts in my head."

My fingers curl in on themselves as she straightens. Her skin is pale, her green eyes shadowed as she begins to speak.

"I don't remember my parents," she says quietly. "I don't remember anything, really. Not when I was a child."

I nod, knowing this from the discussions we've had previously.

She flips open the sketchbook in her hands, staring down at the marks on the page. "I asked Ethan a few days before I left how he managed when I was little, since he doesn't like to be touched. He told me I had a nursemaid called Maria. He'd never mentioned her to me before."

My whole body jerks, and her eyes flick to me. "Sorry," I say hoarsely.

But I recognise that name.

Holding my tongue, I wait for Zella to bring her thoughts together. The little threads to a mystery two decades old.

She looks back down to the page. "Around the same time, I sketched something different to anything I'd drawn before. I always struggled to draw anything I'd never seen, but this...,"

She holds the book out to me. "It just came so naturally," she whispers. "Like it was always there, inside my head."

My fingers shake as I reach for the page. I have my suspicions, but shock still steals my breath as I look down at Maria Cooper's face. I'd know it anywhere.

I've looked at that face every day for more than ten years.

It's a dangerous thing, hope. Almost as dangerous as the absence of it. When you feel hope, opportunities are endless. But as hope begins to fade, those opportunities become like delicate threads. Each one slowly snipped away, until you're left with nothing.

This case consumed my father, pushed him to open up the company we run today, to spend every spare moment searching for answers on behalf of his best friend.

He died without an answer.

My hand clenches on the sketch as I reach into my pocket, tugging out the crumpled photo and holding it out to Zella silently. She stares down at it, at the unmistakable resemblance between the woman in the photograph and the woman in her sketchbook.

"Nineteen years ago," I say hoarsely, "my father's best friend lost his wife and daughter in a fire. It ripped through their home, so much so that they were unidentifiable. But they only ever found one body. The police dismissed it. They couldn't identify the body due to its condition, and they said that because of the heat of the fire, it was likely that the daughter had perished too. They thought it was a simple house fire, and they closed the investigation."

Zella closes her eyes. "I think they got it wrong."

"My father did, too," I say quietly. Her eyes fly open, and I give her a strained smile. "His best friend needed help, and it drove him to open up an investigative company. But he never found any explanation of what might have happened to Maria and Aria Cooper."

Zella flinches, and I reach for her hand. It feels cold in mine, so fucking cold, and I pull her into me. Her entire body is trembling.

"What does this mean?" Her voice is hoarse and shaky as I hold her. "What did Ethan do?"

I rub my hands over her arms, trying to warm her. "I wish I had an answer for you," I say softly. "But we're closer to an answer now than we've ever been."

She swallows. "What do we do now?"

I blow out a breath. "I think," I say carefully, "that a DNA test is needed."

"A DNA test?"

I cup her cheek. "It will tell us if you're really Aria Cooper, Zella," I say, trying to soften my words. "It will tell us if Emerson is your real father."

Her eyes glisten, spilling over with tears. "And if he is?"

"Then," I say softly, "we will think about what happens next. One step at a time, okay?"

It takes her a second to nod. "But... Ethan might have killed my mother. Why would he do that? Did he know them?"

"I don't have all the answers," I swallow, stroking her cheek. "But we're going to get them, Zella. I swear to you."

She straightens. "Can you... call him now? Emerson, I mean?"

"Are you sure, little thief?" Ryder interjects softly. "This is a lot to process in a short amount of time."

Zella shakes her head. "It's been twenty years," she chokes out. "I don't think... I think he deserves to know."

We all exchange glances. "Alright," I say roughly, trying to keep the ache in my throat down. "I'll call him."

Zella slips from my lap, and I glance up. She shifts on her feet.

"I want him to know," she explains wanly. "I just... I don't think I can be in the room for that. Not straight away. Does that make sense?"

"Of course," I acknowledge. "I completely understand."

She holds up her hand to stop Ryder and Enzo as they both rise from their seats. "I just... I'm going to have a bath. And maybe a nap."

She wraps her arms around herself as she leaves, looking so small and fragile that it just about breaks my fucking heart. The others look just as struck, and Enzo's hands are so tight on the arms of his chair I think I hear a crack.

Twenty years. Twenty years of looking for a ghost, of praying for a damn fucking miracle, and here she is.

"We could be wrong," Ryder says quietly, and I shake my head.

"We're not wrong," I say, picking up the phone and bracing myself.

"Wait," he bursts out. "Just... wait."

He looks between the three of us. "This changes nothing," he says hoarsely. "With us. With her."

Enzo taps his hand on his knee, the only outward sign of his anxiety. "Obviously."

He looks to me for confirmation. When I hesitate, he swears. "Fuck, Mav, this is not the time for you to be *noble*."

"It's her choice," I say hoarsely. "It has to be her choice."

He shakes his head. "She makes me want a future," he says, his voice gruff. "I never bothered looking forward until we found her, Maverick. And now I can see it. It's right fucking there. I'm not letting her go anywhere."

"I agree," Enzo chips in, and my eyes close. I can't do this now.

Picking up the phone, I hit Emerson's number and press the phone to my ear.

This is the job. This has always been the job.

We bring them home.

Even if it rips us apart.

"Emerson," I say hoarsely, when he picks up the phone. "I think we've found her."

Zella

Steam rises in gentle curls above the hot water, but I barely feel it.

Huddled over, arms wrapped around my knees, I press my face into my damp skin and focus on breathing deeply, the way Enzo showed me.

It takes a while for my head to stop spinning.

Aria Cooper.

It doesn't feel like my name. I don't feel like I have any connection at all to the little girl in the paintings, any connection to the woman with the vibrant smile and love shining in her eyes, her arms wrapped around a child that might be me.

Maybe it's all a coincidence.

Or maybe Ethan saved me from the fire and kept me safe.

But why would he do that?

I know it doesn't make sense, that I'm grasping, but the alternative isn't something I can face.

Three lives destroyed.

A lifetime of captivity.

But... a *family.* A father.

I wouldn't be alone.

The thoughts threaten to boil over, and I lunge out of the bath, sending water slopping over the sides as my hair slaps wetly against the floor. Tugging on a robe, I move with hurried steps, yanking open my bedroom door and running down to Maverick's room. The door opens before I even raise a hand, and he looks down at me. His blue eyes look like a storm, turbulence swirling. "Zella."

I push past him, my breathing heavy as I turn. My throat feels tight. "Did you tell him?"

"I did," Maverick says heavily. He comes to stand in front of me, and I crane my head to look up at his face. "He wanted to come straight away."

My flinch surprises us both.

"Sorry," I say, clearing my throat. "What did you say?"

"I said no." I don't pull away when he takes my hand, drawing me over to the bed that nearly swallows me when I sink into it. "Here."

I sip at the harsh amber liquid, taking a smaller sip followed by a bigger gulp. The burning in my throat warms me more than the bath did, and I give him a small smile. "Thanks."

Maverick kneels in front of me on the floor, so tall he still towers over me.

"Talk to me," he pleads softly.

"I need to know who I am," I say after a moment. "But I don't feel like I'm Aria Cooper."

There's no lightning bolt of realization. No sudden overpowering awareness smashing into my heart, releasing memories I never knew I had. I just feel... empty.

"Maybe you don't feel like Aria," Maverick suggests gently, "because you're *Zella*. Finding out who you are does not erase who you have always been, sweetheart. This may change your circumstances, but it doesn't change you."

I hold on tight to his words. "I feel like I'm unraveling," I confess, my voice raw and my heart aching as I look to him. "Like my whole existence has been a footnote in someone else's story."

I don't fight him when he nudges me backwards, curling onto my side. The bed sinks as Maverick climbs on, fitting himself around me. His arm slides around my waist as he holds me to him, and the dam breaks.

The first tear falls, and then another. Another.

Until I feel like my body will break under the force of my sobbing. Maverick doesn't say anything, steady and sure behind me as I choke on the knowledge that my entire life has been at the whim of someone else.

Finally, I quieten.

"He killed my mother," I say groggily. Maverick tenses. "Didn't he?"

It makes sense. If I was taken from my home the night my mother died in a fire, kept away from my family, presumed dead for twenty years... it's the only thing that makes sense.

I've spent my life under the control of my mother's murderer.

"I think that's probably the case," Maverick says carefully. "But we don't know anything for certain, Zella. There's a lot to unravel. The most important thing right now is making sure that we're right about this."

I close my eyes, breathing in the comforting scent of Maverick from his bedding. His breathing is slow and steady, and it lulls me into comfort I couldn't find alone in my room.

A thought strikes, and I twist over to face him. His eye cracks open as he glances down at me.

"You said, earlier... about your dad. He set up what you do because of this?"

Maverick's eyebrows draw down. "He did," he says softly. "My father and Emerson, they were great friends. Closer than brothers. My mother was close to Maria, too, but died when I was young. Maria was always very good to me."

My heart constricts at the sorrow in his voice. "How old were you, when the fire happened?"

"Eight." His eyes find mine. "Ask."

"Did... did you know her well? Aria, I mean." I watch as he twists, pulling open a drawer and lifting something out. He hands the frame to me, and I stare at it. Emotion pools in my chest, something tight and uncertain. The little boy, dressed in a crisp white shirt and brown shorts, has a frown on his face, but his body curves protectively over the laughing little girl clinging to him. Her head is thrown back, her face wreathed in delight as she looks up at him.

"She used to drive me mad," he says quietly with a half-laugh. "Always following me around, chattering and singing and dancing. I used to call her my shadow. And then she wasn't there anymore, and I suddenly missed her more than I ever thought possible."

"Maverick," I whisper. My mouth feels dry, my eyes damp, as I picture a lost little boy without his shadow. "I'm sorry."

"Whatever comes," he says softly. "We will make new memories, Zella."

Picking up my wrist, he presses a kiss to the soft underside. "It doesn't matter. If you're Zella, or Aria, or anyone at all. It doesn't matter, as long as you're you. And whatever happens... it brought us to you, Zella, and I will never not be grateful."

He blows out a breath. "We should go down for dinner."

“Not yet,” I whisper. Wrapping my arm around his waist, I curl myself against him. “Five more minutes.”

Zella

My eyes flick up, lips pursing in disapproval as Ryder squirms in front of me.

"Do you think you could stay still?" I ask hopefully.

He lasts a whole minute this time, before raising his hand to scratch at an itch on the end of his nose. Groaning, I throw my hands up in exasperation. "Ryder!"

"Take it from the best," Enzo drawls behind me. He's lounging on a long chair, his legs dangling over the end as he watches my attempts to bring Ryder to life on a canvas. "The more you stay still, the less time it'll take."

Ryder holds his hand up, proudly displaying his middle finger to Enzo and completely breaking the careful pose I placed him in to paint. "You see this? Swivel on it."

My head makes a thump as I bang it into my hands. "This was a terrible idea," I mutter, and yelp as warm hands snake around my waist.

"I'm definitely more of an action person," Ryder murmurs into my ear, making me squirm. "Why don't I lay you down on that comfortable looking blanket and bury my tongue inside you instead?"

I swat his hands away grumpily. "No."

"Princess," he murmurs, and I turn, digging my finger into his chest and making him wince.

"You promised," I say firmly, backing up and crossing my arms when he reaches for me again. "Nope. No sex until your painting is done."

His eyes widen. "I can't last that long."

Throwing my hand out, I wave it at the empty space he just stepped down from. "Your podium awaits," I say sweetly, and he groans.

"Besides," I say loftily, picking my brush back up as he slumps back into his position. "I know exactly what you're trying to do."

"Oh?" Enzo purrs. "And what would that be?"

I turn, leveling him with an even look before dipping my brush into the bronze paint. "You're trying to distract me."

Enzo's smile spreads across his face as he leans forward. "I can think of *far* better ways to distract you than this," he breathes, and I nearly tip the whole palette over as I turn back to Ryder, resisting the urge to fan my face.

Swallowing, I force away the flare of heat between my legs. "I'm very aware that the results will be here today."

Ryder twitches, but he stays where he is when I brandish the brush at him threateningly. His throat bobs as he shares a look with Enzo.

"Stop that." My voice is almost absent-minded as I lean in, trying to get the sleekly curved muscle on Ryder's arm just right. "I'm right here."

"We're worried about you," Ryder says quietly. All mirth has disappeared from his voice, and I flick my eyes up to him and away again. My teeth sink into my lip as I shrug.

"What will be will be," I mutter. My hand twitches, and there's a gleaming line of bronze right across Ryder's left shoulder. "Oh, *shit.*"

"Oooh," Ryder says gleefully. "Profanity. We're corrupting her, Enzo."

I turn my head, biting the inside of my cheek to try and hide my smile. "I think it's more Enzo, to be honest."

Enzo's low laugh sounds behind me as Ryder looks at me with wounded eyes. I can't stop the laugh from slipping free, and his gaze narrows.

"I'm very, *very* good at corruption, I'll have you know," he says slowly. I look up from cleaning my brush. He's advancing on me with a very intent look in his eyes, and I dance backwards with a giggle that cuts off as I hit a hard body.

"You can never be too corrupted," Enzo murmurs in agreement. His hands hold my shoulders, and I swallow as Ryder presses into me, enclosing me between them.

"I agree," Ryder says. His eyes drop to my lips. "So much to teach you, little thief."

His lips have barely brushed mine when Maverick's voice rings out. "Zella."

His tone makes me freeze. Ryder brushes his hand over my cheek as he steps away, and Maverick comes into view. He's leaning against the doorframe, his gaze heavy, and my eyes drop to the envelope in his hands. "It's here?" I ask, my mouth drying.

Maverick nods, holding out the envelope. Enzo squeezes my shoulders again.

"Never alone," he reminds me in a whisper. It's enough to jolt me into reaching forward and taking the heavy cream envelope, turning it over in my hands. It's blank.

"It can wait," Maverick says gently. "If you're not ready."

His eyes are full of understanding, but I force the words out past the lump in my throat. "No, it can't."

This isn't just about me. There are far more people than me waiting for the answers in this envelope. I'm not going to let my own hesitation leave them waiting any longer.

Taking a deep breath, I slide my finger under the tacky strip keeping it closed, ripping it in a jagged slash as I pull out and unfold the cream paper.

It takes me a few seconds to scan the first page, full of tables and numbers that make no sense to me. When I flip to the next page, my eyes drag down to a line.

Probability of paternity: 99%

I expected to feel shock, fear even, but all I feel is numb. I glance up at Maverick. He's hovering, clearly desperate to know.

"It's true," I whisper. "I… Emerson is my father."

And my name, my *real* name, is Aria Cooper.

My father is Emerson Cooper.

My mother was Maria Cooper.

I am Maverick's shadow girl.

He catches me before my knees hit the ground, lifting me up and cradling me gently as he carries me out of the art studio. Enzo and Ryder are close behind, their voices bleeding into one cacophony of noise that sounds like the rush of water on the river.

Maverick's arms are strong around me, and I press my ear to his chest, letting the sound of his heartbeat drown everything out. When

I look up, he's staring down at me, his eyes traveling across my face as though he's seeing me for the very first time.

His eyes are damp, and he closes them when I reach up, catching a tear on my finger.

"Sorry," he says roughly.

"Don't." I swallow. "Don't apologize, Maverick. This is... good news."

"Is it?" He searches my face, his forehead creasing. "Good news?"

My mother is dead, but I have a father. A living, breathing father who desperately wants to see me.

And I still have Maverick. I have Ryder. I have Enzo.

I've gone from having no-one, to having *this*.

Slowly, I nod, and take a breath, letting my lungs fill with oxygen. "Call him. Call Emerson."

If this is a new beginning, I want it to be the best possible start it can be.

***

I'm sitting on the bottom step, gripping Ryder's hand when a pounding sound comes from the front door. Three large bangs make me jump, and I freeze in place as Maverick steps forward to answer it.

His hand pauses on the handle as he turns to face me. "Are you ready?"

Am I?

I'm not sure I'll ever be ready for this. But I nod anyway, keeping hold of Ryder's hand as I stand upright, brushing off my jeans and straightening my top. I drag my braid to the front, playing with it as Maverick pulls the door open. "Emerson."

"Maverick." I can hear the emotion in his voice, the choked sound, and it draws up an answering tightness in my own chest, a burning in my throat. "Is it true?"

Fear roots my feet to the floor, preventing me from moving as Maverick answers him.

Ryder squeezes my hand, and I turn to him, suddenly petrified.

What if he's disappointed?

Ryder sees my agitation, and his face softens as he cups my cheek, reading the question on my face.

"Be proud of who you are, little thief," he murmurs. "I would be proud to have a daughter just like you."

My mind goes blank at that little bombshell, and he presses a kiss to my cheek with a small grin before he turns us to face the man who's stopped in the middle of the hallway.

Emerson Cooper twists a hat in his hands, his eyes locked on my face. His face is wreathed in exhaustion, more so than the last time I saw him. Deep purple circles sit beneath his blue eyes, the lines on his weathered face deep. His mouth parts as I step forward.

We watch each other in silence. I wonder if he's looking for familiarity in my face, searching for the memories of the daughter he lost in the shape of my face, my nose, my cheekbones.

I shift on my feet, uncertain how to approach this. "Um. Hello."

He swallows, the sound audible in the quiet of the hallway. "Hello, Zella."

His voice cracks on my name, and he presses a hand over his mouth as I take a step forward, my hand automatically raising. "I'm – I'm sorry—,"

A tear slides from his eye, and then another, and he buries his face in his hands. "Damn it," he whispers shakily. "I promised myself I wouldn't do this."

The grumbled words remind me so much of myself that it brings a smile to my lips. Carefully, I reach out and take his hands, tugging them away from his face.

"I don't think there's a right or wrong way to do this," I tell him ruefully. "So... maybe we could start with coffee?"

He gives me a relieved smile. "I like coffee. Probably too much."

"Me too."

The guys follow us as I lead Emerson down to the kitchen, and he takes a seat at the table as I start to brew the fresh coffee. I sneak little glances at him, our eyes connecting before we both look away.

The third time, we both laugh. "This is a little awkward," I admit truthfully, taking cups from the cupboard. "I don't know how I'm supposed to act."

"That makes two of us." Emerson nods in thanks as I put a steaming cup in front of him, his fingers curling around it. "I never thought...I never thought something like this would happen. Now that it has, it doesn't seem real."

I take a seat silently next to him, and Maverick looks between us. "We'll give you some privacy," he says softly. Enzo's mouth tightens, and Ryder opens his mouth as if he's going to protest, but they both follow him out of the kitchen, leaving us in silence.

"Will you... tell me about yourself?" he asks quietly. "I'd like to know more about your life."

Ah.

"How much has Maverick told you?"

Emerson shakes his head. "Only the bare bones of what happened. I'll admit that when I found out you were alive... the details didn't matter so much. Now, though... I would very much like to know what happened, Zella, if you're comfortable talking about it."

He swallows, hard. I glance down to where his fingers are gripping his cup tightly, neatly trimmed nails still bearing the traces of paint.

And I start to talk.

I tell him about my childhood, in the apartment. How I grew up surrounded by statues. How much I loved to draw, and how much I loved to watch the sunrise every morning. I try to skirt around Ethan as best I can, but eventually, his name comes up.

"Ethan." Emerson's eyes close. "I never thought... but it makes sense."

"Did you know him?" I whisper, and he nods.

"Very well. The art community is a close one, and Ethan and I have crossed paths many times over the years. If I'd only known then." His face creases in anger. "I never suspected him, but in hindsight, perhaps I should have."

"Why?"

He clears his throat. "He was obsessed with your – with Maria. He'd often say that she was his muse, and it made her uncomfortable. She started avoiding him, eventually, and I asked him to stop coming to the gallery."

He takes a deep breath. "That was a few months before the fire."

My mind races as I stare mindlessly out of the window. "So he may well have started the fire?"

Emerson nods. "I believe so."

Ethan started a fire that killed my mother, and he took me away. Locked me up, and pretended that he'd saved me from some mysterious, terrible fate.

"I never questioned it," I say numbly. "Not until the end."

Emerson's hand brushes mine. "You were a child," he says gently. "None of this was your fault, Zella. I should have looked. You were my daughter, and you were right here, in the same city. All this time... I'm sorry."

"There's only one person at fault," I say softly when his voice begins to shake. "And he's not in this room."

Emerson draws in a shuddering breath. "Maybe not. But we will find him."

His voice is grim, and I swallow down the lump in my throat. I still don't know how I feel about Ethan.

Emerson senses my hesitance and changes the subject. He reaches into his pocket, drawing out a bundle wrapped with a band. "I thought you might like to see these."

My heart jumps inside my chest as he tugs the band off and starts placing photographs down on the table. Images of me as a baby, Emerson holding me up with a grin on his younger face. I pick up a photo of Maria. She's looking out of a window, her hair curling around her face.

"She had hair like yours," Emerson says softly. His fingers brush the photograph. "Not quite as long, though."

I half-laugh, picking up my braid. "I really need to cut it. What was she like?"

"Oh, she was wild." He grins. "She rarely stopped moving. This was an unusually peaceful moment, so I took it while I could. But Maria... she was a whirl of motion. Always looking for new adventures. And her art... her art was beautiful. She was a painter."

"I'd like to see her art." My chest aches as I stare at the photo. "I... I sketch. I never really painted before, but the guys set me up an art studio, and I've been practicing."

He clears his throat. "And they are treating you well? You're happy here?"

I pick up another photo. A small boy is holding a sleeping baby, his eyes wide as he looks down. "Yes," I tell him. "I'm very happy here."

After another hour and a second coffee, Emerson gets up to leave. I walk with him to the front door, and he turns to face me.

"I never thought that I would have this," he says softly. "Seeing you, talking with you... it has been everything, Zella. Would you be willing to come to the gallery, soon? I could show you some of Maria's art. And I'd very much like to see yours."

My cheeks flush. "I'd like that."

He opens his arms uncertainly, before closing them again. "Sorry."

"No," I say quietly. Moving up to him, I wrap my arms around him gently. He smells earthy, a mixture of linseed oil and the slight tang of tarps. Familiar, in a far-off way.

His eyes are glassy when I step back. "I'll see you soon," he says hoarsely.

When I push the door shut, Maverick slips out of his office, pulling the door closed behind him. "How was it?"

"Good," I admit. "It was... good. He's a very kind man."

"He is."

It's a start.

Zella

The rush of cold air sweeps over my face. Autumn is well and truly fading now, melting away to the frosty bite of winter, but I can't bring myself to close my little doors. I'm huddled in the bed of my original room, but sleep is a long way off.

I can't close my eyes, the thoughts tumbling inside my head far too turbulent for that.

It's late, late enough that I should have been asleep by now. Giving up on that idea, I sit up in a huff. My eyes slide to the open door.

Maybe a walk would help.

I debate just going to the main door, but Maverick might still be awake. He's been working late every night, trying to dig up any information he can on Ethan, and where he might be hiding.

My throat tightens. I'm not sure I want them to find him.

I'm not sure I'm ready for what might happen if they do.

This time, at least, I take a moment to pull a thick sweater over my head. I slide my feet into sneakers, carefully tying the laces the way Ryder taught me, looping the bunny ears and tying them into a knot.

It's harder than I thought to descend the wooden slats with shoes on, and I choke as my foot slips, nearly sending me tumbling to the ground. My shoulders slump in relief when I finally land with a thump on the hard ground.

The golden reds of autumn have faded, leaving wilted leaves and bare branches in their place. The moon overhead is bright enough to see by, and I make my way down the same path as before, lost in my own thoughts.

It's hard to reconcile a lifetime of memories with the knowledge I now hold. I had four years of life, *real* life, with a mother and father who loved me, before I was ripped away and placed in that apartment. And I don't remember any of it.

All I remember are white walls, silent sculptures, and Ethan.

"Why did you do it?" I ask out loud. Only the wind answers me, a whistle that lifts my hair. The trees creak and crack in the breeze. It has no answers for me.

And I think that's what I'm struggling with the most. I might never get those answers.

Sighing. I turn back for the house. Twigs crunch beneath my feet, and there's a crack ahead of me. I glance up, in case a branch has broken.

"Zella."

Frowning, I squint. A dark, bulky shadow leans against a tree ahead of me.

"Ryder?" I call. Maybe he followed me again.

I tug at my sweater. "At least I've got clothes on this time," I say playfully.

But there's silence. The hairs on the back of my neck prickle, and my feet slow. "Enzo?"

The figure splits from the tree, and I take a step back as it moves closer. The light from the moon crosses the shadow's face, and my heart stops in my chest.

"Ethan?" I breathe. I blink, just to make sure I'm not imagining him.

Because why would he be *here*?

He pauses a few feet away from me, his hands out in front of him. This man is a far cry from the Ethan I know. He looks filthy, his hair dark and matted, and his usually spotless clothes are worn and crumpled.

I take a step back, and his jaw tightens. "Zella. I just want to talk."

My head whips from side to side. Ethan is blocking the path back to the house, and I suddenly regret my impulsiveness. Maverick *told* me. Told me not to leave without one of them, and now I'm here.

And they're not.

Heaviness settles in my stomach, icy cold washing over my skin.

I shake my head.

"You shouldn't be here," I breathe. He takes another step, and I back away. "You need to leave."

"Zella." His face creases with pain. "I didn't mean... I don't want to scare you."

"So you come here?" I force out. "At night? How did you even *find* me?"

"The festival," he says roughly. "I saw you there, and I followed you back. They didn't see me, but I was there."

My throat tightens. "You've been here? All this time?"

Hiding. Watching. Revulsion washes over me, my breathing so rapid I think I might pass out. Questions pound in my brain, too many to form a single one.

"Why?" I croak finally. Ethan watches me silently, his head tilted. "Why did you do it? The fire?"

He inhales. "So you know, then."

When I nod, he sighs. "I never meant for that to happen, Zella. I just wanted to speak to Maria, but she was so angry. She wouldn't come when I asked her, when I begged her. I knew her better than she knew herself. I knew where she needed to be."

His face twists in revulsion, his fingers tapping against his leg. "She needed to be with me."

His voice twists, going higher as I watch him in disbelief.

This is the real Ethan. I can feel it. This bitter, twisted creature.

And he was *right.*

This world has truly opened my eyes to what evil looks like.

It looks like him. I just never knew any better.

"But you...," he breathes, stepping closer. "You were so perfect, Zella. So pure. They hadn't twisted you yet, hadn't molded you. I knew I could shape you into perfection, and I did. I *did*."

"You caged me," I snap. "Like an animal, Ethan. You *murdered my mother*!"

My voice raises in a shout, and his face darkens. "I released her," he snarls. "I took her from that place, and I freed her, Zella. I sculpted her with my own hands, and she was perfect, then."

My legs shake underneath me as his words filter through. "What do you mean, Ethan?" I whisper. My lips feel dry, my head light and dizzy. "How did you free her? She died in the fire."

Ethan twists away from me, pacing. Slowly, I take another step back, and then another. He doesn't notice, lost in his own ranting.

"They had no idea," he snarls. "They saw a fire, and a body, and they didn't think to look beyond that. But she came, in the end. She followed, for you."

Bile stings my throat. "She went with you," I whisper. "She didn't die in the fire. So where is she?"

He barks out a laugh. "Oh, Zella. Innocent, naïve little Zella."

My hands twist into fists. "Where is she?" I scream. The noise shocks him, and he stumbles back.

A creeping, horrific thought is hovering at the back of my mind. I shove it away, hoping, praying that it's my twisted imagination at play and not the truth.

Ethan straightens, tugging at the ends of his sleeves in a familiar move that jolts at me. "Such a beautiful collection, I had, Zella. All of them, so perfect."

Nausea surges, and I twist, losing the contents of my stomach. A hand lands on my back, and I jerk away, losing my balance and scrabbling over the ground to put distance between us.

"Maria." My face feels frozen. "Maria."

My only companions. My only friends. And the whole time...

My mind feels sluggish, slow, as Ethan comes up to me. I try to push away from his grip, but he holds my face up, turning it from side to side.

"You were my proudest achievement," he murmurs. "Absolute perfection. Untouched. So pure in body and mind, Zella."

He shoves my face away, and it hits the ground, sending a searing pain through my cheek as I cough.

"Ruined!" he roars, and I shrink away as he stalks me. "By *them*. You let them touch you. Let them *defile* you."

"Dante," I blurt, and he stops. "Who was he?"

Ethan is breathing hard. "He was sleeping in the warehouse underneath. Some junkie. So desperate for a fix, he didn't even notice what he was taking when I handed him the syringe."

"Psyche," I whisper. "Cupid?"

He laughs, a shrill, piercing sound that curdles my stomach. "Oh, they were beautiful. They thought they'd found a little love nest, those two. The young love of teenagers. So I gave them one. Together forever."

He advances on me. "I gave them all exactly what they needed," he murmurs. "They didn't thank me for it. They had no idea. But genius always goes unrecognized."

I'm going to be sick again, and I breathe deeply, trying to stop my head from swimming. Piercing pain rings through my face, courtesy of my little trip to the hard ground. "How?" I ask roughly. "How did you do it?"

"I had a workspace," he murmurs, almost dreamily. "Such a beautiful workspace, Zella. And so close, right underneath you. I was always so close to you. I never really left, apart from my little trips abroad."

His hand finds the top of my head again, and he strokes my hair, almost reverently. "You're a masterpiece, Zella," he whispers. "And it's time to come home."

"I'm not going anywhere with you," I force out, and his grip on my hair tightens.

"No more of this. I have a new place now, Zella. I had to start again, but we can do it together. You'll be right there, in the middle of it this time. I have the perfect pose in mind."

My shoulders start to curl over. I know exactly what he means.

And if I leave now, I will never escape again.

One of his statues. Forever.

Enzo

"Are you humming?" Ryder asks with interest.

I ignore him as I head upstairs. He follows behind me, poking my back.

"No," I snarl. "I wasn't humming."

I don't *hum*.

"It sounded like you were," he points out. "Sounded an awful lot like the tune from that film we watched earlier."

I scoff, ignoring him as I continue. I don't hum songs from ridiculous animated films about fish with memory loss.

I don't *hum*, full stop.

Ryder follows me down the hall to Zella's room, and I turn on him with a scowl. "Will you fuck off?"

"Hard pass," he says brightly. "I can't sleep without my little thief."

I grit my teeth. "I wanted her tonight."

He tsks. "Have to learn to share, little blue tang. Don't worry, though. I'll teach you."

He taps on Zella's door before I can respond, and we both wait. And wait.

"It's late," he murmurs. "She's probably asleep."

Disappointment curdles in my stomach, and I shove past him. The door handle opens smoothly under my hands, and we both stare at the decidedly empty room. Ryder sighs. "Ten dollars that she's running naked in the trees again."

I blink, slowly. "Again?"

He shrugs. "She's a free spirit. We should go and find her, though. It's cold out."

The cool air hits my face, and I frown, looking out to the forest before I turn to follow him. I don't like the feeling that just came over me.

We run into Maverick coming out of his office, and he flicks his eyes between us. "Where are you going?"

"To catch a naked Zella," Ryder says promptly. Maverick opens his mouth, but nothing comes out.

Instead, he follows us outside. The three of us fall into step, and Maverick clears his throat. "Do I ask why she's out here with no clothes on? In *winter*?"

Ryder whistles lightly. "Probably not."

"Right." Ignoring them, I pause at the edge of the trees. The forest doesn't sound right. Too quiet. And then I catch it, just barely.

"Wait." My voice is sharp enough that they both silence. The atmosphere changes in a moment.

"What is it?" Maverick says in a low voice. Ryder comes up silently next to me, his head cocked at an angle as he listens. His mouth tightens into lines, and he nods at me.

"She's not alone," I breathe. Maverick turns his head, listening too.

The faintest sound of a male voice can be heard in the distance.

Maverick curses quietly. "Moore?"

"Maybe." I stare out into the darkness, and a smile curls at the edges of my mouth. I take a deep breath, anticipation filling my lungs like oxygen.

"Keep him talking, little prey," I murmur. Ryder and Maverick spread out, the three of us silent as I take the lead. "We're coming for you."

Zella

Ethan tries to pull me up, but I slump to the ground. The act feels all too real. The shaking in my legs feels violent, too violent for me to get up.

A thick black boot kicks the ground, right next to my head, and I flinch. My aching cheek presses into the cool soil, and I breathe it in, praying for something.

Anything.

"Don't be ridiculous," Ethan says dismissively. "I didn't hit you that hard, Zella."

I let out a pitiful groan. "My head..."

Heavy footsteps move away from me, and I blink my eyes open, flicking them around the ground. A snapped off branch sits a little out of my reach.

A hand wraps roughly around my arm, trying to drag me upright. "Get up," Ethan snaps. I crane my head to look at him under my lashes, blinking feebly, and see him looking back over his shoulder.

"It would be an awful shame if that pretty house burned to the ground, Zella."

Icy cold washes over me again. "Don't."

"Don't test me," he hisses. "Come with me now, and I'll leave your little trio alone."

"I will," I whisper, and he pauses. "I'll come with you. Just... let me get myself up. Please."

When he drops my arm, I make a show of trying to push myself up, tipping myself forward before I try it again.

"Enough of this," he snaps.

"Wait!" I cry. "I- I think I've got it."

I push one last time, grunting as my knees scrape over the ground. But the fingers of my right hand close around the branch, my eyes sliding shut in relief.

I grip it as tightly as I can. "Sorry. I think... I do need help."

"Fuck." Ethan grabs my arm again. "This is taking too long."

I have one chance. One chance to get this right. Taking a deep breath, I wait until he lifts me before I twist, driving the branch into him with every bit of strength I have.

His face contorts, his mouth opening on a strangled scream. The sharp edge of the branch slides into his body with little resistance, and I stumble back as he staggers, landing on his knees.

"Zella," he wheezes. Blood, almost black in the muted light, bubbles from around the edges of the stick. I back away, gasping, as Ethan raises his hands to the stick and tries to pull it out.

Hands land on me, and I whirl with a scream in my throat. Enzo is there, his black eyes full of stars as he looks between me and the bleeding man on the floor. "Little prey," he breathes. "Did he hurt you?"

I shake my head, but his eyes move to my face, darkening as he turns. Ryder and Maverick are right behind him, and I sink into them as I turn to watch Enzo move over to Ethan.

He leans over him, his face considering. "A clean shot," he calls. He bends down and twists the stick, and I flinch as Ethan groans. It sounds wet, his chest rattling. "He's got a few minutes at most."

"Zella." Maverick cups my face. "You don't need to see this, sweetheart."

I swallow roughly. "Yes, I do."

When I move past Maverick, he moves with me, his hand on my back as I fall to my knees next to Ethan. He coughs, and I recoil as blood splatters from his mouth.

"Stay… with me," he wheezes. His hand reaches up, and I consider it silently.

"I don't think so," I say quietly. Ethan's eyes widen as I lean forward, and twist the stick as hard as I can. He jerks, a cry of pain forced from his mouth, and Ryder swears softly behind me.

"For my mother," I tell him hoarsely.

Then I twist it again. "For Dante."

And then I pull it out completely as he screams. My hands feel slick with blood as I toss the branch aside.

"He'll go more quickly now," Enzo observes, his voice neutral.

I frown at the stick. "Oh."

"We could stick it back in," he suggests, and Maverick blocks my view, turning my face towards him. His hand feels hot against my skin.

"Forget him," he murmurs. "Let him die alone, Zella."

I nod vacantly. Yes, that feels appropriate.

As I stand, he tries to speak, only succeeding in a choked sound.

I don't respond to his garbled sounds. Instead, I turn my back, walking away. Maverick stays next to me, his arm cradling my shoulders as Ryder and Enzo follow on silent feet.

We walk away from the clearing, and the shaking starts to return to my legs. When I stop, folding over, arms slide underneath me, lifting me and carrying me forward.

"Steady," Maverick whispers in my ear. "We've got you, Zella. You're safe."

"The adrenaline's wearing off," Enzo mutters. "She's gonna crash."

His words are the last thing I hear.

Zella

I move through the days in a haze.

I eat the food that Maverick feeds me.

I lift up my arms obediently when Ryder dresses me.

I lay there listlessly as Enzo runs a washcloth over my arms, his hands gentle.

"Do you see them?" I ask tonelessly one day, and he pauses, turning to look at me. It's an effort to move my head.

His eyes are a void. No stars today.

"See what, little prey?"

"The statues." My throat scratches, and I don't say anything else.

They're everywhere. In every corner of every room, staring at me. I sleep more to try and escape them, but they follow me into my dreams, grabbing at me with hard hands and dragging me until I'm trapped, nothing but a statue myself.

I wake to the sound of my own screams, Maverick wrapped around me, his ragged breathing chasing away the ghosts around us. "Zella," he begs.

I don't know how to stop seeing them.

Another day, I turn to Ryder. He's sitting beside me, pretending to watch the film I haven't looked at while his eyes linger on me.

"They won't go away," I whisper. My voice cracks.

"Who won't, little thief?" His voice is gentle, but it sounds exhausted, too.

"Dante. Psyche. Cupid." I take a breath, but no air fills my lungs. "My mother."

He frowns. "Your mother?"

I nod.

"He made them into statues," I murmur. "They were my friends, and I didn't realize."

Ryder looks at me, and whatever he sees makes his skin turn almost as pale as theirs.

"I would have done something," I whisper. I'm talking to the statue in the corner, her wings spread out behind her. She watches me, judgment in her face. "If I had known. I would have done something."

"Little thief," Ryder says quietly. His voice breaks. "There's nobody there, baby."

But there is. And they're judging me.

I don't blame them at all.

***

"Tell me about the statues," Maverick says. I blink, looking up from my plate.

In the corner, Maria watches me. Dante is right behind Maverick.

"Are they here right now?" he presses. I nod.

"They're always here," I say softly.

A hand grips the back of my neck, and I look at Enzo.

"What do they want?" he demands. I slide my eyes away, looking down again.

I don't know the answer.

Ryder

I jerk awake, my hand moving automatically to the spot where Zella should be.

It's cold.

Awareness is immediate, and I swing my legs out of bed with a curse. The sound of running water comes from the bathroom, and I pull the door open, dread swarming me.

My heart constricts. "Little thief. What are you doing?"

Zella's eyes flick to mine in the steamed mirror. "It has to go," she rasps.

She savagely yanks another piece of hair. Tears track down her face, and I dart to the shower, turning off the hot water.

"Little thief. Princess." I try to stop her, but she pulls away from me, ripping more hair out of her head.

She's breaking my fucking heart. At this point she's more hair than anything else, her cheeks sunken. She's a walking shell of the Zella we knew before.

"Stop," I say firmly. I cover her hands with mine, and she struggles, a sob breaking free from her chest as she weakly tries to pull away. When I don't let go, she collapses into me, her tears soaking my chest. Carefully, I cradle my arms around her.

"Please," I beg. I'll pray to whoever the hell I need to to *help* her. "Talk to me, little thief. What's going on?"

"I can't look at it anymore," she sobs, and as much as my heart breaks, it lifts, too. Because she sounds normal, not the zombie-fied Zella that flinches at shadows and weeps in her sleep.

"Okay," I breathe. "You want it cut, we'll cut it."

I coax her out of the bathroom, and Maverick jerks awake in his chair. Enzo watches us, his eyes hooded, as I sit her down on the bed. She buries her head in her hands, her shoulders shaking and her hair loose around her face.

"Get me scissors," I say over my shoulder, meeting Maverick's eyes. He hesitates, but comes back with a pair in his hands.

Zella

I need it gone.

It hangs heavy on my shoulders, like a shroud, and I can't bear it for a second longer.

I try to pull more out, and hands capture my wrists, holding me.

"Stop, prey," Enzo says firmly. "We're going to cut it, but I need you to stay still. Breathe with me."

I take shuddering, gasping breaths, and for the first time in weeks, I feel my lungs fill as Ryder carefully snips away at my hair. Strand by strand, the strangling weight falls away, and my face crumples in relief.

I can breathe.

Staring at Enzo, I see the purple bruising under his eyes. They all look so tired, and guilt hits me hard. They look like this because of me.

He watches my face carefully. "You with me, little prey?"

I nod, and Ryder clicks his tongue. "Stay still, princess. I'm no hairdresser, but I'm trying."

"I don't care." My throat feels raw, and I cough. Maverick hands me a glass of water, and I gulp it down gratefully, holding it out for more.

His hand brushes my cheek as he hands me another. "There you are," he says quietly.

I don't think he means the water.

I sip this glass more carefully, taking my time. My hands grip it tightly as more hair falls around me, and Maverick gathers up the strands.

"How do you get rid of hair?" I ask absently, staring at it. Ryder pauses.

"Donate it," he suggests. "There are charities."

"What does that mean?" I ask, and he snips away another piece. I glance down to where my newly-cut hair dangles to just below my shoulders, and away.

"There are people out there who make wigs," he explains as he continues. "People lose their hair sometimes, because they're ill or stressed, and they make wigs from the hair people donate."

"I'd like that," I say softly. "To do something good with it."

"Then that's what we'll do." Maverick carefully places the gathered hair on the bed. "How are you feeling?"

Everyone turns to me, and Ryder pauses his cutting.

My hand plays with a loose thread on the bedding beside me. "Tired," I say quietly. "And sad."

"And the statues?" Enzo asks. His eyes dart around the room, as if he can see them too.

"Still there," I say heavily. Although they don't feel as ominous right now. Almost... peaceful. But I'm fairly sure it's not normal to see statues everywhere.

"Zella," Maverick says. He takes a seat beside me, nudging hair out of the way as he takes the glass from me. "You mentioned that... he made them into statues."

Enzo frowns. "Now isn't the time," he snaps, but I shake my head.

"Now is fine." In halting words, I tell them what I found out, that night in the woods. Ryder and Maverick both look paler when I finish, but Enzo just purses his lips, saying nothing.

"Is he gone?" I ask him, and he nods.

"He's gone, little prey. Nobody will ever find him."

I blow out a breath. "Those people... nobody will ever know what happened to them."

"We can look into it," Maverick murmurs. His thumb rubs across my hand in soft strokes. "Find out if they had families."

We could bring them home.

I hesitate. "My mother..."

He swallows. "What do you want to do?"

"We need to tell Emerson," I say quietly. Then my head jerks. "Has he—?"

Maverick nods. "He's called often to check on you. He knows a little of what happened."

"Okay." My heart breaks for him.

"Zella," Maverick says my name carefully, like it's breakable. "We can get you someone to talk to about this. There's a lot to process."

The refusal sticks in my throat.

Maybe it would help.

"Maybe. I'll think about it."

Ryder steps back and tilts his head. His face splits into a small, hesitant smile. "Well, damn. I think I missed my calling."

My hand moves to my head. It feels so much lighter now, white gold hair covering my lap that I collect in a heap and dump on the bed next to me. Ryder holds out his hand and I take it, our fingers curling together as he leads me to the mirror leaning against the wall.

"What do you think?" he asks, and my eyes round as I lean forward.

My hair rests neatly on the edges of my shoulders, framing my face. When I shake it, I stagger, and Ryder grabs my arm. "Steady."

"My head feels so light," I say in wonder, and he huffs.

"That's because you were carrying a whole other person in hair form," he says. "I think we've got enough there for ten wigs, truthfully."

I run my hands through my new haircut, and a laugh escapes me when it slips out of my hand. They're all staring at me when I turn around.

"I like it," I assure them. "It needed to be gone."

It feels like I've shed something heavier than just my hair. As though I've taken control over my own body.

"I'm actually looking forward to washing my hair," I say with wonder. "I always hated it before. It took so long."

"No time like the present," Ryder says promptly. "I'm in need of a shower myself." I let out a shocked noise as he lifts me, his arms gentle. Maverick's voice rings out, chastising Ryder as he follows us to the bathroom with Enzo following.

It doesn't feel quite normal, but something close.

And that's enough.

Ryder

I bounce up and down in my chair. "That one's mine!" I shout, and Enzo holds up the sock-wrapped gift gingerly.

"I wonder what this could be?" he drawls, pulling out the coal. I cackle as he throws it at me, black dust trailing everywhere. Zella yelps as she bats it away, and Maverick steadies her where she sits on his lap.

"Stop," she protests, but she's laughing. "You're mean, Ryder."

I wink at her, reaching behind me and producing a haphazardly wrapped box. "Am I, though?"

She squeals, giving me grabby hands as she looks at the box with covetous eyes. I stifle my laugh as I hand it over and she rips it apart with zero unwrapping finesse, cooing over the vibrant scarf. "I love it!"

"Of course you do." Enzo rolls his eyes but I can see the smile tugging at his lips. "It looks like a unicorn vomited glitter on it."

"It's beautiful," she protests, wrapping the neon pink and purple glitter scarf around her neck.

"It really goes with your socks," I say smoothly, trying not to laugh, and she beams at me. The bumblebee socks stretch up to her knees, and she smooths down the lime green elf dress I bought as a joke… but that seems to have actually made its way into her day-to-day wardrobe.

"And this is for you, jolly old saint prick." I throw another box directly at Enzo's head, but the fucker plucks it out of the air without even raising an eyebrow. He flips it open, and I have a moment of pure satisfaction as his eyes widen. He pulls out the silver dagger, perfectly balancing it on the end of his finger and giving me a begrudging nod that's practically on par with a hug.

I mean, what else do you buy a serial killer for Christmas?

Maverick watches us all, his eyes half-closed, and I toss his gift over, smirking when Zella ducks and it hits him in the face. "For you, old man."

He gingerly unwraps it, his eyes scanning the words before he groans. "For fucks' sake."

"Hold it up," I urge happily. "So everyone can see it."

Zella twists, eyeing the text and sucking on her cheek as she flicks her eyes to the ceiling. I can see her shoulders shaking as Maverick holds up the apron.

"Daddy Mav?" he says drily. "Really?"

"I think it suits you," Zella says seriously, and I hold in the laugh as Maverick winces.

"Thank you," he says evenly, kissing her cheek. He whispers something in her ear, and she flushes.

"I love Christmas," she says dreamily. When Maverick stands, cradling Zella, I frown.

"Where are you going?"

"If you want your present," he calls back, "you'd better hurry up."

"Well, you should've said," I mutter. I jump up and follow, and Enzo loiters behind me as Maverick pulls open the door to the spare room.

My mouth goes dry.

Zella tilts her head to the side. "Who, exactly, is this present for?"

Enzo pushes past me, and I can see the glint in his eyes as he takes in the newly designed room. "Oh, I like this."

Maverick clears his throat. "All of us?" he suggests, and Zella gives him a dubious look. She steps forward, running her hands over the padded bench.

"What's that?" she asks, pointing at the St. Andrews cross on the wall. I smirk at Maverick, but he doesn't blink. Holding her hips, he nudges her backwards until her back presses against the center.

"You place your hands here," he explains, lifting her hands and pressing them against the ridges. Zella's eyes widen, her mouth popping open in a little *o* of understanding.

"And your legs go here." His knee pushes her black and yellow striped legs apart, nudging her feet into position. "You see?"

I see the way her flush spreads deliciously over her face and down into the neckline of her dress. She clears her throat. "I might need a proper demonstration."

"Show her the bench," Enzo suggests. He turns from the wall, and all of our eyes drop to the rope in his hands. "Or maybe a hoist?"

"The bench," Maverick says slowly. He leads Zella over to the padded structure, but he pauses. "I think..." he plucks at the strap of her dress. "That the elf dress needs to come off, now."

"But the bee socks can stay on," I blurt out, and Enzo laughs. "Kinky."

"Have you seen them?" I hiss. She looks fucking delectable.

Zella turns. "I might need some help," she says over her shoulder, and we all leap forward at once. Mav is closest, though, and he slips his hands under her little straps, drawing her dress down until it pools around her waist.

When she turns, I think all of our eyes widen.

"What are those?" Enzo asks, in a strangled tone.

She shimmies, and the little Christmas puddings attached to her nipples jiggle. "Tassels! I ordered them from the googirl."

Maverick half groans, half laughs. "I'm going to confiscate your card."

"I'll give you mine," I breathe in delight. "You can have all of them. All of my cards."

Take my fucking money.

Stepping forward, I carefully peel one of the pasties away. When she pouts, I lean down and suck a reddened nipple into my mouth, groaning as her hands slide into my hair and she pushes herself into me.

I release her with a wet-sounding pop. "Fucking delicious, little thief."

She grins down at me. "What's next?"

Maverick takes her hand, and I step back as he coaxes her into position on the bench. She lays her head to the side, balancing on her knees with her arms down. Maverick runs his hands down her legs, over her socks, and straps her into position, holding her in place with thick leather straps. At the top end, Enzo secures her hands the same way. Her breathing rises in the small space, little gasps that make my dick hard as fucking nails.

"Beautiful," Maverick praises. She whimpers as he runs his hand over the smooth curves of her ass. "And already wet for us. I hope you're not attached to these panties."

The rip of the material rings out, revealing her swollen pink pussy.

Maverick slides a finger through her folds, pushing it inside her as she arches her back with a moan. He adds another, pushing them in and out until she's bucking against his hand.

Enzo unbuckles his belt, flipping open the button on his jeans as Zella watches him avidly. He pulls out his cock, already hard and heavy as he presses the head to her mouth. "Suck, little prey. Show them how well you take my dick like a good girl."

I inhale as his cock disappears inside the warm haven of her mouth. He pinches her nose shut as he pushes in, until her chin brushes his balls, her mouth stretched wide to take him.

"Such a good little prey," he praises, and her eyes squeeze shut. "Gonna fuck your throat now."

It's all the warning he gives her as he pulls out, thrusting in again as she gags around him, her groan reverberating against his shaft.

I step up beside Maverick, adding my fingers to the mix and rubbing her swollen clit as Maverick pumps his fingers, the wet noises filling the air as our little thief moans around Enzo's cock.

"I think, since it's such a special day, that a double gift is in order," I murmur, and Maverick pulls his fingers out, spreading her cheeks wide as his hand moves to unbutton his jeans.

My hand drops down too, and I duck around the bench, leaning over to look into Zella's eyes. She makes a muffled noise, and Enzo pauses his movements.

"You think you can take both of us?" I ask her slowly, cupping her chin. "Both Maverick and I sinking inside you, stretching that pussy and ass wide open?"

Another garbled noise comes from her throat, and Enzo picks up the pace. "That was a yes," he translates. "In case you didn't hear it."

Whistling, I trace my fingers down her spine as I move back to where Maverick has his dick nestled at her opening. He rubs his head up and down her slit, tapping her ass in gentle remonstration when she pushes back against him. "Patience, Zella."

The sound that comes from her throat is one hundred percent disgruntled female, and I grin as I step up to the plate. Maverick sinks into her slowly, his hand settling between her shoulder blades as he holds her down. Sliding my hand down, I gather some of the wetness from her pussy, sliding my hand up and circling her ass with my thumb. It clenches around me when I test it, sliding my thumb inside and feeling the muscles tighten.

"Relax, princess," I murmur. Maverick moves slowly, sliding in and out, finding a rhythm with Enzo's movements as Zella twitches and shakes underneath us. Enzo pulls out completely, and she half moans, half sobs.

"I can't," she gasps. "It's too much."

"You were made for us," I push my thumb in further, stretching her as she cranes her head back to look at me, her eyes heavy and languid. "Made to take us, little thief. So bend over, and take it like a good girl."

She melts at the smallest amount of praise, and it's fucking delicious to feel the way she relaxes around my touch. Pulling out my thumb, I push back in slowly with two fingers, adding a third as she squirms around us.

Maverick's hands flex on the smooth globes of her ass, his fingers tightening into the skin as the tendons stand out in his neck from the urge to thrust. "Ryder."

I shuck my jeans off, stroking my cock in my hand as I climb over him. "Watch the balls, they're delicate," I quip, and Mav swats my ass as I move in front of him.

"Jesus," he mutters, as I wiggle it for good measure.

"That's what they all say." Balancing myself, I take a deep breath as I notch the head of my cock to the tight ring. Enzo slows his movements as I begin to push inside. "Deep breaths, little thief."

She's panting, her body completely lax under us as Maverick holds her steady on his cock and I push inside her, taking my time, until I bottom out.

"Fuck," I gasp, my forehead damp with perspiration. "Feels so fucking good, princess."

I run my hand down her spine, and she arches. Pinned beneath us, she tries to push back as she pulls her mouth away from Enzo. "More. *Harder.*"

Yes, ma'am.

The room fills with the obscene sound of fucking as the three of us find our rhythm, moving in and out. Zella moans, a low thrum, and Enzo curses.

"Fuck, I'm going to come," he says roughly. He tips Zella's head back, and she clenches around us, her muscles fluttering around me drawing a hot prickling from the base of my spine.

Maverick starts moving faster, his hips thrusting underneath me as Enzo roars his release, pumping into Zella's mouth. He releases her with murmured praise, and she buries her head into the bench, her nails sinking into the leather as we push harder and harder.

"Come for us, Zella," Maverick demands, and she cries out as he twists his hips. Her muscles start to flutter, and my release hits like a fucking truck as she cries out, the sound gravelly and raw as we fill her up.

Maverick pulls out first, his release leaking from her as I follow and he grabs my shoulder to help me off the bench. When I catch my balance, he's already unbuckling Zella, Enzo doing the same as she breathes heavily, her eyes closed.

"Best. Christmas. Ever," she breathes.

I completely fucking agree.

Maverick — six months later

I press a glass of champagne into Zella's hand. She spins to me, her face glowing with delight.

"To your achievements," I say softly. I clink our glasses together. "And to all the ones still to come."

She takes a sip, her eyes glassy as we both turn to look down the gallery. Dozens of people are crammed into the space, all of them focused on the canvas paintings hanging at small intervals.

"I can't believe it," she whispers. "They really like it."

"I never doubted it." I watch a couple pause in front of a large canvas. The girl in the painting dances, her toes pointed and her face looking up to a sky lit with hundreds of glowing lanterns. Three pairs of eyes watch her from the shadows. To others, they look like predators, but I know better.

The woman picks up the price tag attached, only to drop it in disappointment, and Zella sighs. "I knew I made them too expensive."

I smile down into my glass. "It's not that. I'm afraid that one's already taken."

Realization hits, and she nudges my arm. "Maverick!"

"Mine," I say softly. Entwining our arms together, we begin to move through the gallery. Zella is stopped often, and I glance around for the others as she chats to an enthusiastic collector. Ryder already declared his intent to charm people into buying each and every painting, and Enzo lingers at the edge of the room, arms folded and his eyes focused on Zella.

Emerson finds us, and Zella encloses him in a gentle hug. They've become closer over the last few months, and he's bursting with pride that Zella's first showing is being held in his gallery.

"Every painting has been sold," he crows, kissing her cheek. "I am so proud of you, Zella."

She blushes. "I think Maverick bought most of them."

"A few," Emerson concedes with a smile, "but we also have a waiting list open for your future work, and it's filling up rapidly."

Zella blinks, looking up at me. "So... does this mean I'm a proper artist?"

Both Emerson and I laugh. Ryder appears to steal her away, and as we watch them stroll away, Emerson leans in.

"I'm proud of you too, you know," he says softly. "And your father would be too, Maverick."

I swallow around the lump that appears in my throat, giving him a nod. "Thank you," I say hoarsely. "I'm sorry it took so long to find answers, Emerson."

His smile is a mixture of sadness and joy. "That was not your doing, Maverick. I had given up all hope. To see Zella now, happy and healthy and here, is more than I ever hoped for."

He gives me a very fatherly look. "Might there be... wedding bells?" he asks delicately. "In the future?"

Smiling, I tip my glass to him and move away without answering, and I hear him laugh behind me. It's a debate we're still having. Zella is content to continue as we are. Enzo doesn't care, but Ryder and I are in fierce competition over who will legally make Zella ours.

My hand dips into my pocket, feeling the edge of the delicate ring.

I'm fighting to win.

Enzo — one year later

"ENZO!"

Ignoring the furious bellow from upstairs, I carefully press down, watching the viscous red liquid flow from the perfect cut I've made along Timothy Chalmer's arm. He wails behind his gag, and I let out a trilling burst of song which roughly follows the sound of his scream.

He shuts up pretty quickly. I'm almost disappointed.

"Cut the other side, so it matches." My little prey is perched on a table on the other side of the room, carefully keeping out of reach of any accidental sprays. Instead, she's offering advice. This is a particularly fun one for both of us, since she acted as the bait.

A perfect set-up.

A dark, quiet alley, a timid girl walking home from work on a late night, and Timmy was hog-tied in the back of the truck before he even touched her.

My prey has a knack for enticing bad men.

I should know.

I was one of them.

Maverick bellows again, and Zella tilts her head. "What did you do?" she asks flatly, and I purse my lips.

"Nothing."

I have a feeling I know what this is about, but I'm keeping my cards close to my chest.

I move on to carving a smiley face into Timmy's chest, using his nipples as a guide. Snot slides out of his nose, and I recoil.

Blood? No issue.

Vomit? Meh.

Snot? Hard fucking limit.

"You're disgusting," I tell him, and I toss a cloth over his head so I don't have to look at his sniveling little face anymore.

The door slams upstairs, and Zella winces.

"Somebody's in trouble," she sings. Really badly.

My little prey is not, in fact, a songbird. It's interesting, all these little things that you learn when you're completely obsessed over someone. Like how she chews the inside of her cheek when she's telling a lie, or how she dances like an awkward chicken.

It's adorable. She thinks she has perfect rhythm.

I'll never tell her.

I sigh as Maverick comes storming in, barely glancing at the beautifully carved soon-to-be-corpse on my table.

"Please, do come in," I mutter.

"You sneaky fucker," he roars.

Zella clears her throat, and he blanches when he turns and she gives him a waggle of her fingers.

"What are you – *why* is she here?" he demands, and I click my tongue.

Who am I to deny the bloodthirsty urges of our soulmate?

When I don't answer, Maverick pinches the bridge of his nose, his eyes closing. "I found the records. You asshole."

Ah.

"What records?" Zella asks, and his mouth drops open.

"You didn't even *tell* her?"

Sighing, I wipe my hands and turn. "Little prey. We're married."

They both stare at me in silence. Zella looks bemused. "Are we? I don't remember. Don't I have to wear a dress for that? And... consent?"

"You *should*," Maverick says darkly. "But somebody decided to change the records at the Clerk's Office. Just went on in and updated them."

"So... we're married?" Zella asks me, her smile growing on her face. I see Maverick's jaw ticking.

"Relax," I say shortly. "We'll get a divorce in a year."

Zella's face falls, and I roll my eyes. "So you can marry one of them," I clarify. "Figured we could take it in turns."

God knows the government isn't intelligent enough to recognize that monogamy is only one of the many options available. Although I did feel a small amount of glee when I saw our names recorded together. Zella decided to keep her name, so she's Zella Aria Cooper on her identification.

Zella Aria Cooper & Enzo Gambino.

I kind of like it.

Zella jumps off the table and snuggles under Maverick's arm. "We'll do it properly," she promises him, laughter in her voice.

He sighs, wrapping his arm around her. "On the beach."

She stiffens, her eyes lighting with interest. "The beach?"

"Mmmm. How's your travel list coming along?"

Zella shifts. "Um. There's a lot of pins on it."

"How many?"

She coughs delicately into her fist. "Maybe... a hundred?"

When we stare at her, she shrugs helplessly. "I can't help it! Everywhere looks so exciting. And the Googirl keeps suggesting new places, and they all look so *good*."

"That fucking Googirl," I mutter, and she points at me.

"Leave her alone," she says firmly. "She's my best friend."

I blink. "You need to meet more people."

Sniffing indignantly, she turns for the door. "You just wait," she calls back airily. "You'll eat your words, Enzo. Our trip is going to be *ah-ma-zing*."

Zella

The breeze skips over my skin, the scent of salt and sand and *warmth* sinking into my nose as I inhale deeply, my eyes closed as I tilt my face up to the sunshine.

Adjusting the large green sunhat on my head, I squint at Enzo's sleeping figure on the sun lounger next to me. His eyes crack open, star-filled irises staring back at me.

They're always filled with stars, now.

"Little prey," he murmurs. "What are you doing?"

"Watching you," I say softly. He looks more relaxed than I've ever seen him. This trip has been good for all of us.

A hoarse shout comes from the sea in front of us and I twist, laughing as Maverick throws himself at Ryder, shoving him under the waves until he emerges with a cursed splutter.

They both turn, and I get the absolutely joyful experience of watching them both strut out of the sea, chests sparkling with water and trunks plastered against their legs.

I beam up at Ryder as he pelts past Maverick, reaching me first and throwing himself down, making me squeal as he shakes his head like a dog and sprays me with droplets. "Ryder!"

He turns until his head is planted in my lap, and I push damp strands of hair back from his forehead as he bats his eyelashes mournfully. "Little thief. Maverick tried to drown me."

"Trust me," he says drily, "you'd be dead if I tried to drown you."

Leaning down, he tips my chin up for a kiss. I hold on when he moves to pull away, and he smiles against my lips. "Patience, future Mrs. Brooks."

"You're not even supposed to see me today," I tell him solemnly. "It's against the rules."

He settles on the lounger next to me, taking a sip from the ice-cold bottle of beer on the table next to us. "I've waited a whole year for this," he says firmly. "I'm not letting you out of my sight for a moment."

Ryder sighs. "I told you, it was only a joke. We didn't actually elope."

We're in Mexico now, but we were in Scotland last month. They have this place called Gretna Green, and Ryder told me it would be an adventure to sneak out without the others.

Maverick caught us right before I said my vows. I don't think he's quite forgiven Ryder yet.

"This is perfect," I murmur. "The perfect place for a beach wedding."

"Have you got your dress?" Maverick asks, and I dig my nails into Ryder's shoulder when he starts to wheeze.

"Yep!" I say brightly. It might not be a traditional white dress, but when I saw it, I immediately knew it was the right one.

I didn't even know they did that shade of yellow.

And it glows in the dark.

Sighing happily, I settle back in the sun, listening to Ryder and Enzo argue over who's going to be the main groomsman, Maverick's patient voice telling them to *shut the fuck up* and *you're lucky you're invited at all*.

"Sorry, Daddy Mav," Ryder mutters, and I bite my cheeks against a laugh.

My life is perfect. Maybe it didn't start out that way, but somehow, I know that I'm exactly where I'm meant to be.

And I'm just getting started.

Stalk me

If you'd like to keep up with the latest releases, you can find my social media by scanning the QR code below!

Playlist

Book playlist (in order)

The Walls Are Closing In/Hangman – The Pretty Reckless

Run – Hozier

Cold Blooded – The Pretty Reckless

Fire and the Flood – Vance Joy

Victim – memyself&i

Tag, You're It – Melanie Martinez

You Put A Spell On Me – Austin Giorgio

Body – Rosenfield

Panic Room – Au/Ra

Flames – Tedy

DARKSIDE – Neoni

Church – Chase Atlantic

Sugar – Sleep Token

Trouble (Stripped) – Halsey

Coming soon

A Murder of Crows

Welcome to Mafia University.

Here, the heirs of the mafia are educated in darkness and violence.

Alliances are forged.
Enemies are made.
Marriages are bought.
And all are bound in blood.

As the sole female heir to my father's mafia empire, I can't let my walls down, even for a moment. The only people I can truly rely on are my enforcer and my best friend.

Every ally could be an enemy.
Every friend could be a traitor.

And the other four heirs are circling, ready to slide a knife into my back.

Luciano Morelli.
Giovanni Fusco.
Dante V'Arezzo.
Stefano Asante.

But I'll never let that happen, because I'm Caterina Corvo.
I am a Crow.
And you know what they call a gang of Crows?
A *murder.*

Also by Evelyn Flood

Knot Forever

The Bonding Trials duet

Denied

Devoted

The Omega War trilogy

Omega Found

Omega Lost

Omega Fallen

Made in the USA
Middletown, DE
28 September 2024

61625108R00220